Robert Scott Burn

The Grammar of House Planning

SALZWASSER
VERLAG

Robert Scott Burn

The Grammar of House Planning

Reprint of the original, first published in 1864.

1st Edition 2022 | ISBN: 978-3-75259-501-7

Verlag (Publisher): Salzwasser Verlag GmbH, Zeilweg 44, 60439 Frankfurt, Deutschland
Vertretungsberechtigt (Authorized to represent): E. Roepke, Zeilweg 44, 60439 Frankfurt, Deutschland
Druck (Print): Books on Demand GmbH, In de Tarpen 42, 22848 Norderstedt, Deutschland

THE GRAMMAR

OF

HOUSE PLANNING:

HINTS ON ARRANGING AND MODIFYING PLANS OF

COTTAGES, STREET-HOUSES, FARM-HOUSES, VILLAS, MANSIONS, AND OUT-BUILDINGS.

1864.

PREFACE.

THIS work is designed to meet a desideratum which has been long and much felt in practical literature. It purposes to place before the reader a wide variety of plans, ranging from that adapted to the simplest COTTAGE and STREET house, up to the more pretentious COUNTRY VILLA and TOWN MANSION. The design or scope of the work comprehends, however, not merely the giving of a series of plans, or suggestions for plans, but also occasional alternative arrangements adapted to one and the same plan; showing how, by altering not only the relative position of the apartments, but parts of the apartments themselves, as position of doors, windows, and fireplaces, certain disadvantages in the one plan may be obviated, and more convenient and more economical arrangements obtained in the other. This *antithetical or contrastive* mode of treatment, the reader will at once perceive, possesses advantages of a thoroughly practical nature; but which, obvious as they appear when alluded to, have not yet—the editor believes—formed a systematic feature in any work treating on House Arrangement. In addition to plans of houses of various grades, designs for Out-buildings and Stables are also given. These will be useful as affording hints to those who contemplate keeping, at their Country Houses or Suburban Villas, a small herd of dairy cattle, or a stud of horses. To serve in some measure as practical hints to the Student of Architecture, and to House Proprietors, as affording suggestions for the style of decoration they would like to adopt, a series of examples are given comprising Doors, Windows, Chimneys, &c.

Still further to render the work practically useful in all departments, brief Essays are given on several important departments of Arrangement, Construction, and Internal Conveniences, as arrangement of Apartments, Ventilation, Lighting, Drainage, Aspect, Soil, and Site, &c. In these, it is believed, some hints of a useful and novel character will be found worthy the attention of the Reader. The work is not designed exclusively for the purpose of conveying the opinions of the Compiler on the various points of which its pages treat, but as a medium also for giving the opinions of others, whose position in the world of Science and Art entitles them to be considered as authorities. To embody this idea the Compiler has, therefore, carefully selected from a wide range of authorities, opinions which cannot fail to be otherwise than useful to the practical man. The sources of these being generally acknowledged in the body of the work, it is unnecessary here to give them in full; the Compiler cannot, however, omit here noting his special obligations to the pages of the "Builder," the "Building News," and to various papers read before the Professional Societies. If the Reader will derive as much profit and pleasure from their perusal as the Compiler has done while selecting them for republication in the pages of his little work, his labour will not have been in vain.

At the same time, while reproducing these opinions of others, the Compiler has not refrained from giving those of his own on the various subjects discussed in its pages. These will easily be distinguished from the other portions of selected matter; and for what they are worth the Reader must take them. It is right here, however, to say, that much of the matter embodying these opinions of the Compiler, formed part of a series of Lectures delivered by him to the members of an important public educational institution.

While noticing his obligations to the pages of the Journals

named above, the Compiler must not omit naming those he is under to the Proprietor of the "Mark Lane Express and Agricultural Journal," for permission to re-publish various plans of Cottages and Farm Houses, with notes and suggestions which he prepared for the pages of that Journal.

With reference to the diagrams in the body of the work which illustrate the arrangements of houses, it may here be noted, that being designed merely as hints or general suggestions, on which the Reader may base properly proportioned plans; and which have, therefore, no pretension to being considered as drawn to scale, the Compiler deemed that the purposes he had in view would be as well met by giving the "type diagrams" as they now appear, as by giving more elaborately drawn plans, which, while they would have added to the expense, would not, he conceives, have added much to the practical suggestive utility of the work. In the Plates, however, a number of plans of various styles of houses are given duly drawn to scale, together with examples of doors, windows, &c. Several of these have been specially prepared for the work, the remainder have been culled from various sources to which the Compiler has had access.

Not further to enlarge upon the scope and scheme of the work, and of the manner in which the Compiler has endeavoured to realize them; and without claiming for it any place as an original or thoroughly exhaustive treatise on the important subject of which it treats, he trusts that the hope may be permitted him that it will nevertheless take a position as one calculated to furnish, if not in a novel, at least in a practically useful and suggestive form, a selection of material which will be of some utility to the man of practice, the student of architecture, and to investors of house property.

TABLE OF CONTENTS.

DIVISION FIRST.

THE SITE, ASPECT, INTERNAL ARRANGEMENTS, AND THE SANITARY CONSTRUCTION AND ARRANGEMENT OF THE MANSION, VILLA, FARM-HOUSE, COTTAGE, STABLE, AND COW-HOUSE.

DIVISION SECOND.

EXAMPLES AND ANALYSES OF PLANS OF HOUSES, FROM THE COTTAGE TO THE MANSION.

DESCRIPTION OF THE PLATES.

PLATE XXIV.—Fig. 1, Section of Cow-house; *a b c* the travis or division between the stalls, *a b* being the head and foot posts; *c* the boarding; *d* the feeding trough; *e* the feeding passage running at the back of the stalls; *f* the gutter in dunging passage. Fig. 2, Part Plan, showing three stalls; *a a* the feeding passage, with rails to run food-trucks on; *b b* the racks; *c c* the manger.

„ XXV.—Fig. 1, Section of Stable; *a a* head; *b* foot-post of travis between the stalls; *c c* tie-beam of roof, to which posts are fixed; *d d* travis-boards; *e* rack; *f* feeding passage; *g* gutter. Fig. 2, Part Plan; *a a* feeding passage; *b b* racks; *c c* travis divisions between the stalls.

„ XXVI.—Examples of Chimneys; scale, 3-16ths of an inch to the foot. Figs. 1 and 7 are Italian; Figs. 2, 6, 8, Elizabethan; and Figs. 3, 4, 5, Gothic.

„ XXVII.—Examples of Gothic Windows — Bay-windows, Figs. 1, 3, 4, 6, 7, 9,; Figs. 2, 5, lower story window, Fig. 13 being upper story window for same; Fig. 8, Triplet-window for lower story in place of a Bay; Fig. 12, upper story window for same; Figs. 10, 11, Attic Windows. Scale, 1-16th inch to the foot; Figs. 1, 3, 1-8th of an inch to 3 feet.

„ XXVIII.—Examples of Doors. Figs. 1, 4, 6, 9, Domestic Gothic; Figs. 2, 5, 7, Italian; Figs. 3, 8, Elizabethan; 1-8th scale.

„ XXIX.—Examples of Towers, Gables, and Perforated Parapets. Fig. 1, Anglo-Italian Tower; Figs. 2, 3, Gothic Tower; Fig. 6, Gothic Gable; Fig. 7, Elizabethan ditto; Fig. 8, Anglo-Italian ditto; Figs. 4, 9, 10, Gothic Perforated Parapets; Fig. 5, Elizabethan ditto.

„ XXX.—Examples of Windows, in Figs. 1, 2, 4, 5, 9, in the Italian Style; of Chimneys in the Gothic.

„ XXXI.—Examples of Windows. Figs. 1, 2, 4, Italian; Figs. 6, 8, Elizabethan; Figs. 7, 9, Gothic.

THE GRAMMAR

OF

HOUSE PLANNING AND CONVENIENCES.

DIVISION FIRST.

THE SITE, ASPECT, INTERNAL ARRANGEMENTS, AND THE SANITARY CONSTRUCTION AND ARRANGEMENT OF THE MANSION, VILLA, FARM-HOUSE, COTTAGE, STABLE, AND COW-HOUSE.

CHAPTER FIRST.

THE MANSION, VILLA, AND FARM-HOUSE.

1. It would be an easy matter to dwell upon the importance of the subjects above indicated, but this is not necessary, so abundantly evident must it be to any one who gives even the briefest consideration to their bearing on the comfort of the inmates, and on the every day labours of the servants inhabiting those classes of domestic structures. We do not, in the notes which we are about to present to the reader, propose to exhaust thoroughly the discussion of the various points connected with the arrangement and construction of various classes of domestic buildings, as indicated above; it is only to the most important of these that we propose drawing the attention of the reader, and enough will be done if we succeed in making our remarks not novel or striking merely, but practically useful and easily available. There are many points which are commonplace enough when stated, and some remarks which may appear to

be mere truisms to which every one will easily assent, but which, nevertheless, bearing as they do most closely on the subject, and being indeed of the highest practical importance, are, it is somewhat strange to say, frequently overlooked or ignored. To a few of these we hope to be able to attract the attention of the reader—not only pointing out how certain things should be so, but why they are so—a double way of viewing things highly productive of benefit in practice. Without further preface then, we proceed to the discussion of the subject, taking up first the consideration of some points connected with the *mansion*, the *villa*, and *farm-house;* premising that our remarks are based on the supposition that these structures are to be of a superior class; it being obviously an easy matter to modify our recommendations to suit those of the inferior kind. We have classed these three styles of structure together, as the major portion of our remarks in this chapter will apply equally to all three. Wherever any specialty of arrangement exists, applicable to one only of these classes of houses, we shall, of course, make specific allusion to it. It is deemed desirable to give such remarks as we may have to offer in connection with the Cottage in a separate chapter. It is right, also, to draw here special attention to the fact, that we purpose adding to our own remarks a variety of hints culled from various professional periodicals and works; so doing because our aim is rather to provide the reader with a carefully selected digest or compilation of authoritative remarks, possessed of a high practical value, than ambitious to make these exclusively our own. Much of what we give will obviously be useful—and designedly so—to the non-professional reader, who we suppose to be anxious to know some of the points necessary to be attended to in order to insure comfortable, safe, and economically constructed dwelling houses. Much, however, designed for this class, will, it is hoped, be not altogether unsuggestive to the professional reader of our pages.

2. THE PLANNING OF THE HOUSE.—It seems to be stating a very commonplace truism, when we say that "seeing a house is a place in which to live, it behoves the man who proposes to live in it, so to consider its arrangements that he may live in it comfortably." And yet it is a truism which, like many others we might name, is often ignored or over-

looked; so often, indeed, that of many it may be said that they think a house is more to look *at* than to live *in*. Yet seeing how much of his time a man has to spend in his house, and how often, therefore, he is to be pleased with its comforts or annoyed by its defects, it does seem odd that he should rarely know whether he has to enjoy the one or endure the other until he takes possession, when knowledge comes too late for remedy. For it should never be forgotten, that the mistakes made in the *planning* of a house cannot be rectified when the plan is perpetuated in stone or brick and mortar, or if rectified, rectified only at large expense and much trouble. This consideration then should urge all men proposing to build to consider well *what* they really are going to build. Necessary in all cases is this, but more especially necessary in the case of large-sized houses, where defects in arrangement not only affect *the* comfort of the inhabitants, but *may add* greatly to the labour of the domestics; this last consideration being of no small importance in such establishments where labour is necessarily great. When we see badly planned houses—and their number is by no means a small one—it is difficult to know who is most to blame, the architect or his client. That architects often commit gross mistakes in planning is true enough, yet it is equally true that clients have put it in their power to do so, when by the exercise of a little examination of the plans, and of some thought as to their peculiarities, they might have prevented it. With some architects, fortunately not with many, the rule often is to make the elevation or external design dictate the plan, rather than the plan dictate the design. The point seems unimportant, but a glance at its bearings will show that it by no means is so. In his endeavour to please the client by the picturesqueness of its outlines, such an architect may think first and chiefly as to how the building will look when finished; prompted thus the outline shapes itself in his mind, and is finally decided upon. And the outline thus obtained must be filled in with apartments as best it may. A plan thus obtained may be good and convenient, but the chances are equally that they may be bad and inconvenient. A part may be useless, or if useful, may be inconvenient; but that part must not be sacrificed as it may be detrimental to the elevational character or design. Thus it happens often that the plan is cramped, cabined, and confined, in consequence of the requirements of the design, which design has been foreshadowed in the architect's mind from the beginning, and which has more or less markedly influenced the whole internal arrangements. Seldom as this process may be done, it has nevertheless been done sometimes, and being likely to be done again it is worth while to warn the reader of the dangers of the practice, and make him aware of the advantages of the converse mode of proceeding, namely, to let the plan dictate the design. We are far from ignoring the importance of having a design beautiful to look at—far, indeed, for we deem it of essential importance, in a merely mental point of view, that we should not have anything staring us continually in the face which causes regret or uneasiness. But we hold, that if we obtain the essential conveniences in a plan, that a clever architect will be able to give that plan a character distinctive and pleasing in elevation. We simply insist upon this as the *primary* consideration, that your house shall in its arrangements add to your comfort while living in it, and to the convenience of your servants while working in it. And these can only be obtained by the arrangements calculated to promote them being carefully considered in the plan. Whatever else you obtain you will be sure to obtain this, a characteristic outline, which will tell its own story and give evidence of mind, and where that is we defy a house to be a mistake. As regards its external characteristics or style of design, no truly experienced architect will have any difficulty in designing a good elevation to such a carefully matured plan as we here insist upon.

3. To secure perfection in the plan do not plan in a hurry, and as in order to ensure good building you should build in the spring and summer; let your winter evenings be dedicated to frequent talk over your plan. A writer possessed of a keen knowledge of human nature states in one of his admirable Essays, that he believes there is no enjoyment so real as that obtained while discussing at the winter's fireside the various arrangements of the house you are to live in in the following season. And there is, we have reason to know, a vast deal of truth in the remark. Discussion is sure to elicit opinion, and from a variety of opinions you can elicit practically valuable hints. If

you have the good fortune to have the society of ladies at your fireside, take them into counsel over the matter. Ladies generally have a much better idea of what constitutes real comfort in a house than gentlemen; and on all points connected with the relative arrangement of apartments so as to save labour on the part of the servants, we would far sooner take the opinion of an intelligent female than that of the cleverest architect who ever handled drawing square and pencil. Sure are we that many of the absurdities of house arrangement which we have seen perpetrated in houses, the plans of which have come from the studios of some architects, would never have been made had a female acquainted with house arrangement, and possessed of some powers of thought, been consulted in the matter. In discussing, as we recommend you to discuss, the proposed arrangements of your house during the winter, omit no opportunity to scribble in your note-book such modifications in your plan as may be proposed from time to time. You may get a capital hint quite casually which you fancy you can bear in your memory, but on trying to bring it back again after the lapse of a few hours only, you will be often mortified to find that you can no longer grasp it. Your various scribbles of plans or notes of suggestions will be a register to which you will refer with advantage, and it will help you greatly to mature your plan. All this may appear to some to be unnecessary as it may appear to be trifling, but nothing is trifling which is important; and to say that the arrangements of the house you are to live in, which will at all times minister to your pleasure, or add to your discomfort, are not important, is to display an utter ignorance of the great truth, namely, that life, comfort, and happiness is more influenced by little things than by great ones. All this fine attention which we here recommend you to give to the plan of your house may appear unimportant to one who is not to live in it; but to you who are, the matter assumes a very different aspect. You may say of it in the words of the classical poet—"How small to others, but oh how great to me."

4. But the importance of carefully maturing the plan at first, before the final drawings are made, or a brick or stone laid, may be urged from another point of view. If, after the house is begun to be built, you find that you would like certain altera-

tions to be made, or find, as some do, that they *must* be made, so gross being the mistake in planning which has given rise to the necessity; you thus break through the contract, and open the door to charges for *extras* being made by the builders. Now, there is nothing so unsatisfactory as these extras; no matter how large may be a man's means, he is always dissatisfied with any addition to the original estimated cost. It seems to be a principle of human nature, that if a man is told that a thing is to cost so much, he is disappointed if it comes to cost more, even although the extra sum may be trifling in the extreme. Architects are often blamed for causing the final cost of a house to exceed its estimated cost; but clients are to blame as often as, nay, oftener than the architect. Remember that the contract with the builder who engages to erect your house for a definite sum is only binding so long as the specifications and plans are rigidly adhered to—these once being altered, even in the most trifling degree, the contract is no longer binding, but extras are allowed. Mature your plan then well before you hand it over to your architect for the final drawings and specifications to be made from it; and being decided upon, let no inducement urge you to alter it, that is, if you really wish to have your house constructed at the estimated cost.

5. CONSIDERATIONS CONNECTED WITH THE CHOICE OF A SITE FOR THE HOUSE.—(1.) *Position of site.*—(2.) *Aspect of house.*—(3.) *Position of house with reference to the road.*—(4.) *Trees near the house.*—(5.) (6.) *General considerations.*—The plan of the house being decided upon, the next point for consideration is the *site* which it is to occupy. This should not be hurriedly decided upon; and one point we would urge upon you is, when you personally inspect the proposed site, that you *should inspect it in the worst weather you can have.* If the site in any way favourably impresses you then, you may make sure that it will impress you more favourably afterwards. It is a bad plan to choose your site on a fine day, for nearly every place looks charming under the influence of clear air and bright sky. As a house set upon the top of a hill cannot be hid, so neither can the surrounding scenery be hid from the house; *the highest part of rising ground* would, therefore, be considered—where taste alone is the standard—*the best position for a house.* But

many things come in to modify this rule; elevated positions are generally exposed to blustering winds and to dashing rains; and they involve labour in reaching them either on foot or in conveyance. It does not follow, however, that a low position is more sheltered; for it is true enough that a stronger wind may rush through a valley than along the sides or top of the hills which enclose it. In this matter of site the middle course will be the safest to follow. Let the elevation be moderate, and let it be near a road; and if in a valley, or rather on the sloping sides of it, let it be on the southern side. A low site near a marshy spot must be carefully avoided, and one also on the immediate margin of a piece of stagnant water or the banks of a slowly running stream. In these situations not only does damp arise from the surface of the water, but it frequently happens that the ground rises from the margin up to the surrounding land, so that the drainage of it is brought down to the site of the house, rendering it damp. A moderately elevated site not only admits of refreshing breezes to blow round the house, but of the water of the soil being drained easily away, as well as the sewage matters. Wherever you build, look out for the finest view; it is truly lamentable, at times, to see a house with its face turned from an enchanting prospect. But even in thus securing a fine look out, regard must be had to the *actual aspect of the house.* Light has such a remarkably good influence on the health of man—we mean, direct light from the sun, not reflected light—that we hold it to be an essential point in selecting a site that it should have a sunny aspect. That is best secured by placing the *principal front*, out of which the living rooms look, *south-east.* But while having the majority of your principal rooms fronting thus, let one of them have as due a western look-out as you can get. For an afternoon room nothing can be pleasanter than to have the windows commanding a full view of the western sky, with all its marvellous beauties of light and shade, and the gorgeous colouring of sunset effects. We have said that the site of your *house should be near a road;* but not too near. There is an essential vulgarity in placing a house so close upon the public pathway—let the reader remember we speak of rural, not street districts, where compulsion as to site is a rule—that it shoulders itself like a rude fellow into notice, forcing, as it were, your criticism upon it, and speaking, as walls can speak, as plainly as possible, "here I am; admire me." A retiring position for a house, like a retiring disposition in a man, is always pleasant. But, while a near retirement and accessible seclusion are aimed at, these should not be pushed to an extreme. We like a house to be seen, but seen at the trouble of some looking for it; we therefore would counsel you to give the public glimpses of it through shady trees and clustering shrubs, partly seen and partly hid; showing, that while the occupier has resources within himself of books or company, rendering the gazing out upon the public pathway for amusement unnecessary; he is still accessible. We have no sympathy with the selfishness which dictates a man shutting his house out from public gaze, hid behind frowning walls or exclusive palings. It is in these things, and such as these, that a man's house may be an index to a man's character. *Trees upon a site always improve* it, but they should not be too numerous or too near the house; if so, they will obscure the light too much, make the rooms gloomy, and will tend somewhat to make the house damp, by dashing moisture upon the ground near it and preventing the warmth of the sun's rays to act upon it. It is a disputed point whether it is best to have a site on which trees already grow, or one free from them, so that you can plant at will. Where the site possesses a few fine old trees, with spreading branches and gnarled trunks, retain them there by all means. To cut down trees of this sort—unless they actually encroach upon the site—is like taking away a life. Thickly wooded sites are by no means common in this country; but where they are, these are certainly advantageous, as a writer on site well points out, as they give "a basis for ornamental operations." "It is," as he remarks, "a great saving of time and labour to buy your shade-trees already grown. All you have to do in such cases is to cut out roads and walks wherever they are wanted, to open up a prospect here, and plant a denser thicket there, and so to smooth out the tangled locks of nature as to develope her finest charms. This is all very well where it can be done, but such situations cannot always be found combining also the other important features to which we have just alluded. And where they cannot be found we would select one possessing the other desirable qualities, and then proceed at once to plant the ground with the best trees and in the best manner. Whether one lives to see his trees attain great size or not, is really of no consequence. There is more enjoyment in planting trees and watching their yearly improvement, than in sitting idly under trees already grown. A thousand associations spring up from year to year, and cluster around such trees. They are *your* trees; you selected them, planted them, nursed them in their feebleness, defended them from their enemies, rejoiced in their prosperous growth, and now you gaze upon their spreading boughs and thickening shade with a sort of paternal pride and affection, which you feel towards no other trees." There is much true knowledge of human nature displayed in these remarks, and we commend them to the attention of the reader. There is such a desire implanted within us to create, that we believe more satisfaction will be derived from clothing your house site with the beauties of green leaves, spreading branches and fragrant flowers, than by choosing a site where all this is already done for you. Allen, in his work on 'Rural Architecture,' has such admirable remarks on the subject of trees near a house, that we give them here:—"Nothing is more common than to see a man build a house, perhaps in most elaborate and expensive style, and then plant a row of trees close upon the front, which when grown will shut it almost entirely out of view; while he leaves the rear as bald and unprotected as if it were a barn or a horse shed—as if in utter ignorance, as he probably is, that his house is more effectively set off by a *flanking* and *background* of tree and shrubbery, than in front. And this is called good taste! Let us examine it. Trees near a dwelling are desirable for shade; *shelter* they do not afford except in masses, which last is always better given to the house itself by a veranda. Immediately adjoining, or within touching distance of a house, trees create dampness, more or less litter, and frequently vermin. They injure the walls and roofs by their continual shade and dampness. They exclude the rays of the sun, and prevent a free circulation of air. Therefore, *close* to the house, trees are absolutely pernicious, to say nothing of excluding all its architectural effect from observation; when, if planted at proper distances, they compose its finest ornaments.

"If it be necessary to build in good taste at all, it is quite as necessary that such good taste be kept in throughout. A country dwelling should always be a conspicuous object, in its full character and outlines, from one or more prominent points of observation; consequently all plantation of tree or shrubbery in its immediate vicinity should be considered as aids to show off the house and its appendages, instead of becoming the principal objects of attraction in themselves. Their disposition should be such as to create a perfect and agreeable whole, when seen in connection with the house itself. They should also be so placed as to open the surrounding landscape to view in its most attractive features, from the various parts of the dwelling. Much in the effective disposition of trees around the dwelling will thus depend upon the character of the country seen from it, and which should control to a great extent their position. A single tree of grand and stately dimensions, will frequently give greater effect than the most studied plantations. A ledge of rock, in the clifts of which wild vines may nestle, or around which a mass of shrubbery may cluster, will add a charm to the dwelling which an elaborate cultivation would fail to bestow; and the most negligent apparel of nature in a thousand ways may give a character which we might strive in vain to accomplish by our own invention. In the efforts to embellish our dwellings or grounds, the strong natural objects with which they are associated should be consulted, always keeping in view an expression of the chief character to which the whole is applied." In so much as you surround your house with shading shrubs or trees, you, while shutting yourselves comparatively in, shut out correspondingly the view. This will, however, be the case as regards the lower rooms only; and even in their case partially, for, we presume, the reader will follow the suggestions we have already dwelt upon as to having his house retiring, but not utterly secluded. Through the gaps then, admitting the gaze of the passer by, you will see the outer view, and in the way best suited to please you—for it is a curious thing, that half concealed charms heighten the pleasure, and that in the inherent yearning after mystery, we desire to know what is not fully revealed to us. This principle is much overlooked in landscape gardening, and in setting out the environments of a house. If you wish to have the full and expanded beauties of the view, you can ascend to the upper storey, or better still the prospect tower with which we advise, if not every country house, at least every farmhouse of a superior order, to be provided. We can speak from experience, not only of the pleasure derived from a vantage point of this sort, but of the value of it; for you can look fully down upon your farm buildings, and take in at a glance the general features of your adjacent fields. Nor is such a place a bad place for the quiet contemplation which all right-thinking men desire to have at times—aided, as it may be, in the genial summer time, with the quiet whiffs of a cigar.

In addition to what we have already said upon *site and aspect*, the following extracts from able architectural authorities will be valued by the reader as conveying much that is of immense importance in connection with these two points:—

"The selection of a site," says an able writer in the '*Building News*,' "is generally made by the building owner before the architect has been consulted, and he consequently has to make his proposed design suitable for its intended position. In villa architecture the nature of the landscape must, to a certain extent, guide him in the character of the edifice about to be erected. It is essential that it should harmonise perfectly with the scenery surrounding it, that it should blend as it were with the productions of nature which encircle it, and that it should unite with her to form a complete whole, yet remain in itself as a production of man and an object of utility pleasing to the eye. The arrangement and laying out of the gardens and lands around the house is a duty often intrusted to the architect, and no other person is, or ought to be, so well able to do it tastefully, and in accordance with the requirements of what has been termed landscape gardening. Simple as it may appear, it is nevertheless necessary that some thought should be bestowed upon it, and the effects of a refined fancy should be made visible in the works produced. It is needless to speak of the absurdity of Italian terraces and walks, with their classic balustrades being placed round a Gothic building, or, on the contrary, of a Gothic feature being worked round an Italian building. Yet this has been done over and over again, and we do not doubt that notwithstanding its absurdity it will be as often repeated.

"The Greeks paid great attention to the position of their temples and public buildings, and also to their private residences.

The larger edifices were placed generally in an elevated spot, both commanding a fine view and in return exposed to the observation of all around. The Egyptians, on the contrary, buried their temples and other large buildings in obscure dells, where they were hidden by enclosures and dark masses of foliage which threw their deep and solemn shades upon them; their love for the mysterious prompted this, and the priests, who were ever striving to enshroud their religion and religious observances in a gloomy superstition, were of course the originators of this practice. In our own land the Medieval architects were not unmindful of the additional and pleasing effect to be derived from a judicious selection of their building sites. They were sensible of the influence scenery has upon the mind, of the tendency it has to raise the thoughts from the earthly to the celestial, and they accordingly made use of that knowledge in the position of their churches and other religious edifices. Even the savage is not insensible to the influences of scenery; though unable to define the impressions it makes upon him, yet he feels its power and is moved by its irresistible charm. He is melted by that something which he cannot describe, and he is fascinated by the poetry which lingers in the bosom of the forest. He feels subdued, yet he knows not what it is that subdues him. He feels a kind of awe, yet he knows not what inspires it; and he seems surrounded by some invisible yet irresistible agency which makes him sensible of the existence of a greater than he. These impressions become deeper as we become more civilised, and the more refined the taste the more do they affect the feelings, and the more intelligible do they appear. It is, therefore, essential that due attention should be paid to the positions of villas and mansions, in order that they may be ornaments to the landscape in which they rise, and also that they may command as fine a view as circumstances will permit—of course convenience must be consulted. Drainage and the supply of water,—together with a ready means of approach, will of necessity be considerations which will have great weight in the selection, and which must not be forgotten, for on these requirements being met well, perhaps, depend the comfort of the future residents in the building to be erected."

Mr. Allan, from whose work we have already quoted, has also the following on site:—

"A fitness to the purposes for which the dwelling is constructed should, unquestionably, be the governing point in determining its position. The site should be dry, and slightly declining, if possible, on every side; but if the surface be level, or where water occasionally flows from contiguous grounds, or on a soil naturally damp, it should be thoroughly drained of all superfluous moisture. That is indispensable to the preservation of the house itself and the health of the inmates. The house should so stand as to present an agreeable aspect from the main points at which it is seen, or the thoroughfares by which it is approached. It should be so arranged as to afford protection from wind and storm to that part most usually occupied, as well as be easy of access to the out-buildings appended to it. It should have an unmistakable front, sides, and rear; and the uses to which its various parts are applied should distinctly appear in its outward character. It should combine all the advantages of soil, cultivation, water, shade, and shelter, which the most liberal gratification, consistent with the circumstances of the owner, may demand. If a site on the estate command a prospect of singular beauty, other things equal, the dwelling should embrace it; if the luxury of a stream, or a sheet of water in repose, present itself, it should, if possible, be enjoyed; if the shade and protection of a grove be near, its benefits should be included; in fine, any object in itself desirable, and not embarrassing to the main purposes of the dwelling and its appendages, should be turned to the best account, and appropriated in such manner as to combine all that is desirable both in beauty and effect, as well as in utility, to make up a perfect whole in the family residence."

The following remarks from a contemporary work on the *aspect and prospect* of the house are also so exceedingly suggestive that we reproduce them here:—

"Nothing," says Messrs. H. and J. Repton, is more common than for those who intend to build to consult many advisers and collect different plans, from which they suppose it possible to make one perfect whole, but they might as well expect to make an epic poem by selecting detached verses from the works of different poets. Others take a plan, and fancy it may be adapted to any situation, but, in reality, the plan must be made, not only to suit the spot, but it ought actually to be made on the spot, that every door and window may be adapted to the aspects and prospects of the situation. It was a remark of my venerable friend, Mr. Carr of York, after four-score years of experience as an architect, that to build a house we had only to provide all that was wanted, and no more than to place the best rooms to the best aspects and the best views. Simple as this apothegm may appear, it contains more truth in theory and more difficulty in practice than all the rules that have ever been laid down in books by architects, or the remarks of all the admirers of rural scenery, with whom I have conversed. The former never think of aspects, and the latter think of nothing but prospects. I will therefore beg leave to enlarge upon these two subjects.

"I consider the aspect of infinitely more consequence to the enjoyment and comfort of the inhabitant than any prospect whatever; and every common observer must be convinced that in this climate a southern aspect is most desirable; but few are aware of the total difference in the effect of turning the front of the house a few points to the east or to the west of the south, because, although the south-east is the best, yet the south-west is the worst of all possible aspects, for this reason, that all blustering winds and driving rains come from the south-west, and consequently the windows are so covered with wet, as to render the landscape hardly visible. My attention was drawn to this subject by travelling so much in post carriages, and often remarking the difference betwixt the window to the south-west and the window to the south-east, during a shower of rain or immediately afterwards, when the sun shining on the drops, causes an unpleasant glitter, obstructing the prospect, while the view towards the south-east remains perfectly visible.

"At Organ Hall, in Herefordshire, the living room was towards the south-west, and, during a heavy storm of wind and rain, we accidentally went into the butler's pantry, which looked towards the south-east, where we found the storm abated and the view from the windows perfectly clear and free from wet; but on returning into the other rooms the storm appeared as violent as ever, and the windows entirely covered with drops which obstructed all view. On considering the prevalence of south-west winds, it was determined to reverse the aspects of the house, by changing the uses of the rooms, thus making a very comfortable house of one which, from its aspect before, was hardly inhabitable, since no window, nor hardly any brick wall, will keep out the wet where a front is exposed to the south-west; for this reason, it has been found necessary, in many places, to cover the walls with slates, and to use double sashes to the windows so situated. If we had only one front or one aspect to consider, our difficulty would soon vanish; but the prevailing partiality for variety of prospect seems to require that in every direction the views should be retained; and as the opposite side must be parallel, and the corners, and right angles, we must consider the effect on each of the four sides as in the annexed diagram.

"First, the aspect due north is apt to be gloomy, because no sunshine ever cheers a room so placed.

"Secondly, the aspect due east is not much better, because there the sun only shines whilst we are in bed.

"Thirdly, the aspect due west is intolerable, from the excess of sun dazzling the eye through the greatest part of the day.

"Hence we may conclude that a square house, placed with its front opposite the cardinal points, will have one good and three bad aspects.

"Let us now consider the effect of turning the principal front towards the south-east; in this case the opposite front will be to the north-west, an aspect far better than either due north or due east, because some sunshine may be preserved when its beams are less potent than in the west, and the scene will be illuminated by those catching lights so much studied by painters, especially when the landscape consists of large masses of forest trees, and thickets richly hanging down the sides of an opposite hill. An aspect open to the north-east would be objectionable during the cold winds of spring, unless the building could be effectually sheltered by an impenetrable screen of trees, rising ground, or other defence against the wind."

The author further remarks that the south-west aspect should be sheltered by a plantation, and the offices should be erected in that situation, and again says:—"It is very common for admirers of landscape or natural scenery, to overlook the difference between a tree and a pole, or between a grove of old trees and a plantation of young ones. We fancy that time will reconcile us to the difference, but alas! we grow old as fast as the trees, and while we dot and clump a few striding saplings on an open lawn, we indulge hopes of seeing trees, while in fact, we only live to see the clumsy fence by which for many years they must be protected. Happy is the proprietor of the soil who becomes possessed of large trees, already growing on the land he purchases, since no price can buy the effect of years, or create a full grown wood, and without this we may possess a garden or a shrubbery, but not a landscape. This consideration alone is sufficient to attach us to the venerable avenue, which it would be a sort of sacrilege to desert, and whose age and beauty will give an immediate degree of importance to the house, which could never be expected in any more open part of an estate."

Mr. Kerr has also in the '*Builder*' pointed out, as follows, the importance of considering the position, aspect, and prospect of mansions,—"and the singular neglect of this principle in most cases; observing that every room whatever has not merely a right aspect as opposed to a wrong, but generally a very limited range of suitable aspect as against the entire remainder of the compass more or less unsuitable. We also alluded to the great value commonly assigned to considerations of prospect, for which those of aspect were probably too often sacrificed, without at least sufficiently drawing upon ingenuity to accommodate both demands. The general question of aspect, he further said, is threefold,—as regards sunshine, weather, and prospect. The sun being south at noon, east at six A.M., west at six P.M., and so on, such rooms as require coolness and shade at any particular time of the day must be aspected accordingly. As to weather, west being generally the wet quarter, and east the dry; north, gloomy; south, sultry; south-west, exposed to boisterous winds; south-east, the quarter of mild winds, and so on, the various rooms must be again aspected with reference to this. Lastly, speaking of prospect, as a southward view in the daytime has the sun in the picture, while a northward view has the landscape in full light, and the like with other quarters at different hours of the day, there must be one more question with reference to which the aspect of windows ought to be determined; the problem here being to secure at a given time an approved clieroscuro for the landscape in view."

The subject of the relation of the *garden* to the house has been singularly overlooked by many authorities. The following remarks by an able authority, Mr. S. Huggins, as given in the '*Building News*,' will be valued by the reader. He begins his remarks by pointing out that the arrangement of Pliny's summer villa in Tuscany was such, that it was scattered in detached apartments over the ground, and then connected only by porticoes; and that the modern houses of Persia are much in the same way, the apartments being intermingled with gardens, trees, &c. Our climate, of course, precludes this arrangement; but, as Mr. Huggins remarks, although we cannot obtain this in its full completeness, we may have our garden arrangements much more in keeping with fine taste than they are at present. The house need not be exposed in the winter time to every rude blast that blows, making all its garden accessories exposed, as they are else as so "many unmeaning mockeries." We may, in the first place, have such accessories so distributed and connected by "sheltering features, walls, verandas, and covered walks, porticoes, loggies, and pavilions," that we can enjoy them even in bad weather. The house, if small and compact, might occupy the centre of the garden; which should be sheltered by fence walls; if, on the contrary, "large and straggling," it might have attached to it at one or more sides, a sheltered spot, "forming either wing or tail with the garden entrance opening into it"—this inner garden being the private one, sacred to the family, while the outer one would be more for the public eye to gaze upon, and be ornamental. But the close and intimate relation of the garden to the house aimed at by Mr. Huggins, is that in which the house is so fashioned that it will include the garden in it "as it were in its bosom." "There are circumstances," says Mr. Huggins, "with which advantage might be found in arranging the parts of a country house around a garden court, planted with flowers and cloistered or otherwise, which might be made a most beautiful and delight-yielding feature.

"Near to a town where, from its dearness, the plot of land is limited in size, instead of placing the house in its *centre* exposed to every wind that blows and to observation from all points, I would build it on its *circumference;* that is to say, I would have it enclosing rather than being surrounded by, the garden, which, for eight months in the year, must be a nuisance instead of a pleasure; or, if not entirely surrounding it, encompassing it on two or three sides, leaving it to a wall 9 or 10 feet high, to do the rest; which would render the garden perfectly private and secure from the blast. Stables and offices might make up a part of the circumscribing pile, as they assisted to form the quadrangle of the old manor-house.

"There is this difference between the requirements of our houses and those of the Italians; our apartments must not be entered immediately from the court, and without the intervention of a corridor. Lobby or corridor there must be; and the garden should be disposed with an eye to rendering it as accessible as possible to the sun, and as inaccessible to the severer winds.

"The one-story arrangement, in spreading out the house over greater space, is most favourable to the surrounding of a garden in the way I suggest; and there is infinitely more convenience in a house in which all the occupied rooms, including bed-rooms and offices, are on one floor, than there is in one of two or three stories. There is less of the danger to life and limb, which constantly going up and down stairs must occasion, less toil and confusion and other advantages, more especially felt by elderly persons and invalids. The staircase is a feature susceptible of great beauty, and in most town residences and in many country residences stairs are unavoidable. But they are an evil to be eschewed where it is possible, and in neighbourhoods where the cheapness of land renders it practicable, I think the additional cost incurred by having all the needful rooms on one floor is well repaid by the daily convenience.

"But to return from what is somewhat of a digression: if the embracing of a garden in the centre of a house can seldom be accomplished, there is nothing to forbid the enclosed side gardens. For these, while they could have all the shelter necessary to render them available for pleasure and recreation, the greater part of the year, would not necessitate any radical departure from the usual anatomy of a house.

"What has hitherto operated against their introduction has

been, I believe, those enemies of true taste and fitness both in architecture and horticulture—vanity and fashion—the vanity that is solicitous to show off the entire house and its beauties of style to every stranger that approaches it, and would have no evidence of its cost—symbols of its owner's wealth—hidden from the public gaze. What I suggest, however, can be done without any sacrifice of architectural display in the exterior of the house: the walls that are built to enclose the side gardens may be made architectural, and receive as much embellishment by niches, pilasters, or sculpture as any other part. They may become an extension of the decorated walls of the house, so that the garden is really embraced by the external architecture, and made an interior feature.

"As to the effect of the garden artistically upon the house, however it be connected with it, whether it embrace it as a girdle, form wings to its sides, a tail to its back, or a court within its bosom, no more fitting, or beautiful and poetic appendage to an architectural scene can be conceived, than a refined and cultivated garden of choice flowers—those beautiful objects sent expressly to gratify the senses, and in the formation and adornment of which are united in perfection the graces of colour and shape, freshness and fragrancy. Nothing can be more assisting to the decorative composition than the enchanting picture that floral and sylvan elements would compose and furnish. Much, I take it, of what we dream, or fable of fairyland, might be realized in a scene where every vegetable beauty and delicacy are at the command of an artist, and may be employed as materials and elements along with those of an art on which the taste and genius of nations have been lavished. Indeed, we can only reach the utmost possibilities of art when we call in the aid of nature, not only as an instructress in all that is great and beautiful, but as a contributor of her rich gifts; in other words, when we can make large quotations from the works of the Great Architect, and successfully combine them with our own. 'Art and luxury,' says Emerson, 'have early learned that they must work as enchantment and sequel to the original beauty of nature. Only so far as the masters of the world have called in nature to their aid have they reached the height of magnificence. This is the meaning of their hanging gardens, villas, garden houses, islands, parks, and preserves—to back their faulty personality with these strong accessories.' To nature's magical aid, I would add, is owing much of the boasted beauty of the Southern and Eastern houses. What would the Moorish palaces of Spain be, beautiful as they are in themselves; what would they be, notwithstanding their elaborate stone lattices and richly carved arcades, without the orange and pomegranate trees and sweet flowers of Andalusia, and the ever-springing fountains of cool water with which they are beautifully mingled?"

(5.) *Soil of the Site.*—Avoid by all means of avoidance, if possible, having anything to do with a heavy tenacious clay soil. It is almost impossible to have a house dry where the soil is of this nature, unless at a great outlay. A gravelly soil is the best of all. "A damp situation," says a writer in a professional journal, "above all things is to be avoided, both for the sake of comfort and of health. Nothing can be more injurious than a damp atmosphere and damp locality: the evil effects are too well known to require enumerating. We all know that chills and colds are the foundations on which are built more than half the sickness and disease to which the human race is subject; this is more especially the case with children and young persons, who are more susceptible than those of a more advanced age, and to them a damp house or a damp atmosphere often proves fatal. Besides this we generally find the soils in these localities are bad for foundations, consisting for the most part of clays which are totally unfit to receive any superstructure without extra preparation being made and additional means being taken to secure its safety, and thereby necessitating the expenditure of money that might otherwise have been saved. The economising of funds in our day is a question which is looked at most rigorously by building owners, who have imbibed a morbid fear of every work which they commence being the ultimate cause of their ruin." But in whatever soil you build, it is essential that you specially *drain* the site. While the evil of a damp house is so universally feared, and deservedly so, it is a marvel that so simple an expedient as the thorough drainage of its site has not been more insisted and acted upon than it has. It is usual to recommend courses of slate laid in cement, or sheet lead to be laid on the course of stone or brick just above the ground line, sometimes trenches filled with concrete to some depth in which to build the footings or foundations of the wall, and in some cases, layers of smithy clinkers to be used in place of concrete. All these are but partially acting preventives of the disease of a damp house; and may very well be used, and used with some good result, if in conjunction with the thorough drainage of the site we have alluded to. The site of the house—and by this we mean a space of ground some yards wider on all sides than the immediate space occupied by the building—should be surrounded completely by a cincture of tubular drains leading into the main drain. These form or act as the catch drains intercepting the water coming from all parts of the surrounding field to the plot in which the house stands, while the water of the plot itself must be led off by drains, more or less numerous, intersecting either its transverse or longitudinal section according to the slope of the ground, and leading to the drains encircling the plot. This complete drainage of the site we look upon as essential in close, tenacious, and what we call, retentive soils; but may be modified in the direction of simplification in proportion as the soil of the site approaches the character of extreme dryness and lightness, in which case, drainage may be dispensed with, and the usual method of building good foundations trusted to, for the prevention of damp. Damp, in its worst form, generally arises from the moist condition of the soil; being worst near the ground, and gradually extending upwards. Damp, however, sometimes gets into walls where exposed to long continued battering blasts of rain. Dryness of wall, in this case, is often attempted to be secured by covering the wall exposed to the prevalent storms by slates; these, however, look ill, and are expensive, and are, moreover, not always efficient. By far the best method is to ascertain the direction of the prevalent storms, and specify that the walls on that side shall be of increased thickness, and be what is called a cavity wall. Indeed, this "cavity wall" system is possessed of such peculiar advantages, that we strongly recommend its adoption throughout. An excellent plan to secure dryness is to have the house, or part of the house, *cellared under.* The following remarks on preventing damp in houses from the pen of an able writer in the '*Building News,*' will be of service here:—

"*Damp* may be guarded against by his adoption of a judicious form of roof; as for example, if the building be on an eminence, by the use of good overhanging eaves, which will serve to protect the edifice from the effects of heavy rain storms. The health of the inmates may be seriously endangered by the neglect of all proper precautions for excluding moisture; and the presence of even one thin wall or ceiling, pervious to the external damps of rain or fog, may cause great annoyance and sickness. In such case it will often be found that the moist state of the air out of doors becomes generally distributed indoors; and the whole residence, walls, wooden partitions, doors, and indeed every exposed surface, will break out, as it were, into a sweat; and the damp be seen to run down everywhere in streams. In exposed situations it will always be desirable to adopt a roof of simple form, and to avoid all land-gutters, lantern or sky-lights. Cross-gutters are in country houses very often resorted to: they should be carefully eschewed. Of course it is of consequence that ample water-courses or gutters should be provided, and everything be done by the architect to render the roofs capable of carrying off the rain-fall; but, in isolated country houses, especially such as lie embowered amid trees, assurance against accident from rain-storms, by not only the sufficiency of down-pipes and other means of exit, but their careful protection against obstruction by leaves, birds' nests, and the like. The dryness of the walls will naturally be a thing of the first consequence in building on an exposed site; and here it is that architects often get into difficulties with their clients; caused by that fruitful source of quarrel, the architect's estimate. This, in the case of a country mansion or other isolated dwelling, is too often based upon the known cost of some town or suburban residence, where comparatively thin walls might possibly entail no evil on the occupants; but, in exposed rural districts the case is very different; and, to surround the dwelling with walls of extra thickness, adding greatly to the expenditure, is a positive necessity.

"Where brick or stone are costly materials, all kinds of expedients are resorted to, in order to obtain a cheap, weather-tight wall, by their merely partial adoption. The thin wall may be built hollow; it may be coated externally with compo; it may be *slated* outside; or, it may be battened inside; and each of these expedients may have its own especial advantage of economy or other desideratum in building; but, for our own present purpose—*healthy building*—there can be no question about it; and nothing can be so desirable as a very thick wall of good brick or stone. We say 'good,' because in some districts, though the latter material may be very plentiful, it is not of a good quality: thus in some of our northern counties (Westmoreland for example) so faulty is the quality of the stone that, to render the work weather-tight, the masons, or 'wallers,' are obliged to lay the stones with their top and bottom beds inclining outward from the inside of the wall.

"Descending from the use of thick walls to the next preferable substitute, we should consider inside battening the best process for rendering a building dry. Hollow walls have within the last few years become very general; but, unless great care is taken by the workmen, this expedient is liable to offer a harbour for rats and other vermin; which in time will create an unwholesome stench within the dwelling, not easily obviated, as it ordinarily can be when the evil occurs behind internal battening.

"'How to *cure* damp walls,' to judge by the advertisements we so often see, has now become a stock or standard problem of our day, and one that has long taken rank with our old friend, 'how to cure smoky chimneys.' We have no particular recipe to offer for the *cure* of damp walls; but would urge builders to use every precaution for their *prevention*. In clayey soils it will be always desirable to introduce dry areas well drained, outside all walls, enclosing underground rooms; and to observe the precaution, now so general, of inserting between the joints of the work, at certain levels above the ground, a layer of lead, of slate, or of asphalte, to prevent the moisture caused by contact with the earth from rising up the wall."

Another, and a great advantage, from having an underground cellar, to which we have already alluded, is in having places in which to store away provisions. We all know the difficulties there is to keep meat fresh and cool in summer time, and of all the expedients adopted to secure this there is none so completely effectual as an underground cellar. We write in a district in which cellars are almost universally made to houses, even of the lowest class; and we are simply giving expression to the fact, when we say, that by their means a large saving is annually effected in the keeping of meat in good condition till it can be conveniently used, which would otherwise be rendered useless. We can conceive of no house in its arrangements being perfect without one or more cellar apartments. In the cellar should be placed a stone table on which to salt meat, &c., when required. While upon the subject of prevention of damp—we would here point out one frequent cause of damp walls in the neighbourhood of the sea, that is, using the sea-sand in the preparation of the mortar. The affinity of salt for moisture is so well known that we need not enter further into an explanation of the matter. We know at present where the residence of one Earl is now uninhabitable, from sea-sand having been used in the mortar with which it is built. In localities, then, where the builder may be tempted to take sea-sand, let him be looked sharply after that he does not yield to the temptation. Let the use of clean sharp river sand be always specified; and if river sand be not obtainable easily, and the sand be obtained from a pit, let it be examined to see that it is not highly impregnated with salt, which it may be from being in a locality at one time submerged by the sea in ancient times. We have seen a sand-pit opened, which, fully one mile from the sea, was used for building purposes, although in reality sea-sand. Where the quality of the sand is doubtful, it is a good practice to wash it with water. In sea-side localities we have known parties tempted to use stones for building purposes—for cottages more especially—which had been exposed to the waters and the salt breezes of the shore. Such stones are sure to effloresce, and give out saline dampness in certain conditions of the weather. Such stones, if in abundance, may be considered good enough for cottage work; that we hold them not to be, for health is of as much importance to labouring men as to us, and health cannot exist where dampness is.

6. Ventilation.—We have now to draw the attention of the reader, and briefly, to this important subject, about which so much has been written, and of which so little is practically thought in every day life. Upon that importance we need not now take up time by insisting, only stating, that if comfort and health are desiderated it will not be neglected; and further, we say, that if all knew the organic impurities which defile impure air, we should find as general a horror of breathing dirty air as there

is of drinking dirty water. How little it is attended to, or rather how grossly it is neglected, the following few sentences from the '*Builder*' most graphically show:—

"With regard to sanatory science in house construction we moderns have made little progress. In some respects we have 'advanced backwards.' That is, the perfection of workmanship and of materials in modern houses is an evil. Flooring-boards are stove-dried, close-jointed, and laid double; skirtings are of cement; door-casings, window-casings, and doors and windows are 'the perfection of workmanship.' The entire house, from basement to roof, is sound and air-tight in walls, in floors, in doors and windows, and in roof; but, and herein consists the evil, arrangements for ventilation there are none. The openings from the grates to the flues are low; the ceilings are high; but means for a never-ceasing change of the internal atmosphere there are none. We have the most costly material and the perfection of workmanship spoiled in our house building, because we make no provision for permanent ventilation. Better far for health the old houses of our great-grandfathers, with a chimney so wide that the family coach might have been hoisted up it: with a fire on the hearth so big that an ox might have been roasted at it; and with chinks, with cracks, and with openings in floor, in walls, in doors, in windows, and in roofs, letting in streams of fresh air sufficient to drive a small windmill. Our great-grandfathers may have shortened their lives by gluttony and strong ale; they may have suffered from rheumatism; but they did not die prematurely of close rooms and foul air."

In the same journal the following is given as to the quantity of air necessary to be supplied to apartments:—

"It has been proved that each person consumes about 14 cubic feet of air per hour, and by exhausting the vital element, oxygen, and producing carbonic acid to the extent of from four to five per cent. vitiates 100 cubic feet more. But the provision of this quantity would be so near upon the point of danger, that authorities are of opinion that twenty times this should be supplied per hour. The prisoners at Holloway receive from thirty to forty times this quantity, and the supply is not too large. In our public hospitals, from 1,000 to 1,700 cubic feet of space are allowed to each person, and when the area is lessened, injurious effects speedily follow. Dr. Bence Jones found that in the dormitories in St. Pancras workhouse, when only 164 cubic feet per head were allowed, the air contained about thirty times its proper amount of carbonic acid, and the closeness of the atmosphere was most oppressive, so that the inmates sickened of fever. Even in such of the barracks as have 500 cubic feet of space allowed, the air becomes charged with poisonous matter."

We might here give at length the various theories on which ventilation is assumed to depend, and upon the modes by which their requirements are met in practice; but we reduce as follows the matter at once to its simplest elements, both in its theory and in its practice. Air when breathed becomes warmed, and when expired rises upwards. The apertures made for its exit from the room must therefore be made near the ceiling. But fresh air is required to take its place, and this should be admitted at or near the level of the floor. Two classes of apertures are therefore always required before we can secure ventilation; for ventilation does not mean merely the taking away of foul air from a room, any more than it does not mean the supply of fresh air to it. It includes both, and both of which are, or should be, in coincident operation. By far the best way we know of to withdraw the foul air from a room, is to have double flues carried up from the fireplace; or rather the second or ventilating flue to start at a point above it some foot or 18 inches from the ceiling. An opening is made into the ventilating flue near the ceiling which may be covered with an ornamental grating. Where perfect efficiency is, however, required, the aperture to the flue should be such in its relation to the level of the ceiling, that the air should have the easiest possible access to it. It should be remembered that warmed air has a difficulty in dipping down just as water has in rising up to pass over an obstacle. Indeed air has to be cooled before it will dip down. Hence the desirability to have the apertures leading to the flue at the same, or at a higher level, than that of a ceiling. To secure this, the better way will be to perforate the cornice at the breast of the chimney, close to the line of the ceiling, with a number of apertures, these leading to a tube, closed at the ends, and communicating at its centre with vertical flue running up alongside of the chimney flue. These double flues are now made in pottery. It is right, however, to state, that we shall never be able to carry off, in the easiest way, foul air from our rooms until we have our ceilings made in such a way as to take advantage of the ascensional power of warmed air. Nothing is so easy as to get rid of foul air if we only allow it to escape; our present form of room ceilings is admirably contrived to *prevent* this escape. As regards the supply of fresh air, the fittings of our rooms are, upon the whole, pretty well adapted—not designedly, however—to meet this. Doors and windows do not fit so tightly, but air enough, in many instances, finds easy access to the rooms. But such is the English "horror of draughts"—a refined mode of expressing the horror of fresh air—that modern improvements so-called, in house construction tend chiefly to the closing up of air passages to rooms. Moreover, air admitted at once from the outside atmosphere has certainly this disadvantage, that it is cold in winter. The best method then to supply a room with fresh air warm in winter, is to use one of the many forms of what are called ventilating grates. By the use of these the air is taken from the outside, brought in contact with the back part of the grate, heated thereby, and thence sent into the room through convenient apertures.

7. Drainage of Town Houses and Districts.—While ventilation has for its object the conveying rapidly the foul air from within, *drainage* is carried out to prevent the production of foul air without the house. The principles and practice of drainage will be found fully explained and illustrated in "Working Drawings in Architecture and Building;" A. Fullarton & Co.,—the scope of the present work precluding these being given here. The following will, however, be valuable, as presenting a *vidimus* of the points to be attended to in carrying out schemes of drainage. They are the practical suggestions issued by Mr. Rawlinson, C.E., for the aid of local surveyors, connected with the draining works in progress, or to be undertaken under the powers of the Public Works Act. They may be found of service in a wider area than Mr. Rawlinson originally contemplated:—

"Before a scheme of sewerage is devised, the district should be most carefully examined so as to obtain a correct idea of the drainage area, or the several drainage areas; inquiry should then be made to ascertain how surface water has passed off up to the time of such examination, and with what effects to property. Main sewers and drains need not have sectional capacity equal to the volume of surface flood water over the whole area, but may be adapted to the length of streets, number of houses, surface area of house-yards and roofs, number of street gulleys and volume of water supply. Sewers and drains, in wet subsoil, should be made to act as land drains. The following rules are general; but each surveyor must use his own judgment, and make the best arrangements possible, under the circumstances, with each special area, and with the materials at command:—

1. Natural streams should not be arched over to form main sewers.

2. Valley lines and natural streams may be improved, so as to remove more readily surface water and extreme falls of rain.

3. Main sewers need not be of capacity to contain the flood water of the area drained; such flood water may be passed over the surface, in most cases, without causing injury.

4. Main sewers should be laid out in straight lines and true gradients, from point to point, with manholes, and flushing and ventilating arrangements at each principal change of line and gradient. All manholes should be brought up to the surface of the road or street, and should be finished with a cover easily removable for inspection.

5. Duplicate systems of sewers are not required. Drains for storm waters to natural streams in valley lines may be retained, and may be improved.

6. Earthenware pipes make good sewers and drains up to their capacity. Pipes must be truly laid, and securely jointed. In ordinary ground they should be joined with clay. In sandy ground, special means must be used to prevent sand washing in at the joints.

7. Brick sewers ought to be formed with bricks moulded to the *radii*.

8. Brick sewers should, in all cases, be set in hydraulic mortar. In no case should any sewer be formed with bricks set dry, to be subsequently grouted.

9. Main sewers may have flood water overflows wherever

practicable, to prevent such sewers being choked during thunder storms or heavy rains.

10. Sewers should not join at right angles. Tributary sewers should deliver sewage in the direction of the mainflow.

11. Sewers and drains, at junctions and curves, should have extra fall to compensate for friction.

12. Sewers of unequal sectional diameters should not join with level inverts, but the lesser or tributary sewer should have a fall into the main at least equal to the difference in the sectional diameter.

13. Earthenware pipes of equal diameters should not be joined, but the lesser pipe should be joined on to the greater.

14. House drains should not pass direct from sewers to the inside of houses, but all drains should end at an outside wall and have means of external ventilation.

15. Sinks and closets should be against external walls, so that the refuse water, or soil, may be discharged into the drain outside the main wall. Down-spouts may be used for ventilation, care being taken that the head of such spout is not near a window.

16. Inlets to all pipe drains should be properly protected.

17. Side junctions should be provided in all sewers and drains. The position should be sketched, and indicated by figures in a book or on a plan. Side junctions should be carefully closed for subsequent use.

18. A record should be kept by the surveyor of the character of the subsoil opened out in each street sewered or drained.

19. All sewers and drains should be set out true in line and in gradient. All the material used should be sound, and the workmanship should be carefully attended to.

20. 'Sight rails' should be put up in each street before the ground is opened out, showing the centre line of each sewer and the depth to the invert.

21. Sewers having steep gradients should have full means for ventilation at the highest points.

22. Tall chimneys may be used with advantage for sewer and drain ventilation, if the owners will allow a connection to be made.

23. Sewer outlet works should be simple in form, and cheap

in construction, so as to remove all solids, sediment, and flocculent matter from the sewage.

"It is of the utmost importance to impress upon local surveyors the necessity of care in setting out main sewerage works and house drains with accuracy, in choosing sound materials, and in properly superintending the works during their progress. House drains should be so arranged as to be capable of removing all water, soil, and fluid refuse from yards, roofs, and interiors of houses to the sewers, without any risk of gaseous contamination to such houses. Street sewers should be capable of conveying all sewage to some common outlet, without retaining sediment in them. All sewers and drains should have arrangements for full ventilation, at such points and in such manner as not to cause any nuisance. Charcoal (as proposed by Dr. John Stenhouse) may be used to filter and disinfect sewage gases, at all manholes and other ventilators. If the fluid sewage can be applied to land for agricultural uses, means should be provided for effecting this purpose."

8. Drainage of Rural Houses.—While of course drainage cannot be carried out in the country in the complete way in which it is in the town, it should not on any account be totally neglected. The foul water, &c., arising from domestic operations must be carried away somewhere, and it is well to carry them away quickly; and that somewhere should be the "liquid manure tank." As the drain tubes are apt to become choked, we should recommend the line of their direction to the tank to be carefully marked; so that they can be easily got at for the purpose of cleansing. This will be greatly aided by using lidded or capped drain tubes.

9. Cesspool Ventilation and Trapping of Drains.—But in providing for country and suburban houses a place of final deposit for the foul water of the house, as the liquid manure tank, let this not degenerate into the *cesspool.* It is also essential to provide thorough ventilation of drains. Generally speaking, enough is thought to be done if the drains are "trapped;" but the following suggestive extract from the '*Builder*' will show that great evils are apt to arise if trapping alone is trusted to. "There are frequent complaints of bad smells being perceived from drains, from closets, from sinks, from street gullies,

and there is a loud outcry for 'trapping.' But trapping alone is a delusion and a snare. Foul gases are not destroyed by such means, but are concentrated,—made far more deadly, and are forced into houses through every rat-hole, crack, or imperfection in sewer, drain, wall, and floor. By far the safest remedy is external ventilation, free and abundant at any point where there is the least chance of harm, remembering that foul gases admitted to the open air are diffused into space, and seldom injure, but that foul gases admitted within houses are diffused through the rooms, and injure at all times, but especially at night and during sleep. We often read that gullies have been removed or trapped, because foul gases escaped, to the annoyance of some one; and we have learned that the Queen, in driving about Windsor, detecting a stench from some of the gullies, ordered them to be trapped. We most sincerely hope her Majesty, at the same time, ordered better and fuller ventilation to be provided; as, also, the sewers to be examined, cleansed, and improved. If there are foul smells from any sewers, sinks, or closets, there is something wrong, requiring constructive improvement, and full and free external ventilation. A ton of gunpowder permanently stored beneath any dwelling-house would be neither safe nor desirable, but it might work far less mischief than foul sewers, with foul drains, thoroughly trapped. We would prefer the gunpowder, which might go off once, to the fever poison, which is acting always."

CHAPTER SECOND.

GENERAL HINTS ON THE INTERIOR ARRANGEMENTS AND CONVENIENCES OF HOUSES.

10. Lighting—Windows.—It is quite evident, that however careful you may have been in the choice of a site, and however fine may be the prospect obtained from it, you will not secure all the benefits of this care unless your house have good windows, and these disposed of in the most advantageous way. A dark ill-lighted room has a most depressing effect upon the spirits, and is the exciting cause of very distressing and peculiar forms of diseases. We have already given in the first division a yet

notes on aspect of the house; but the following from an article on the Sanitary Arrangement of Buildings from the '*Building News*,' will not be out of place here as bearing on this point of lighting of rooms:—

"Of course in town buildings the owner has no alternative: his plot of ground is already fixed for him, and usually presents but two frontages; one of them dictated by the line of street in which his premises are situated. In selecting even a town dwelling, however, we should ourselves make its salubrious aspect a primary consideration. This is seldom done; and what is worse, it is seldom that, when a new town is built, or an estate laid out for building upon, its projectors give the healthy aspect of the streets a moment's reflection. Even in setting out a detached mansion on an open ground, we too often neglect the salutary precaution of so placing it with reference to the points of the compass, as to ensure (so far as the precaution *can* secure it) the future health of the occupants. But if this precaution be needed in the case of a single dwelling, how much more so in that of a sanitary asylum, a workhouse, or a barrack? As a general rule such structures should never stand with their windows looking due north and south: it is safer always to place them *diagonally* to the four cardinal points; so that, at no 'look-out' will a living or sleeping room be all day deprived of the sun's rays, nor all day exposed to them. There is a remarkable case on record—that of a large Russian barrack—that should serve as a warning to all architects. In the case of this barrack it was found that the soldiers placed in the wing lighted from the north were those most frequently attacked with sickness; while their comrades in the wing facing south were remarkable for their healthy condition. By way of experiment as to the cause, the men were made to exchange quarters; when it was at once seen that the invalids transferred from the north wing grew well, and its new occupants, transferred from the south wing, became invalids.

"The necessity of providing sufficient *light* has already been alluded to as an item of *convenience* in building; but its influence on health also ought not to be lost sight of. Dark rooms, dark cellars and passages are always harbingers of sickness; if for no other reason than this—that they help to discourage cleanliness; to say nothing of their adverse influence on the health and spirits of their occupants; plenty of light being justly accounted as essential to health as plenty of pure air."

11. *Connection between aspect and prospect.*—In addition to the above, the following, from a paper read by Mr. Kerr, before one of the Architectural Associations, will be of service, as drawing attention to a point too often overlooked, namely, the connection between "aspect" and "prospect:"—

"Every room whatever has not merely a right aspect as opposed to a wrong, but generally, a very limited range of suitable aspect as against the entire remainder of the compass, more or less unsuitable. Great value is also commonly assigned to considerations of prospect, for which those of aspect were probably too often sacrificed, without, at least, sufficiently drawing upon ingenuity to accommodate both demands. The general question of aspect, he further said, is threefold, as regards sunshine, weather, and prospect. The sun being south at noon, east at 6 A.M., west at 6 P.M., and so on, such rooms as require coolness and shade at any particular time of the day, must be aspected accordingly. As to weather, west being generally the wet quarter, and east the dry, north gloomy, south sultry, south-west exposed to boisterous winds, south-east the quarter of mild winds, and so on, the various rooms must be again aspected with reference to this. Lastly, speaking of prospect, as a southward view in the day-time has the sun in the picture, while a northward view has the landscape in full light, and the like with other quarters at different hours of the day; there must thus be one more question with reference to which the aspect of windows ought to be determined, the problem here being to secure at a given time an approved *chiaro-scuro* for the landscape in view."

12. *Position and size of Windows.*—Windows, therefore, should be large and well-placed; and, above all, the sills should be low, so that while sitting you can easily, without effort, see out upon the scene before you. To secure this, the height from the floor should be 18 inches, but not exceed two feet. As regards the proportion of a window relatively to the size of the room, it is difficult to give precise rules. It is better to err in excess than in deficiency, for this very common sense reason, that if you

have too much light, you can easily exclude it in any degree you wish; but if your window is so small as to give too little, you cannot at will increase it. At the same time it should not be overlooked, that much window surface makes a room cold in winter. The width of all the windows throughout should be uniform. By this one set of window blinds will suit all; if this is not attended to, considerable labour to the housewife will be involved. Again, it is of importance to study the relation of the window or windows of a room to the fire-places in it. We have known the window of a room placed in the same wall in which the fireplace was, and close beside it; the result of which was, that only one half of the room was well lighted. The matter assumes greater importance in kitchens where operations are carried on incessantly at the fireside; and yet so often is the point overlooked, that it is no difficult matter to find houses where the window is placed in the position just now described; the result of which is, that the cook has no direct light to aid her. The matter is not much mended, if any, by having the window placed immediately in front of the fireplace, for in that case the cook will stand in her own light. The best position for the window is to the right or the left. Windows are generally placed in the centre of the walls of a room; but if, in addition to the central window or windows, we could, by having one in a corner, command a fine or an additional point of view, we would not hesitate to place it there; although any architect might tell us we were destroying the symmetry of the room. Some of these corner windows we have come across have been the most delightful lounging windows in the house. For entertaining rooms, those deeply recessed bay or bow windows, now so generally introduced, are most admirable contrivances, and add immensely to the pleasures of a house.

13. DOORS.—*Position of the doors* of a room materially affects the comfort of the inhabitants. It is usually a bad position to have a door in the centre of the wall, for in this case you will probably find, especially in small-sized rooms, that you have not space on either side for articles of furniture you would like to place there. This attention to the position of a door is of even greater importance in the case of moderately sized bed-rooms. We have known a door so placed, that the only position for the bed was jammed

up against the window. Close by the side of a fireplace in an entertaining room is also bad, for in this case, those sitting near the fireplace are more or less disturbed every time the door is used to allow of parties entering or leaving the room. The hanging of the door is also a matter of some importance; if hung, for instance, so that the hinges are at the side nearest the window, the door will, on opening, throw a shade upon the party entering. The light of the window should fall on the face of the door which is on the outside or passage side when it is shut. The doors of small places, as water closets, dressing rooms, &c., should always open into the passage or the largest room if they are entered from one room. They should never open into the closets themselves, as this only reduces the internal space of the closets.

On this subject of doors we give the following suggestive remarks of Mr. S. Huggins, extracted from a valuable series of papers on "Plans and Planning," contributed by him to the pages of the '*Building News:*'—"I have seen a greater look of comfort, and more of the elements of all that is calculated to excite pleasing emotions, in the single day-apartment or house-part of a labourer's cottage, than is to be found throughout the numerous apartments of many a modern mansion; where the number and disposition of the *doors* show either ignorance or disregard, on the part of their designers, of what constitutes a comfortable and cheerful apartment. I have noted plans of recently erected noblemen's and other mansions, showing four or five doors opening into one room of but moderate dimensions, sometimes two of them in the same wall with the fireplace, which must render freedom from draughts impossible, and give all ideas of domestic enjoyment to the winds that ride rampant through them. At one of Her Majesty's present residences, if it be not belied by the engraved plan of it, scarce one of the rooms contains a snug corner, so numerous are the doors opening into them in every direction, one-half of which might be built up with great advantage to the place. The sense of comfort and undisturbed tranquillity cannot be gratified in such rooms, nor in any rooms beyond a certain very moderate size. A room so large that the returning wall is four or five yards from the fireplace, can only be rendered fit for domestic occupation, or reception of a family group, by screens round the fire, forming as it were a room within a room. Where is the snug and comfortable nook in the large symmetrical wildernesses called coffee-rooms or dining-rooms of our club-houses, which, generally speaking, must be dreary substitutes for a genuine English home? A measure of architectural character and display was, no doubt, necessary in these rooms; but too much seems to have been sacrificed to obtain it. Instead of one large coffee or dining-room, what was there to hinder a series of smaller ones being provided?

"A due recognition of the principle here insisted on would, I think, more frequently lead, in the better class of houses, to having ante-rooms and retiring-rooms to sitting and bed-rooms, which somewhat unusual apartments, while they give a most charming sense of privacy, seclusion, and quiet, so grateful to the feelings of a studious person or invalid, do away with the necessity of having every room to abut on a lobby, and thus decrease the difficulty of planning."

14. Bed-Rooms.—Let the intending house-builder be most careful in attending to the bed-room department. We make no objection whatever to the house being well provided with public entertaining rooms, and these of ample dimensions; but we do most strongly object to the system, too often adopted, of obtaining these at the expense of cramped passages, staircases, and above all, confined bed-rooms. As we have in another place remarked, —"Nothing adds so much to the comfort of a man's life as good roomy bed-rooms, and nothing to the convenience of a family as plenty of them. Architects, in claiming, and unfortunately getting, ample space for the public rooms, and giving the least dimensions to the bed-rooms, seem to forget that in no room does a man spend so much of his time as in his bed-room. It should, therefore, be so large as to give plenty of room, and to have the bed so placed, that when the window or door is opened, it should not be in the line of direct draught. Ask a physician, and he will tell you, that in cases of severe illness, there is nothing he dreads so much as the confined room in which his patient is placed; the air in it is always foul, and can only be made fresh at a fearful risk. Looking at the question from all sides we are strong advocates for large bed-rooms, indeed, for their being the best rooms in the house—for the confined closets which our architects and builders often deem right to give

us we have a profound contempt." The following hints about bed-rooms from Sir James Clark's work on the "Sanative Influences of Climate" will be useful here:—"Their small size and their lowness render them very insalubrious; and the case is rendered worse by close windows and thick curtains and hangings, with which the beds are often so carefully surrounded, as to prevent the possibility of the air being renewed. The consequence is, that we are breathing vitiated air during the greater part of the night; that is, more than a third part of our lives; and thus the period of repose which is necessary for the renovation of our mental and bodily vigour, becomes a source of disease. Sleep, under such circumstances, is very often disturbed, and always much less refreshing than when enjoyed in a well-ventilated apartment; it often happens indeed, that such repose, instead of being followed by renovated strength and activity, is succeeded by a degree of heaviness and languor which is not overcome till the person has been some time in a purer air. Nor is this the only evil arising from sleeping in ill-ventilated apartments. When it is known that the blood undergoes most important changes in its circulation through the lungs by means of the air which we breathe, and that these vital changes can only be effected by the respiration of pure air, it will be easily understood how the healthy functions of the lungs must be impeded by inhaling for many successive hours the vitiated air of our bed-rooms, and how the health must be as effectually destroyed by respiring impure air, as by living on unwholesome or innutritious food. In the case of children and young persons predisposed to consumption, it is of still more urgent consequence that they should breathe pure air by night as well as by day, by securing a continuous renewal of the air in their bed-rooms, nurseries, schools, &c. Let the mother who has been made anxious by the sickly looks of her children, go from pure air into their bed-rooms in the morning before a door or window has been opened, and remark the state of the atmosphere—the close, oppressive, and often fetid odour of the room—and she may cease to wonder at the pale, sickly aspect of her children. Let her pay a similar visit some morning after means have been taken by the chimney ventilator or otherwise, to secure a full supply and continual renewal of the air in the bed-rooms during the night, and she will be able to account for the more healthy appearance of her children, which is sure to be the consequence of supplying them with pure air to breathe."

15. *Bed-Rooms for Sick Persons.*—On the subject of bed-rooms, Mr. Huggins has a capital remark or two which we here give:—"As to bed-rooms, I know not whether Lord Bacon's suggestion of having an infirmary, in case 'the prince or any special person should be sick,' has ever been acted upon in modern mansions; but I think it is one that might be adopted in most houses of any size, so far as devoting a suite of detached or semi-detached bed-rooms to the use of a sick person, where he might be more secluded than he could be elsewhere from the noise and bustle of the house, and in which provision might be made, by double sashes and double wall, to exclude the sound of the elements without. The value of such infirmary would be doubly felt in a case of contagious disease.

"In large country houses, where provision has to be made for reception of staying visitors, each stranger's suite of sleeping apartments ought to comprise, besides bedchamber and dressing or private room, a lobby, bath-room, lavatory, and closet, all exclusively devoted to him. In the mansions of those whose means are abundant, and sufficient water can be obtained, a large apartment, 8 or 10 yards square, with 'swimming bath' on the door, would look more sensible and rational, and represent more true enjoyment than a billiard-room, which, if it did not give way to so unusual an introduction, might at least be sometimes substituted by something of a higher or more useful character."

16. Kitchens—Sculleries.—If small and inconvenient bed-rooms are to be avoided in houses; not less so are small and inconvenient kitchens and sculleries. It is painful at times to witness how little regard is shown to the convenience of our domestics in the matter of affording them ample space and abundant convenience to carry on their work with ease and comfort. If we expect them to do their work well, is it too much to say that we should give them the means of doing it? The following remarks, for which we are indebted to the pages of the '*Building News*,' will be useful on this subject:—"From these rooms we pass to the kitchen, that department which the good housewife always wishes to see as perfect and as 'unique' as possible. The ar-

rangement of this portion. therefore, is of some consequence if these dwellings are to obtain favour with that sex whom it is always our wish to please and conciliate. It must be obvious, therefore, that to become skilful in this peculiar portion, an architect should not pass his days in single blessedness. Not that we think for one moment that it is necessary for the married members of the profession to be always at their wives' aprons, ciceronied at all times through the mazes of these culinary operations in which every lady should be, if the lords of the creation are to be supremely blessed, an adept; far from it; but because, through an interchange of ideas with a sensible and good housewife, a great advantage may be made in the knowlodgo of those 'little things' which go to make up the comfort and convenience of this truly domestic portion of an Englishman's castle. Truly the knowledge to be acquired by one who would honestly and skilfully discharge the duties of his profession are multifarious and perplexing. We may talk of fine art architecture, and pass our lives in preparing, reading, and hearing papers upon the applicability of various styles to various purposes; we may study the strength of materials and make ourselves thorough masters of the divers manipulations required in bringing them into the various forms we require; we may study the harmony of colours, and their application to internal and external decoration; we may 'engineer' as much as we like in all the malleable metals, and broach new applications of them in the science of house building, and yet not succeed in applying our varied and useful stock of knowledge so as to secure for us an honourable position as 'architect,' or win golden opinions upon our talents as artists and skill as designers, from the fairest of the fair. So true is it, that if we do not devote some little time and attention to that place which the gentle sharer of man's joys and sorrows takes special delight in—that is, those who are brought up with a proper knowledge of the duties devolving upon womanhood—no matter how fine we may have made the building, how well and compactly we arrange the several parts, how perfect we make the groupings, or pure the ornamentation, of the house and its offices, the sharp critique and biting sarcasm (more severe because clothed in gentle form) will find us out, and after many exclamations of delight as to drawing-rooms, boudoir, &c., the criticisms upon the generally, but falsely, assumed inferior portions will rob them of all their delight, and make us feel sorely and acutely that one great end and aim of our mission has been forgotten, or the means to that end made palpably and fearfully deficient. Many a skilful artist and master of 'constructive science,' has been ready to shrink into a nutshell at the pertinent remarks of one, who, untouched by the grand displays of skill he may have presented her, yet can detect at a glance all the shortcomings of which he may have been guilty in the non-production of a good and useful culinary laboratory."

17. *Relation of kitchen to Rooms.*—The position which a kitchen should occupy with relation to the entertaining rooms should be well considered. It adds to the comfort of a house, that those sitting in the public rooms should not be annoyed by the noise or by the smells proceeding from the working rooms; hence the latter should be placed as far as convenient from the former. We say as far as convenient, for we should not forget how much we add to the labour of our domestics, when we cause them to traverse long passages or mount many steps. The necessities of the case will be met by placing all the working apartments completely at the back, and isolating them by a door at the end of the hall or lobby. To ease the labour of the servants, we would strongly urge the adaptation of "speaking tubes" to the public rooms and bed-rooms leading to the kitchen. "Bells," as we have elsewhere remarked, "are all very well, but we would use them chiefly to draw the attention of the servants to what we wished to tell them. The saving of labour by the adoption of this simple apparatus would be very great. If you analyze the reason why you want your servants, you will find that in the great majority of cases you want them to bring something which is actually within their own domains; when, therefore, you have only a bell, you ring for the servant to come; and after she has came, she has again to go back for the article you require; then to return with it, and finally to go back. With a "speaking tube," one journey will do the work of four. These considerations may seem very trifling ones, but they are not so,—far, indeed, from being so. It is our duty to save our domestics from unnecessary and fatiguing labour."

18. *Scullery Position and Arrangement.*—This should be near the kitchen, and where possible should, as remarked by a writer in a recent publication, "open into it, having another door leading into the yard or open court. If the house be built of brick, plastering here will be unnecessary, and to have the brickwork well pointed and whitewashed will answer much better, and, if done carefully, will look equally well, besides preserving its appearance much longer, for plaster on scullery walls is continually being broken-off and damaged. When the walls are of stone, plastering becomes more necessary, and it has also the advantage of being much cheaper than working a good face to the stonework.

"The drainage and supply of water to sculleries should be well attended to, and the experience of the late severe frost should be an extra inducement to keep the pipes as much sheltered as possible, for we have all seen the numerous inconveniences and annoyances that have arisen from their exposure. The floors should be laid with a good fall in order to allow the water to pass off rapidly without lying on them in pools and thereby constantly keeping them in a damp and moist condition. We have seen sculleries which are continually in this state, and which present a most miserable appearance, all occasioned by the flatness of the floor, from which the water has no chance of passing away. Sculleries, in addition to this, should be well lighted and well ventilated, as should every other portion of the house, light in this case being very essential. The pantry and larder should also be placed near the kitchen, and should have a north aspect, their principal requirements being a dry and cool situation, and one in which fresh air can be easily obtained."

19. *Servants' Bed-Rooms.*—We have already pointed out the importance of giving large and healthily arranged bed-rooms for the superior parts of the house; be careful that they are equally supplied to the working department. It is one of the disgraces attached to plans of many of our large houses, that no attention has been paid to the sleeping accommodation of the servants. On this point the following, from a letter to the '*Builder*,' will be suggestive:—

"Can a small room, without a fireplace, or any means of ventilation, except the window or the door, be possibly adapted for a dormitory? Is not a sleeping-room as important to health as a sitting-room? Is it right or humane to place a servant or children in nooks and corners where their strength must inevitably be undermined?

"In several new houses attics without fireplaces were supposed to be fit sleeping-rooms for servants, the only way to ventilate which was by opening a skylight. It is obvious that such windows must remain sealed ones in wet, damp, and cold weather.

"Well may consumptive and bronchial ailments make the ravages they do if poor human frames are stowed away in such utter disregard of sanitary principles.

"Inspectors are appointed to prevent overcrowding amongst the lower classes; but in too many cases I fear that evils commensurate with overcrowding exist in the dwellings of the middling classes.

"As no limit can be placed upon the number that may be lodged in our houses, is it not essential to have a clear definition of what constitutes a bed-room, and at the same time incumbent upon all builders and occupiers to recognise the definition in its integrity?"

20. *Water-Closets.*—"There is no greater convenience," says a writer in the '*Building News*,' "in a house than a water-closet when properly managed, or no greater nuisance when improperly attended to. Their position in the plan of a house should be well studied, care being taken to place them where they can best be lighted and ventilated. We do not like the plan of placing them where they are dependent on borrowed lights; but their proper position is against the outside wall of a house, where the window will open into a yard or unobstructed space. The window should be carried up close to the ceiling, if the water-closet be not provided with ventilation, in order to allow of all the foul air escaping from the house, and not *into* it, as is too often the case. These windows should be left partly open during the night, for it is then even more than during the daytime that the close, unhealthy air from a water-closet pervades the house, and is kept within it by every aperture being closed. The practice of papering the walls of a water-closet we do not think so advisable as painting them. Paint

can be more readily cleaned and kept in order, and is for obvious reasons more suitable for this purpose than paper. The plan of having two doors to each water-closet is an excellent one, and is becoming pretty general. The space between these doors is made to answer the purpose of a small lavatory (a desirable accompaniment), and added to its convenience it has a suitable appearance. There should, we think, be a water-closet on every floor, the one above being situated over the one below, without necessarily disturbing the arrangement of the rooms on either floor. Independent of these there should, in the case of a villa or country residence, be a privy to every house. It should be situated near the main building, but screened from the more frequented portions, and be constructed on the principle of a water-closet, having the vault some little distance from it, in order to render it as healthy as possible, and also prevent its becoming a nuisance to the house to which it is attached. There are many persons who object to water-closets in a house; but the generality of people think otherwise, and it would, we think, be an act of folly to design or carry out a building without one, which, whether used by the household or not, would be found of great use in the case of invalids or aged persons. It is hard to remove a prejudice, and the question of introducing these conveniences into our houses has before now been warmly contested; but it is now almost universally allowed in the civilized world that they are indispensable, and the objections urged against them have been overruled by the advantages derived from them."

21. *General Hints on the Arrangement and Conveniences of Houses.*—The following extracts are culled from various authorities, and will be a useful conclusion to this division of our work.

Mr. Wightwick, in his "Hints to Young Architects," (Lockwood and Co., London), has the following remarks:—"In allusion to a few matters of COMFORT and CONVENIENCE we would hint at the virtue of *being a match for the occasional violence of gusty weather;* in so contriving that two doors shall be passed before you are fairly in the body of the house. Thus an enclosed porch will enable you to shut the outer or porch door, before the inner or passage door is opened. An entrance vestibule should, if possible, have only one outer door, and one inner door leading into the staircase or hall of common internal communication.

The interception of thorough draughts cannot be too attentively considered. A range of doors, all opening one way, in a long passage with a window at each end, will often exhibit the very perfection of the evil; and you may not expect your lady patroness to give much eulogy to the perspective of your corridor if she loses her cap in passing through it, and only gains in return a sore throat. The air that can quietly and courteously insinuate itself into rooms under the bottoms of the doors, in the chinks between the casements and rebates, and through the fireplace, is a welcome and necessary guest; but when it takes to slamming doors, breaking windows, and carrying hearthrugs up the chimney, it is a symptom of some great want of caution in the architect.

"The *best situation for fireplaces in a large room* is, unquestionably, in the centre of the longer side; and, *for doors*, close to the extremity of the same. The worst position for doors is at the extremities of the walls at right angles to the fireplace side, looking directly over the length of the hearth. Where doors communicate between rooms, they will be best placed in that part of the partition walls nearest the window side, and furthest from the fire. In smaller rooms, where there is scarcely sufficient room for a central fireplace, and *two* doors equidistant from it on the same side, it is often better to put the fire opening in the centre of the length between the one door and the end of the wall. It is not only more comfortable, but, where there is no projecting chimney breast, more sightly. Under some circumstances a perfect preservation of centrality may be preserved by the use of breaks or pilasters and ceiling beams, as the adjoined figure exemplifies. (Not here given.)

"If any method of *general warming and ventilation* be required, it will be for the architect to choose from the number of patents and practices in vogue, and to prepare for them in his first plans. An early conference with the patentees or professors of these methods should be, of course, secured, and their proposed operations duly provided for.

"The *perfection of kitchen and office comfort* is, perhaps, a 'consummation' more 'devoutly to be wished' than any other; for all others are especially dependent on it. Expect no master or mistress to be happy while a cook, housekeeper, and butler, are discontented. Keep the smell of the mutton fat, cabbage water, and chopped onions, out of the main house, for the sake of the hostess and her guests; but, for the united sake of all parties, make your kitchen, scullery, larder, store-room, and pantry, replete in all tho sufficicncy of space, fittings, and communication. Old servants may have accommodated themselves to old defects; but the success of new and better arrangements will, for a length of time, remain problematical. Your only chance is to flatter old servants by consultation. Learn from them the merits and demerits of their present accommodation; submit the result of your ingenuity, and of their exactions, to the upper house; and then deduce a well-studied plan, to be again modified till you *think* both houses are satisfied. Forget not the *cook's closet, the still room, the china closet.* Remember that,—besides a larder for cooked meat,—another for hung meat, and a salting room, may be required. The *dairy* may be insufficient without a scalding room and a churning room. The *butler's pantry* may be incomplete without a separate glass-washing and plate-cleaning room, and a strong closet for the security of plate not in constant use. Enable the housekeeper to have an eye on the cook, and the means (by a sliding door) of communicating with the kitchen without necessarily going into it. Keep the servants' hall and the back entrance out of the way of the operations and runnings to and fro during the bustle of dinner; but, at the same time, 'handy' for a speedy advance to the front door of the main house. Remember that a butler's satisfaction is improved by *well arranged cellars for beer, strong ale, wine in casks, and ditto in bins;* and that a master's comfort is enhanced by ready access to the said cellars from his own part of the building. Forget not that it will be well if the brew-house is connected by pipes with the cellars; and especially bear in mind, that pipes of wine which are from 5 to 6 feet long have to go lengthwise down an inclined plane and through door-ways into the cask cellar. A corking room, and a bottle room follow of course. Let your *coal and fuel stores* be prompt for the supply of offices and main house, and consider that coals are of at least two qualities, and must exist divided. Let your gallantry think of pretty maids carrying coal-scuttles in their hands without bonnets on their heads, and provide covered ways for their benefit. To the *boot and knife house* it may be well to add a brushing room with a good stove in it, or a drying closet for wet clothes. Let the *wash-house* yield its cleansed linen readily to the laundry, and the *laundry* its mangled and ironed ditto to the linen room. Consult propriety in keeping the maids and the men servants in a state of respectful separation, with separate staircases to their respective dormitories. Let the housekeeper's and butler's sleeping rooms respectively command those of the former.

"Returning into the main house, we may mention the convenience of a *waiting room* connected with the master's private room; and again, connected with the latter, a fire-proof strong closet and a *gun closet*. A gentleman's bath and water-closet will be well added to this nest of conveniences; a second bath and closet for ladies being provided on the floor next above. On each floor a *house-maid's closet* will be most welcome, with a pipe from the great reservoir in the roof to supply each with water for the bed-rooms. The convenience of a ready supply of water from one or more reservoirs (to be filled, when not supplied by the rain, with water ejected from the tank below by a force pump) will be obvious. The *water-closets, baths*, butler's room, &c., will be jointly dependent on it. The matter of water, though mentioned late in this Essay, will be among the first things considered by the young architect, who has, no doubt, an adequate knowledge of well-sinking and steining. It only remains to hint at the policy of providing ordinary closets wherever a recess in the masonry may allow it; for, among the stronger impulses of woman is a passion for closets, shelves, rails, and pegs. To crown the ridge of this part of our fabric of hints, we simply allude to a good and well-located dinner bell."

22. Mr. Kerr, in his paper already alluded to, and as reported in the '*Building News*,' has the following on various points connected with the arrangement of houses:—

"Taking up, fourthly, the matter of elegance and importance, it was carefully pointed out as being a fundamental consideration with the class of English gentlemen, and their ladies no less, that decoration and display must be confined within strict limits, architects being as a rule difficult of restraint in this respect, and somewhat pertinacious in introducing precisely what their clients desire to avoid. Perfect neatness and grace must always be studied, but ambitious artistic effect decidedly spared; that there may be no interference with homely comfort, and no suspicion of ostentation suggested. Even in cases where rank and wealth surround themselves with costliness and luxury, simplicity and subdued power will still be preferred, and the glare of mere pomp despised. An effect of due importance, however, will always be expected to be produced; exaggeration being distasteful, but the exact proper value for the cost expended, exhibited in a spirit equally removed from ostentation and meanness, being the rule. In the interior something like license might be taken, although not with the rooms, with the thoroughfares, such as the hall, corridor, and staircase; indeed, as matter of dignity, this would often be not only permitted, but encouraged, the instances being many where an injudicious management of these portions of the house have given to a mansion the inferior appearance of a cottage, while, on the other hand, a little expansion in other cases have conferred upon a cottage all the importance of a mansion.

"Turning now to the detailed characteristics of apartments, the lecturer proposed to touch briefly upon the principal of these, so far as time would admit.

"The *dining-room* of an ordinary mansion was described as a spacious and comparatively stately apartment, to be cool and free from the glare of sunshine at the hour of evening dinner, and as regards external position, somewhat retired. The best aspect would be north or north-east, or east but for the east wind, or south-east but for the sunshine during the day; south, south-west, or west being altogether objectionable. The lecturer then explained the preference for side windows over end windows, as primary light of the room; the advantage of end light in addition in a large apartment (looking east rather than west); the compromise of aspect for prospect, and the danger of over-estimating the value of the latter, and the great service of the bay window as a means of accommodating conflicting demands of this kind. The process of determining the width and length of a dining-room was then described, and the principles of arrangement for the sideboard, fireplace, and doorway; the uses of the service-room were also set forth, and the relation of such an apartment to the dining-room on one hand and the kitchen on the other.

"The case of a *dining-room used as the family sitting-room* was likewise treated of, where what may be called drawing-room elements must be introduced, not only in furniture, but in aspect more especially; the south-eastward being now decidedly preferable, the fireplace also requiring to be disposed on new principles—namely, those of the sitting-room and the fireside. The general design of a proper dining-room, it was also remarked, ought to be massive and substantial, as if of masculine importance, although not devoid of cheerfulness.

"Speaking of the *morning-room*, it was remarked that this served to relieve, in a manner, both dining-room and drawing-room, being used as a breakfast-room, and also as a sitting-room for the ladies during the early part of the day; and in more homely establishments being still more used. For breakfast the aspect might best be eastward, a south-east window taking, at 9 A. M., the sunshine full in front; but for a sitting-room south-east would be preferable, keeping the sun from morning till 1 P. M. due south—being the extreme.

"The *drawing-room* was next discussed, as essentially the ladies' apartment, the modern form of the ladies' withdrawing-room of the olden time, its purpose being for the reception of visitors, the assembling of the family and guests before dinner, the evening circle afterwards, the reception of evening parties, and so on. This room might be said to be, perhaps, the simplest in the house, as respects principles of plan, there being only one kind of drawing-room with little difference, except in dimensions and luxury, between that of the duchess and that of the homeliest gentleman. The character to be aimed at must be especial cheerfulness, refinement of elegance, and lightness of style; decoration, therefore, requiring to be comparatively minute and delicate, and the whole effect, so to speak, entirely ladylike. The dining-room and drawing-room would thus be in contrast. As to aspect, this must avoid equally the wet west, the bleak east, the afternoon sultriness of the south-west, the shadow of the opposite quarter, and so on, the south-east becoming thus the nearest approach to perfection, cheerful and pleasant early in the day, shaded from the level sunshine of the evening, and exposed only to the mildest winds; south being sultry, and west taking little else than the evening glare and the rain. The principles of side windows, as laid down for a dining-room, would still apply with end windows in addition for large rooms. Prospect would be always worthy of serious consideration, although best to be dealt with by end windows (if compromise of aspect be required), which may be south-west or even west if necessary, east or north-east; the eastward views having the especial advantage of presenting the landscape in the afternoon and evening, well-lighted pictorially, and the southward views for full daylight effects being placed at a disadvantage. The use of the bay window might now be still more advocated, the most serviceable form being not three but five sides of a regular octagon, whereby it is always possible, by closing three sides against the sun, to have two uncovered. Further remarks were made in explanation of the particular principles of plan governing a sitting-room so as to produce a comfortable fireside by the judicious relations of fireplace, light, and entrance, a result often found to be extremely difficult of accomplishment, especially in a small room, unless it be nearly square. The question of doors of intercommunication generally was also touched upon, these being frequently demanded for family convenience, but nevertheless, as a rule, to be discouraged by the architect.

"After describing the *library and boudoir*, the lecturer treated of the gentleman's *business-room*, and of the *study* in such a case as that of a parsonage; adverting to the difficulty sometimes experienced in finding a place for writing which shall be properly situated as respects the light, the door, and the fire, and laying it down as the best rule that the occupant, when seated at his desk, shall have at his back a blank end wall or bookcase; on his right, the fireplace near that end; on his left, the window, near the other end, and in front the door. The secondary entrance for the business-room was also described.

"Speaking briefly of the *family thoroughfares*, attention was first directed to the porch, more particularly as to the correction of a blustering aspect for the entrance—south-west, north-east, or the like; the plan in such cases being to place the outer doorway with an aspect at right angles to that objected to; the northwest being, however, particularly unfortunate in this respect, inasmuch as both the aspects at right angles to it—namely, north-east and south-west, are equally bad with itself.

"The *entrance-hall* was alluded to as an apartment existing in so many characteristic varieties as to be a sort of criterion of class for the house as a whole. Two very different principles of plan were to be found developed in contrasted buildings; in the one case the route of entrance being central, leading directly forward through a symmetrical hall and vestibule to the staircase or some other chief object; while in the other case, symmetry and directions are avoided, the outward doorway being in one corner, for instance, the inward doorway at some point of contrast rather than correspondence, and the latter entering the corridor in an equally one-sided manner. The first plan must alwyas be more classical and stately, the other being considered to exhibit more domestic convenience; but although it may not be desirable to sacrifice comfort for mere symmetry, yet to carry irregularity into affectation must be still more unrefined.

"The *gallery or corridor* of a mansion was next spoken of, the desirableness of side windows rather than end ones, the objections to ceiling light as cheerless, the propriety of a centrical position for the principal staircase, the necessity for avoiding complex forms of plan, and so on. The *internal relation of the rooms* to each other being the relation of their doors, it must be always best to place the doors of the chief apartments in prominent positions, so that they cannot be mistaken. The route between the entrance and the drawing-room ought also to be well arranged; the same of the route between the dining and drawing-rooms, avoiding that twisting of the line which occurs, for example, when both doors are on one side of the corridor. The preservation of the corridor as far as possible in privacy was also a thing to be carefully attended to, the routes of the servants being kept clear of those of the family as far as possible."

23. *Arrangement of City Houses.*—The remarks which we have given above by the eminent authorities named—and the principal points of which, we have taken the liberty to *italicise* for the greater convenience of our readers—have reference chiefly to villas or mansions in the country, or in suburban districts. The arrangements of a city house will obviously be much controlled by the peculiarities of site. The following remarks on

this subject from the '*Building News*' will be useful here; they give a very lucid comparison between city or street, and rural or suburban villas. Other points of importance are also well handled.

"In city houses," says the writer, "it is generally found necessary to have the *kitchen in the basement*, as space does not often permit of its being placed on the ground-floor, but in villas this arrangement should not be, as the inconvenience of running up and down steps is a sufficient obstacle to its being adopted, besides which there is no possible excuse for it when there is plenty of room for it above ground. The great thing is to have it as near the dining-room as possible, without bringing it into the front and best part of the house, and on a level with it, steps either down or up to it should never be allowed where it is possible to avoid them; they become a continual source of annoyance to the servants, whose comfort and convenience it is of course necessary to consult, and they prove very fatiguing to persons who have constantly to pass up and down them. Some writers go so far as to recommend the abolition of steps altogether, and have both sleeping and living rooms on the same floor, but we do not agree with this, and cannot see the wisdom of the proposal. We, however, do perceive the necessity of avoiding them when they can be avoided, and also the advisability of keeping every room in each story on the same level.

"In *street architecture* we generally find the *drawing-room* on the first floor, an arrangement which, in nine cases out of ten, is compulsory. In villa architecture this is not imperative, and we think that the ground floor is more suitable for it. It should be situated in the pleasantest part of the house, and should have an air of comfort about it, and the appearance of being cool in summer and warm in winter. French casements may here be introduced with advantage; when well constructed they have an elegant and convenient look, which is both pleasing and effective, yet there are many who are prejudiced against them as others are against Gothic casements, but without the slightest cause, for experience has taught us that when they are constructed properly and with well-seasoned materials, they are everything that could be desired; and in point of appearance are, in our opinion, infinitely superior to the common sash.

"*Libraries and picture galleries* are generally made to face the north, this being considered the best for light, which of course is the principal thing to be provided for. The library should be as distant from noise as possible, and in town buildings should be placed at the back of the house and not in the front, where the bustle and rolling of carriages is likely to disturb the occupier. What is more annoying to a student than a continual din, which is constantly disturbing him in the midst of his deep studies, when he requires everything to be as still and motionless as the inner sanctuary of an Egyptian temple, or the centre chamber of an Egyptian pyramid? Many persons feel it impossible to devote themselves to profound study when the slightest noise or confusion prevails. The nerves are very sensitive on this point, and it is therefore desirable that the most retired and private part of the house should be the position of the study.

"The situation of the *morning-room, billiard-room, and breakfast-room* will be dependent on circumstances, and possibly on the site of the house or the whim of the owner. There is no recognised law respecting the placing of these apartments, but the architect will, of course, select the most suitable part. In large buildings, where there is a central hall of sufficient size, it would be well for these rooms, together with the dining and drawing rooms, to open into it, thus affording an easy communication one with the other. There is, perhaps, no more imposing feature in a house than a good staircase hall. When well arranged it has a look of grandeur, which produces a favourable impression on the visitor, and leads him at once to conclude that the house is a superior one. As Palladio says, a stranger should be compelled to pass through the best portion of the edifice before he reaches the staircase, in order that he may be impressed by the grandeur of the structure. This is sound advice, and where it can be followed it would be well to do so, for first impressions, whether favourable or unfavourable, are more lasting than any others, and linger longer in the mind and memory—in fact, they are seldom entirely forgotten or wholly effaced. The staircase in any house is susceptible of much beauty and artistic treatment where the funds will permit. In whatever style it may be, or in whatever character of building it may be placed, still it affords one of the best opportunities for a display of taste."

CHAPTER THIRD.

ARRANGEMENT AND ACCOMMODATION OF THE FARM HOUSE.

24. *Kitchen and Scullery.—The working part of the farm house* should have the following accommodation, and the dimensions stated may be taken as average ones for a farm 500 to 600 acres in extent. First, a kitchen 18 feet by 16. This should be entered by a door from a passage which should divide the kitchen from the public rooms. The best form of fire-grate, both for economy in the consumption of fuel and for the facilities it gives for cooking purposes, is what is called the *kitchener*. The only objection to it is, that it is rather expensive, and, looking at the material and workmanship in it, often unnecessarily so. It will be long, we fear, before the prejudices of our servants, and we may say of ourselves, will enable us to use the much cheaper, and, in every way as efficient, cooking ranges, or rather stoves, used on the Continent and in North America. Having seen the working of these in the houses of the middle and poorer classes of France, Belgium, and in America, we can with confidence recommend them as the cheapest in first cost, and the most economical in working of all the forms of cooking apparatus we have met with. The kitchen should be provided with a large dresser, the best material for the top of which is sycamore or plane tree. The under part should be fitted up with a cupboard in the centre, the doors of which should open right and left, and drawers of various depths on each side. Abundance of cupboard room should be given to the kitchen—and hooks and shelves. The scullery, 12 feet by 10, should enter from the kitchen, and be provided with a furnace and double copper, and a slop-stone or sink ranged along the wall and near the window, so that plenty of light may be thrown on it. The scullery may also be used as a wash-house, in which case the wash-tubs may be set on the slop-stone when being used. We would, however, recommend a small set-off from the scullery to be appropriated as a wash-house, in which wash-tubs should be put up as fixtures, and supplied with hot and cold water at same pressure. The scullery should have a door leading to the back part of the premises, and near this should be placed the *fuel store*.

25. *The milk-room or dairy* should be separated from the kitchen and scullery by a narrow passage, which may be partly fitted up as a closet or cupboard; so that the heat of these apartments shall not affect its temperature. A door entering from the dairy to the scullery might be useful when the utensils are to be washed, but the danger of this is that it admits of vapours, smells, &c., to enter the dairy. It will, therefore, be better to go round through the kitchen. A dairy cannot be too perfectly isolated from apartments in which tainting vapours arise; the readiness with which milk absorbs these, and is spoiled by them, is something remarkable. The aspect of the dairy windows should be north or north-east; the latter is the best, and will be easily secured, by making it at the back of the house, the aspect of which we have before recommended you to make south-east. For the walls of a dairy we know of no materials equal to the glazed tiles, which can be had now very cheaply. Flooring tiles, with a glazed or rather a hard vitrified surface, will be useful. The best shelves for the milk pans will be marble; where the expense of this is objected to, slate may be used, which is nearly as good. Both are kept easily from stains, especially the former, which flag-stone is not.

Water in abundance should be applied to the dairy. From the dairy a small room should enter, in which the butter can be made up, and in which it may be stored. The cheese-press may be placed in this. From this closet or room a "lift" should lead to the cheese room in the floor above, in which also should be the servants' bed-room and closets. It is usually the practice to give the servants' rooms a complete isolation from the rest of the house, by a stair entering near to or from the kitchen. While we would give this stair for direct communication, we would insist upon a door to enter the servants' floor from the bed-room floor of the house,—as we look upon it as essential that the mistress of a house should be able at any time, and in the easiest way, to inspect every part of the house. The reasons for this are obvious enough on consideration. The isolation considered necessary may easily be obtained, by providing a door to this entrance to the servants' floor.

CHAPTER FOURTH.

ACCOMMODATION OF THE LABOURER'S COTTAGE.

26. As regards the *accommodation* which should be given to a labourer's cottage, much has been written, and more said, and yet less of the one or the other might have been done, and more practical results might have followed. The truth is, that no rule can be set down applicable to all circumstances. When we are building houses for ourselves, we build them in accordance with our wants, or likely wants; why should not we adopt this simple common-sense rule in the case of cottages, and have *different sized cottages for different sized families?* For cottages with the *smallest* accommodation, a kitchen or "living room," as it is most frequently called, and a single bed-room, will make up the accommodation required; for cottages of the *medium* accommodation, a living and two bed-rooms; while for cottages with the *maximum* accommodation, a living room, and three bed-rooms, will be required. In addition to these, we wish the reader to understand, that other conveniences in accommodation will have to be given; what these are we shall presently point out. While having cottages of different sizes, built either separately or in rows, we prefer the separate or detached, or at most the semi-detached mode. It will be advisable to have cottages built with unequal accommodation, that is, a cottage having the maximum with a cottage—all under the same roof having the minimum accommodation.

27. *Living Rooms.*—Leaving the question of extent of accommodation to be decided, as it should be decided, by local or other considerations, let us glance at a few of the essentials to be carried out whatever may be the extent of the accommodation to be decided upon. On the subject of the *living room* or kitchen we need say but little; it should be well lighted from two sides, if possible the windows to throw the light on the fireplace. It should be provided with a dresser amply supplied with drawers; and have a liberal allowance of shelves on the walls, and hooks from the ceiling. The fireplace should have a boiler and oven, and the best form we know of is what is called the "Lancashire Range;" this is at once cheap and efficient. A description of

this we purpose giving in the section on materials in the present series of articles.

28. *Scullery or Wash-house.*—Aiding mightily the efforts of the good housewife in her attempts to keep the house orderly, is this same convenience; adding also to the attractions of home by getting rid of the annoyance of washing in the living room. Habits of cleanliness and order can never be characteristic of the labouring classes so long as the structural conveniences—or rather inconveniences—are such as to prevent them having their houses "clean and tidy;" and which have the effect of accustoming them to filth and disorder. It is a huge folly to look for habits of a superior order where there is every inducement to the cultivation of, or, at least, the toleration of those of an opposite kind. The "scullery" should be large enough to enable washing to be done; and if there is room for a small furnace and boiler so much the better, a step higher in the rank of "healthy homes" will be attained. We look upon this facility for "washing," apart from the "living room," as a matter of great importance in dwelling places for the labouring classes. Few but have *heard* of—and these are the lucky portions of *mankind* who have only *heard*—and many are they that have known of the discomforts which the operations of a washing day invariably and unfailingly bring to a household. It needs not here to be stated the evils thus arising—they have formed alike the burthen of "song," and of "complaint;" and, we may add, have not unfrequently acted as an incentive to or been hailed as an excuse by the labouring man to leave his own fireside for the evils, but, alas! attractive ones, of the public house. Let everything then be done to counteract such attractions, and to make a man's own fireside the brightest thing in his memory when he is absent from it; and the greatest attraction when he is at his house. And this addition of a scullery and wash-house will in no small degree tend to make his home attractive, because it will tend to make it comfortable.

29. *Cupboards or Presses.*—As tending to add materially to the comfort and conveniences of the cottage, "*cupboards*"—or, as they are called in the north, *presses*—should be given in abundance. It is simply absurd in us to find fault with the untidy habits of cottagers for not "putting things away," as the phrase goes, if we give them no place in which to put them. Let us be

reasonable in all things. It puts us in mind, when we hear grave recitals of poor folks' untidiness, of the lady who, when she saw one at dinner performing with a knife such wonderful feats in eating, in her profound ignorance of the habits of some of the working population, asked the question, "*why does not the man use a silver fork?*" Truly, silver forks are just as easily had, we mean in some poor men's cottages, as cupboards and presses. Give then the cottages cupboards, and if after that you see untidiness, be unsparing in your fault-finding; we have no mercy for confusion when order *can* be carried out; only with reference to the state of things examination is reasonable before we indulge in condemnation.

30. *A Porch or small entrance hall*—leading from the open air to the *living room*, tends to make that apartment more comfortable; and economizing as it does the heat of the fire in winter time, it economizes the cottagers' means; and if we can, by such a simple matter as a porch, do this double kindness to the man, why should not we? May we ask if ever any of our readers have spent a few hours in a room of which the door opened at once upon the street or road? If they have, they will understand why we insist upon a porch forming part of every cottage plan; if they have not, they may believe us when we tell them, that it is no pleasant position. We have seen snow drifted half way up the living room through the door.

31. *Separate Entrances to Bed-Rooms* we deem of essential importance, not only in a healthy, but a moral point of view. One room should never be entered through another. That privacy and isolation which is imperative where the claims of decency are attended to, cannot be obtained by having one bed-room pass through another; and in times of sickness, the inconveniences are multiplied ten-fold.

32. *Pantries.*—We have spoken of the advantages of cupboards. We must not forget the important matter of a *provision pantry.* For storage of provisions, we know, however, of no contrivance equal to the *cellar.* Almost every house in Lancashire has a cellar, even a cottage, letting at a shilling or eighteen-pence a-week. Meat can be preserved in cellars for a much longer time than in pantries placed in the living floor. But they also add to the dryness of the house, a most important consideration.

33. *Lighting of Rooms.*—But whatever else you have in a cottage, see that you have plenty of light to the rooms; for not only does it exercise a healthy influence upon the inhabitants, but it enables the house to be kept clean. For an ill-lighted house is always a dirty one; believe this to be true, reader. Let the windows then be large and well placed, so that every corner may be lighted, and dirt will fly at its approach; so that, at any rate, if the housewife allows it to lie there, she cannot have the excuse of not having seen it, to plead for its continuance.

34. *Drainage—Water-Closets—Sink in Scullery—Liquid Manure Tank.*—The physical evils arising from accumulation of filth and refuse are now well understood, or at least admitted. In the language of sanitary science, "the immediate and direct cause of fever is a poison generated by the decomposition of animal and vegetable matters." It is, therefore, of prime importance, to have arrangements in all cottages by which the refuse of the kitchen, &c., can be stored up in a place, and in such a way, as to prevent all noxious exhalations emanating from it. The ashes should be stored up in an ash-pit, which should be in close connection with the *privy*, and both of which should be the greatest distance possible from the house—we mean, of course, within the limits of the back premises. We at one time advocated the use of *water-closets* for cottages; but later and more extended experience has shown to us that they are not adapted for rural districts. There a supply of water cannot be kept *constantly* on, and at pressure —so that all modes of supplying them from cisterns we find likely to be neglected. Indeed, even where a supply of water is most easily obtained, a difficulty is sometimes met with in the fact that the cottagers will not take the trouble to turn it on. We have sometimes been disgusted beyond measure at the state of matters we have seen in water-closets, not less so at the abominable laziness or carelessness which caused it. All the sanitary requirements of the case will be pretty fairly met if the privy and the ash-pit are placed in the garden. If the cottagers can be persuaded to throw in from time to time the ashes of the fireplaces into the privy, the contents will, to a certain extent, be deodorized. By using dried earth—after Mr. Moule's fashion —perfect deodorization will be obtained, and an excellent ma-

nure in no way disgusting to handle will be available for the garden.

The waste water from the kitchen should be led by a drain pipe from the *sink* in the scullery to the *liquid manure tank* in the garden. Both of these are essentials in a well arranged cottage. The sink, if of stone, and of ample dimensions, and not of a greater depth than two inches, will be of immense service in housewifery operations. The tank may be of the simplest possible construction, and will soon repay itself in the excellent manure it will yield.

35. *A cistern for catching and storing up the rain water draining from the roof* should never be omitted. Rain water is by far the best for washing clothes and for ablution; indeed those who have been accustomed to wash with rain water take ill when they are forced to use hard water.

36. The *piggery* is an essential part of a working man's cottage in the country. The pig-stye, the ash-pit, and the privy, will form, when put together, the outhouses, to which should be added a place for coal and lumber.

37. SIZE, MATERIALS, AND FORM OF THE COTTAGE.—There are some points connected with the construction of cottages to which we would like now briefly to draw the attention of the reader. The cheapness of a cottage depends upon several considerations—the size, the materials of which it is composed, and the form or way in which these are put together. The *size* of the house depends upon the number of apartments it contains, and the dimensions of these. There is a maximum and a minimum dimension, for the apartments in a cottage, but it is difficult accurately to define what is the medium. A room too large is almost as bad as one too small; the over large room is difficult to warm; and there is a difficulty in managing household matters in too small rooms, where convenience alone is consulted. We confess that we should rather have any room err in excess than in deficiency of space; like the sailors, we love plenty of sea-room. *A good size for a living-room* is generally now accepted at 144 square feet of floor surface. This will give a square of 12 by 12 feet; we, however, prefer 14 feet by 12 as the better size. Two rooms of exactly the same size may however be very different in the accommodation they give; thus, if the door enters

in the centre of one of the sides, the space of floor at each side will be so cut up that it will afford little room for articles of furniture, which, therefore, will have to be put away in some other less convenient part of the room. The door, if possible, should be placed at the corner. The *size of a bed-room* is generally set down at 10 feet square—dimensions, we think, by far too small, and for the following reasons. As a workman spends by far the greatest portion of his time in his bed-room—we mean, of course, the time he is at home—we are strong advocates for making it as large and convenient as any room in the house. We are dead set against all bed-closets, or bed-rooms so small as really to be closets; well named *close-sets*—for that is the original term—are they. We believe that many a poor man gets severe cold from being stewed up in a close-set place all night, and rushing off at early morn into the cold and damp air. In cottages, the principal bed-rooms above should be allowed to remain the *same size as the room below*. The walls running vertically up dictate this, and we therefore deprecate all cutting up of these rooms, at least by partitions. The *height of the living-room and bed-room stories* should be the same; indeed, if health is the main object to be considered, the height of the bed-room ceiling should be greater than that of the living-room, for the reason that we have already stated—namely, that a man spends most of his time in it. Let us then, in the planning of cottages, remember this important department; and in thinking of our own comfort, let us not forget that of others, and of the time

> " When dumb night goes softly by
> Towards the fiery western sky,
> A-lulling birds, and shutting up
> The daisy and the buttercup;
> And men go to lay their heavy heads,
> And weary bones, upon their beds."

We deprecate altogether the notion, which unfortunately is very wide spread, that closets are quite good enough for bed-rooms or rather sleeping *places*. A height of 10 feet we consider the best then for the ceilings. Economical reasons have generally such sway, that the height of bed-rooms is crushed down to seven feet six, or eight feet, a height absolutely absurd. The *size of the scullery* is of importance, as in it many operations are carried on. We take 10 feet by 8 to be a very convenient size.

38. The question as to whether a cottage should be *single or two storeyed*, influencing the cost of the house, should be considered. Much depends upon the accommodation in it. If it is a single cottage for a man and his wife alone, it will be better to make it single storeyed; if two cottages of this sort are required together, it would make a nicer-looking house to build them two-storeyed, one above the other, the one entering from the back. But the rule, in my opinion, is decided; wherever the cottage has more accommodation in it than a living-room, bed-room, and scullery, then build a two-storeyed cottage without any debate upon the point. Roof-space is saved, and roof-space is always a costly thing to cover. By spreading out the rooms in one floor you vastly increase the roof-space; and more than that, you place your bed-rooms in the worst possible position—next the ground. Bed-rooms should always be in the second floor. By putting them there you have merely the vertical walling to pay for; for the roof, which could only cover the living-room, &c., on the ground floor, if single-storeyed, now covers both living-room and bed-rooms. As to attics, our advice is decided,—have nothing whatever to do with them; they bring about a wretchedly paltry saving in the cost of construction, and afford, at the best, miserable rooms, overcold in winter, and overheated in summer.

39. The *materials* of which it is composed exercises an important influence upon the cost. Bricks, when they can be had cheap, afford the best material. They are warm, not half so easily affected by damp as stone; and require no preliminary working like that material before they can be set up. Where excuses are made so frequently as to the cost of cottages forming an obstacle in the way of building them, as if—as it seems to do with some—cost settled a man's conscience, we wonder why the American style of *framed houses of timber* is not introduced. Of course national prejudice at once comes in to pooh! pooh! the suggestion. But calling a project fudge, or pooh poohing it, will not destroy the facts upon which it is based. Now we happen to know something about American frame houses, or houses composed of timber planks. We have lived in them, and can vouch for the fact that their inhabitants are as keenly alive to the comforts and elegancies of life as we ourselves are. And if any objection is made on the score of

climate, assuredly we cannot lay claim to the degree of cold which graces an American winter. Winds bluster and rains dash as they do with us; but frame houses, notwithstanding, oppose bravely the one and resist successfully the other. We have visited a millionnaire, whose establishment was kept up at no small expense—twenty or thirty thousand dollars we have no doubt—yet he lived in a frame house. Certainly by far the worst frame house we ever saw in America, and it looked so ill constructed, that, to quote the Irishman, "bedad, it looked as if somebody had made it;" was a palace in point of sound external construction, and a Turkish divan in point of internal comfort compared to those wretched tumble-down, pig-stye, dog-kennel-looking structures we have met with in our rambles in *this* country, and called by courtesy cottages; and which, in the words of a fellow-labourer in this field of agricultural economics, we may describe now, as having "mud or wattled walls, on swampy sites, low walls, roof; if thatch, rotten with age, or green with fungoid vegetation; if timber, decayed; if of slates and tiles, these broken and abounding in holes; doors, windows, and fittings matching the roof in decay, and vying, with the dirt and smoke of years, in colour with the mud floor." If then landlords object to give their labourers cottages more consistent with the dignity of man—even if he be not so good as themselves—than with the grovelling of a beast, for the wretched reason that they cost too much to build—build or erect them timber ones—that will be cheap enough, and we shall gladly guarantee that they will be comfortable. It is right, however, to say, that timber cottages are on the increase; and if properly constructed, they will last a long time, and be in every way more fitted for the residence of thinking beings than the wretched huts which they replace. In Sweden and Norway—and surely in these regions the cold is severe enough to stand any comparison with that we have here—these timber houses are much used; they build them with a cavity or space between what may be called the outer and inner skin of planking—which space is filled up with moss. A very strong and fire-proof mode of erecting timber, or rather combined timber and stone houses, we recommended years ago. In this the vertical framing posts are first put up, and the spaces crossed with rough timber battens so as to form a series of pigeon holes—no matter of what shape or form these are. Into these holes stones, broken bricks, or the like, are inserted, and the interstices well filled in with mortar. When this sets, a sound and durable wall is obtained.

40. *Raising of the floor above the ground level.*—Of course in timber constructions—and the remark applies to other materials with as much force—it is essential that the floor shall be well raised above the ground. We have a great horror of cottages placed squat upon the ground. This absurdity in house construction, too often seen exemplified, is not only silly, but it is highly mischievous; for so built, cottages must be more or less damp. Every cottage then should be entered by two steps at the very least, but three we are inclined to place as the safer minimum.

41. The *form of the cottage* exercises an influence upon its cost. The form of an exact square is the cheapest, as it encloses a larger space than any other figure. With the same quantity of walling in a square you secure a larger amount of internal accommodation than by any other form. Another great advantage is the simplicity of the roof of a square house. Where look is not desiderated, you have only to raise gables, throw a ridge-pole across, and put up your rafters; all is of the simplest construction in carpentry. On the other hand, a square cottage is the ugliest you can build; it almost invariably suggests itself as an exemplification of what has been called graphically, if not truly, the "tea-box" style of architecture. If then you require the cottage to be of somewhat pretentious looks, build it with breaks and projections; these always give a pleasing outline, and as a set-off to their extra cost in construction. You will find in their nooks and corners admirable opportunities for giving closets, cupboards, and pantries; on the utility of which we have already made some remarks. On the point of *elevational character or design* we have little to say. No attempt at architectural design should be made aiming at elaborate effect—*simplicity in appearance should be the great characteristic of a cottage;* and we know of no ornamentation so cheaply obtained, so perfect of its kind, and so satisfactory in its results, as the effect of simple trellis work covering the porch or masking the window, up which creep-

ing plants can be grown. With their graceful foliage set in relief against the white-washed wall, and the flowers in front in the tiny garden, a cottage, to our mind, is complete. And, if further effect is desired, give a background to the *north* in the form of a clump of trees, against which the smoke from the chimney may "rise a twisting blue," as a western poet exquisitely expresses it; and then you have all that the eye of the painter or the taste of the most fastidious may desire. We have thus thrown a few hints together on the subject of cottage accommodation for the labourers of the farm, and for rural and suburban districts; and, in conclusion, we would take the liberty to impress upon the reader its great importance, and entreat of him to bear in mind, that while it is doing the poor a vast injury to bring them up with the notion that everything will be done for them, and that they need not trouble themselves with self help, as they will get enough of neighbour help; there are some things in which the poor cannot by any possibility help themselves, and that this matter of obtaining good house accommodation is one of the most important of them. They cannot build houses, they must be built for them. The evils connected with the sanitary condition of our rural labouring population will not be healed by the hand of time,—time will only render them the more malignant. There is no self-contained power of recovery in the case; and if it exists now, each succeeding day weakens its force and abates its energy. The cure, if cure is to come, must come from without. We see, therefore, no hope of the condition of our labouring poor being ameliorated in this direction, if to the poor the task of improvement is left. We write strongly on this matter; for we feel most thoroughly convinced that the question is one which has a close and important bearing upon the future of our social life.

CHAPTER FIFTH.

THE STABLE, COW-HOUSE, AND DAIRY.

42. *Stables.*—The floor of the stable is the first point to be considered; and here, at the outset, it is necessary to say, that it is a disputed point amongst farming authorities, whether the floor of a stall should be level or inclined. A slight inclination

of three inches in the whole of the length of the stall—9 feet —is recommended; but it is worthy of remembrance, as well pointed out by that shrewd authority in farming matters Mr. Henry Stephens, that when horses have a freedom of choice, they invariably prefer to stand upon level ground. The following are the remarks of the above authority upon this point:—

"Some veterinary writers say that the position of the feet of the horses imposed by the rise, does not throw an injurious strain on the back tendons of the hind legs. This may be, but it cannot be denied that in this position the toes are raised above the heels much higher than on level ground. I admit, that a rise of 3 inches is necessary in stalls in which geldings stand, as they eject their water pretty far on the litter, but in the case of mares, so great a rise is unnecessary. It is indisputable that a horse always prefers to stand on level ground, when he is free to choose the ground for himself, and much more ought he to have level ground to stand on in a stable, which is his place of rest. It is no argument in this case to call for instances in which the horse has been lamed by standing in a stall having a great declivity; for the question is, not whether or not the horse can be rendered lame, in any degree, or in any way, but how to afford the greatest ease and even comfort to the work-horse while in the stable."

43. The desiderata in the floor of a stable are hardness and roughness of surface, the former to resist the action of the horses' feet, the latter to prevent their slipping; to these must be added a capability to resist the absorption of the urine. An excellent floor can be made of bricks set on edge, and if of unequal width, the narrowest should be placed between two of the broadest ones

thus, affording foot-holding for the horses. The desiderata for a stable floor are well met in Musgrove's Stable Flooring bricks, as illustrated in fig. 32, Chapter Sixth. An excellent form of stable floor is that introduced by Mr. Forbes, and manufactured by Clayton of the Altas Works, London. They serve the purpose of drainage bricks. The gutter of a stable is placed immediately behind the stall-post; it should be smooth in its upper surface, and should have a gentle fall to the outside of the wall, where it should communicate with the drain leading to the liquid manure tank. This old-fashioned form of open gutter is fast becoming disused, and is being rapidly replaced by the closed gutter or drain tube; the liquid reaching the interior of the drain tube through gratings placed at intervals in the open gutter running along the foot of stalls. These gratings, in the best constructions, are trapped, which prevents the issue of bad smells from the drains to the interior of the stables.

44. The stalls are *generally* placed in stables so that the heads are right against the back wall. There is no doubt that this plan is not so beneficial as where a feeding passage is placed, running along the heads of stalls, as in the following type diagram:

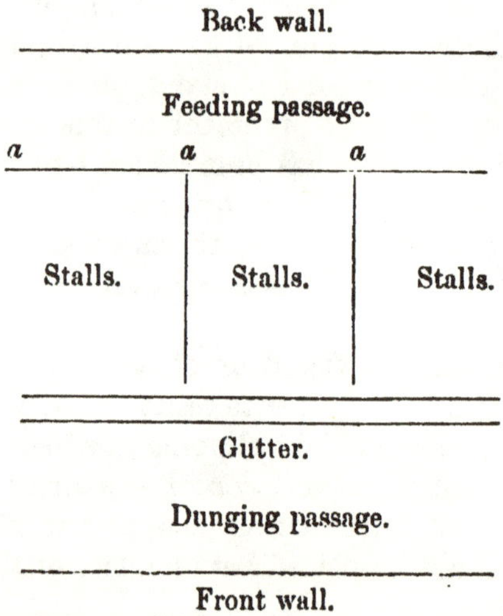

On this point of having a feeding passage at the head of the stall, Mr. J. L. Morton has the following remarks:—

"Hitherto it has usually been the practice of architects to place the stalls against a dead wall; and, accordingly, the animals, in breathing, are compelled to reinhale the corrupted air which, on leaving the animal, is obstructed by the wall. In the injurious effects which result from the ammonia of the manure coming into contact with the lime of the building and affecting the eyes of the horses, we see another objection to this mode of placing the stalls. A wall at a little distance from the horse's head, especially if it happens to be an outside one, must, by its condensation of foul vapours, and the obstruction of circulation, greatly add to the impurity of the whole interior. . . . It is generally admitted, that cattle stalls arranged with a central feeding passage are preferable to those having a wall in front of them. It has been alleged, no doubt, that in cases where cattle in two ranges are placed head to head, with only a five feet passage between them, there is some risk, in the event of contagious disease breaking out, of its being rapidly communicated from one animal to another, in the act of expiration. Where the ventilation is very defective, the fouled air from the lungs of the animals facing each other will fill the whole open space in front; but if an infectious disease once gets into a byre, it will soon pervade every part of it, whatever way the cattle stalls may be arranged. If cow stalls having a front feeding passage are found of advantage in facilitating labour, in supplying the animals with food, and, in some degree, promoting ventilation, the same arrangement ought surely to be adopted in stables, where these advantages are of still greater importance."

45. The stalls are divided from one another by what are called *travises*—evidently a corruption of the word traverse—the travises are made up of boards running horizontally, and tongued and grooved; they are supported by the "head-post" placed 18 inches from the wall or against the wall. The head-post is made up of two battens, 4 inches by 2½ inches; these battens hold the ends of the travis boards between them. The upper ends of the "head-posts" are secured to the joists of the roof or truss of the stable; while the lower end is morticed into holes made in the stone rest, which should run from head to foot of the stall. On the upper side of this rest a groove should be cut to admit of the lower board of the travis being placed in it. This is a much better plan than to place the lower board of the travis immediately in contact with the floor of the stall exposed to all the wet of the litter. The end of this stone-rest nearest the gutter is provided with a hole, into which the lower end of the "heel-post" is fixed; the upper end of which is

secured to a beam running along the whole length of the stable. The heel-post should be made circular, say 5 or 6 inches in diameter; if rectangular, the corners should be rounded off to prevent accidents to the horses. *All angles should, indeed, be rounded off, and "bull-nosed" bricks used at the jambs of all doors opening into stock houses.* The thickness of the travis boards should be 1½ or 2 inches; the height at the end nearest the "head-post" 7 feet, and at "heel-post" 5 feet 6 inches. The upper edge of travis is usually curved in outline, and finished off either with an oak rail, or with a strip of iron with rounded edges. In cases where a feeding passage is placed at the heads of the stalls (see last diagram); the "head-posts" are placed at intervals, corresponding to the width of the stalls, as at *a a*. The space between these posts at head of stalls should be made up of boards to a height of five feet to keep undue draughts from the horse's head; and to admit of a sliding door being made, through which the hay and food are passed to the racks and mangers. In fig. 33, Chapter Sixth, we illustrate the method of combining iron and wood in the construction of stable travises, as introduced by Messrs. Musgrove and Brothers, Ann Street Iron Works, Belfast; and in fig. 34, another form in which is adapted a barrier sheath. In this is placed a rod which can be pulled out on either travis, forming a very readily made "loose-box."

46. The *position of the hay rack* is one of the disputed points of stable architecture; some advocating the high position for it, so that the horse in eating will have to raise its head in order to pull out the hay; others advocating the low position as the best. A due consideration of the natural features connected with the horse while feeding, will, we think, result in showing the great advantages of the low position of the rack.

On this question of high and low racks, Mr. Stephens has the following:—

"The prevailing opinion may be learned from the general practice, which is to place them as high as the horse's head, because, it is alleged, the horse is thereby obliged to hold up his head, and he cannot then breathe upon his food. Many better reasons, as I conceive, may be adduced for placing the racks low down. A workhorse does not require to hold up his head at any time, and much less in the stable, where he should rest as much as he can. A low rack permits the head and neck, in the act of eating, to be held in the usual position. He is not so liable to put the hay among his feet, from a low as from a high rack. His breath cannot contaminate his food so much in a low as in a high rack, inasmuch as the breath naturally ascends, and as breathing is employed by the horse in choosing his food by the sense of smell, he chooses his food from a low rack; whereas he is first obliged to pull it out of the high one, before he knows he is to like what he pulls. He is less fatigued eating out of a low rack than from a high rack, every mouthful having to be pulled out of the latter, from its sloping position, by the side of the mouth turned upwards. For this reason, mown grass is much more easily eaten out of a low than a high rack; and lastly, I have heard of pease falling out of the straw, when pulled out of a high rack, into an ear of a horse, and therein setting up a serious degree of inflammation."

47. Fig. 35, Chapter Sixth, shows the mode of fitting up a small court with a rack and manger, as introduced by the Messrs. Musgrove. The same principle of arrangement is also applicable to stable stalls. From the open hay-rack, as in fig. 35, Chapter Sixth, the horse, while eating, is apt to pull out much of the loose hay, and scatter it abroad, and waste it in his stall. Various forms of fittings have been introduced to prevent this being done. In Bruce's stable fittings, as manufactured by Messrs. Ransomes and Sons of Ipswich, a self-acting hay-rack is introduced. This consists of a rack in the corner of the stall, made up of vertical bars, with a horizontally barred top. The hay is kept continually pressed up against this barred top so tightly, that the horse cannot pull out any as loose stuff; and this by the following simple means,—the hay rests upon a moveable platform, which slides up and down within the rack, and is kept acted upon by weights which are connected to the ends of chains, which pass over pulleys, and are fixed to the platform on which the hay rests. In fig. 36, Chapter Sixth, we illustrate in section, Messrs. Musgrove's sliding hay-rack, which, in a simple manner, secures the hay firmly against the sides of the rack.

48. In the old-fashioned mode of fitting up stables, the manger is placed immediately under the hay-rack; and to a ring fixed in front and in the centre of manger the "horse-tie" is attached.

The rope or halter from the horse's neck passes through this ring, and is provided at its lower end with a weight. The object of this weight is to keep the rope taut, and out of the way of the horse; if loose, the probability is, that his fore-feet would get entangled in it, and serious accidents ensue. In Fig. 37, Chapter Sixth, we illustrate Musgrove's horse-tie, in which an india-rubber ring is attached to the upper end of balance-weight, by which the noise is deadened as the horse pulls the weight up against the bottom of the bucket.

49. *Ventilation* is of the utmost importance in a stable; of the practical details required to ensure this desideratum, the reader will find ample description in Essay Fifth—"Working Drawings in Architecture and Building." A. Fullarton & Co.—which takes up the whole subject. The following from an agricultural journal will, however, be useful on this subject:—"Until within the last quarter of a century it was considered absolutely necessary by farmers to have the stable as completely shut up and warm as possible, neither access nor egress being allowed for air, the bottom of the door even had to be packed with straw; and what with narrow stables, contracted stalls, and low ceilings filled with hay or straw, a horse had barely a chance to live instead of thrive. It is observable that old stables of farm steadings generally are only about 16 feet wide, with stalls from 5 to 5½ feet wide, and the ceiling in many cases not more than 8 feet high, as a hay loft above was reckoned indispensable for comfort to the horse and readiness for supply. The space, therefore, allotted to each animal did not exceed 700 cubit feet, and if 600 feet be the smallest quantity requisite to keep a man healthy, how is it possible, a horse which breathes double that quantity could remain in health with only 700 feet of space allotted to him? it could only be to his superior strength. However, it is gratifying to know that scientific and practical men are now exposing this fatal mistake, and that horses are beginning to get a purer atmosphere to breathe when resting and feeding, though many farmers are still of opinion that it is dangerous having *holes* in a stable for giving horses cold. Having some experience in the erection of farm stables, it may not be unworthy of notice to state the simple mode used for ventilating. The stable is either 19 or 20 feet wide according to the size of horses used on the farm; walls 10 feet high; no loft

allowed, but open to the ridge; stalls never less than 6 feet wide, so that each horse has 1,600 cubic feet of air at least, and when the stable is 20 feet wide, 1,680. One window is allowed for every 3 horses, the under third of window being fitted with luffer-boards; horizontal ventilators 2 feet by 2 inches, slanting upwards towards the inside, are formed in the back wall every 12 feet, about 8 feet from the ground, and placed opposite each alternate travise, thus dividing the opening and giving each horse 12 inches. Zinc ventilators, 9 inches square, are placed in the ridge every 12 feet, and exactly between the ventilators in the wall, so causing the current of air to take an oblique direction, and thus make a circulation through the entire upper part of the stable where the respired air rises to. It will be observed, that by this mode, a thorough and simple system of ventilation is effected; the air passing through the luffer-boards carries off the effluvia from behind the horses, without allowing it to commix with the pure air, which comes in by the horizontal openings, and these openings being placed near the horses' heads, supply a continued stream of fresh air from without, at the same time conducting the breathed air through the zinc ventilators. The stables ventilated in this manner have given entire satisfaction, and lessened disease amongst the horses to a very great extent."

50. Of all the modes yet introduced for *lighting* stables, that invented by the Messrs. Musgrove of Belfast, to whom we are indebted for illustration of so many admirable fittings of stock houses, is by far the simplest and the safest; we illustrate the mode in fig. 38, Chapter Sixth; a hollow rod is made to run from one end of the stable to the other; and in the lower side of this a slit is made; a catch slides along this, and is connected by means of an elastic balance with the stable lamp, as shown. The lamp can instantly be moved from one part of the stable to another.

51. *Dimensions of Stable Fittings of Timber.*—Where hay-racks and mangers are made of timber—is cases where there is plenty of home timber obtainable—the following notes of dimensions will be useful:—The distance of bottom rail of hay-rack from wall 6 inches; scantling of rail, 4 inches by 3 inches; the scantling of top rail is the same, and its distance

from the wall 2 feet; this will give a slope of the front bars of the rack of 18 inches. The front bars should be circular—they are however generally made flat, and fitted easily into the upper and lower rails. The dimensions of manger are as follows:—15 inches wide at top, 9 at bottom, and 10 inches deep; made of 1½ inch stuff, and usually stretching from side to side of stall. The *dimensions of stall* have not yet been alluded to; but in arranging these regard should be had more to the care and comfort of the animal than to the economization of space,—a point of comparatively little importance in country districts, where ground space is easily obtained. The dimensions, therefore, we would recommend, are, width of stall, inside measurement, six feet; length of stall from *front* of fittings, hay-rack, manger, &c., to front of the heel post, 9 feet. The other dimensions of stable and stable-fittings are: total width of stable 18 feet maximum, 17 feet minimum; height from floor to ceiling 10 to 11 feet; window width 3 feet 6, height 4 feet 6 inches; width of door, 4 feet 6 inches; height, 7 feet 6 inches, with bull-nosed jambs. The dimensions of a loose-box, 12 feet by 18 feet.

52. *General Remarks on Stables.*—The following remarks from an article on "Stables and Horses," in the '*Builder*,' reviewing Mr. Haycock's excellent work—(The Gentleman's Stable Manual, or a Treatise on the Construction of the Stable, by W. Haycock, M.R.C.V.S. Routledge, Warne, and Routledge: London,) will be useful here:—"A stable, to be well placed, should be built upon rising ground; with the front to the south, and the inmates facing the north. If possible, have the heads of the horses due north. Have the windows a good size, both in width and height. Many, not aware of the great importance of light, and its influence upon the health of animals, have their stables nearly dark. This is a great mistake; for light is as essential to the continued health and vigour of animals as it is to vegetation. On this account a north aspect for the stable should be avoided if it be possible. The number of windows necessary will, of course, depend upon the size of the stable: as a general rule, however, there should be one good-sized window for every three stalls. Again, the stable should not be closely surrounded with large trees: they impede the light and the air, and in addition they afford shelter to flies and annoying insects, and also, by their foliage, they

attract much moisture, which constantly tends to keep the building and the surrounding air damp and unhealthy.

"As to the height and width of the stable within, 11 feet of height is quite sufficient. A greater height is objectionable on account of the chilliness it might occasion; while, if lower to any considerable extent, it would be dark, and perhaps might prove unhealthy. In width (or from front wall to back wall), it should not be less than 22 feet. Many speak of 18 feet as being sufficient, but experience shows that 18 feet is too narrow.

"He would have the doorways 7 feet high, and about 4 feet 6 inches in width. The doors should either be made to slide, or —what perhaps is better—should be made in two halves, and the hinges fixed on the outside; that is, if it be not within the control of the Metropolitan Building Act. The doors of all loose boxes should be suspended so as to open on the outside.

"The door jambs should be *rounded* at the edges, to prevent a horse, when going into the stable, or when coming out, from injuring the hips, should he make a rush, or become alarmed during the act.

"Stalls, where space of ground will allow, should be 6 feet in width; but certainly not less than 5 feet 8 or 9 inches. As to height, 7 feet 6 inches, at the highest part, is abundantly sufficient for the largest-sized horse, and about 6 feet at the lowest end.

"A common practice with many is to have the stall-post to proceed from the ground up to the ceiling. This is objectionable on two grounds: it looks ugly; and a large-sized horse, placed in the stall, and made to turn quickly round, would be very liable to strike his head against it, and possibly damage an eye, or knock out a tooth.

"The stall partitions should consist of boards 4 or 5 inches in width, and about 2½ inches thick. They should not be tongued and grooved, but simply fitted close and compact to one another. The length of the stall partitions, from the back of the manger to where the boards join the stall-post (that is to say, the length of the stalls from the hay-rack to the heel-post behind), should be 9 feet.

"Our author inclines to the old arrangement of hay-rack and manger, with some alterations, and does not recommend a water-trough. On these points, in a letter to us commenting on one of his reviewers, he says,—

"'Water-troughs, filled with water close to horses' heads, are a great nuisance, and I never recommend them. Hay-seeds and straws of hay fall into them, and the horses are always slobbering in the water, and in a very short time the fluid becomes so disgusting that the horses will not look at it. It is a very nice thing in idea to always let your horse have water beside him, but I never knew any one who allowed such things to remain in his stable more than twelve months. Fault has been found with me by one reviewer for recommending the old style of rack and manger. He says that the low racks are better, and horses do not waste near so much hay as with the old racks. Now, I will tell you why I recommend the old form of hay-rack. I have had several cases where horses have been severely injured in consequence of their getting their fore feet fast in the low rack: in one case a horse, that cost the owner £100, was so lamed and the ligaments of the fetlock joint were so much torn and lacerated, that the animal was never worth £10 afterwards. For these reasons (and I think they are good ones) I recommend the old form of hay-rack.'

"Mr. Haycock wisely dwells at some length on the necessity for a regular and copious supply of pure air in stables, and recommends the following mode of ventilating amongst others:—

"'Make an opening ten inches square through the wall in front of the heads of the inmates. Make it behind the woodwork dividing the hay-racks from one another, or immediately behind where the divisions of the stalls commence. One opening in the position named, and of the size specified, will be sufficient to afford air for a single horse. To modify the current, and prevent the entrance of foreign bodies from without, place an iron grate against the outside of the opening. Where it is impracticable to cut through in the manner directed, the difficulty may be obviated by carrying tubes made of iron or wood through the roof, taking care to cover the upper opening of the tube with perforated caps. A corresponding number of openings of the same size are next to be made through the wall *behind* the horses, These openings must be cut within a few inches of the ground, and protected by grates fixed on the outside, as directed above.

Each opening must terminate in a square tube, placed within the stable. Each tube must be five feet high, having an upright position, and secured to the wall by means of holdfasts. They should be five or six inches square, having three sides of wood, the fourth being formed by the wall against which they are fixed. On the top of every tube, fix a thick plate of zinc, well perforated with small holes.'

"Mr. Haycock says there is no surer indication, in a general way, of a badly ventilated stable than the fact that in it '*scarlatina readily supervenes upon catarrh.*' He speaks of this, doubtless correctly, as a common occurrence; scarlatina following catarrh because of the want of sanitary arrangements in the stable! Some of our medical friends will try to make us believe that some other horse suffering with scarlatina must have communicated it. We should have been glad to find our author pronouncing positively against the use of living-rooms over the stables. Experience has shown us that it is most hurtful to the occupants. He contents himself with pointing out that care should be taken in such cases to provide an entrance to the rooms quite separate from the stable, and that the floor should be double. We have ourselves a very strong adverse opinion on the arrangement."

53. *Cow-Houses.*—Many of the points connected with the fittings of stables, just discussed, are obviously applicable to cow-houses. It should be noted, however, that the part of the stall from the front of the manger to the heel part of travis must be comparatively soft; to prevent the knees of the cows being hurt when rising up or lying down. This part, therefore, may be boarded and covered, if deemed desirable, with kamptulicon, or with cocoa matting; or it may be made with earth well beaten down. The width of the stall for a single cow should not be less than 4 feet 6 inches, but five feet if possible—for two cows 9 feet. We would, however, never recommend stalls for two cows to be adopted. A study of the habits of the animal will show that the best way by far is to give a stall to each cow; and let this stall be roomy enough; it is a great mistake to cramp animals up in a small confined space. The divisions or travises between the stalls are generally made of stone, as shown in the building to the right hand of the drawing in Plate of Cow-House,

at the end of this work; the length being usually 6 feet, and height 3 feet. The best way of arranging the stalls of a cow-house is by giving a feeding passage at the head. Stalls are often placed foot to foot, with the dunging passage and gutters behind. An excellent arrangement of a cow-house, as fitted up by Messrs. Musgrove on the Ulster Model Farm, is illustrated in fig. 39, Chapter Sixth. The mangers run from end to end of the stalls; and the supply of water is secured by a pipe and tap; a brass plug is fitted to one of the mangers nearest the drain. The feeding passages are provided with rails on which the trucks run. Ventilation is secured by openings in the walls, and by swing sky-lights in the roof, as shown. In figs. 40 and 41, Chapter Sixth, we illustrate other modes of fitting up cow-houses introduced by the Messrs. Musgrove. In fig. 40 the stalls are provided with mangers only; each stall being for two cows; dwarf partitions are made, dividing the length of manger into two parts; while head-plates, as shown in the stall to the right, may separate the stall from the feeding passage. In fig. 41 racks are provided; which have this advantage, that the hay or grass is kept separate from the turnips or meat in the manger, and does not become heated or breathed upon by the cattle, which is often the case when the fodder and roots are all given to the cattle in the manger. Wood travises or divisions are thought more highly of by some authorities as affording a material freer from damp, and more comfortable to the animal.

54. The following dimensions will be useful for those who contemplate fitting up the stalls of home-grown or other timber, in place of purchasing the stall fittings, such as we have already illustrated. A stone curb, six inches deep, should run from end to end of stall; provided at the upper and lower ends with mortice holes into which the head and heel posts are fixed. The dimensions of these posts are—height 4 feet 6 inches or 5 feet—scantling 4 inches by 3 inches. The boards to be of $1\frac{1}{2}$ inch plank, tongued and grooved, or dowelled and cramped; and the ends let into grooves made in the inner face of head and heel posts, and the lower board into a groove made in the face of stone curb. The manger should rest upon a stone or brick base 18 inches high. The dimensions of the manger, length 3 feet, or stretching from side to side of stall; depth 12 inches; width

at top 15, and at bottom 10 inches; made of inch and half stuff. Each stall should be supplied with a water-trough; this may be made either of cast-iron, slate, or stone; and each should have a brass plug by which the water can be withdrawn from the trough at pleasure; and an overflow pipe by which the waste can be allowed to pass into the drain. A constant supply of water to the trough is advocated by the highest authorities as being the best for the animal; as it can thus drink when nature prompts it.

55. The cows are secured to the stalls in a variety of ways. An excellent plan is illustrated in figs. 39, 40, and 41, Chapter Sixth, in which a slot or vertical opening is made near the head of the stall; in the centre of which is fixed a rod which passes through the ring to which the chain is attached. Another method, where the travis boards are of wood, is to make a rod of iron with pointed ends, turned in at right angles to the length, the ends being driven into the travis boards near the head of stall, the ring being previously passed up the rod. The rod being thus free from the face of the travis boards, allows of ample space for the up and down movement of the ring and chain as the animal moves.

56. *The Calf-House.*—The position of this should be such as to secure ample light and fresh air, and a space before the door to admit of a small court-yard being enclosed. The house is usually fitted up with a series of small enclosures, some four feet six inches square; the divisions between each being made by light frames or hurdles, the frame to the front being hinged so as to open outwards like a door. The following type diagram shows an arrangement of calf-house and court-yard. *a a* court-yard, entrance to which is at *b*; *c c* shelter shed; *d* entrance to calf-house; *e e* calf pens; *f f* dunging passage; *g h* doors:—

57. *The Piggery.*—The usual form of pig-styes is well known. The inner or shelter shed being 6 feet long by 4 feet wide; the court or yard being 7 feet by 4 feet or thereabouts. The court is fitted up with a manger or feeding trough, and provided with a door. The arrangement in fig. 42, Chapter Sixth, is admirably adapted for piggeries.

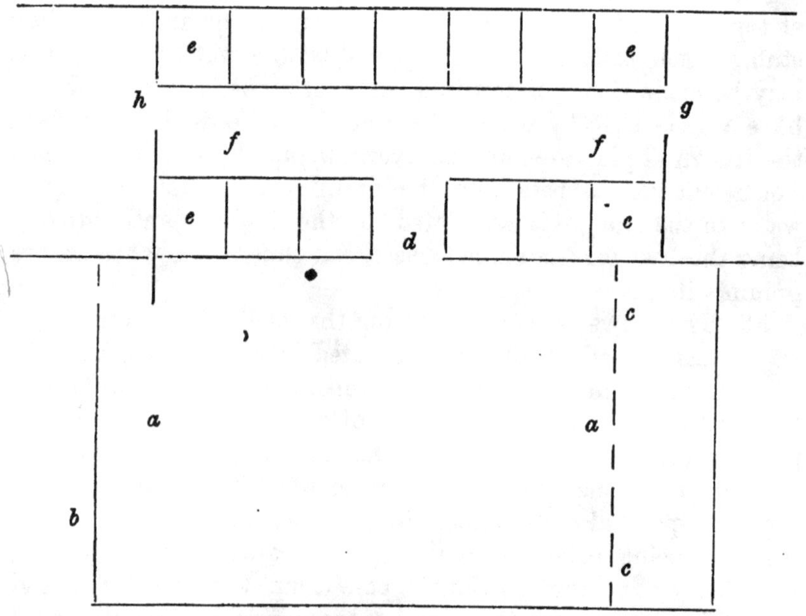

Plan of Calf-house and Court-yard.

58. *The Dairy.*—This, in many farm-steadings, forms part of the farm-house; in others it is an isolated building, or made

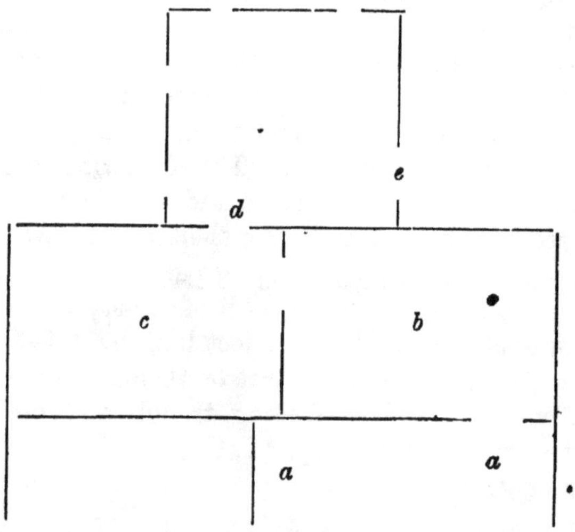

Ground Plan of Dairy.

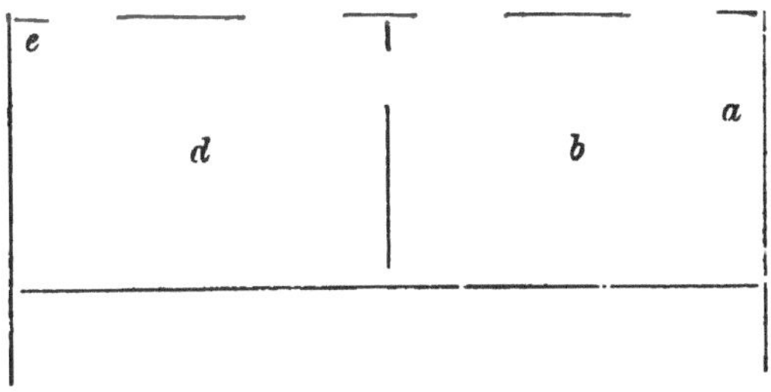

Upper Plan of Dairy.

to form part of the steading. "The apartments required in it," as we have elsewhere stated, "are—1. milking-room; 2. churning-room; 3. cheese-making room; 4. a wash or boiling room, where water may be boiled, and the utensils of the dairy washed; 5. a cheese-drying and storage room.

"The aspect of the dairy should be north; but if this cannot be accomplished, due east must be obtained—a southern aspect is totally inadmissible. In the diagram above we give the plan of the dairy part of a farm house; *a a* the kitchen, with door leading into boiling and wash house *b*; *c* churning-room; *d* milk-room, with external door *e*; in the upper plan—*a* the position of stairs leading from boiling room below; *b* the cheese-making room; *e* a lift in the corner, by which to bring up material from the milk-room below; *d* the cheese-storing room.

"If a convenient locality can be obtained at once near the farm-house and the cow-house, and yet completely away from all noxious smells, &c., of the farm-yard, where an isolated dairy can be erected, more satisfaction will be secured. It is unnecessary to give a plan showing an arrangement of this isolated dairy; the requisite apartments being secured in it, they will best be arranged by the architect according to his notions of convenience of working, or of those of his client.

"The floor of the milk-room, and the benches on which the milk-cans are placed, should be of slate—every pains being taken to secure coolness, and, at the same time, freedom from damp. Ventilation should be carefully attended to, many of the contrivances specially described in former papers, being obviously applicable to this apartment. All breaks, as in cornices, skirtings, &c., should be avoided, as these only afford spaces on which dust lodges; all the internal fittings should be flush with the walls, and the corners of the room and the junction with the ceiling should not be at right angles, but made with curves. The windows, if possible, should be double, the outer one being made with perforated zinc, the inner glazed as usual, and double hung with pullies and sash lights.

"The churning-room and cheese-making room should also be fitted up in the same way, and the floor of the washing-house should dish from all sides to the centre, to permit all slops, &c., to drain rapidly away. Ventilation should be ample to carry rapidly off, and preventing their finding access to the other rooms, all steam and vapour. A small open shed should be provided near the door of the wash-house, under the roof of which the utensils can be placed to dry and get the air."

CHAPTER SIXTH.

ILLUSTRATIONS OF BUILDING CONTRIVANCES USEFUL IN THE CONSTRUCTION OF HOUSES AND THEIR OUTBUILDINGS.

Fig. 1.

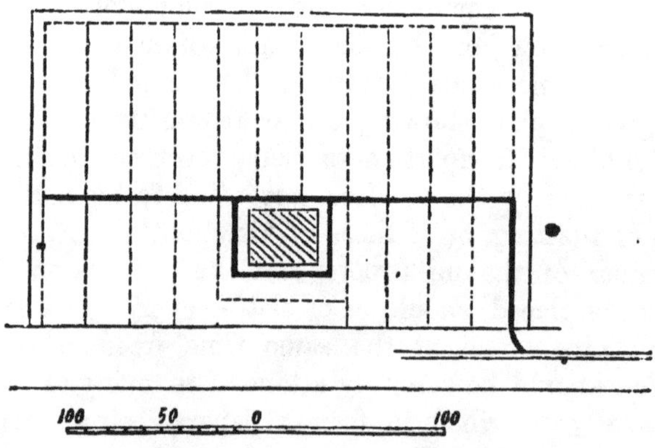

Diagram showing the Site Drainage of a Detached Villa. (See par. 5, p. 18.)

Fig. 2.

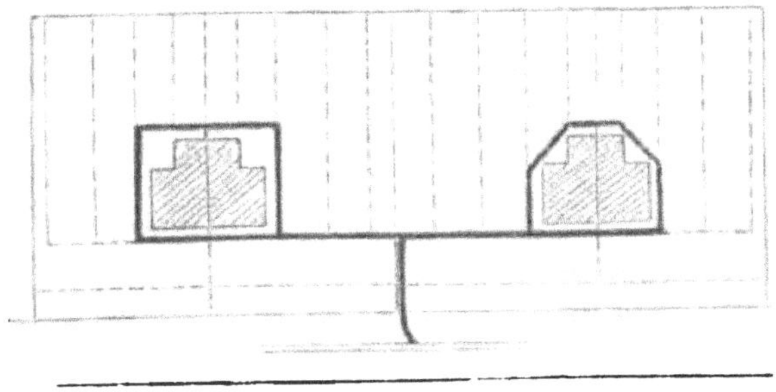

Diagram showing the Site Drainage of Two Semi-detached Villas. (See par. 5.)

Fig. 3.

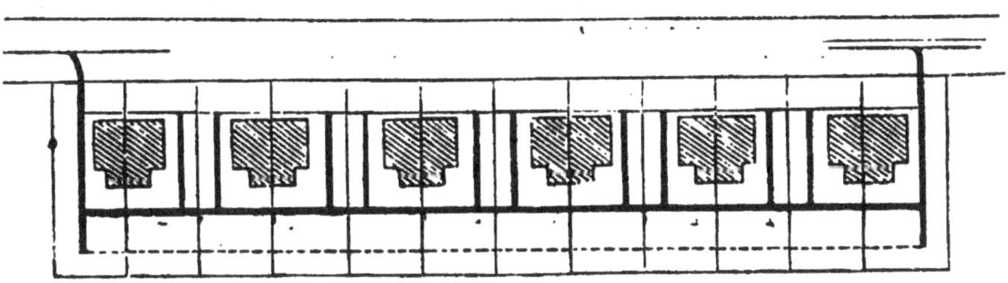

Diagram illustrating the Site Drainage of a row of Six Semi-detached Villas. (See par. 5.)

Fig. 5.

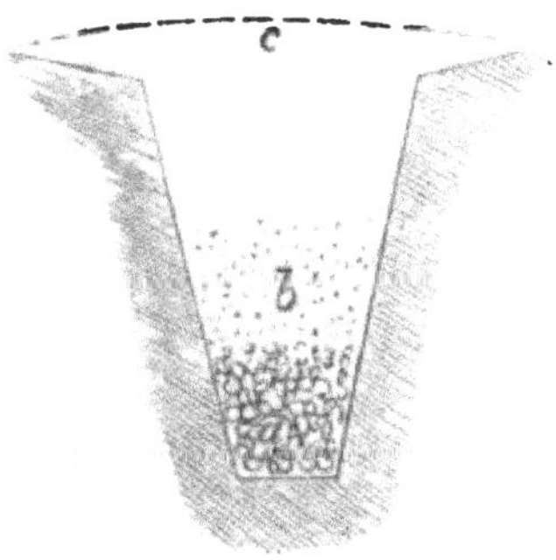

Broken stone filled drain for drainage of sites; *a* stone filling; *b* gravel and soil; *c* upper filling.

Fig. 4.

Open surface drain for fields for sites.

Fig. 6.

Flat stone drain for drainage of site, filled up with stone, gravel, and soil.

Fig. 7.

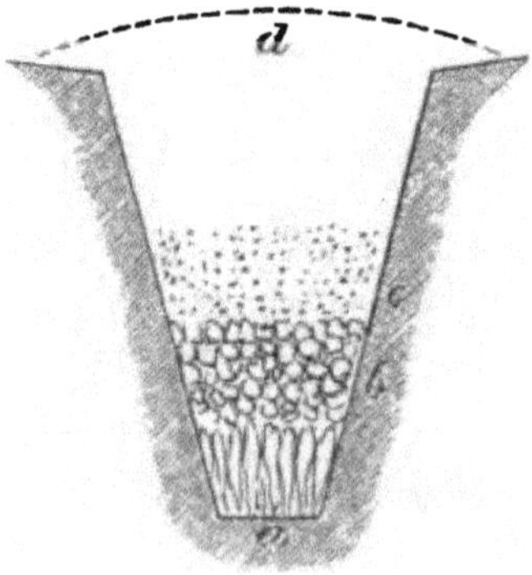

Stone filled drain for drainage of site, with flat stones at bottom, and broken stones, gravel and soil.

Fig. 8.

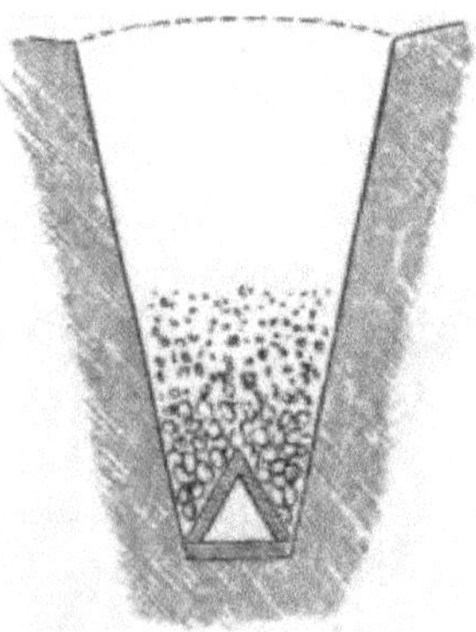

Triangular-shaped drain for drainage of site; formed of flat stones, with gravel and soil filling up.

Fig. 9.

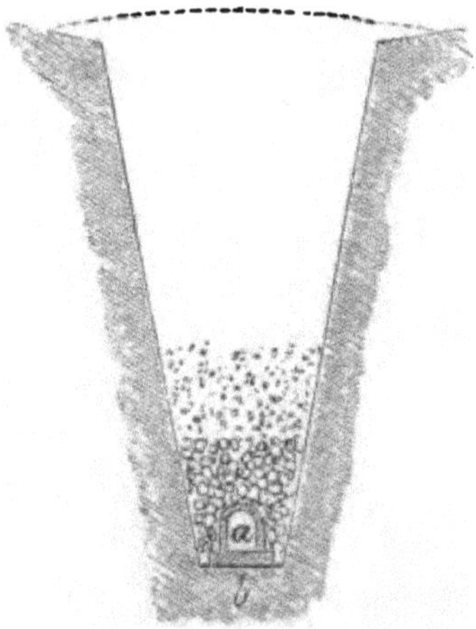

Tile (*a*) and sole (*b*) drain for site drainage.

Fig. 10.

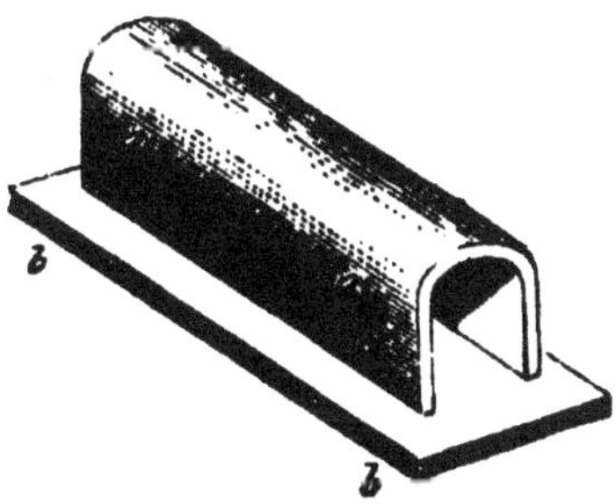

Separate view of tile *a a*, and sole *b b* in fig. 9.

Fig. 11.

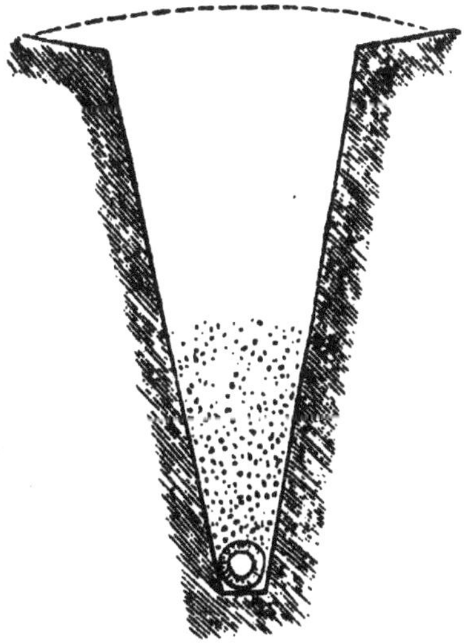

Tubular drain tile for site drainage.

Fig. 11 a.

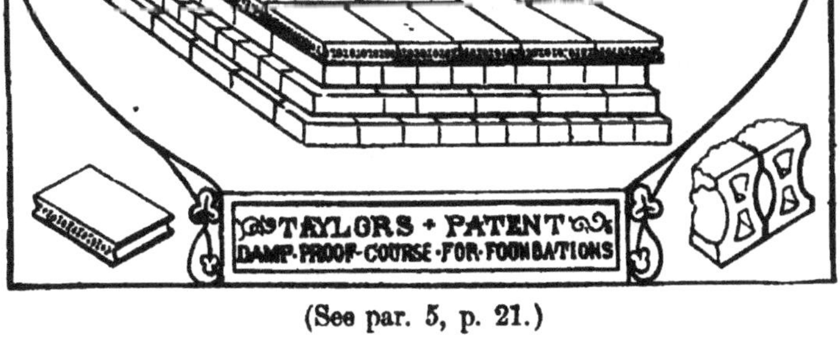

(See par. 5, p. 21.)

Fig. 11–b.

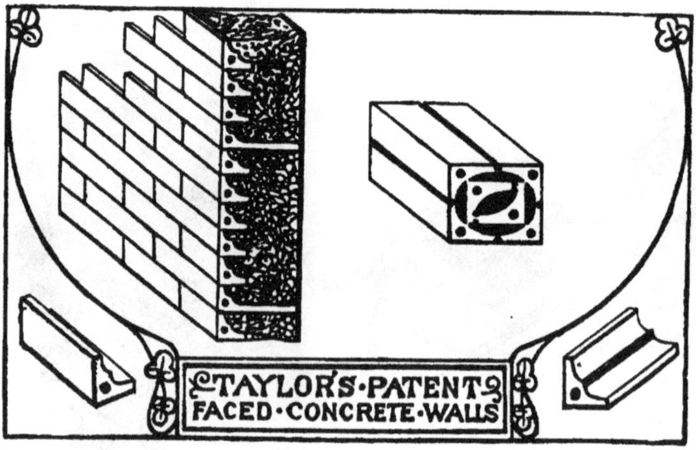

Fig. 11–c.

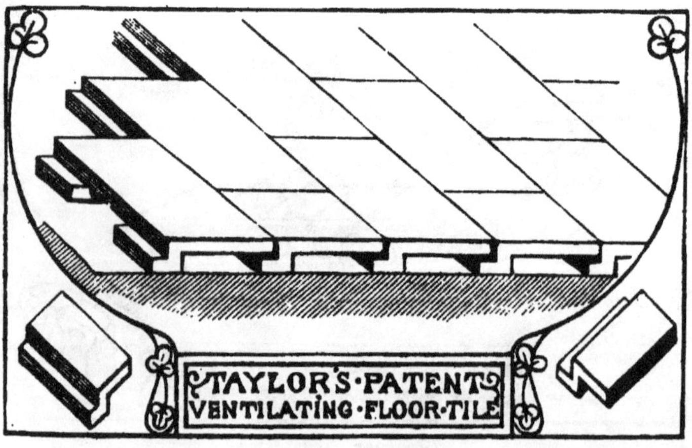

Fig. 11-d.

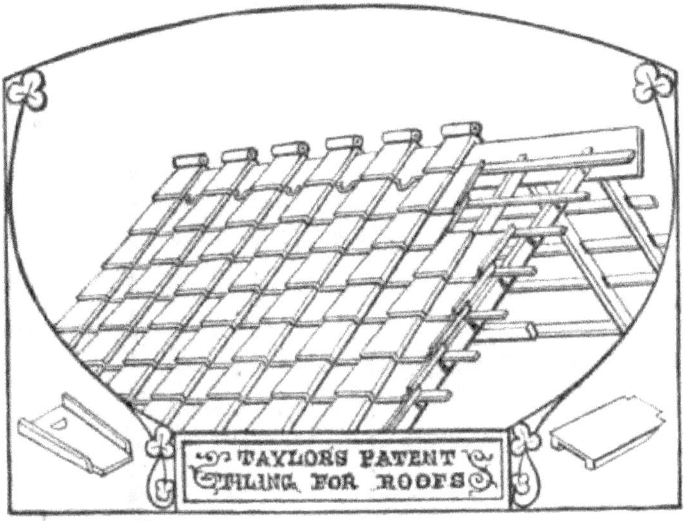

Fig. 12.

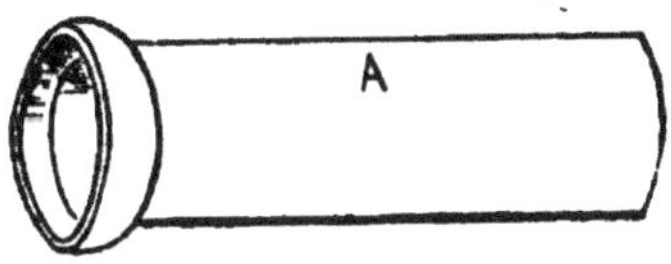

Impermeable Drain Tube for House Sewage (see par. 7, p. 27.) having Socket.

Fig. 13.

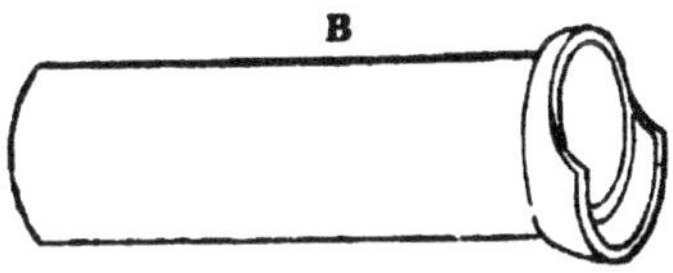

Do., with Rebated Socket.

Fig. 14.

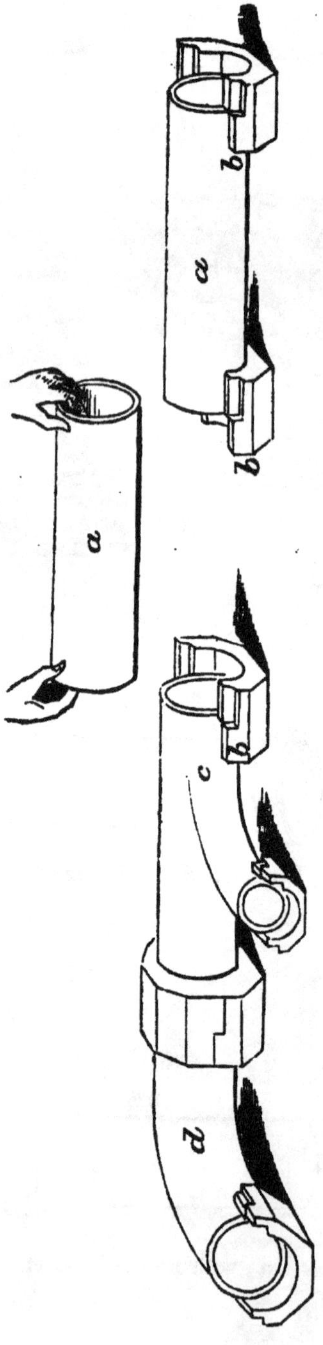

Cooper's Drain Tubes *a a*; and Saddles *b b*. Curved Junctions *c d*. (See par. 8, p. 30.)

Fig. 15.

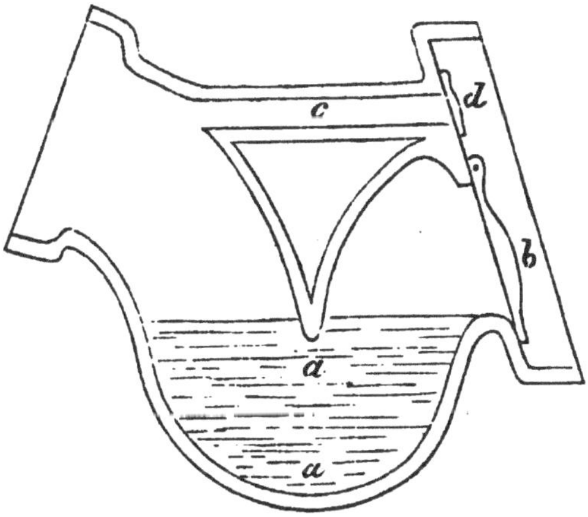

Lovegrove's Trap; *a a* body of Trap; *b* lower water valve; *c d* air passage and valve. (See par. 9, p. 30.)

Fig. 16.

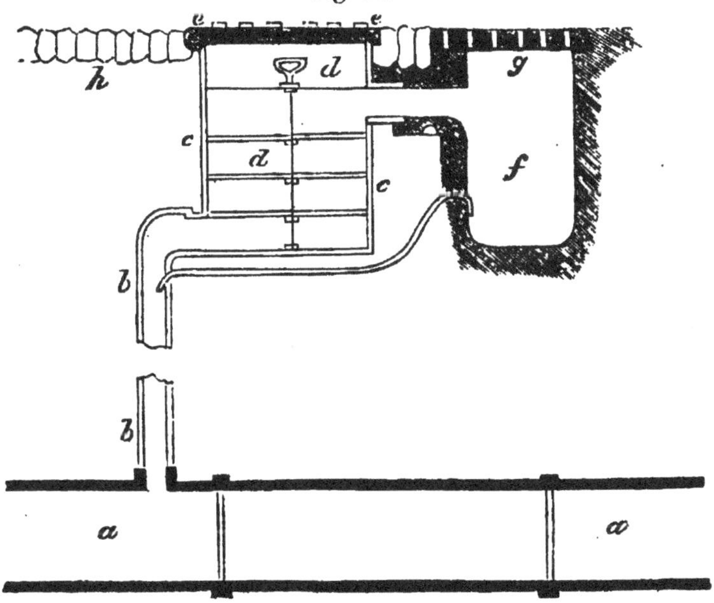

Charcoal Ventilation for Drain (from the '*Builder*'); *a a* drain; *b b* tube leading air to the ventilator *c c*, containing shelves *d d*, supporting the charcoal, *e e* cap to do.; *f* gully cesspool; *g* gully grating; *h* street paving. (See par. 9, p. 30.)

Fig. 17.

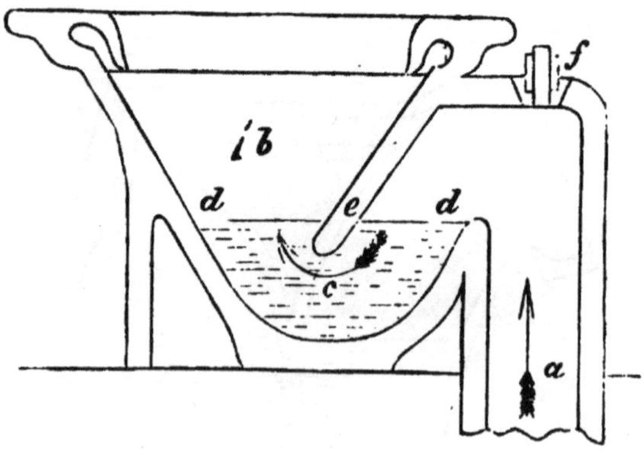

Water Closet Pan Basin; *a* pipe leading to drain; *b* body of seat; *c* water trap; *d d* level of water; *e* division; *f* pipe leading foul air to chimney of house. (See par. 20, p. 42.)

Fig. 18.

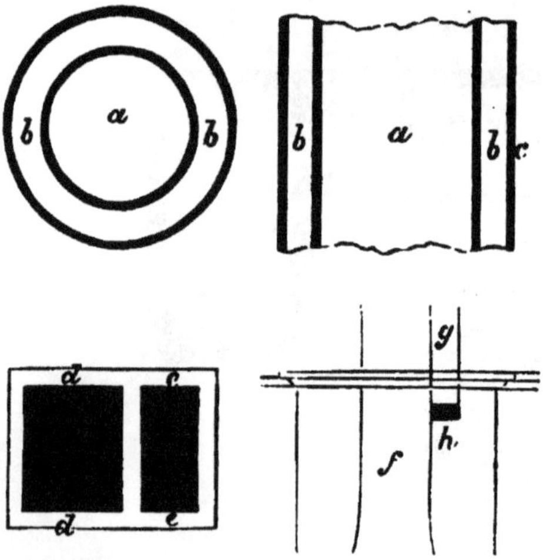

Ventilating Chimney tube (see par. 6, p. 26.) *a d d* the smoke flue; *b b e e* the ventilating flue in plan; *f* flue; *g* ventilating do. in elevation; *h* aperture near the cornice of room to admit foul air to the flue *g*.

Fig. 19.

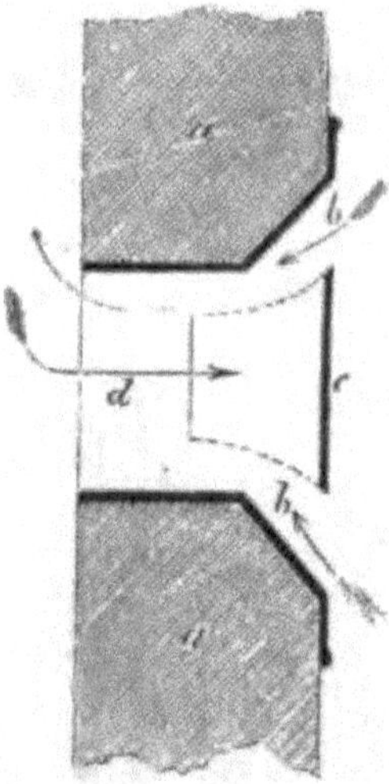

Brydon's Ventilator for Chimney flues. *a a* chimney breast; *b b* metal ventilator with solid centre piece *c*; *bb* ring perforated with holes. The down draught in chimney sends the smoke against the part *c*, which prevents it from entering the room.

Fig. 20.

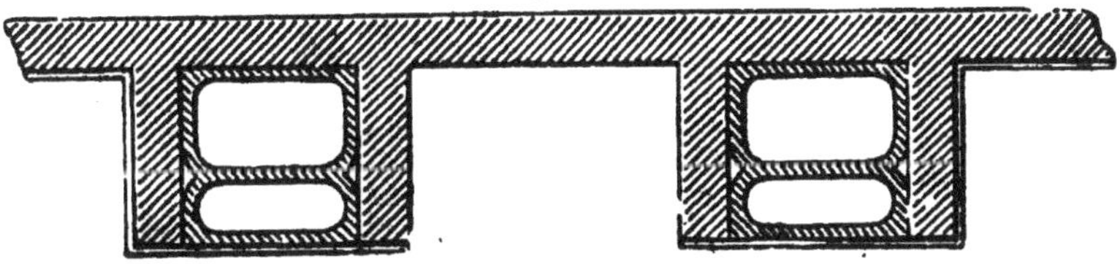

Walker's Ventilating Flue and Smoke Flue Combined.

Fig. 21.

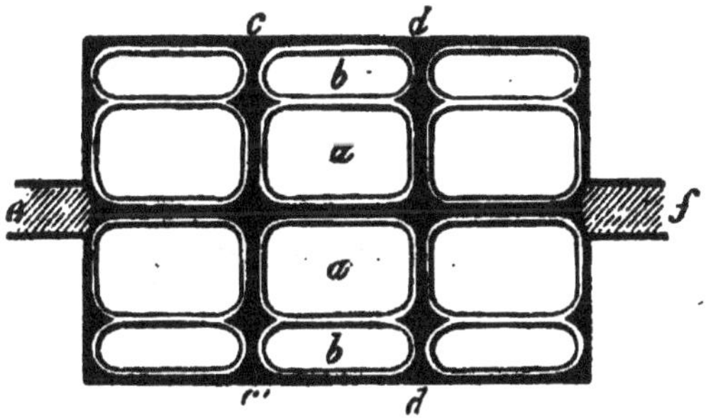

Stack of six Flues

Fig. 22.

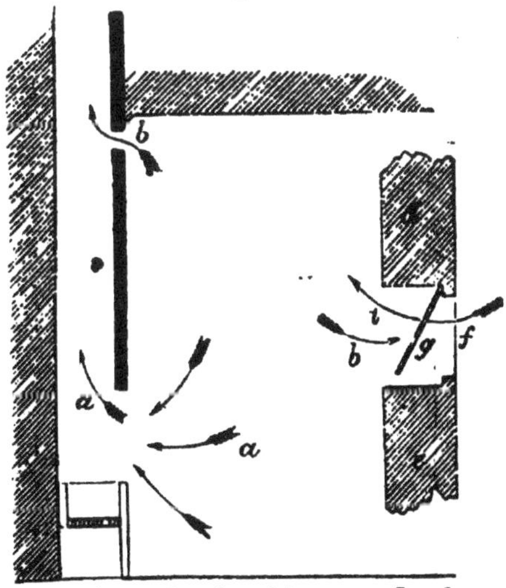

Arnott's Ventilating flap-valve for chimney. In place of having a simple opening *b* into the flue of the fireplace *a a*, a flap of silk *g* is placed in the opening *f*. This is the arrangement used for cottages. For superior rooms the valve is of metal, and nicely balanced.

Fig. 23.

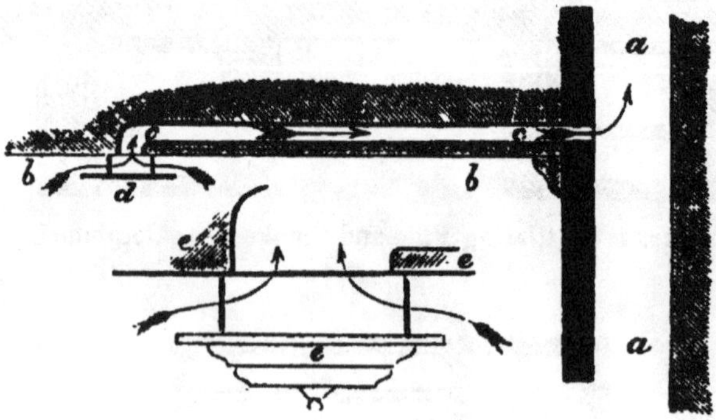

Plan of ventilating a room from the centre of ceiling. *a a* the chimney; *b b* ceiling; *c c* tube above do.; *d* deflecting plate, shown in larger scale below.

Fig. 24.

Cooke's Window Ventilator, in which a diaphragm of flexible material closes or expands as the sash is raised or lowered.

Fig. 25.

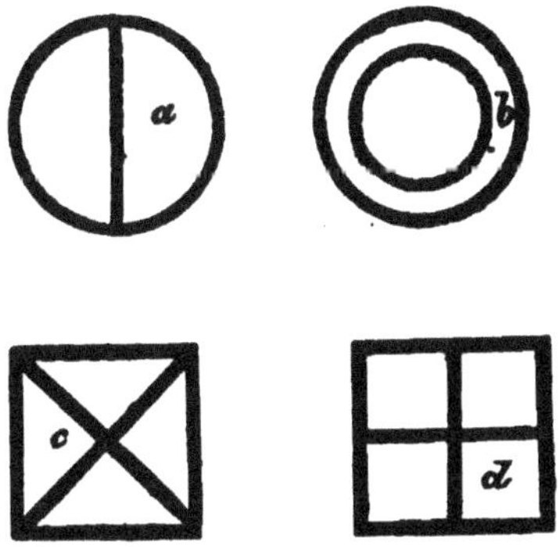

Sections of Moor's Ventilation Tubes divided by plates, one of the divisions serving to supply fresh, the other towithdraw foul air.

Fig. 26

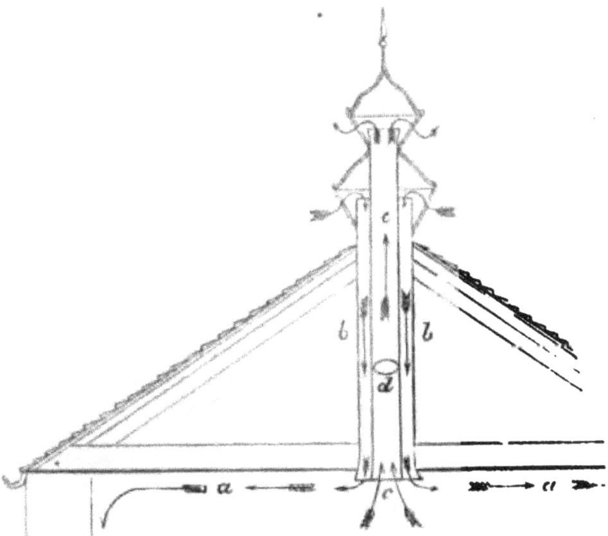

Section of M'Kinnel's Ventilator. *a a* ceiling line; *b b* external tube supplying fresh air; *c c* internal tube taking away the foul; *d* a valve.

Fig. 27.

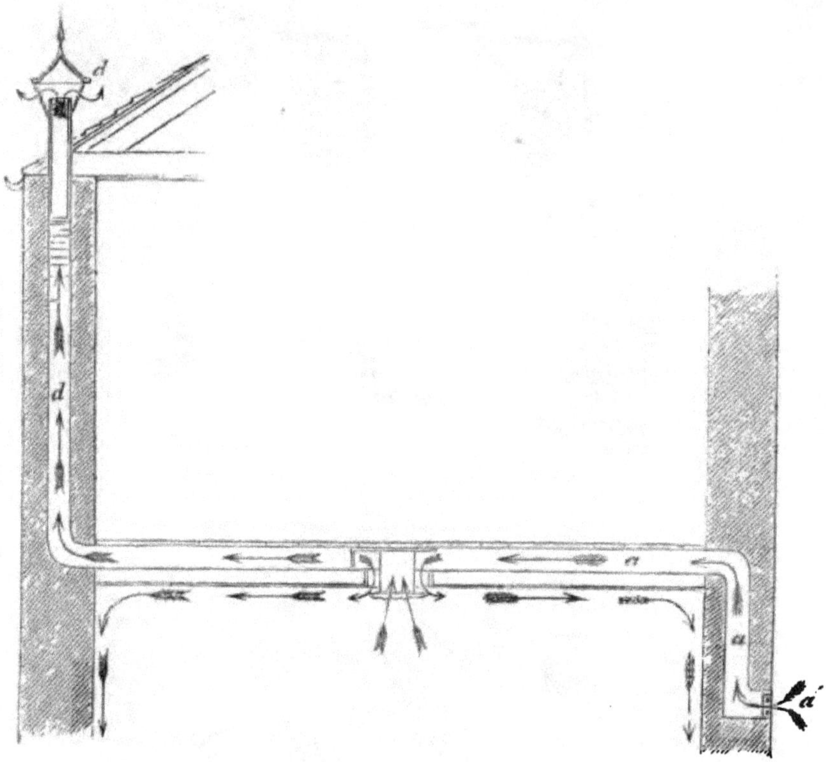

Section of M'Kinnel's Ventilating System. The fresh air is supplied by the channel *a a*, and the foul withdrawn by channel *d d*.

Fig. 28.

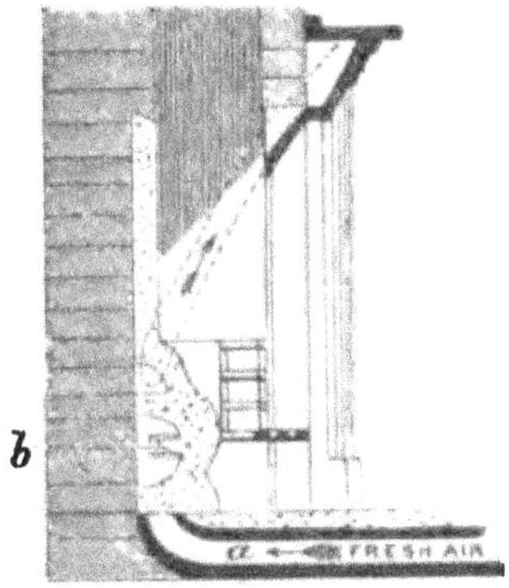

Section of Pierce's Ventilating Grate. The fresh air is led by the channel *a a*, behind the fire-lump *b b*, at back of grate; and, when warmed, passed off to the room by the channel as shown.

Fig. 29.

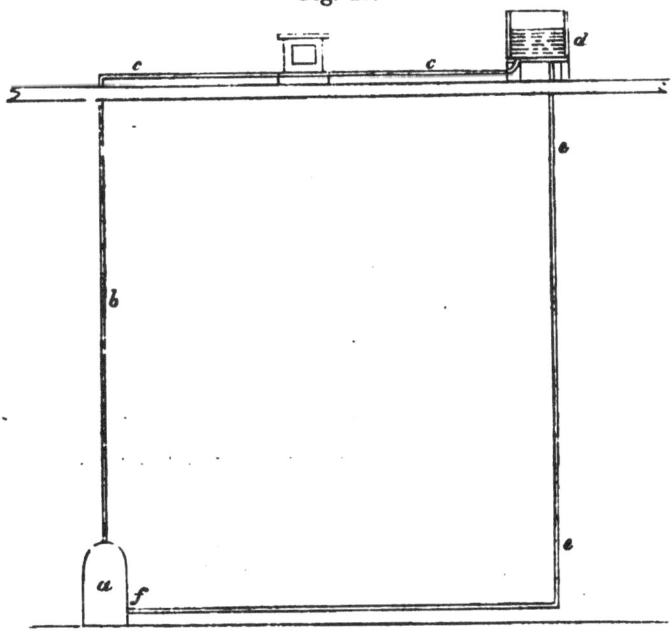

Diagram illustrating Low Pressure Hot Water Apparatus. *a* boiler in the lowest apartment; *b* ascending or flow pipe; *c c* upper part of do. heating room in upper floor, and led into the lower part of the open cistern *d*. As the water cools it flows down the return pipe *e e* back to the boiler; and thus a constant circulation is kept up in the pipes.

Fig. 30.

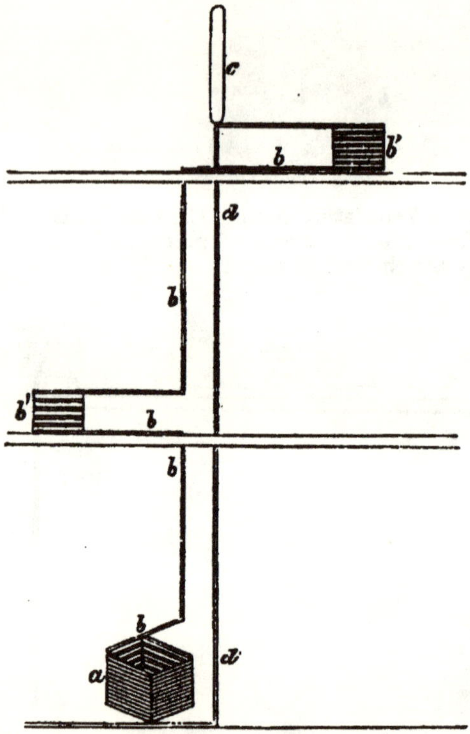

Section illustrating High Pressure Hot Water Warming Apparatus. The boiler is made up of a coil of pipes *a*; *b b* the flow or ascending pipe; *b'* a coil of pipes—which are covered with an ornamental case with perforated sides—to heat the rooms in which they are placed. The pipe *b* terminates in an expansion tube *c*, from which the cooled water returns to the boiler *a* by the pipe *d d*.

Fig. 31.

Section of Hot Water Stove heated by Gas. *a a* the gas-jet; *d d* internal dome—the heated air passes up the tubes *e e* to the space *f f*, and is led off by the chimney *g*. The whole heating surfaces are surrounded by water; *h h* space for expansion. This stove, in addition to warming a hall, may be used to supply heating tubes in adjoining apartments; in this case flow and return pipes will be necessary—as *i* the flow; *j* the return pipe. A section of the gas pipe is shown at *a*, and the disposition of the jets or pipe *a a* at *b b* and *c*.

Fig. 31–a.

Cottage Cooking Range.

Fig. 31–b.

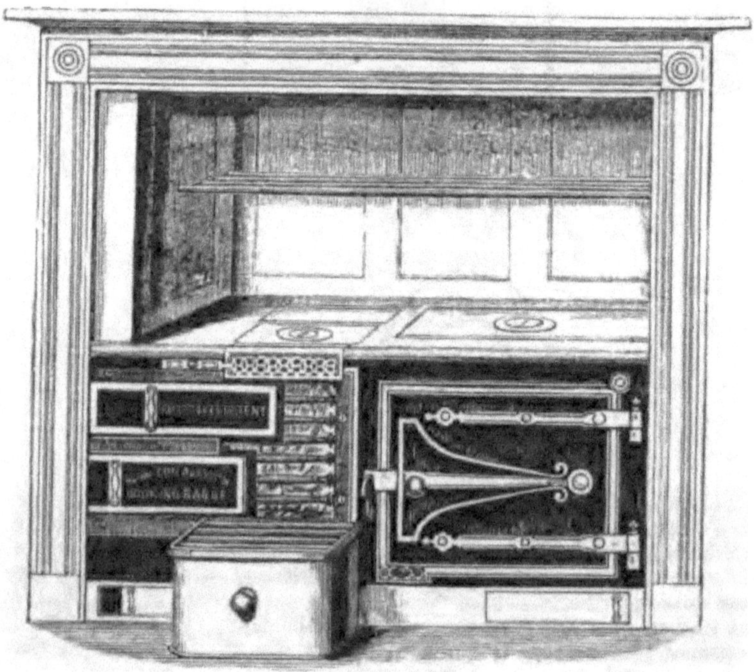

Musgrove's Cooking Range.

Fig. 32.

Brick for Paving Stables. (See par. 43, p. 65.)

Fig. 33.

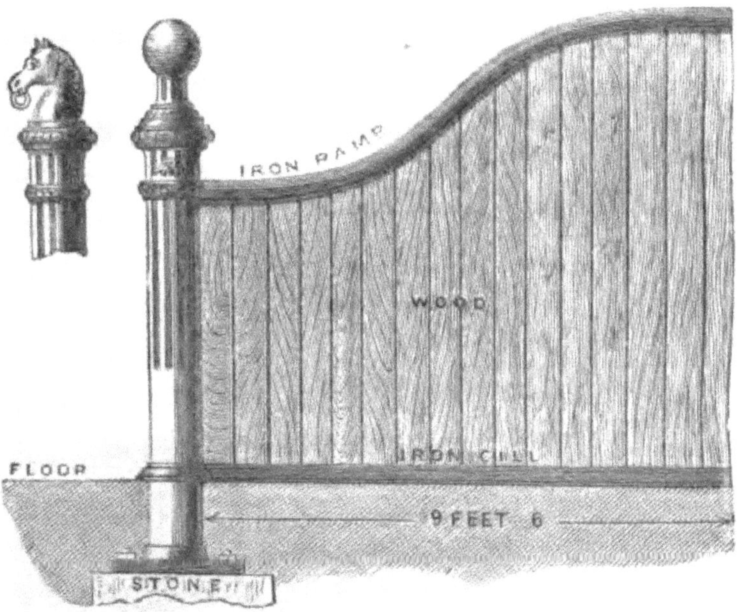

Musgrove's Stall Division or Travis of Wood and Cast-iron. (See par. 45.)

Fig. 34.

Musgrove's Iron and Wood Stall Division with Patent Barrier. (See par. 45.)

Fig. 35.

Musgrove's Rack and Manger. (See par. 47.)

Fig. 36.

Musgrove's Sliding Hay - Guard. (See par. 47).

Fig. 37.

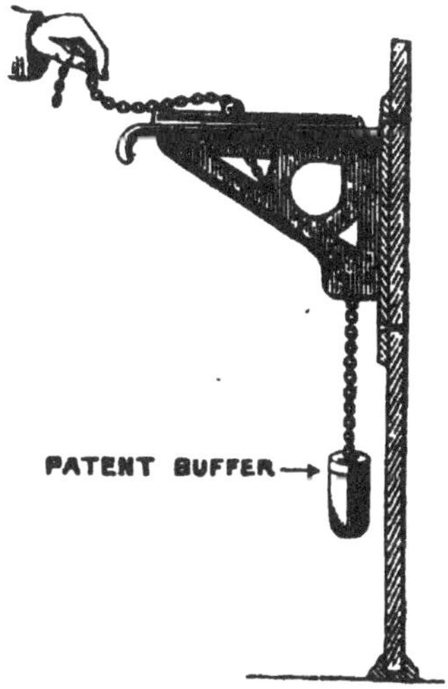

Musgrove's Horse-Tie. (See par. 47).

Fig. 38.

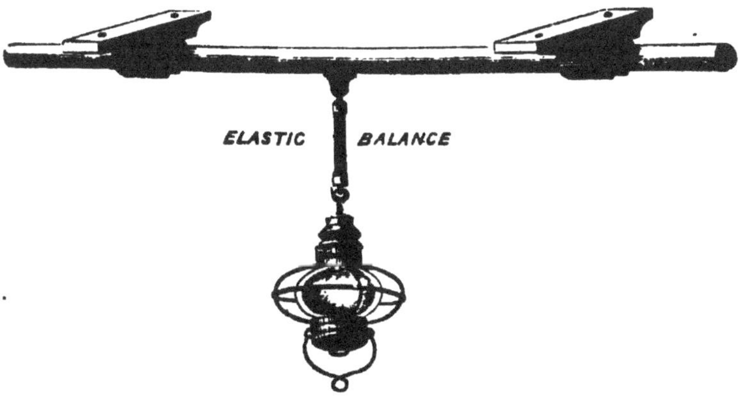

Musgrove's Lantern Slide for Stables. (See par. 50.)

Fig. 39.

Interior View of Cow House with double range of Stalls, erected at the Ulster Model Farm; erected by Musgrove Brothers of Belfast.

Fig. 40.

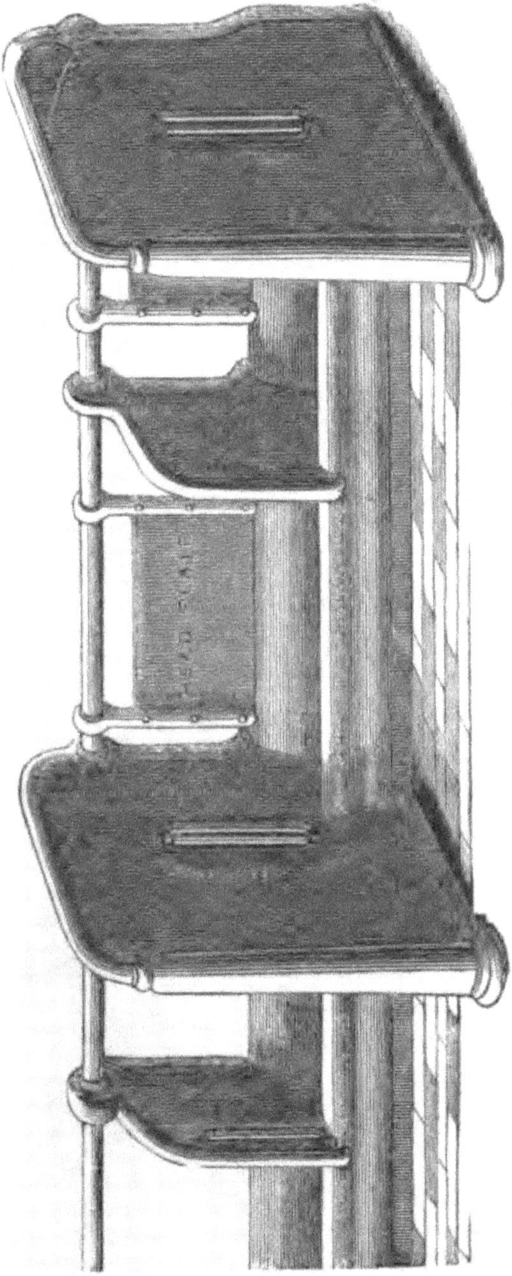

Musgrove's Patent Cow House Fittings with Manger, but without Fodder Rack. (See par. 53.)

Fig. 41.

Patent Cow House Fittings with Fodder Rack. (See par. 53.)

Fig. 42.

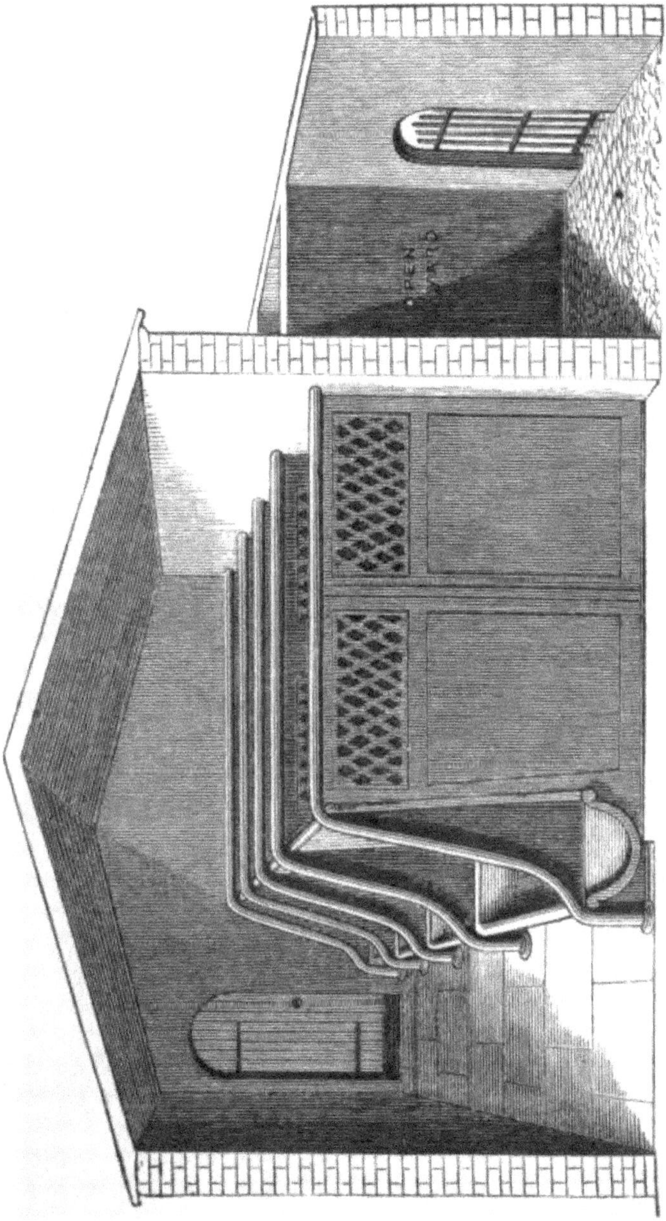

Musgrove's Piggery. (See par. 57.)

Fig. 43.

Ransome's Circular Pig Trough.

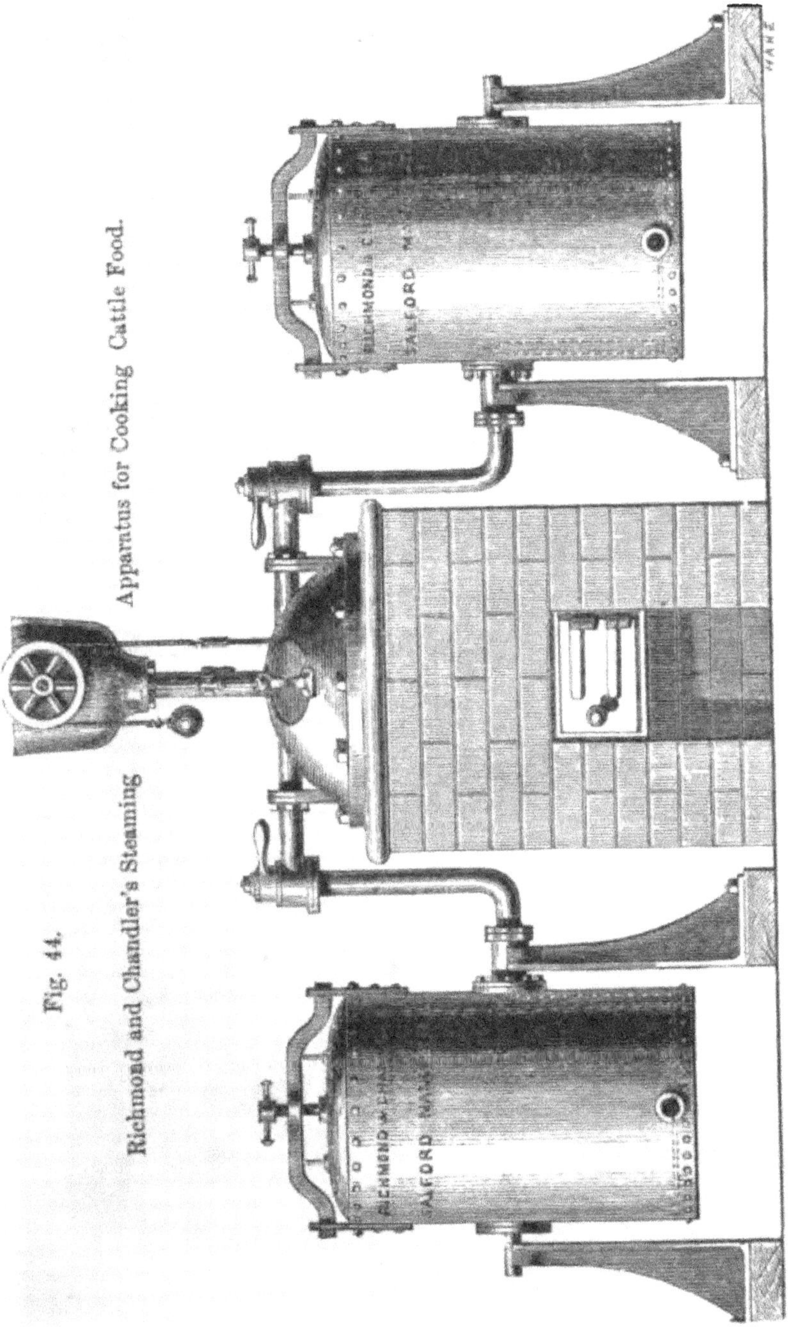

Fig. 44.

Richmond and Chandler's Steaming Apparatus for Cooking Cattle Food.

Fig. 45.

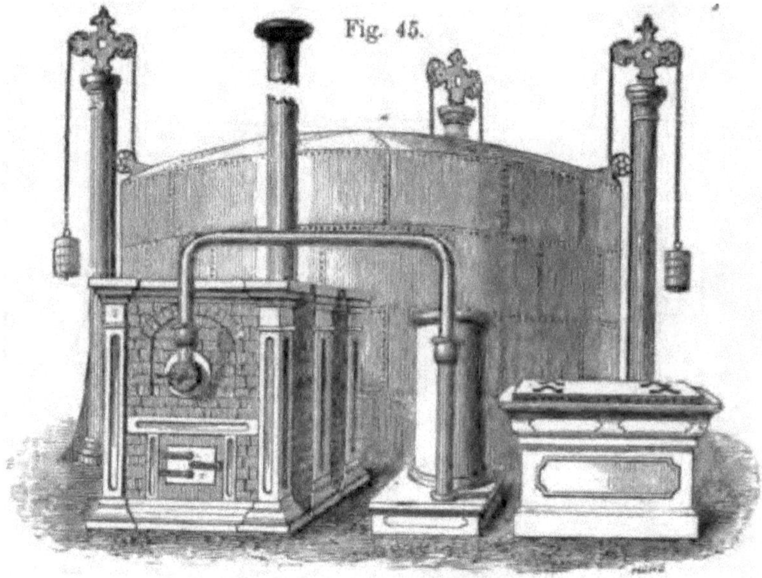

Porter's Portable Gas-Making Apparatus.

Fig. 46.

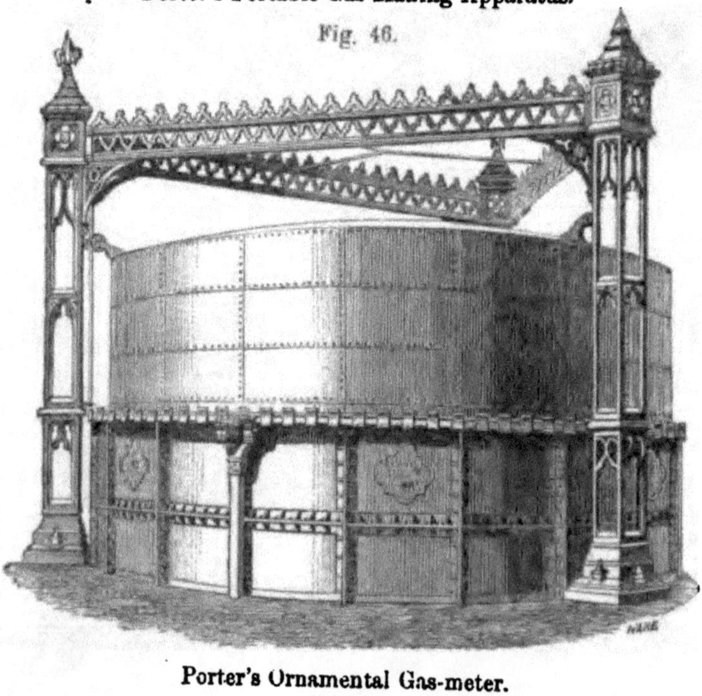

Porter's Ornamental Gas-meter.

Fig. 47.

Front View of Mr. Taylor's Smoke-consuming and Ventilating Grate.

Fig. 48.

Section of Mr. Taylor's Smoke-consuming and Ventilating Grate with Front View removed.

DIVISION SECOND.

EXAMPLES AND ANALYSES OF PLANS OF HOUSES, FROM THE COTTAGE TO THE MANSION.

CHAPTER FIRST.

COTTAGES—RURAL AND SUBURBAN.

1. We begin * by giving the simplest possible arrangement of a cottage, the single-roomed one—a type, we regret to say, of that form too often met with in many districts. In the plan in fig. 1 the door enters at once from the outer air, so that the cottage in winter weather will invariably be cold and comfortless. An

Fig. 1.

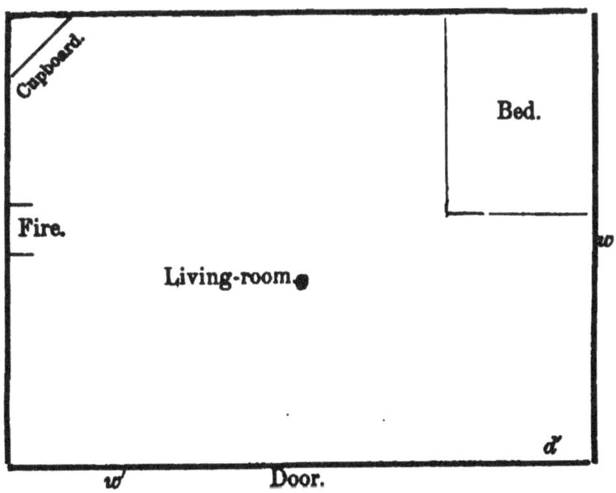

Plan of Single-roomed Cottage.

* In all the type or diagrammatic plans given hereafter, we indicate the position of doors by the letter "*d;*" that of windows by the letter "*w;*" and that of fireplaces either by the letter "*f*" or the word "Fire."

immense improvement would be the addition of a porch, as shown in fig. 2, the door entering this being at the *side*, not at

Fig. 2.

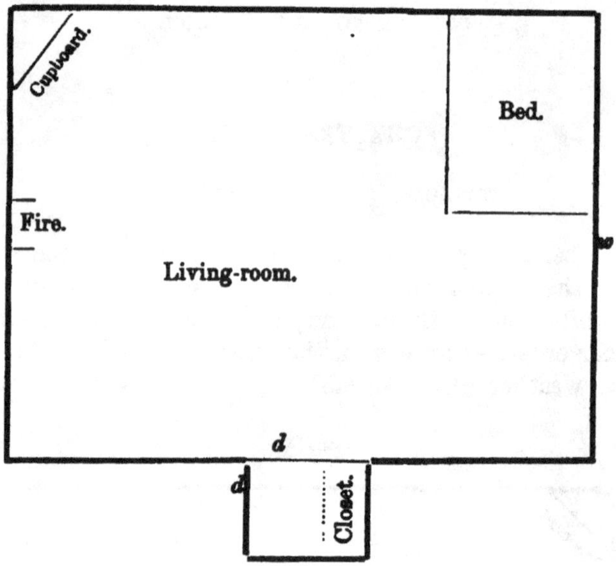

Cottage in Fig. 1 with Porch and Closet.

the end opposite to the internal door. This side arrangement of the door is one of those little things often overlooked in house planning, but which, nevertheless, is just the thing which makes all the difference between comfort secured and comfort missed. By putting the door at the side, the wind never can blow directly into the cottage by the *interior* door. Another advantage obtained by having a porch is a space for a small cupboard or closet, as shown in fig. 2. We may derive a few lessons, as to the effect of placing of doors and windows in various positions, by further studying even such a simple plan as that in fig. 1. The position of the window *w*, with reference to the fire, is the worst possible so far as convenience for cooking, &c., is concerned, inasmuch as the party at the fire will always obscure the light from the fire; but by placing the window—or *a second* window—in the position shown in fig. 1 at *w′*, we bring about a very different arrangement. Another advantage will be obtained by changing the position of the window from *w* to *w′*, namely, the power of placing the bed in the centre of the wall opposite the fireplace, or giving space there for a second or children's bed, while the large bed could be placed in the centre of the wall opposite the door. In many bed-rooms in large houses, for instance, the arrangement is as follows :—where *d* in fig. 3 indicates the position of door entering

Fig. 3.

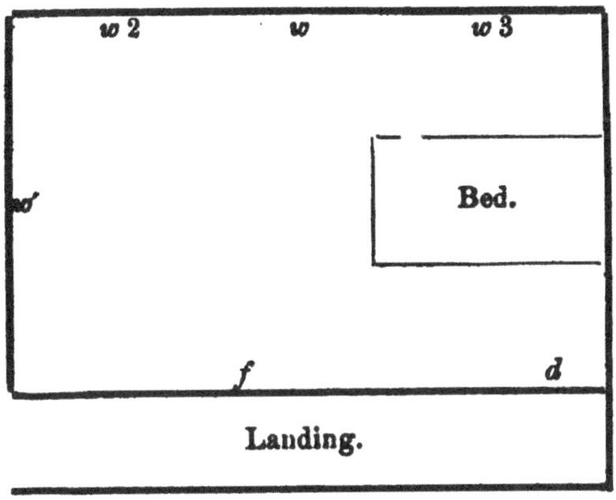

from the landing, *f* that of the fireplace, and *w w* the two windows. Now, this arrangement, while it gives a pleasant, well-lighted room, obviously restricts the position in which the bed can be placed to the one as shown. Now, every *housewife* knows the value of being able to arrange the bed in a bed-room *in more than one* position. Let us suppose that we do away with the windows *w w′*, and still giving two windows to the room, place them at *w* 2 *w* 3. We can now have three positions in which the bed can be placed, one as shown in fig. 3, which is the worst, as the direct draught of the wind passing through the door will blow upon it. The second position will be at *w′*, and the third at *w* between the two windows. But another arrangement is still possible; if we move the fireplace from its position in fig. 3 and place it at *w* between the two windows *w* 2 and *w* 3, we then have an exceedingly pleasant position for it; as, however, we sit at the fireplace, we shall always have a pleasant light, and by putting the bed in the position at *f* we have plenty of space in the room, and at the same time place it out of the reach of the draught between door and window, and this is an immense advantage in a bed-room, for in cases of sickness, by opening the window or windows, a thorough draught can be established through the room without being felt by the patient in the bed placed at *f*. Returning now to the plan of cottage in fig. 1, we notice that by placing, as suggested, the window at *w′*, we throw it and the door so near that we cut up very much the space between them useful for placing furniture, &c.; this disadvantage will at once be obviated by placing the door at *d′*

2. In fig. 4 we illustrate a mode of giving extra accommoda-

Fig. 4.

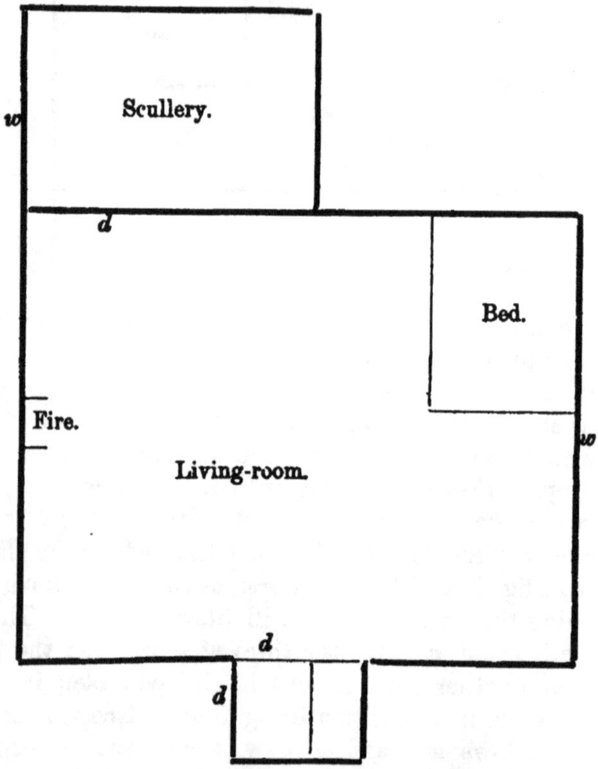

Plan of Fig. 1 with Scullery attached.

tion to the cottage in fig. 1 by building a small offset at the back, affording room for a scullery. By doubling this we obtain, as in fig. 5, a space for a small bed-closet. Both of these rooms enter

Fig. 5.

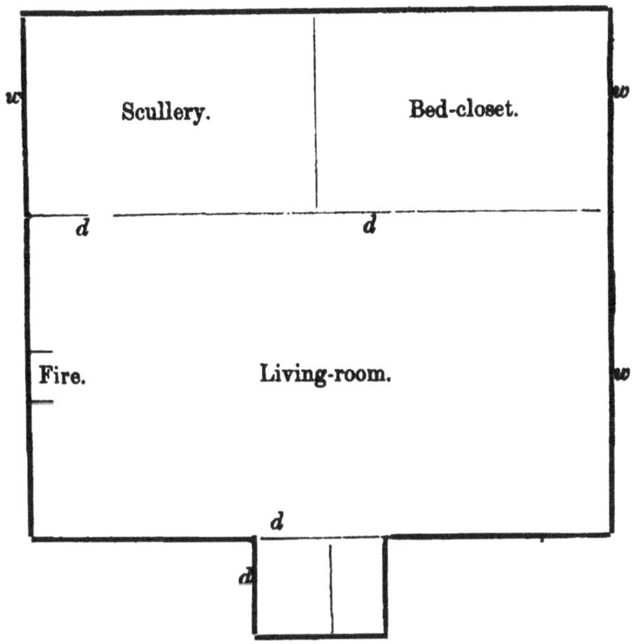

from the living-room. By making the scullery in fig. 5 a bed-room, and adding an offset, as in fig. 6, to the right, we obtain space for a porch, a scullery entering from the porch, a bed-room entering from the living-room, and next the bed-room a pantry or store closet. All these plans in figs. 2, 4, 5, and 6, are improvements on the cottage in fig. 1, by simply adding certain offsets to it.

3. In all these the great disadvantage is met with of the bed-rooms entering from the living-room, which is an arrangement in all cases to be avoided in planning *new* cottages. In fig. 7 we give the plan of a single-storied cottage, in which independent entrances are obtained to all the apartments from a central passage or lobby, as shown. In this plan the two fireplaces are

Fig. 6.

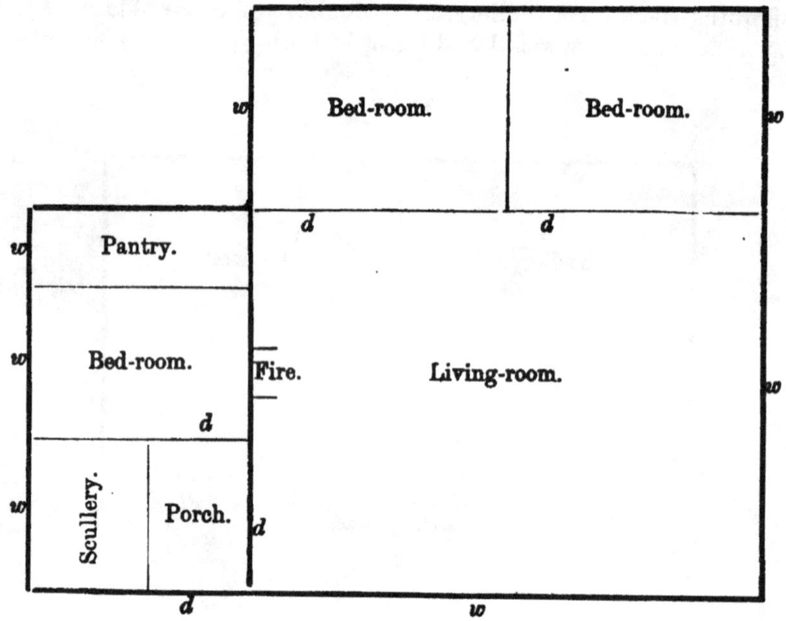

Plan of Fig. 5 improved with Bed-rooms and Scullery.

Fig. 7.

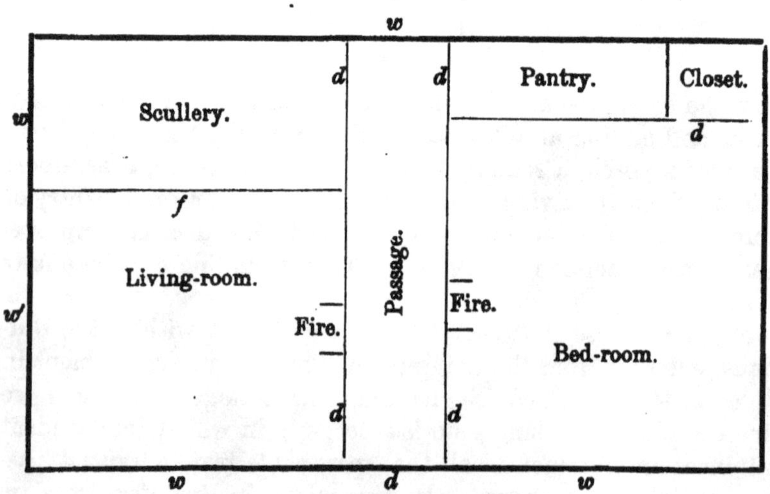

Plan of Single-Storied Cottage.

put against the two walls of the passage; it is questionable, however, whether, in the case of the living-room, the better arrangement would not be to place the fireplace at *f*, which would enable a small fire-place to be given to the scullery or wash-house. In this case a window should be placed at the point *w*. In the plan, as arranged in fig. 7, we have shown the entrance to scullery as leading from the passage, and this for the convenience of being able to remove articles from it without passing through the living-room. Although this is an advantage, inasmuch as it keeps the living-room as private as possible—a point of no small importance, even to a working man—still, some would prefer the scullery to be entered *from* the living-room. In place of the window shown at the end of the passage in fig. 7, some would prefer giving a back door; this, although in many ways convenient, will create a strong current through the inside of the house, which, though considered an advantage by some, is not so deemed by others. A fault in the plan in fig. 7 is the absence of a porch; this addition is shown to the left of fig. 8, with the extra accom-

Fig. 8.

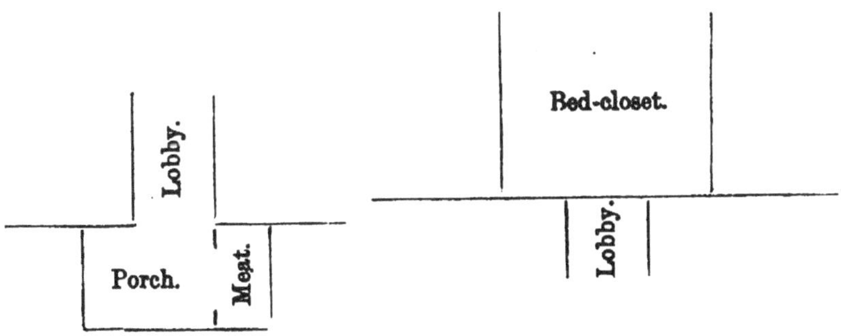

Additions to Plan in Fig. 7.

modation of a meat closet. The sleeping accommodation in fig. 7 being also very limited, a bed-closet may be added in an offset made at the back, and which will be entered from the end of lobby, as shown to the right of fig. 8. Further additional accommodation in bed-room space will be obtained by extending the house towards the back, and giving two bed-rooms, as shown in fig. 9. The closet accommodation in this house (fig. 9) is ample; and,

Fig. 9.

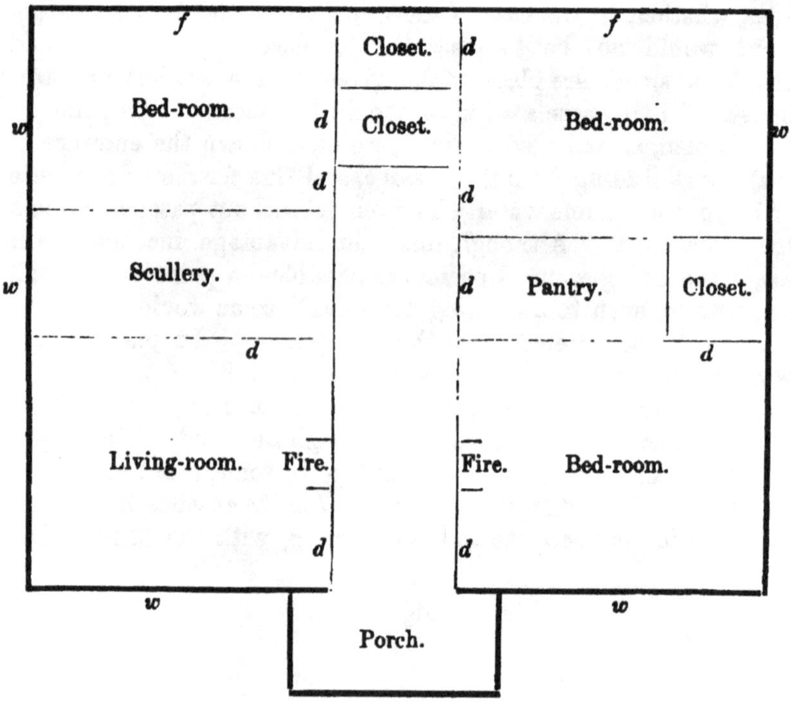

Plan in fig. 7 with additional accommodation.

Fig. 11.

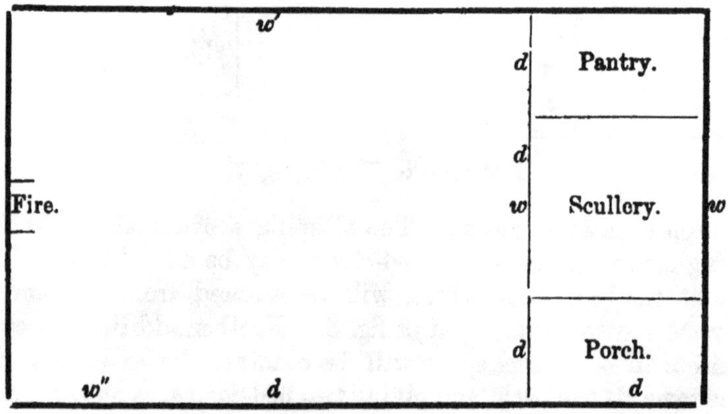

Improved Plan of Fig. 1.

indeed, the plan, as a whole, may be taken as a fair example of a convenient way of filling in a square enclosed space.

4. In fig. 11 we show another mode of improving the plain one-roomed cottage in fig. 1 by the simple addition of a wide passage at one end, giving space for a porch, a scullery (or bed-closet), and a pantry or store. The window (*w*) will, however, be blocked up, necessitating its removal to either the point *w′* or *w″*. Fig. 12 shows how to this house extra accommodation can be given.

5. In fig. 12 we give the plan of a single-storied cottage

Fig. 12.

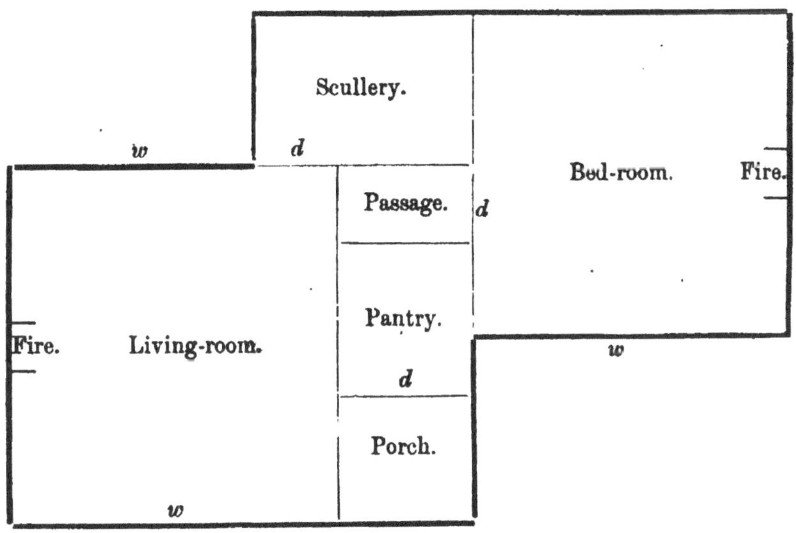

Plan of Single-storied Cottage.

of an irregular form or outline. But in this the great fault is the position of the rooms with reference to the entrance porch, necessitating every one to pass through the living room on going to or leaving the other apartments. This can be overcome by the arrangement shown in fig. 13, changing the porch in fig. 12 into a store-closet, and making the pantry and passage in fig. 12 so that the space will be partly the porch and partly filled up

Fig 13.

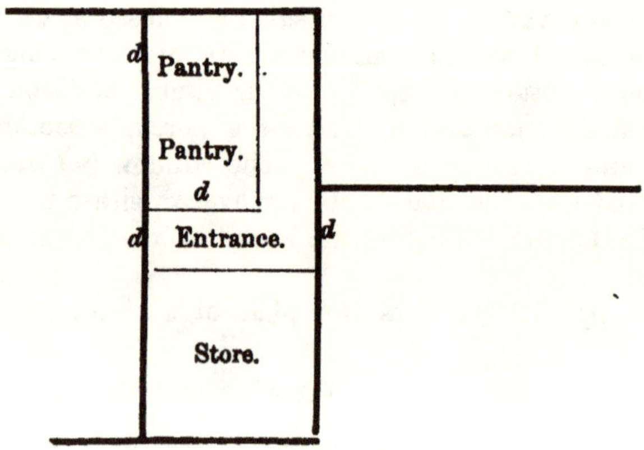

Fig. 14.

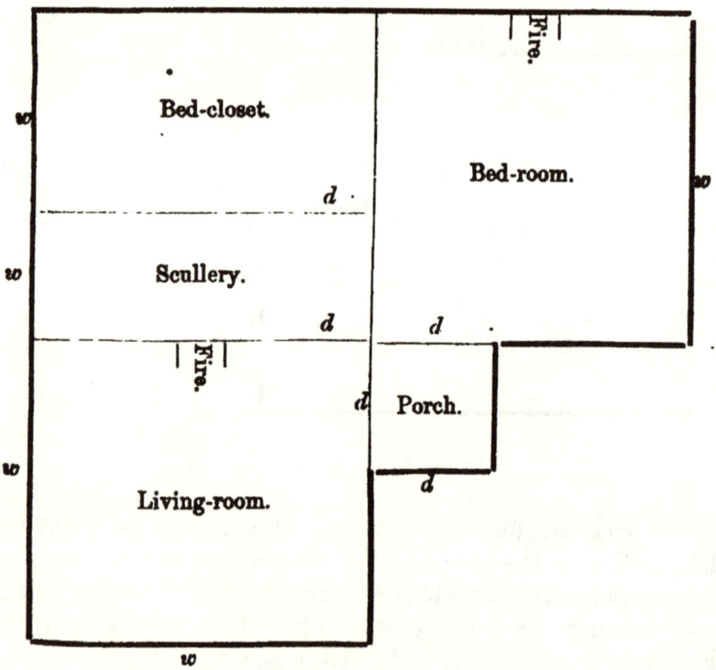

Plan of Single-storied Cottage.

with a pantry; distinct entrances can thus be obtained to the scullery, bed-room, and living-room. Fig. 14 shows still another arrangement by which the one-roomed house in fig. 1 may be converted into a very convenient house; the objection, however, still adheres to this plan in part which belonged to others we have given, the bed-closet being entered from the bed-room, and all exit from and entrance to the scullery obtained only from the living-room; these defects can be obviated by the simple plan of taking off a narrow passage from the bed-room, as shown in fig. 15, *d* being the door to bed-room, *d′* to scullery, and *d″* to the

Fig. 15.

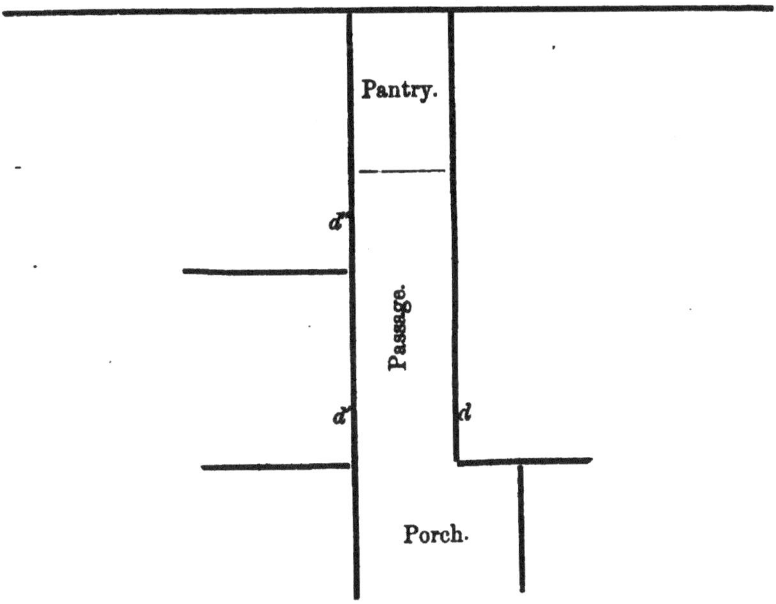

bed-closet. A capital pantry may be obtained at the end of the passage, as shown in fig. 15.

6. We now give a variety of plans of cottages culled from various sources, to which the reader should apply the principles of criticism, which we have above endeavoured to elucidate.

In Fig. 16 we give, to the left, half ground plan, and to the right, half chamber plan, of a pair of semi-detached cottages de-

Fig. 16.

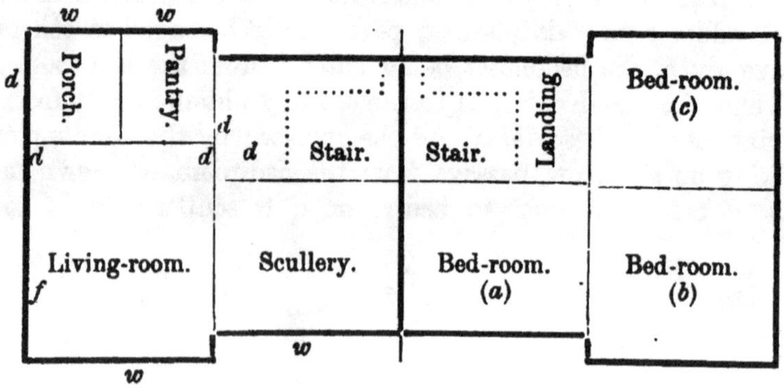

Ground-floor Plan (half). Bed-room Plan (half).

Fig. 17.

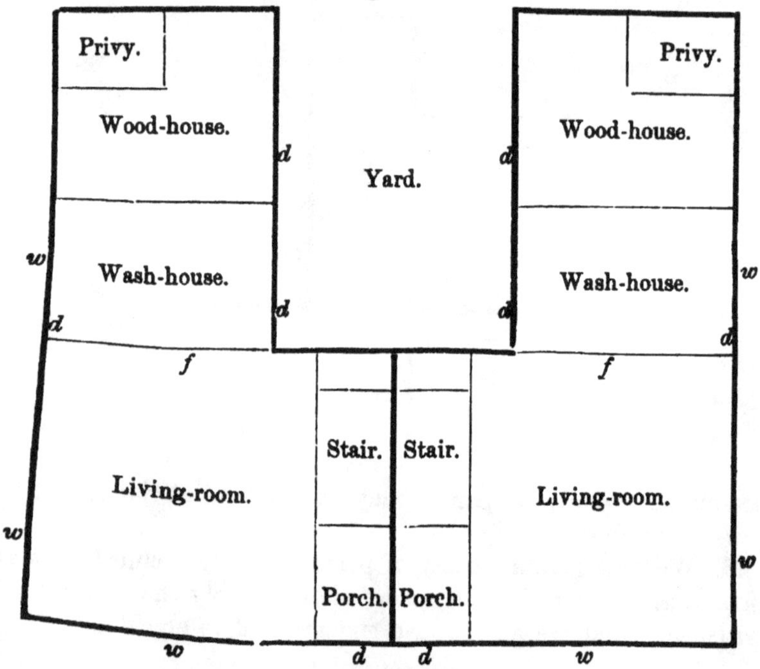

Ground Plan.

signed by Mr. Goddard, architect, of Lincoln, and to which the prize of the Royal Agricultural Society of England was awarded. The dimensions of the apartments named are as follows:—Porch, 5 feet by 3 feet 3 inches; living-room, 11 by 13 feet; pantry, 5 by 4 feet; scullery, 8 feet 6 by 7 feet; bed-room (*a*), 8 feet 6 by 7; do. (*b*), 11 feet by 10; (*c*), 11 feet by 7 feet 6 inches.

In Fig. 17 we give ground plan, and in Fig. 18 chamber plan, of the celebrated cottages erected on the estate of the late Duke of Bedford, than whom no one has done so much towards improving the condition of the agricultural labourer, in so far at

Fig. 18.

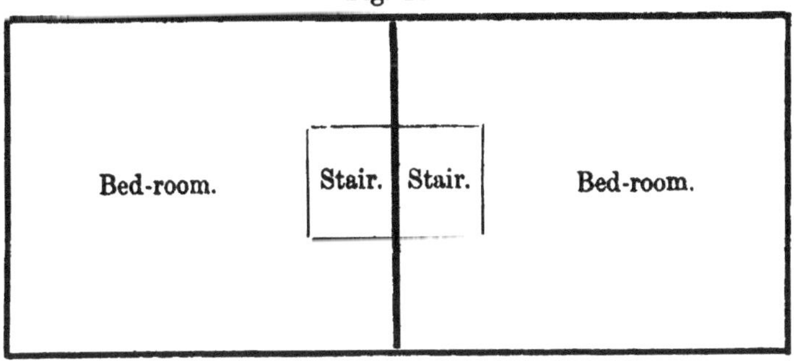

Bed-room Plan.

Fig. 19.

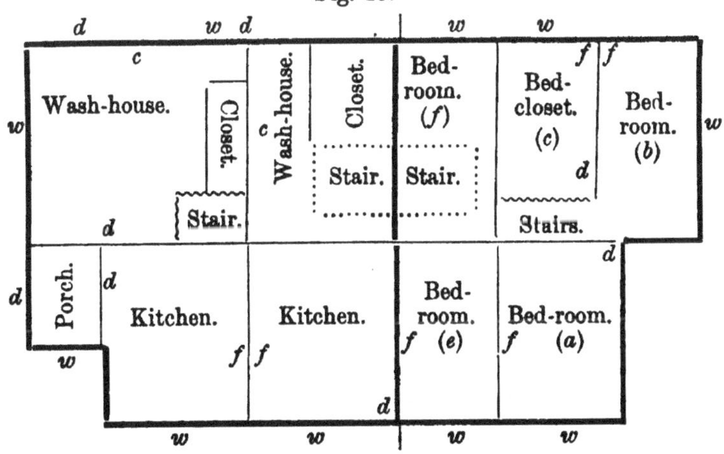

Ground Plan (half). Bed-room Plan (half).

least as his house accommodation is concerned. The dimensions are as follows:—Living-room, 11 feet square; wash-house, 10 feet by 6 feet; wood-house, ditto.

In fig. 19 we give half ground and chamber plan of another arrangement of the "Bedford Cottages," in which four cottages are placed together, two of these having three, and two having two bed-rooms. The kitchen is 11 feet square; the wash-houses, in the end houses, are each 15 feet 1 inch by 12 feet; in the central houses, 12 feet by 8 feet 6 inches. The two end houses are entered by porches. In the ground plan the letters *c c* indicate the position of wash-boiler or copper. Bed-room (*a*), 11 feet square; do. (*b*), 9 feet 6 inches by 7 feet 6 inches; do. (*c*), 12 feet by 7 feet 6 inches; do. (*e*), 11 feet square; do. (*f*), 12 feet by 8 feet 6 inches.

In Fig. 20 we give ground plan, and in Fig. 21 part chamber plan, of another arrangement of the "Bedford Cottages," showing three cottages together, two of which have three bed-rooms, and one of which has two bed-rooms. The kitchens are each 10 feet by 11 feet, and the wash-houses 15 by 11 feet.

Fig. 20.

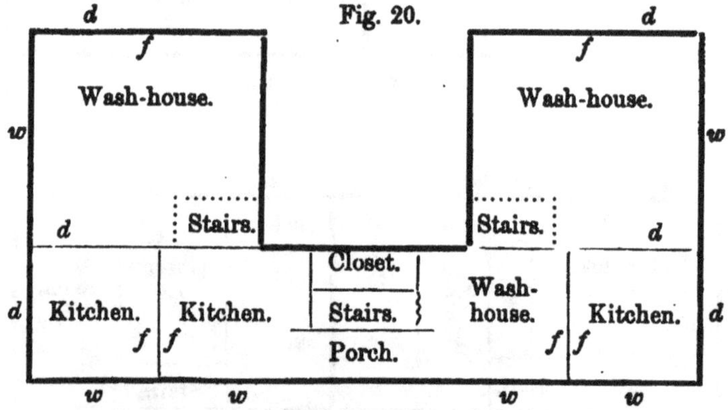

Ground Plan.

In Fig. 22 we give half ground and half chamber plan of the cottages (semi-detached), designed by Mr. Hine, of Nottingham, and for which the prize of the Society of Arts was awarded. In the scullery *a* denotes the position of fire-place, *b* that of the wash-copper, and *c* that of the oven.

Fig. 21.

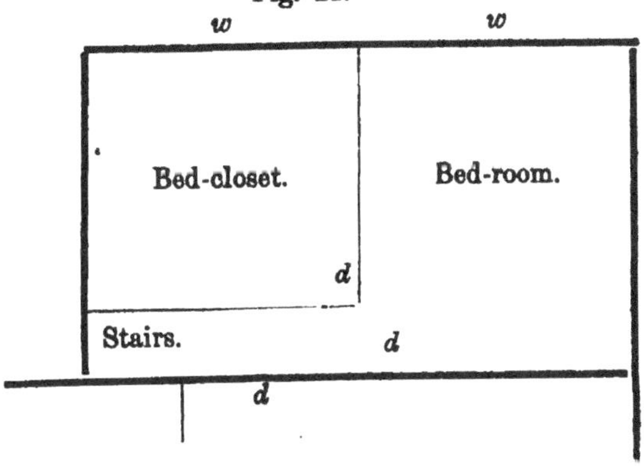

Part of Chamber Plan.

Fig. 22.

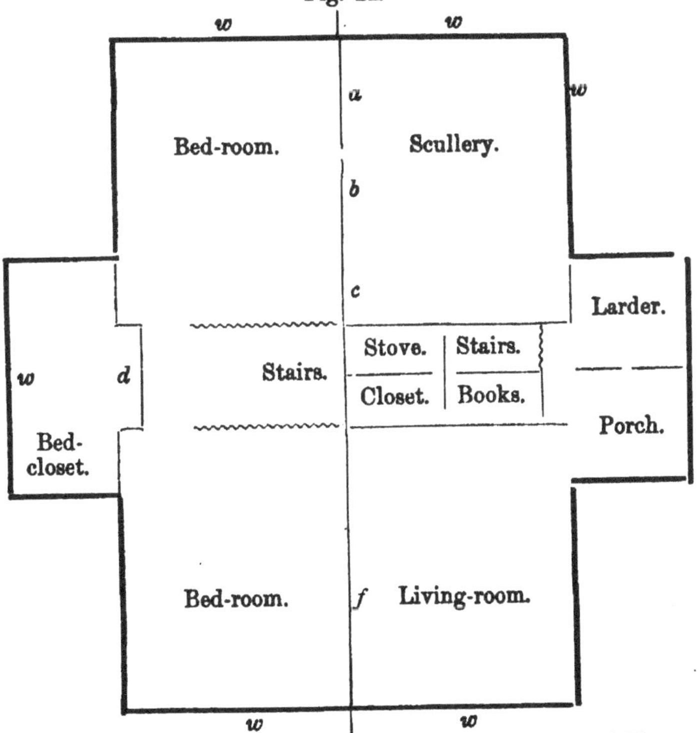

Half Chamber Plan. Half Ground Plan.

In Fig. 23 we give the ground plan of semi-detached cottages,

Fig. 23.

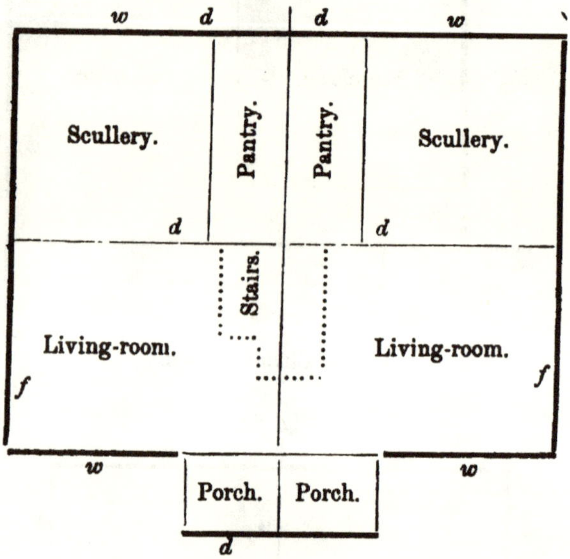

Ground Plan.

Fig. 24.

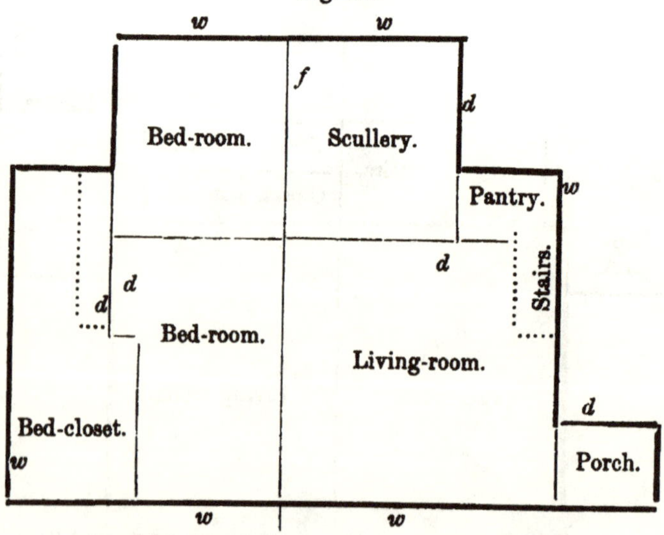

Chamber Plan. Ground Plan.

designed by Mr. Nicholls, and to which also a prize was awarded by the Society of Arts. In the chamber plan the space occupied by the pantry and scullery in the ground plan is divided into two, so as to obtain two bed-rooms.

In Fig. 24 we give half ground and chamber plans of the plan which obtained the prize of the Bath and West of England Society.

In Fig. 25 we give half ground and chamber plan of the cot-

Fig. 25.

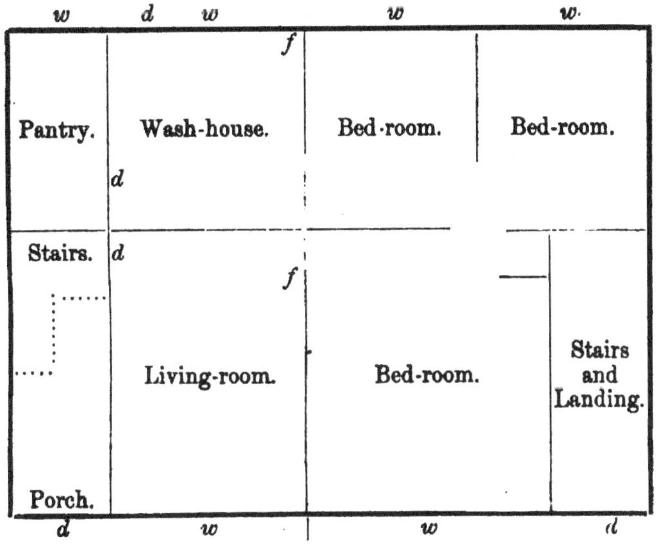

Half Ground Plan. Half Chamber Plan.

tage designed by Mr. Isaac, of Bath, and which is published in the prize essay of the Journal of the above-named Society.

In Fig. 26 we illustrate the plan of cottage (semi-detached) designed by Mr. Strickland, and which enjoys a high reputation amongst authorities on the subject, as combining in a marked degree the advantages of economical construction with compactness of arrangement.

In Fig. 27 we give the plan of a one-storied single cottage, recommended by the Scottish Association for the Improvement of the condition of the Agricultural Labourer: and in Fig. 28

Fig. 26.

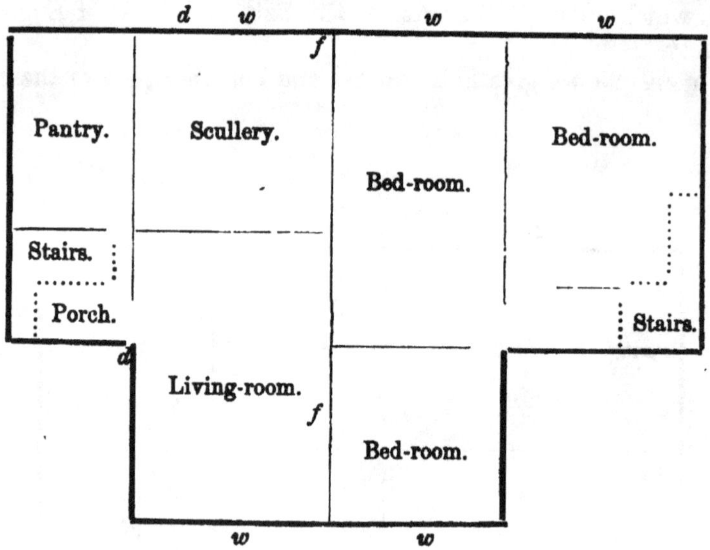

Half Ground Plan. Half Chamber Plan.

Fig. 27.

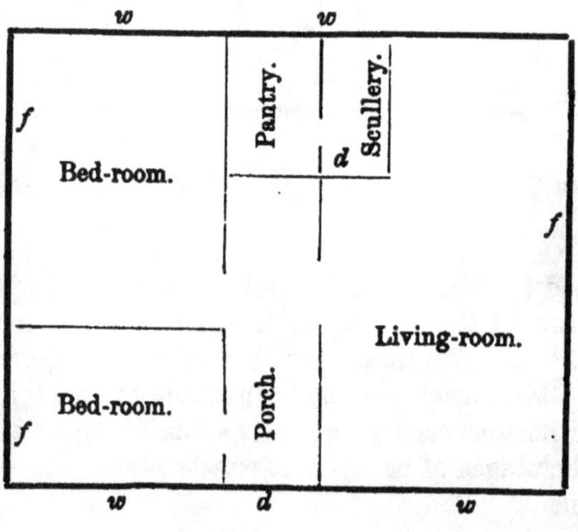

ground plan of pair of cottages, with attics, plan of which is given in Fig. 29.

Fig. 28.

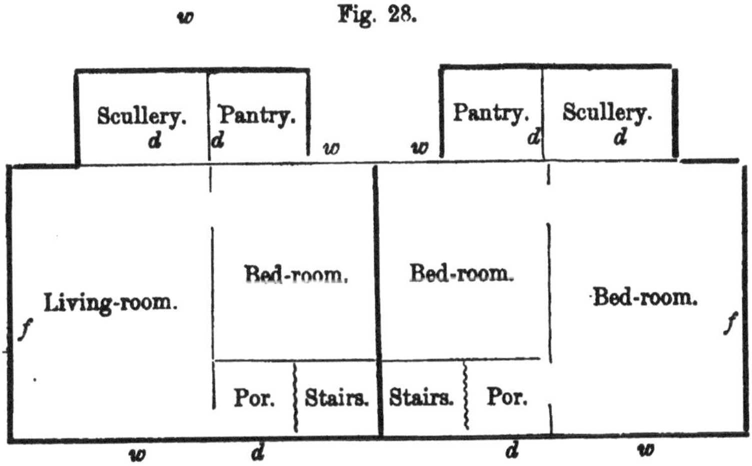

Ground Plan.

Fig. 29.

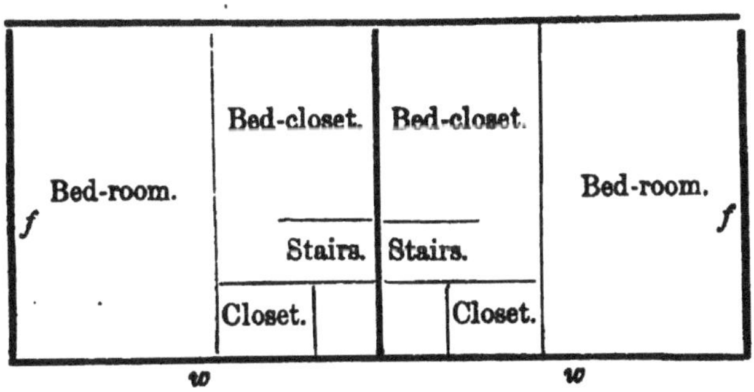

Attic Plan.

In Fig. 30 we give a sketch plan of a one-storied cottage erected at Saughton Mains, near Edinburgh, by Mr. Dickson.

Fig. 30.

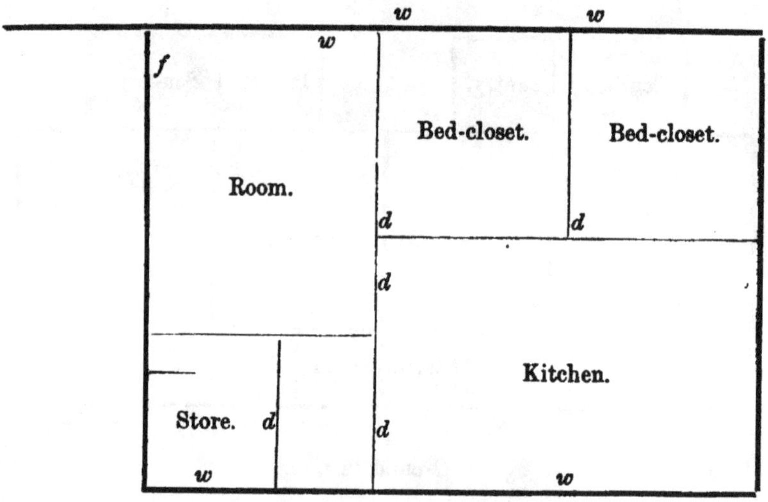

Plan of Single-storied Cottage Semi-detached.

Fig. 31.

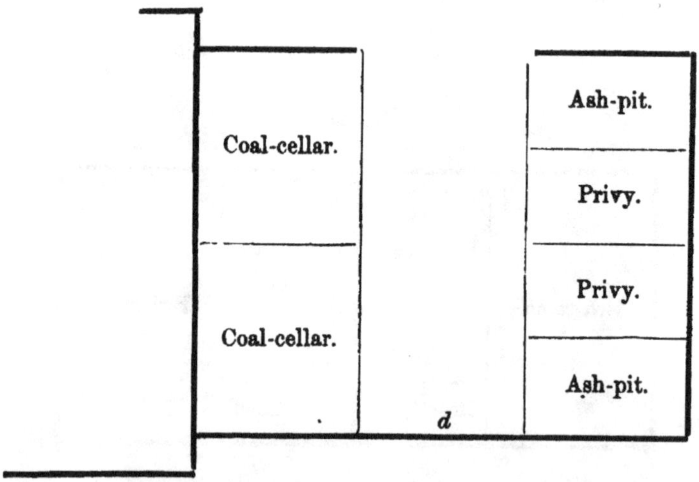

Outbuildings for Cottage in fig. 30.

Fig. 32.

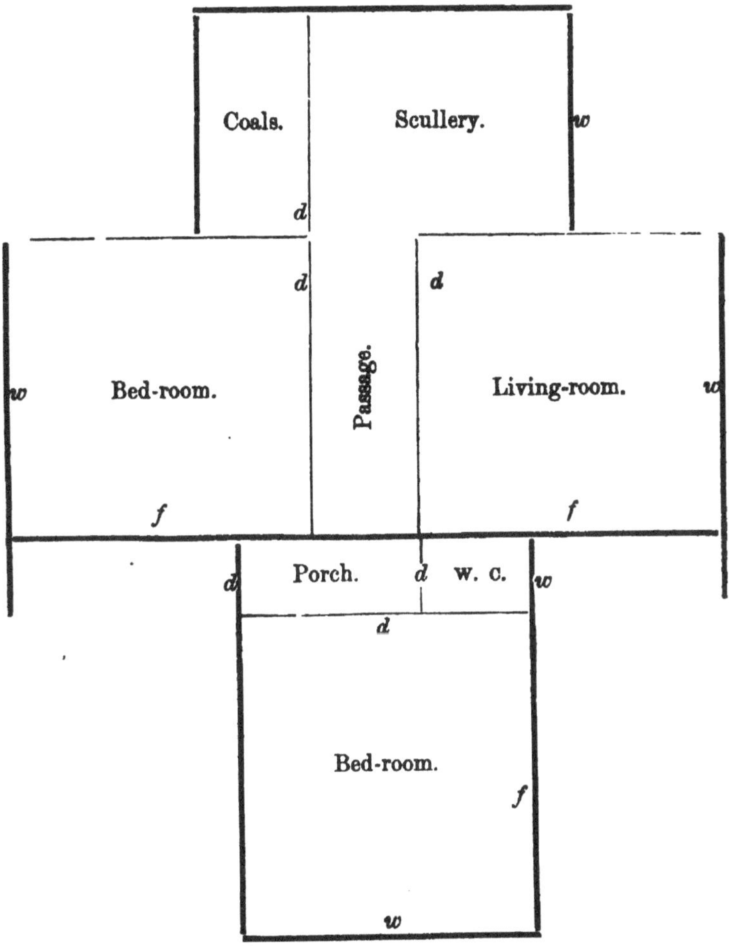

Plan of Single-storied Cottage.

Fig. 33.

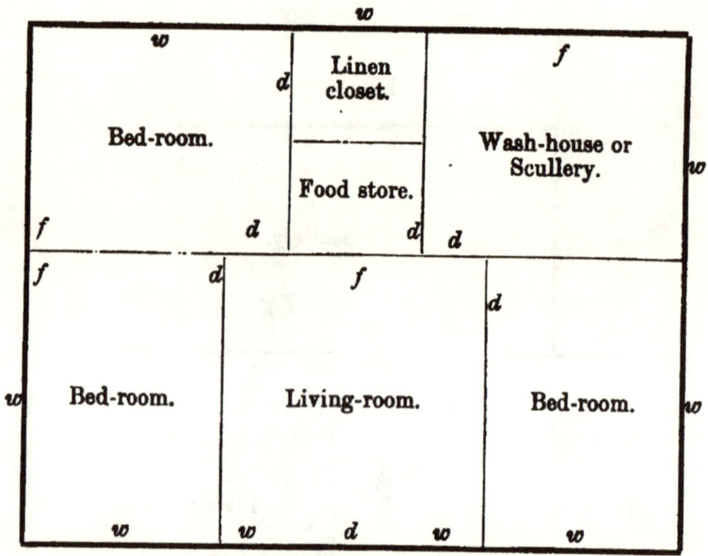

Plan of One-storied Cottage.

Fig. 34.

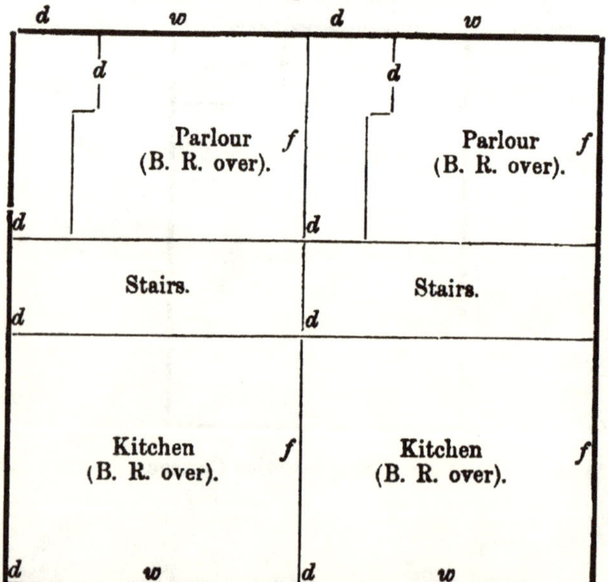

Ground Plan of Leeds Society Cottages.

Fig. 35.

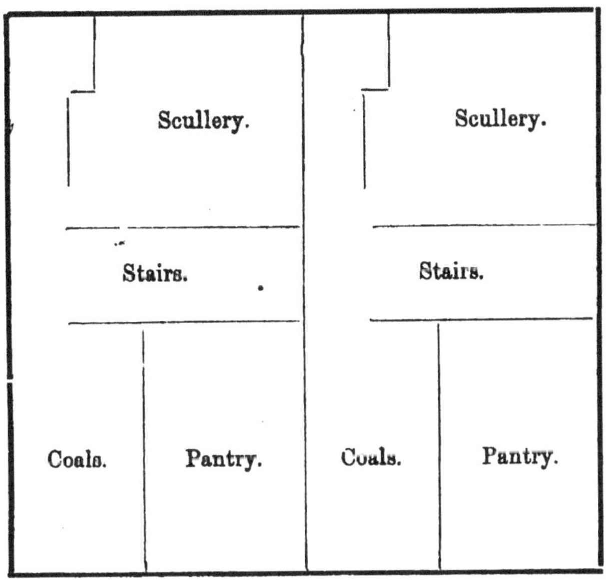

Basement Plan of Fig. 34.

CHAPTER SECOND.

STREET-HOUSES AND RESIDENCES.

Fig. 36.

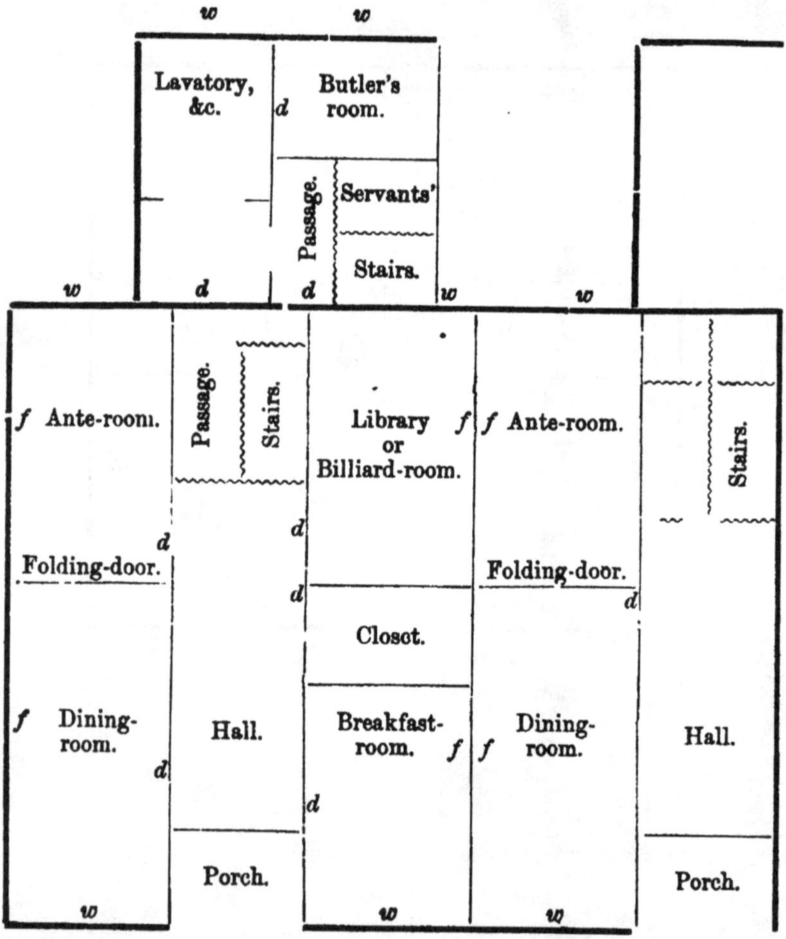

Semi-detached Street Residence—Ground Plan of one and part plan of another.

Fig. 37.

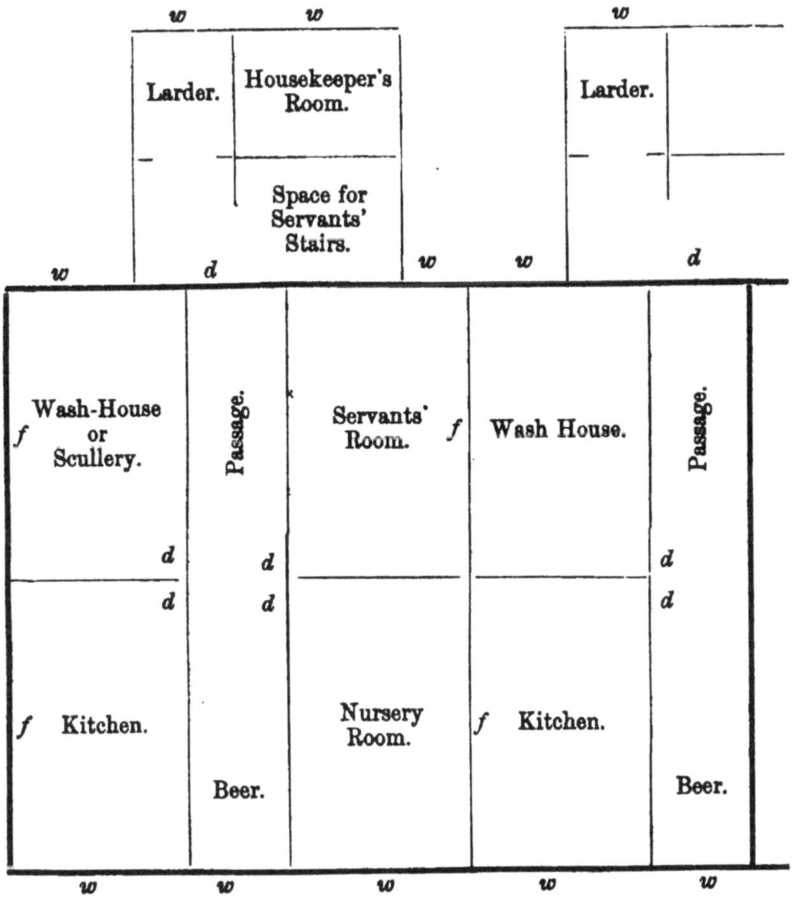

Basement Plan of Semi-detached Residences. Ground Plan in Fig. 36.

Fig. 38.

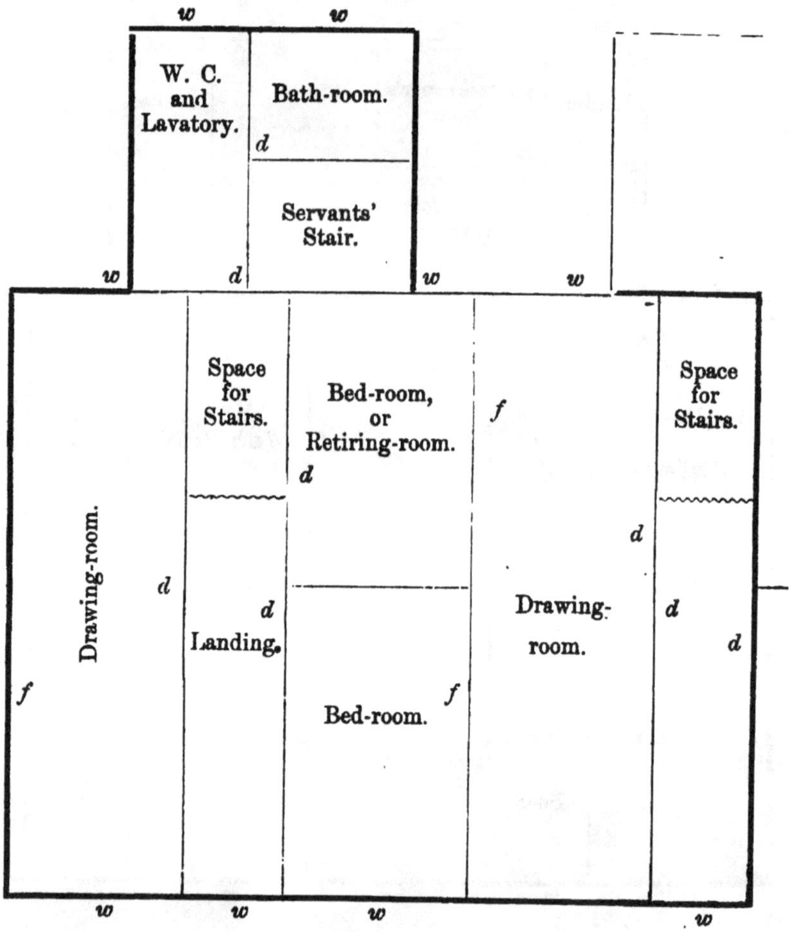

First Chamber Floor of Semi-detached Street Residence. Ground Plan in Fig. 36.

Fig. 39.

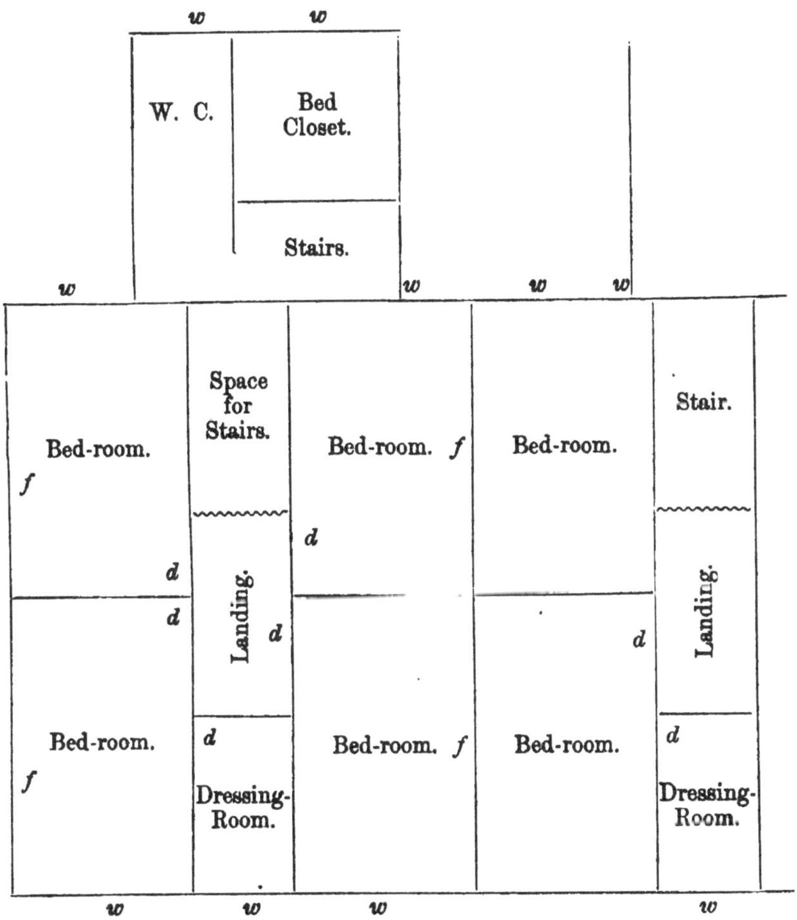

Second Chamber Floor of Semi-detached Street Residences. Ground Plan in Fig. 36.

Fig. 40.

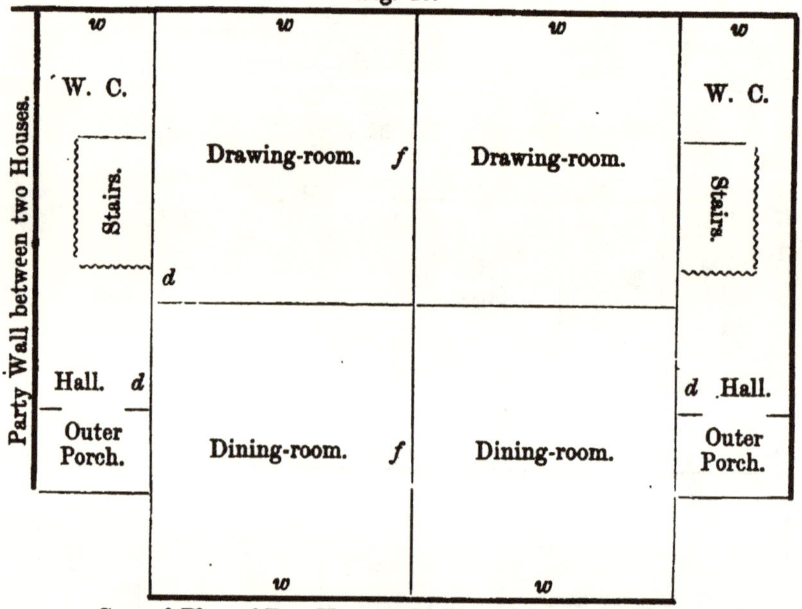

Ground Plan of Two Houses of a Row of Street Residences.

Fig. 41.

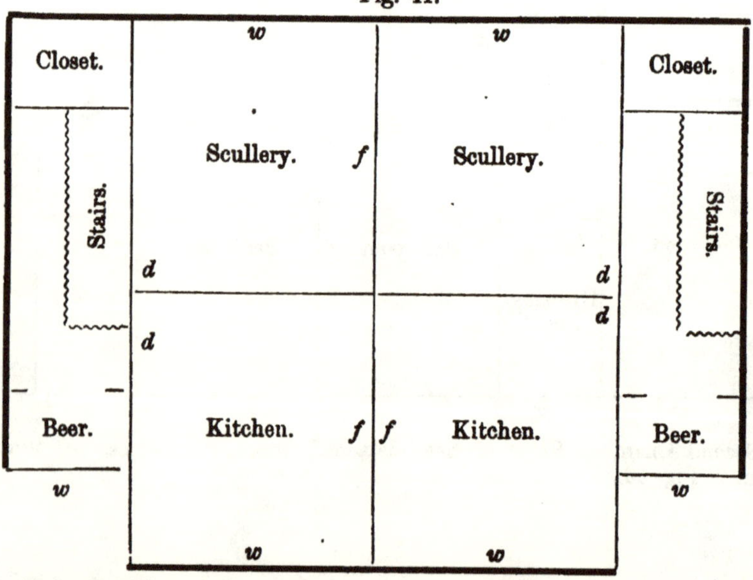

Basement Plan of Two Houses of a Row for Street Residences. Ground Plan in Fig. 40.

Fig. 42.

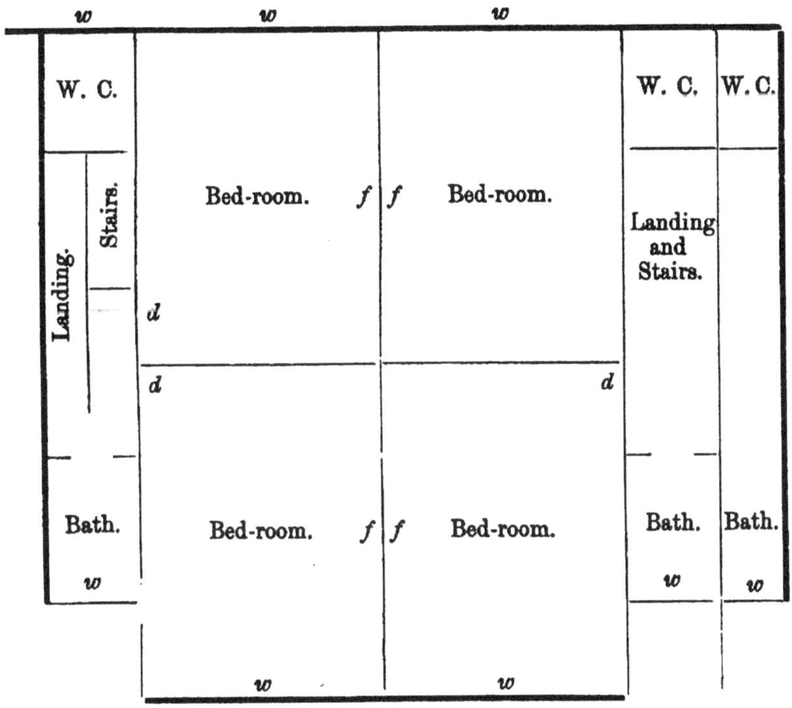

Plan of 1st and 2d Chamber Floors of Two Houses for Street Residences.

Fig. 43.

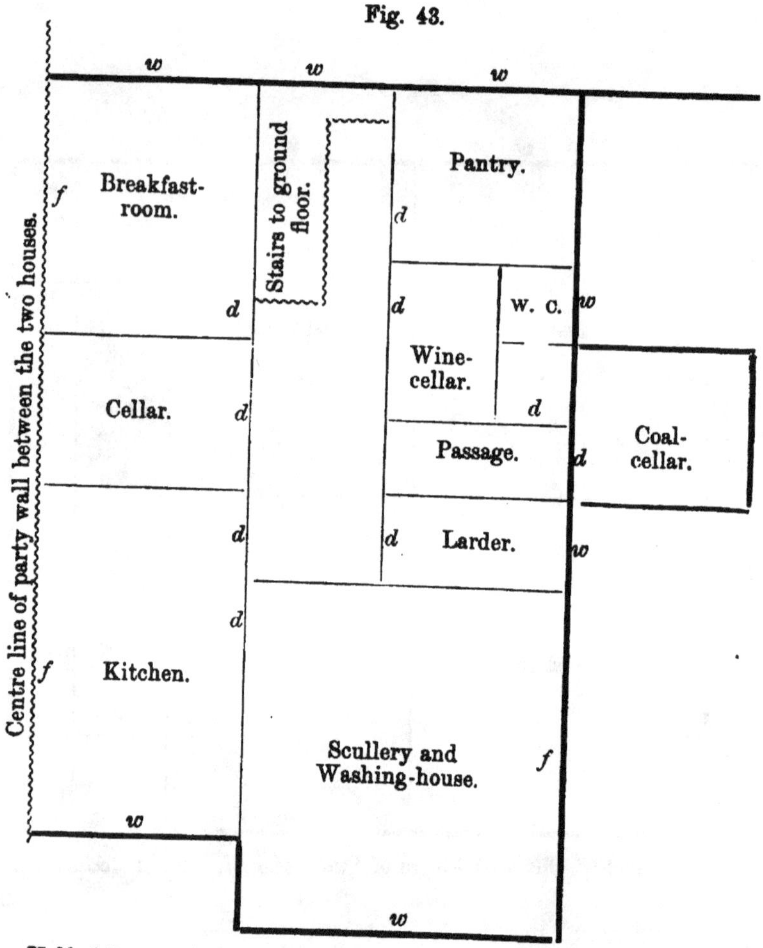

Half of Basement Plan of Semi-detached Town or Street Residences.

Fig. 44.

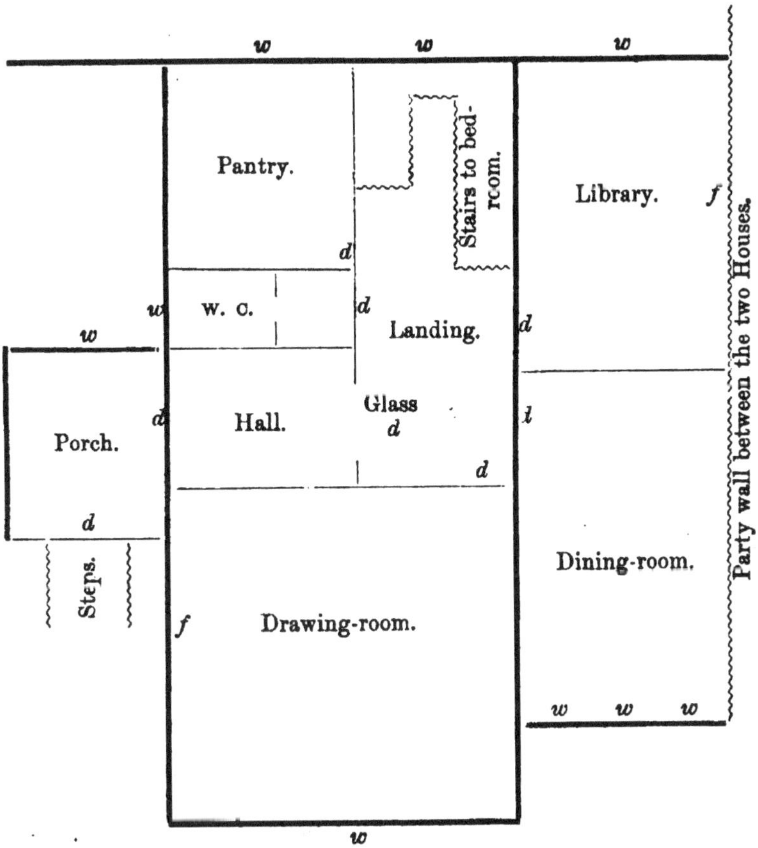

Half Ground Plan of Semi-detached Town or Street Residences.

Fig. 45.

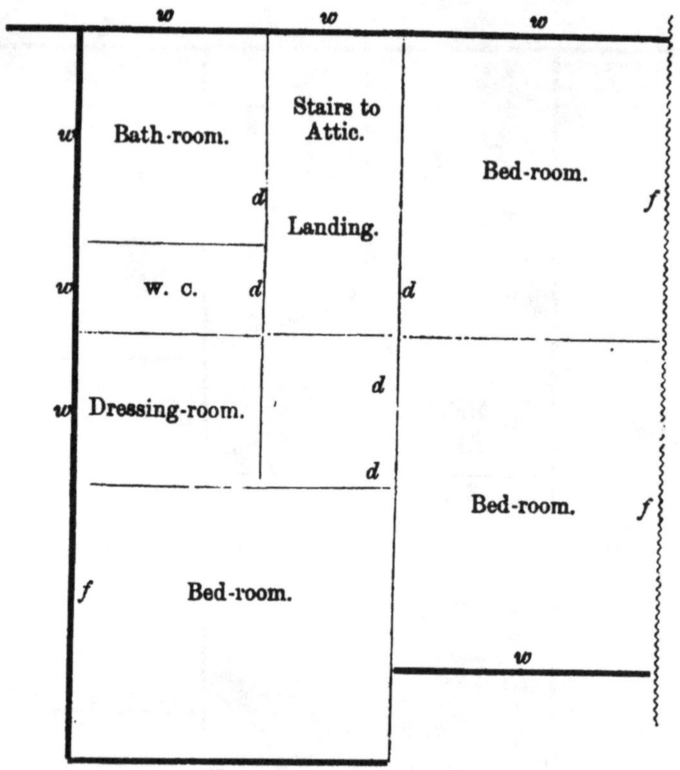

Half Plan of Chamber Floor of Semi-detached or Town Residences. Ground Plan in fig. 44.

Fig. 46.

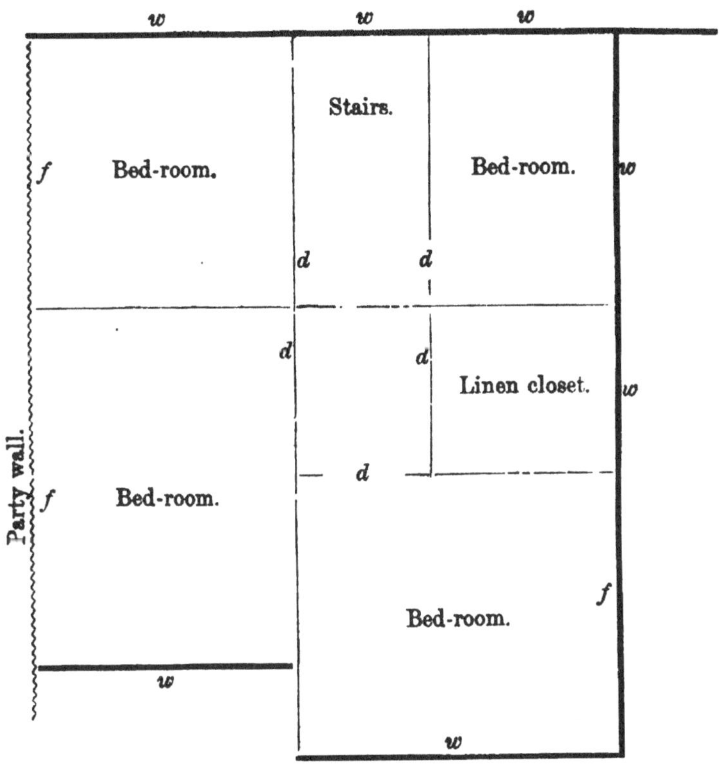

Half Attic Plan to Semi-detached Town or Street Residences.

Fig. 47.

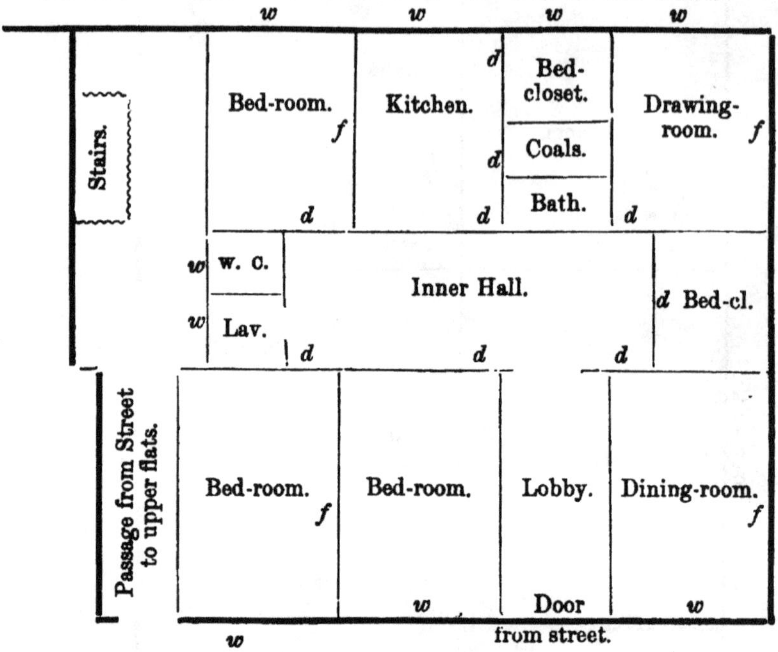

Ground Plan of Street Houses in Scotch Plan (1st Class).

Fig. 48.

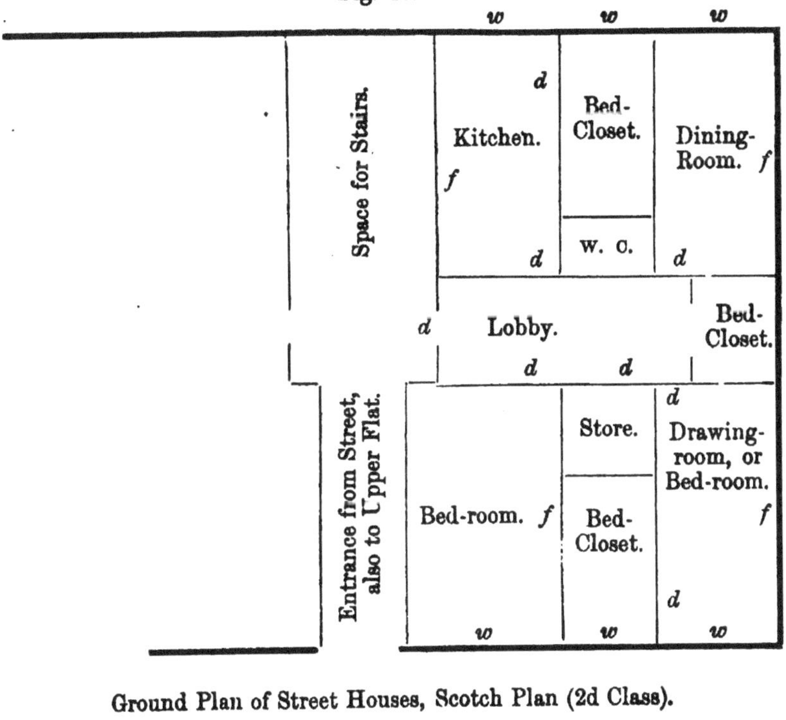

Ground Plan of Street Houses, Scotch Plan (2d Class).

Fig. 49.

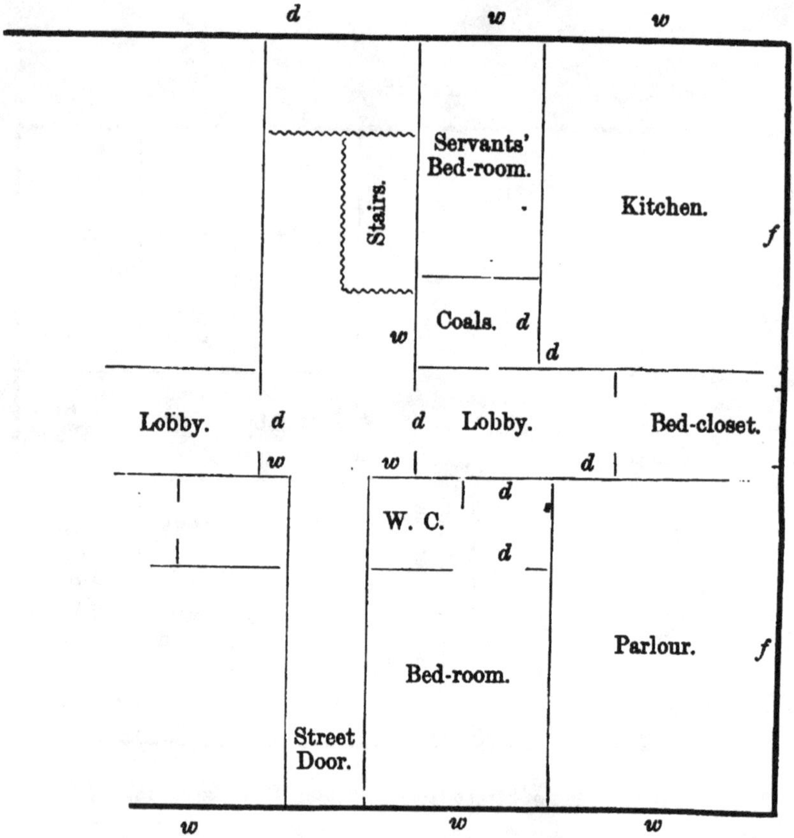

Ground Floor of Street Houses on Scotch Flat Plan (3d Class).

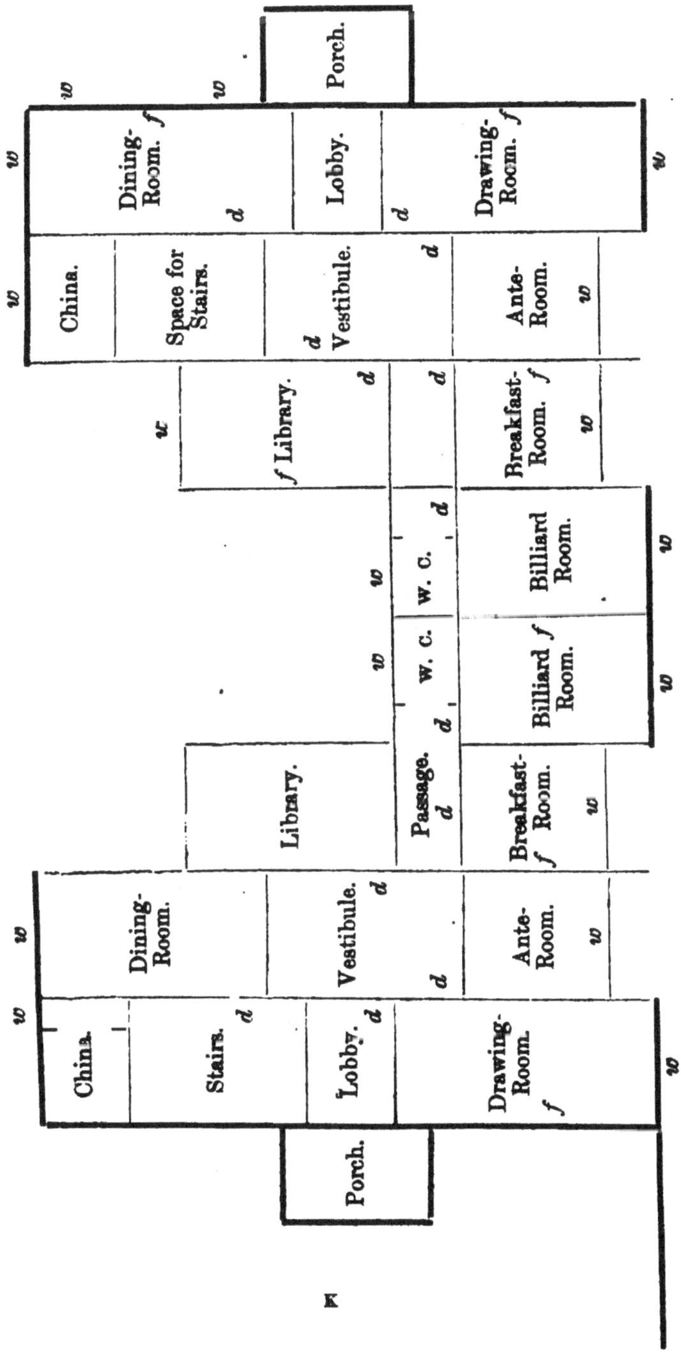

Ground Plan of a Semi-detached Town Mansion.

K

CHAPTER THIRD.

VILLA RESIDENCES.

7. In fig. 3, Plate II., we give the plan of a simple cottage villa residence; the disposition of the apartments of which are indicated by the lettering. In analyzing this, it may be remarked, that the position of the stairs in the lobby necessitates the having one position only for the door to the drawing-room. This being placed as shown in the drawing, cuts up the space on the only side which can be clear, as to leave very little room for the placing of any piece of furniture, as a pianoforte, &c. It will be observed, for instance, that three sides of the room are so arranged that the wall space is interrupted—first, by the bay window; second, by the side window; and third, by the fireplace—so that it would be difficult to find much furniture space on any one of these sides. And from the position of the "set-off" or projecting part of the wall of the room, the door entering from the lobby is thrown so far from the bay window, and so near to the fireplace, that the fourth wall is also cut so very much up, that any piece of furniture, as a piano, would be thrown too near the fireplace. By placing the stairs on the right hand in place of the left hand of the lobby, the door could then be made very near the fireplace, so that ample space could be obtained between it and the corner next the bay window for any piece of furniture. This change of position of the stairs would, however, effect a change of disposition of the doors of the apartments in the bed-room plan, which by many would not be deemed advantageous. In Plate III., fig. 2, the bed-room plan is delineated; but if the stairs were placed as above suggested, the door to the bed-room on the right hand side of the landing could no longer be as shown; and if placed nearer the window of the "bath-room," as thus—

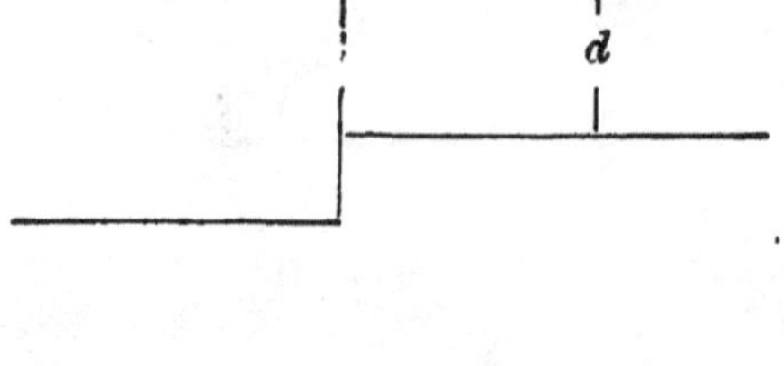

that convenience will have to be done away with, and the bed-room to the right of the landing will have to be entered thus—

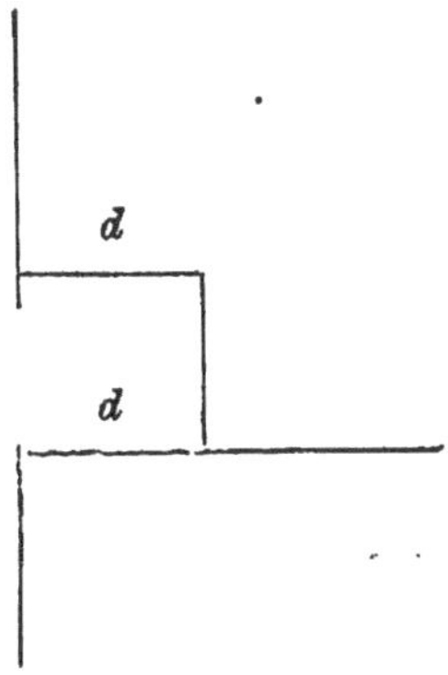

taking off so much of the space from the back right hand bed-room. These remarks are here offered, as showing what a great change in the disposition of the conveniences of some apartments may be made by a comparatively unimportant change in one apartment or part of a house; and how often true it is, that a choice of evils is only left to the architect, and that without any fault of his. In the plan, fig. 1, Plate IV., an alternative arrangement is shown, by which in the dining-room, or what may be called the drawing-room, one side wall is left completely entire, so that there is ample space for any piece of furniture which it may be considered desirous to place there. The fault of this arrangement is, that we have no longer a scullery as in the plan, fig. 3, Plate II.; this, however, may be obviated by widening the space backwards, which is given to the apartments marked "pantry" and "coals," in fig. 1, Plate IV., and making the "coal" place into a scullery, entering this from the pantry, which may be made to give space for a door thus—

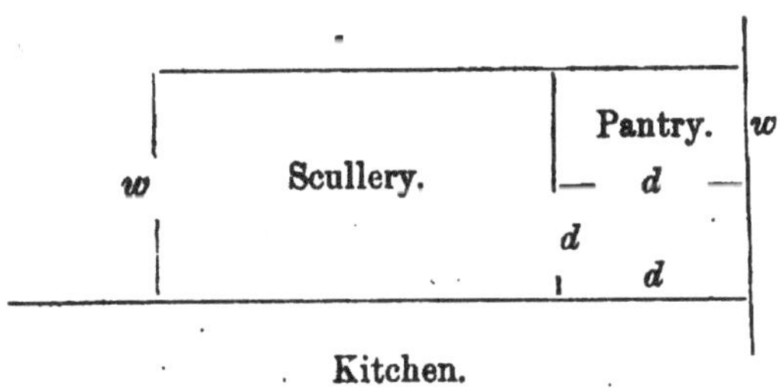

Another arrangement is shown in fig. 1, Plate VI., where the scullery enters from the kitchen, and one wall of the drawing-room is left entire.

8. The arrangement in fig. 2, Plate V., of the stairs gives a free unencumbered lobby or entrance hall, which some would consider advantageous. It necessitates, however, as will be seen on examining the chamber plan in fig. 2, Plate VI., an arrangement of the space over the kitchen which does away with the opportunity of having a good-sized bed-room over that apartment. It is a question, therefore, whether the more economical arrangement of the space would not be the placing of the stairs in the front lobby, thus—

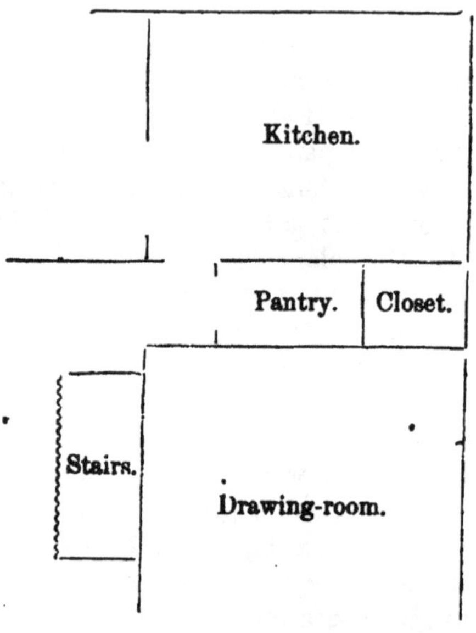

by which a pantry and closet would be obtained in the space occupied by the stairs in fig. 2, Plate V., or this space might be given to the kitchen, making it larger. We should, however, recommend the space to be given to a pantry and closet, as shown above; as a house can scarcely have too many conveniences of this sort; indeed, the great fault of the plan in fig. 2, Plate V., is, that it possesses no conveniences of this description.

The arrangement, then, of the stairs, as suggested in the above diagram, necessitates a new arrangement of the bed-room space, as now shown. We here obtain a large bed-room, the same size

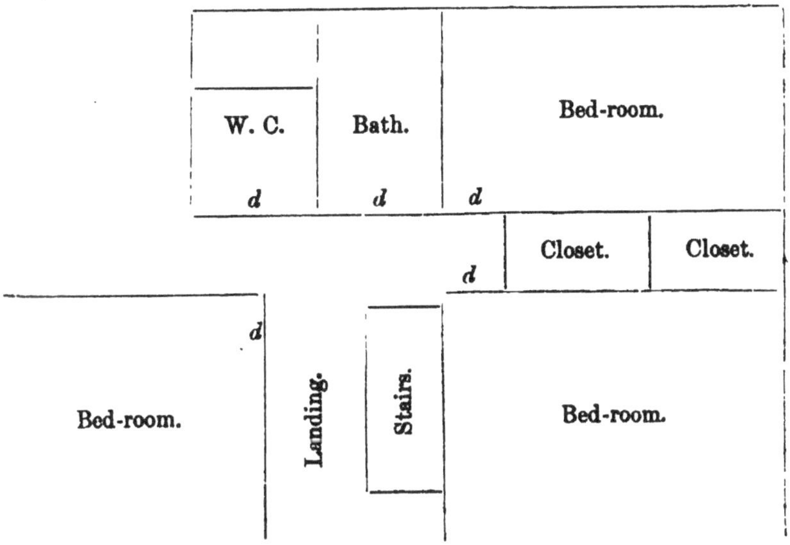

as the kitchen below; and if we consider the W. C. and bath essential, we place them in the small room over the scullery, and arrange them as in the diagram. In the space between the front and back bed-rooms we get two closets, as shown. In fig. 2, Plate VI., a small dressing-room is obtained at the end of the landing over the lobby; but by having the stairs as in the diagram above, the entrance to the right hand bed-room can no longer be obtained as in fig. 2, Plate VI.; we have therefore to enter the right hand bed room by a door opposite to that by which access is obtained to the bed-room over the kitchen. The well-hole of the staircase may be made sufficiently short to admit of the dressing-room being retained, as in fig. 2, Plate VI., and yet give sufficient head-room.

9. In Plate X. we give the ground plan of a villa, the arrangement of which is calculated to secure a fairly convenient residence; it is, however, we take it, deficient in conveniences, as pantries, and it has also one great defect—it has no water-

closet. For many families the accommodation would be much more convenient if the arrangement was altered so as to give the conveniences as shown in the following diagram. The bed-room arrangement would still be the same as in Plate XI.

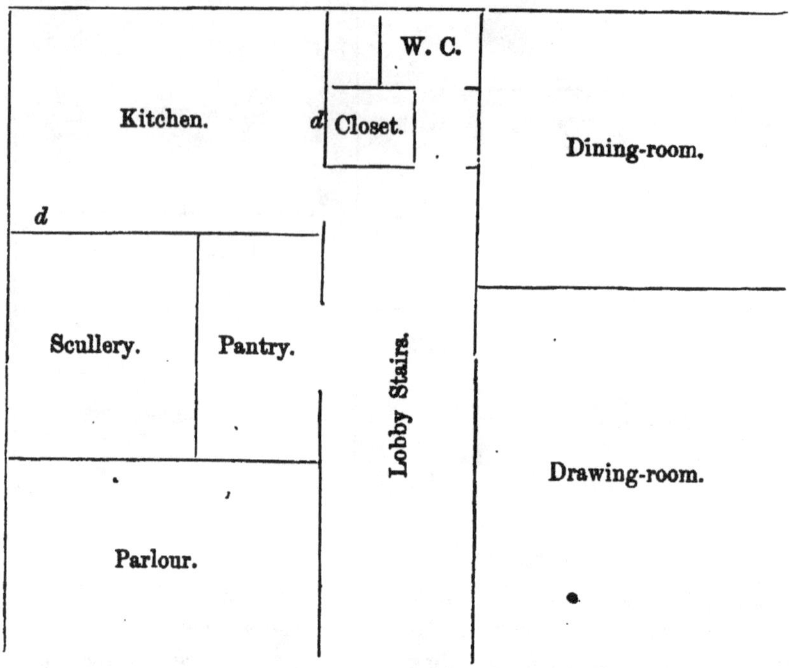

10. The arrangement of the house in Plate XII. would be greatly improved by placing the stairs in the front lobby or entrance-hall, and giving the space now occupied by the stairs to a store-closet and pantry, while the corresponding space above would be given to a water-closet, thus—

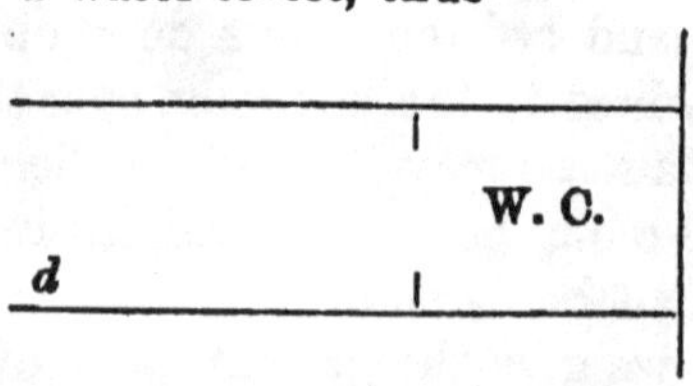

The door to the bed-room being moved to the position as shown in the above diagram. The placing of the stairs in the front lobby as suggested, would, however, lessen the space now given —in the chamber plan, Plate XII.—to the closet; still, sufficient head-room would be obtained, and the closet retained—though less—by shortening the well-hole of the stair.

11. In the plan in Plate XIII. it might be advisable, in like manner, as above suggested, to bring the stairs to the front lobby, thus giving a greater size to the scullery. This would, however, be prejudicial, in so far that the closet arrangement in the chamber plan, Plate XIV., would be done away with. The following diagram shows an alternative arrangement of the ground plan in Plate XIII.

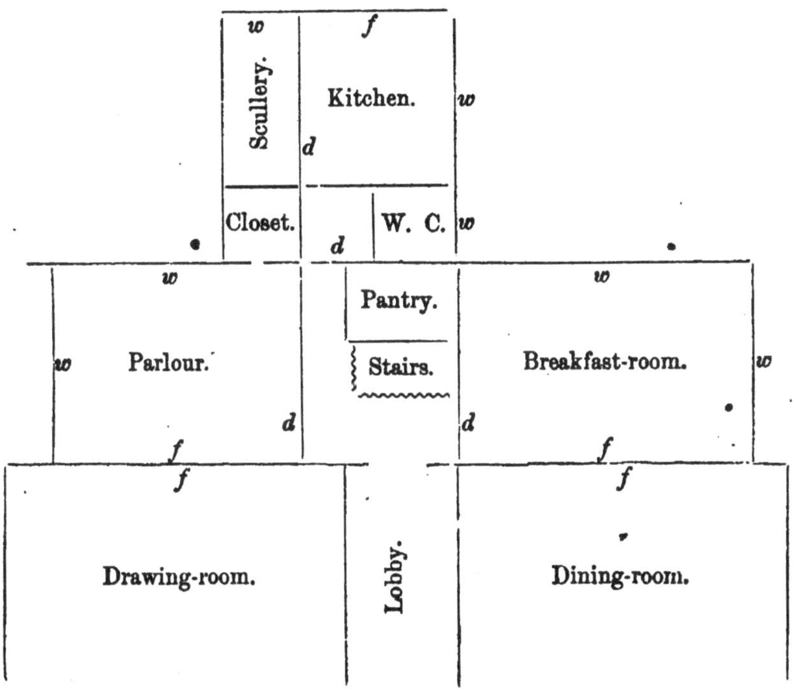

The bed-chamber plan arrangement will be the same as in Plate XIV., with the exception as now shown:—

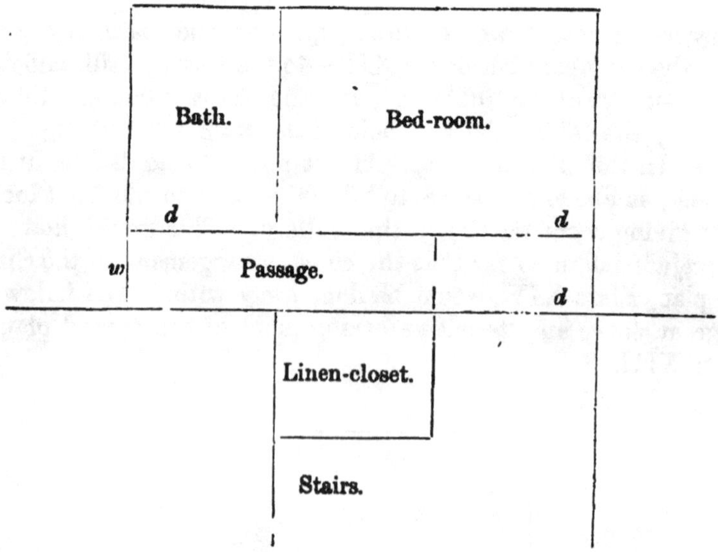

12. In Plate XVII. we give the ground plan of a villa, the accommodation in which, so far as rooms are concerned, is very

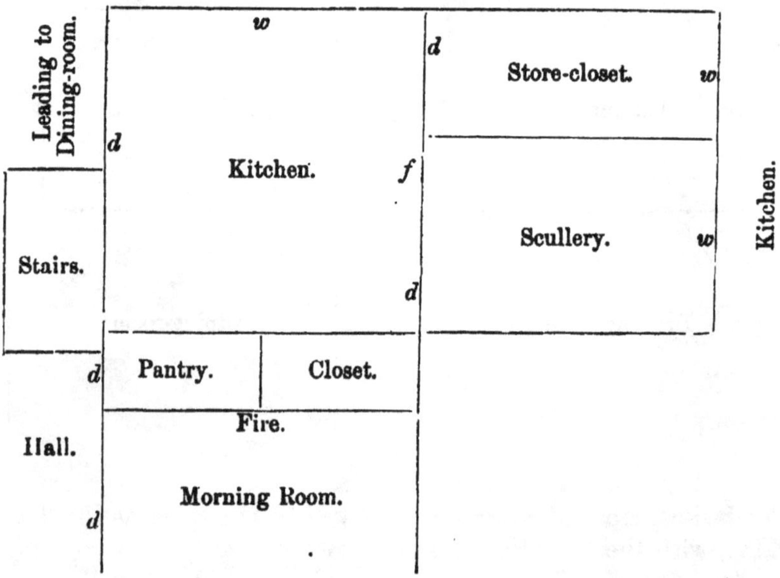

complete ; the fault, however, we have had to find with other plans passed under notice—namely, want of closet conveniences—we have also to find with this, for it will be noticed that there is absolutely nothing of this kind given in the plan as in Plate XVII. Two cupboards may be made at the recesses, on each side of the projecting fire-places, but these can only be made in the morning room and in the kitchen, as they would be out of place in the drawing and dining room. The alternative arrangement, as given at the bottom of preceding page, would give space for closet conveniences. In the bed-room plan, the space given to the pantry and closet in the ground plan would give ample space for a lavatory and bath-room. In Plate XVIII. the scullery walls are not brought up to the roof level, but they might be continued up so as to form an excellent bed-room. The only objection to this would be gaining access to it through the bed-room. The following arrangement would, however, obviate this, and give a separate access to the bed-room over scullery :—

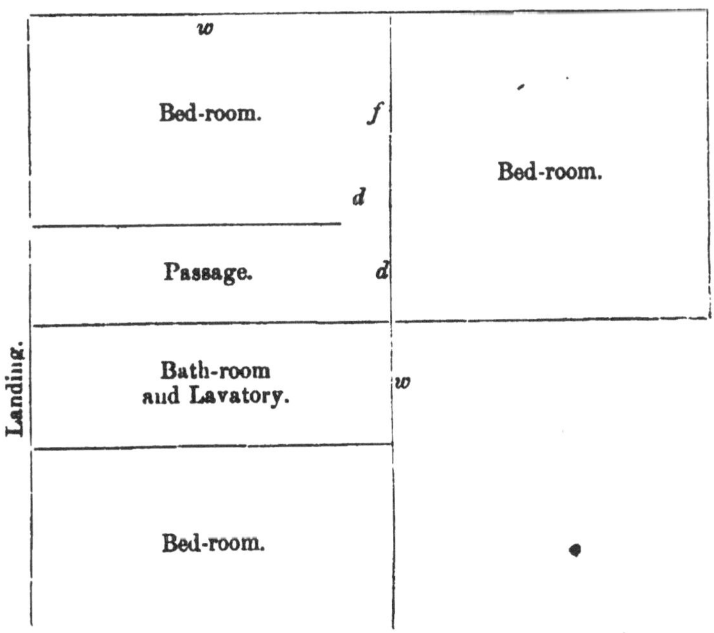

13. In Plate XIX. we give the ground plan of a three-floored villa. Another arrangement might be made of this, in which

the stairs would be placed at the end of the hall, butting against the wall of the scullery; the space now occupied by the stairs in the offset at the end would then give space for a smoking-room. The door at the end of the dining-room leading from the kitchen might be done away with, affording space for the side-board to be placed in the centre of the end wall, a position which cannot be obtained for it as the room is arranged in Plate XIX. Doubtless the door now shown is convenient, as giving ready access from the kitchen to the dining-room. The position of the fireplace in the drawing-room might be changed with advantage to the side opposite to that at which it is now placed, thus affording an opportunity of throwing out a side window, or leaving an unbroken wall for furniture to be placed against.

14. We are now prepared to offer for the study of the reader a variety of plans suggestive of arrangements for villas of different sizes, and to which he should have no difficulty in applying the analytical principles we have endeavoured to elucidate:—

Fig. 51.

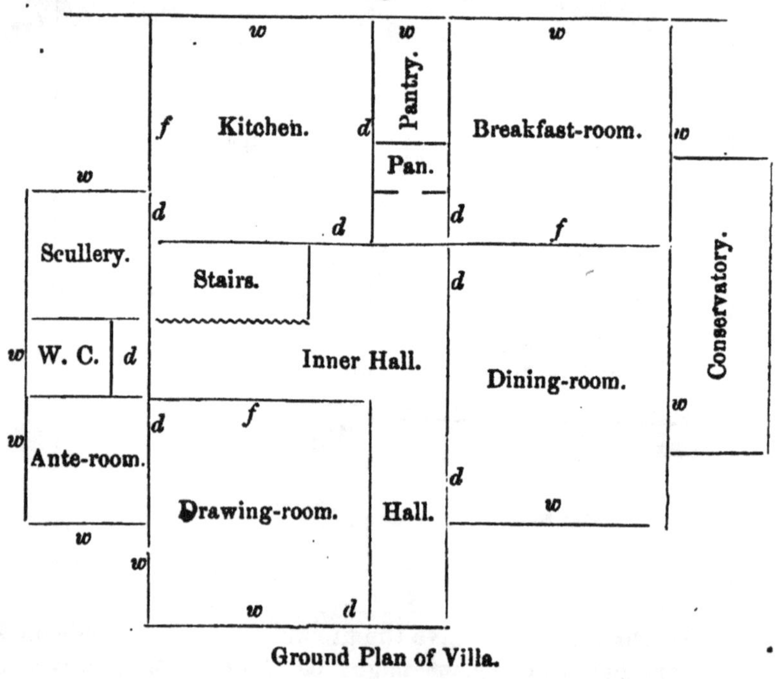

Ground Plan of Villa.

Fig. 52.

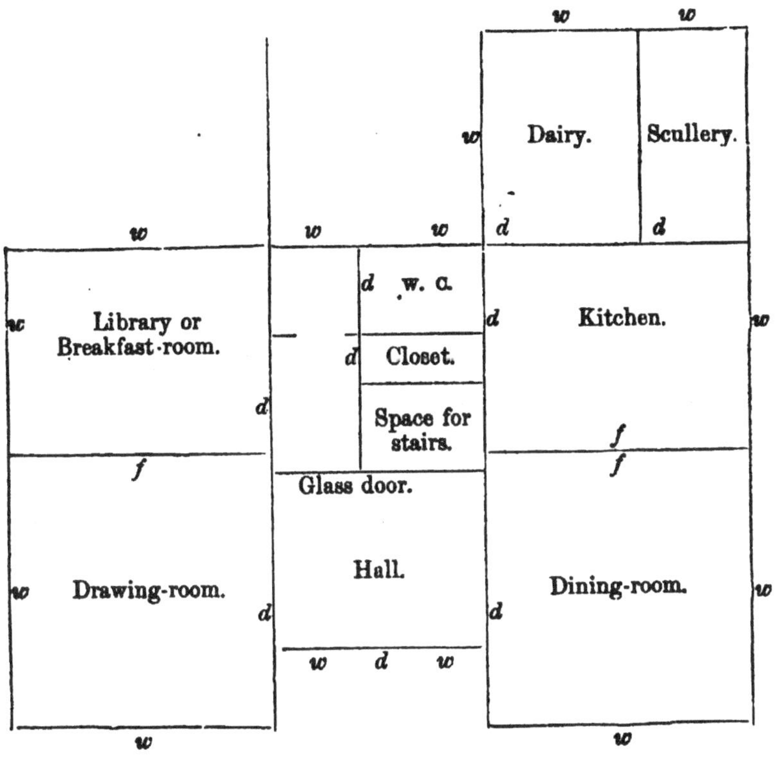

Ground Plan of Villa.

Fig. 53.

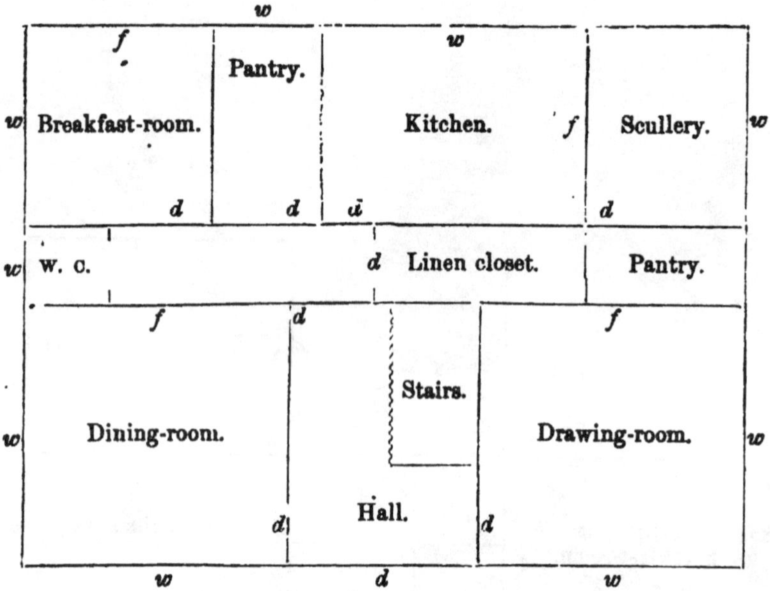

Ground Plan of Villa.

Fig. 54.

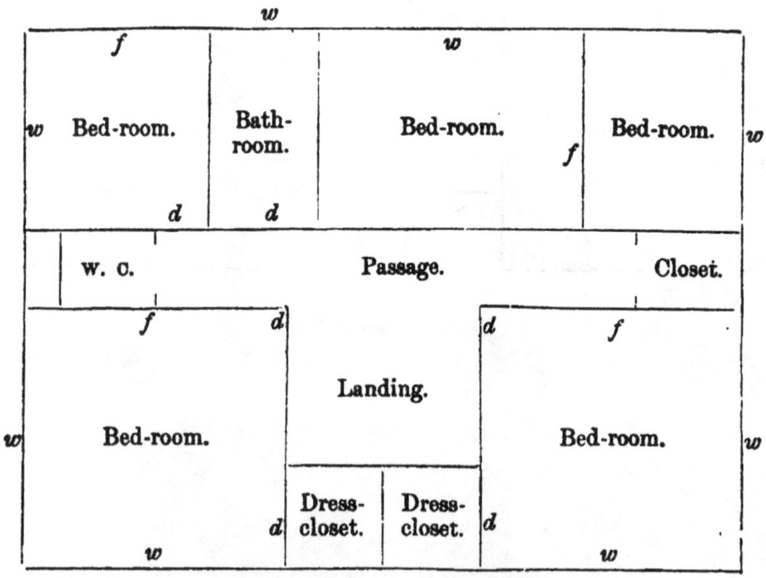

Chamber Plan of Villa in fig. 53.

Fig. 55.

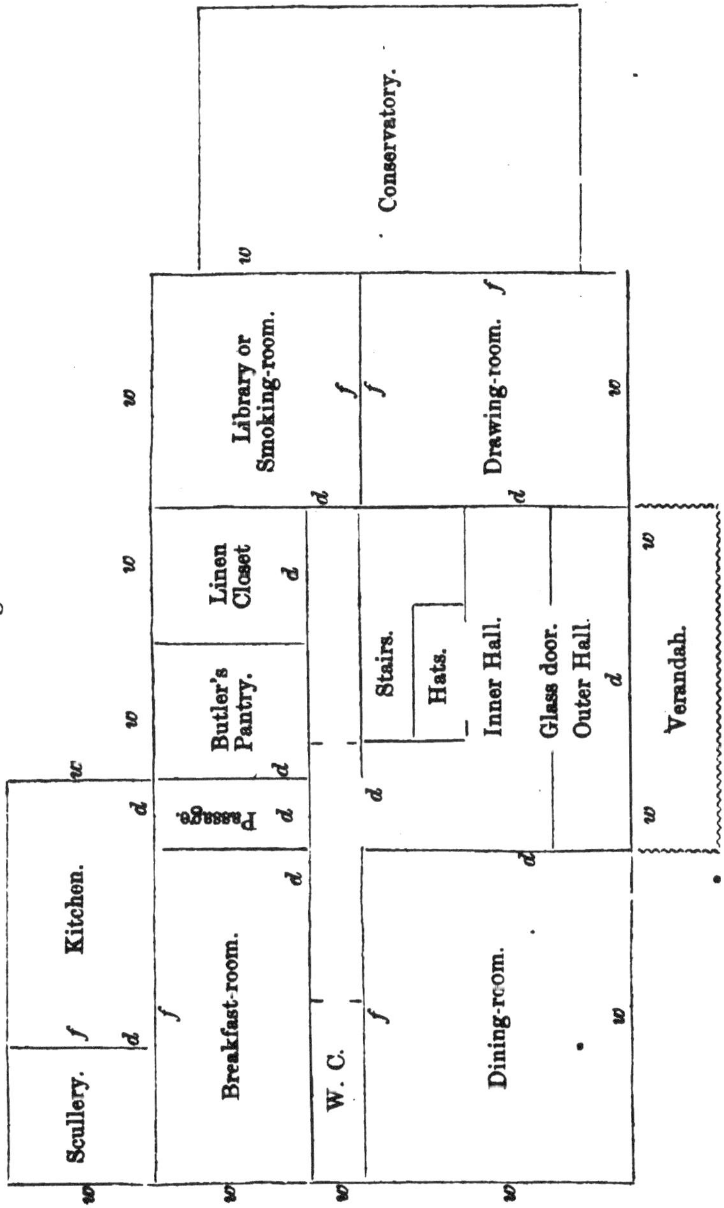

Ground Plan of Villa.

Fig. 56.

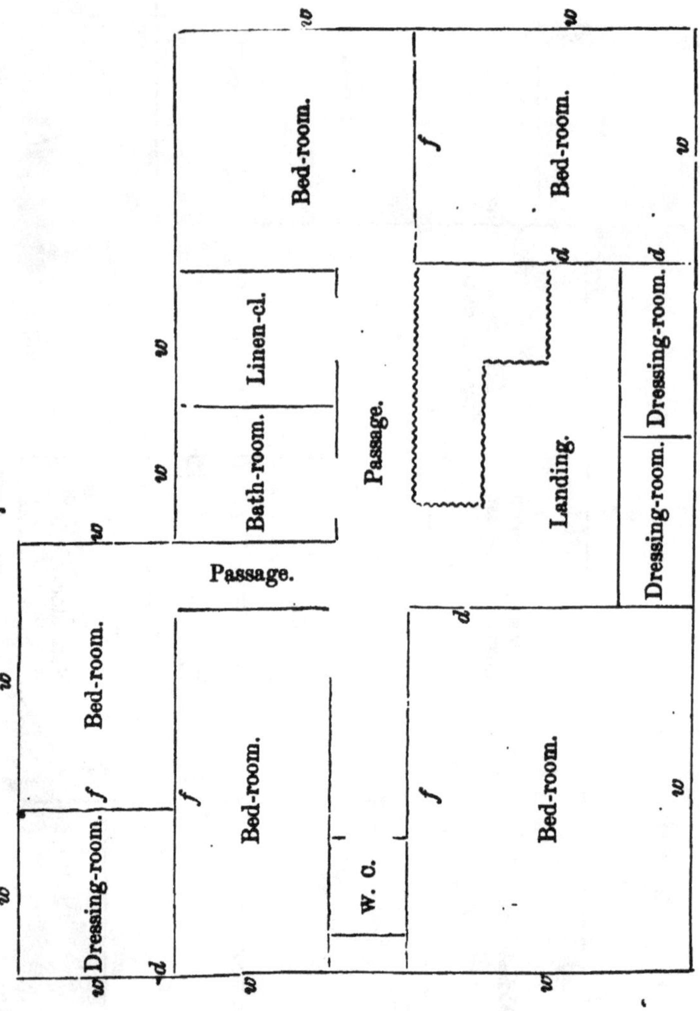

Chamber Plan of Villa in fig. 54.

Fig. 57.

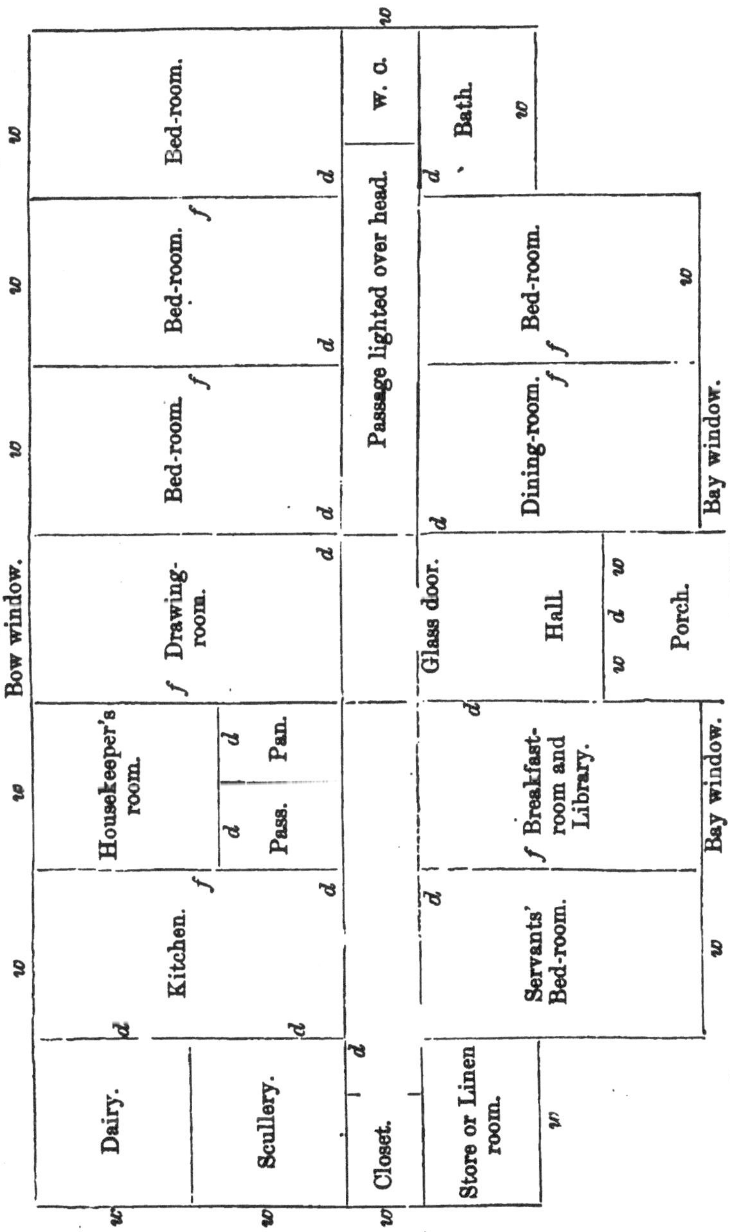

One-storied Villa.

Fig. 58.

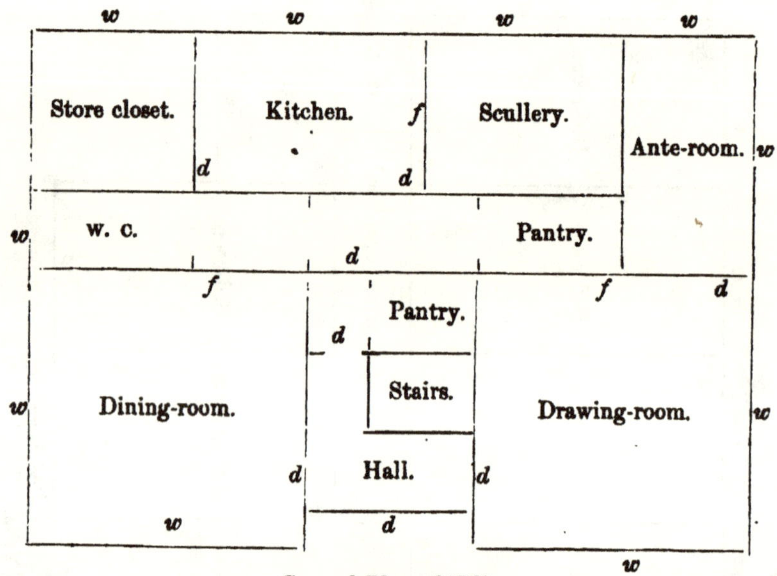

Ground Plan of Villa.

Fig. 59.

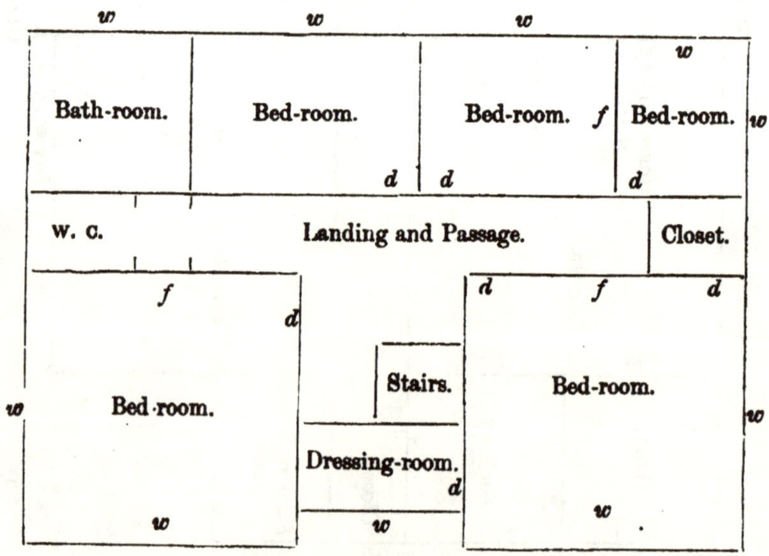

Chamber Plan of Villa in fig. 58.

Fig. 60.

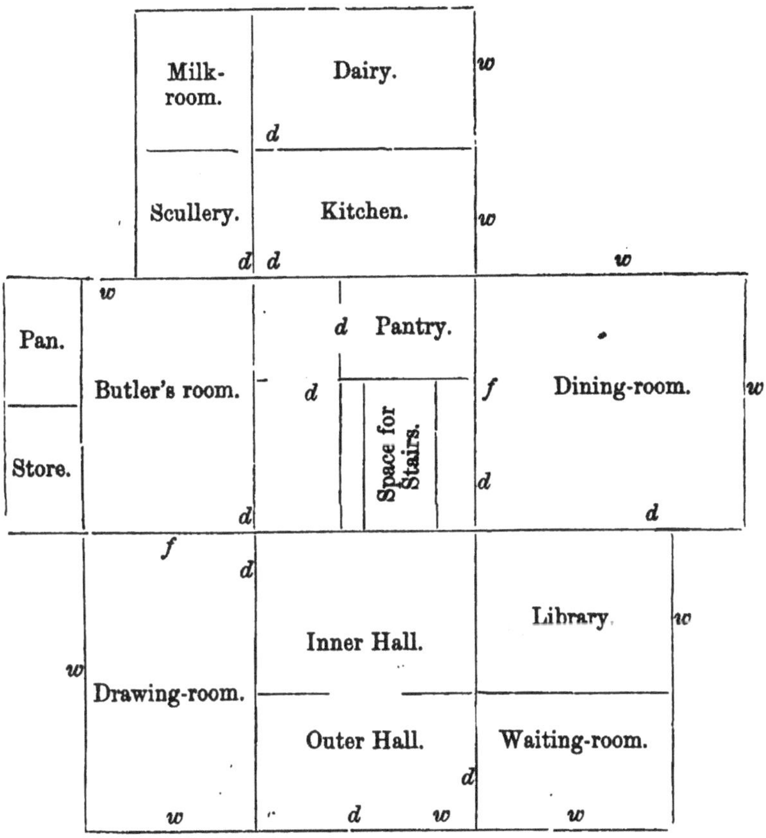

Ground Plan of Villa.

Fig. 61.

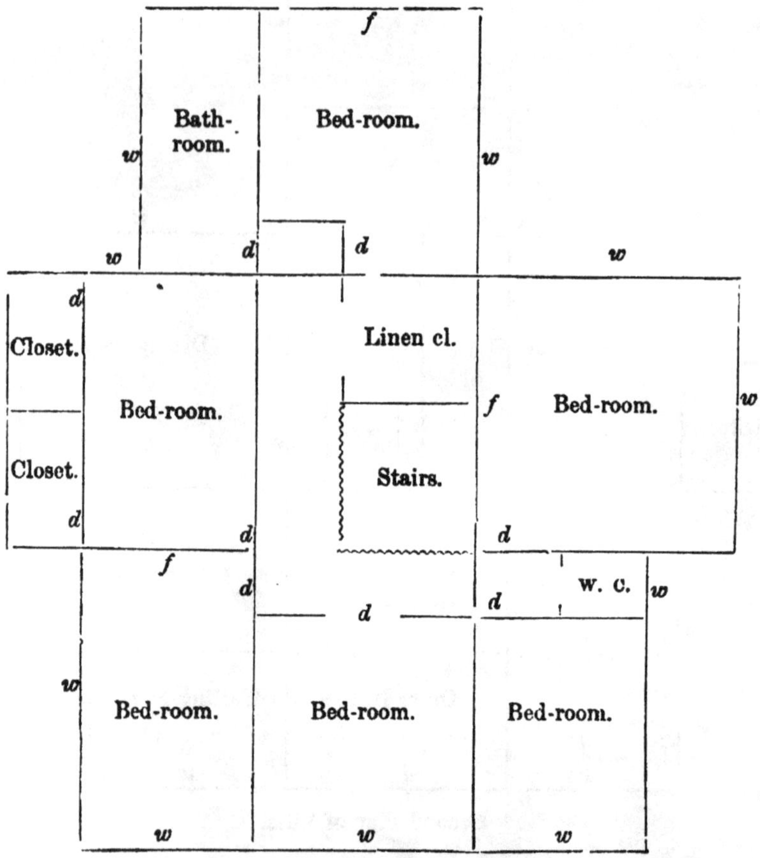

Chamber Plan of Villa in fig. 60.

Fig. 62.

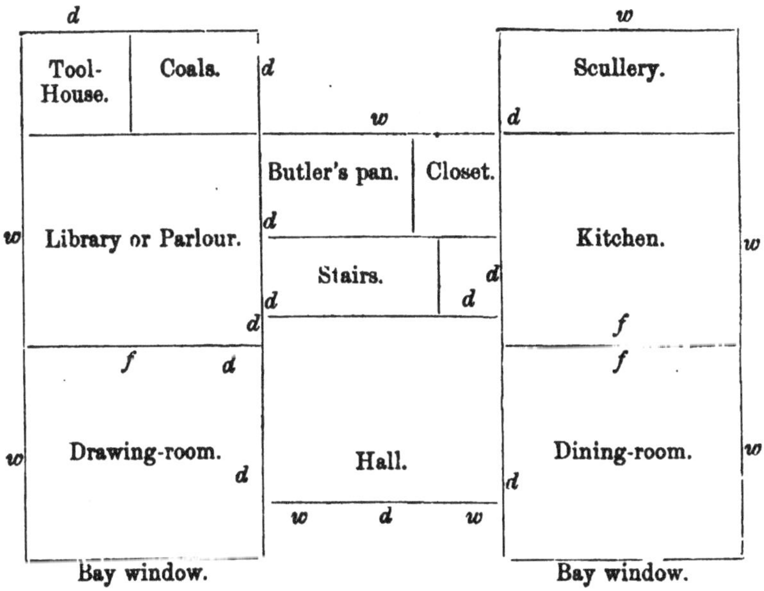

Ground Plan of Villa.

Fig. 63.

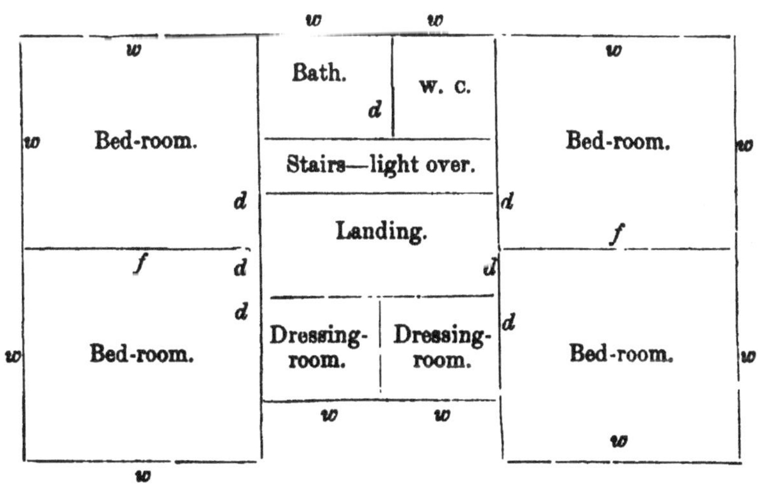

Chamber Plan of Villa in fig. 62.

Fig. 64.

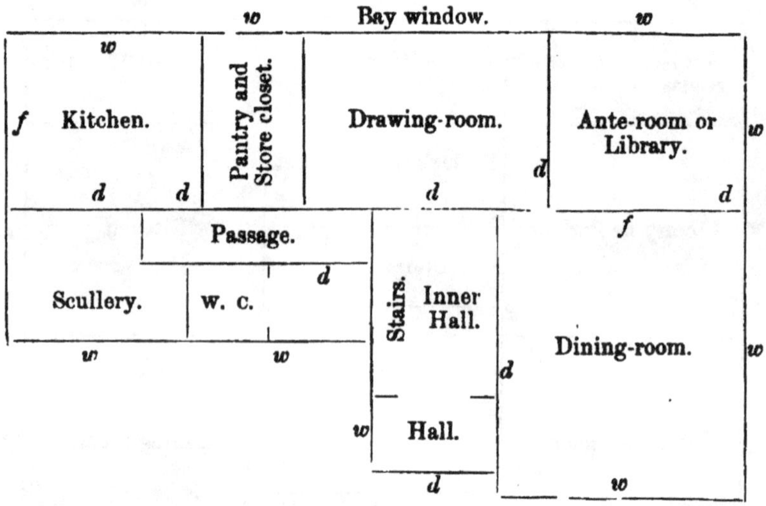

Ground Plan of Villa.

Fig. 65.

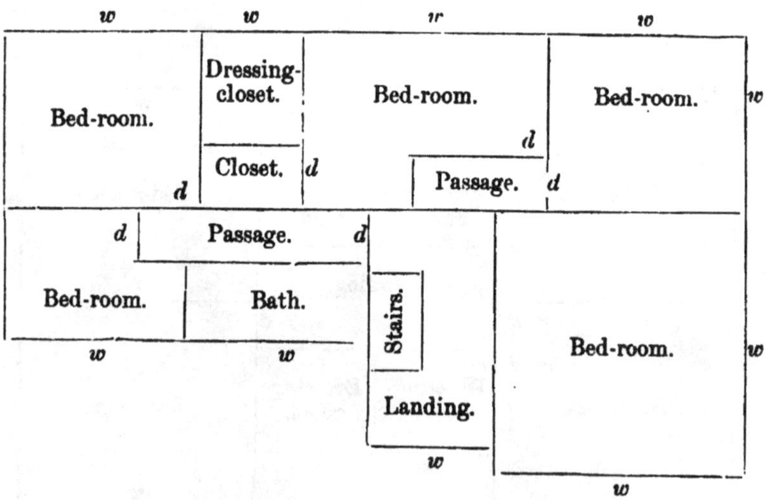

Chamber Plan of Villa in fig. 64.

Fig. 66.

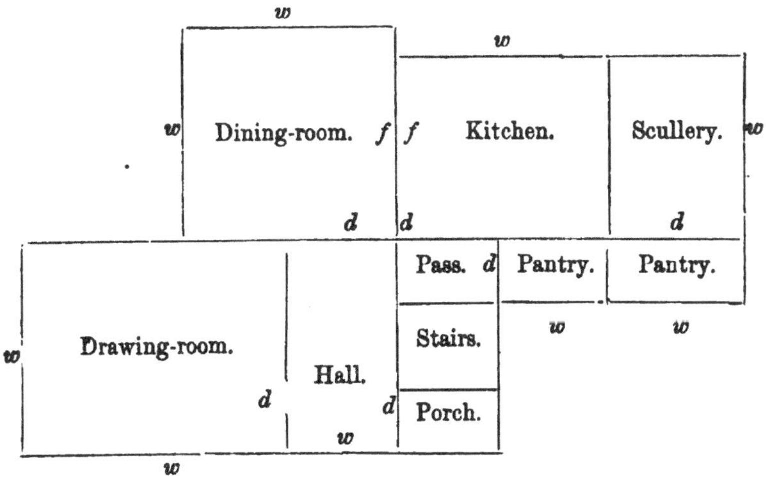

Ground Plan of Villa.

Fig 67.

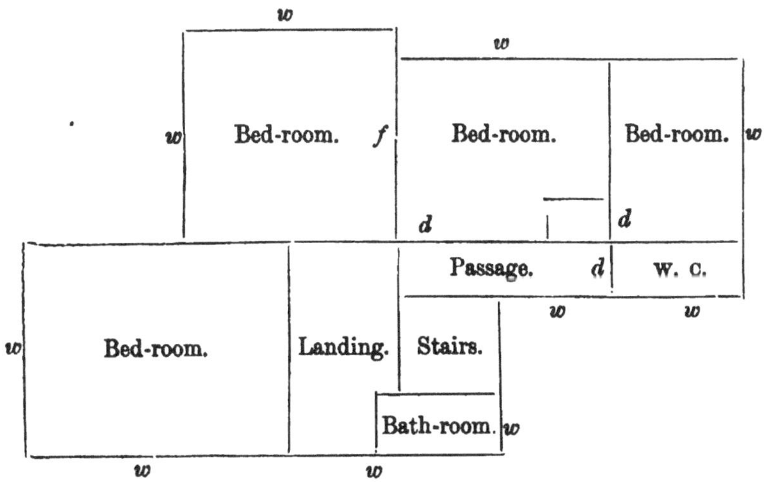

Chamber Plan of Villa in fig. 66.

Fig. 68.

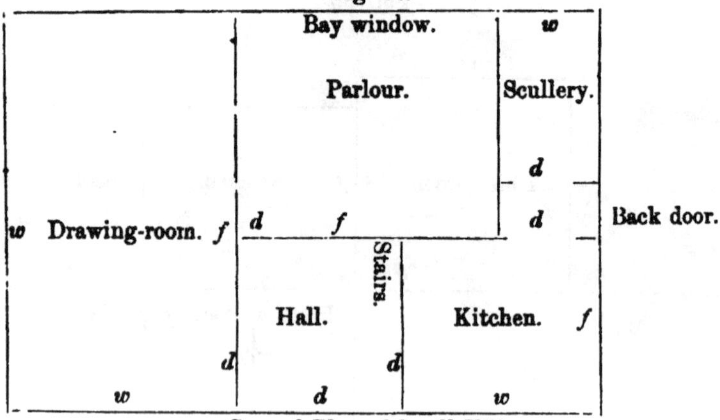

Ground Plan of Small Villa.

Fig. 69.

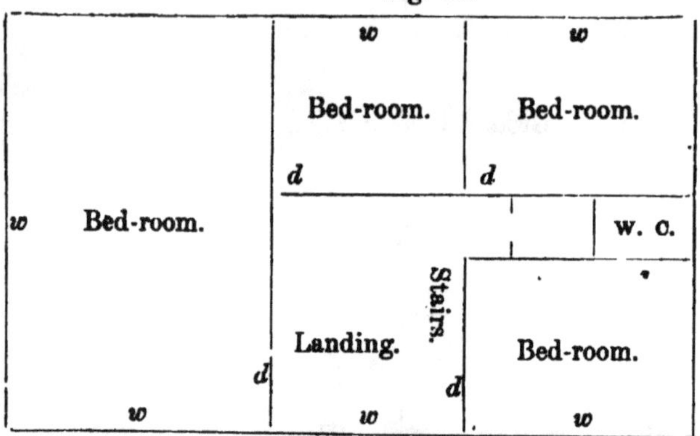

Chamber Plan of Villa in fig. 68.

Fig. 70.

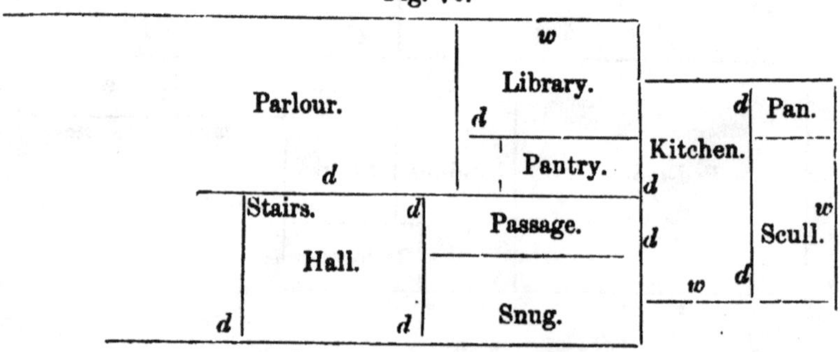

Alternative Plan of fig. 68.

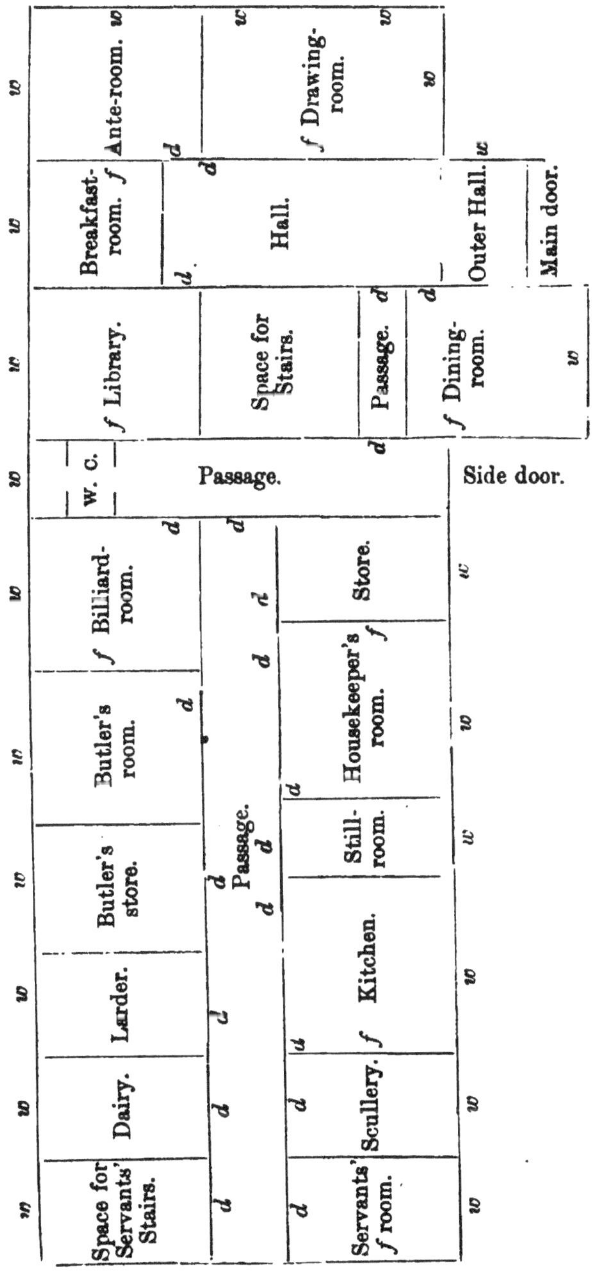

Fig. 71.

Ground Plan of Villa.

Fig. 72.

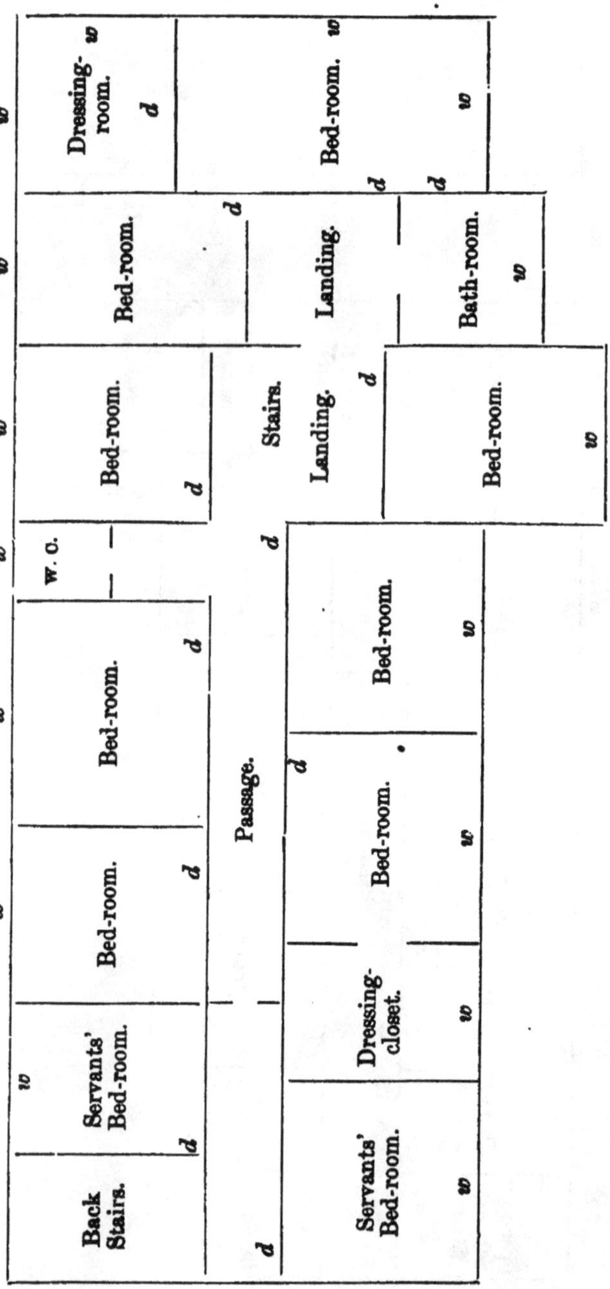

Chamber Plan of Villa in Fig. 71.

Fig. 73.

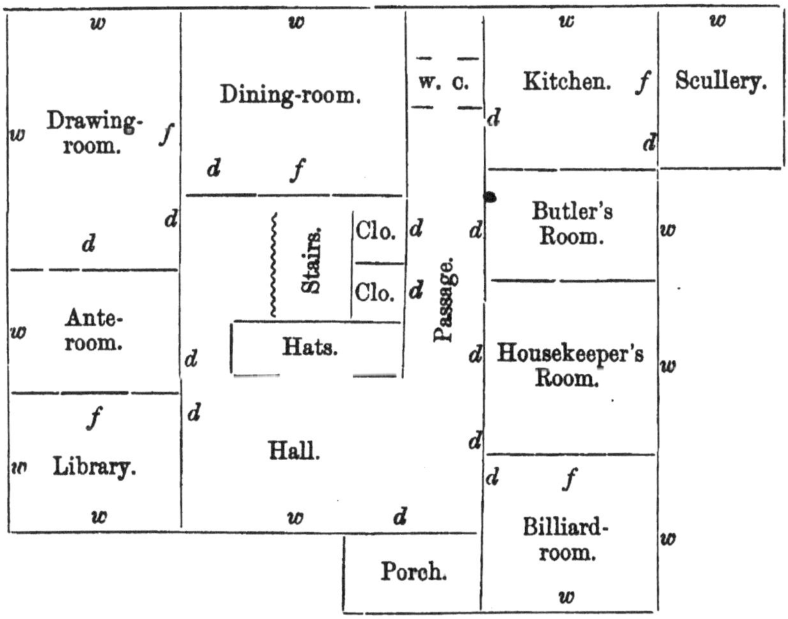

Ground Plan of Villa.

Fig. 74.

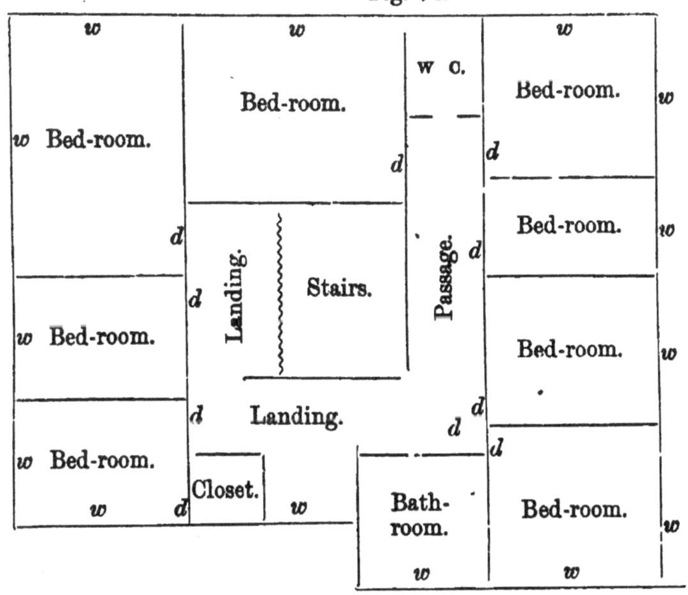

Chamber Plan of Villa in Fig. 73.

Fig. 75.

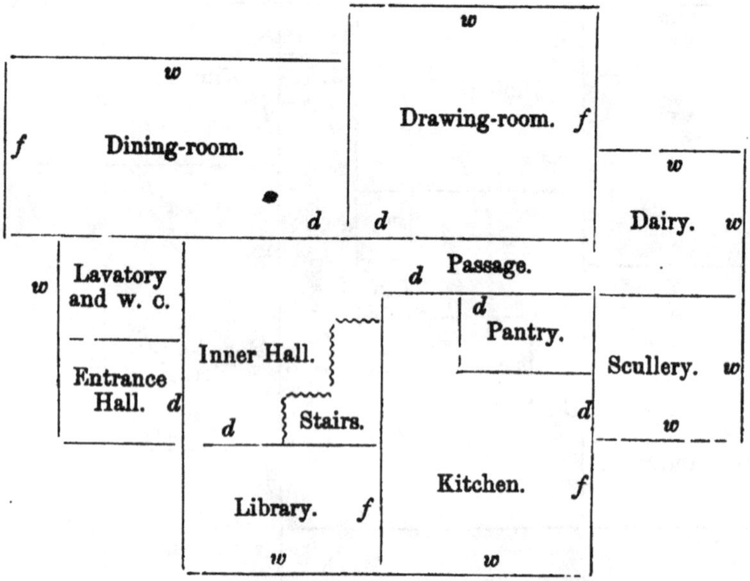

Ground Plan of Villa.

Fig. 76.

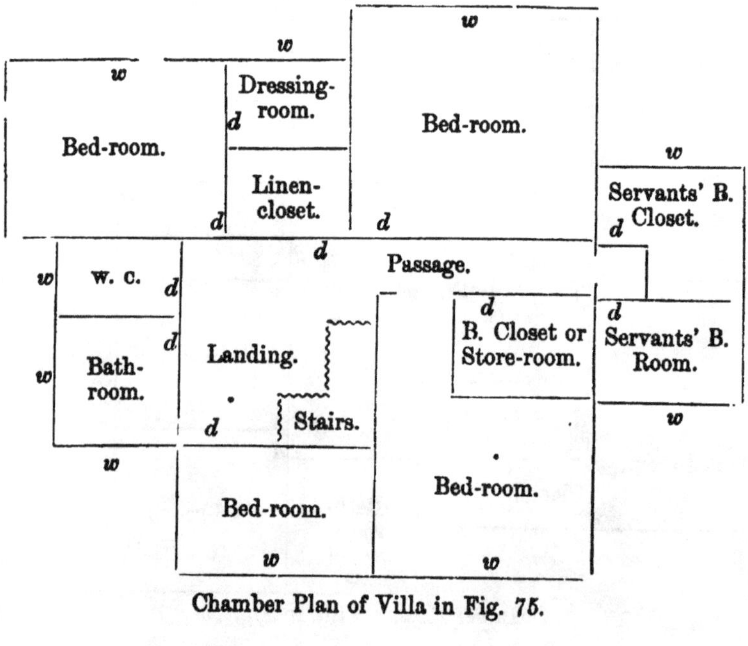

Chamber Plan of Villa in Fig. 75.

Fig. 77.

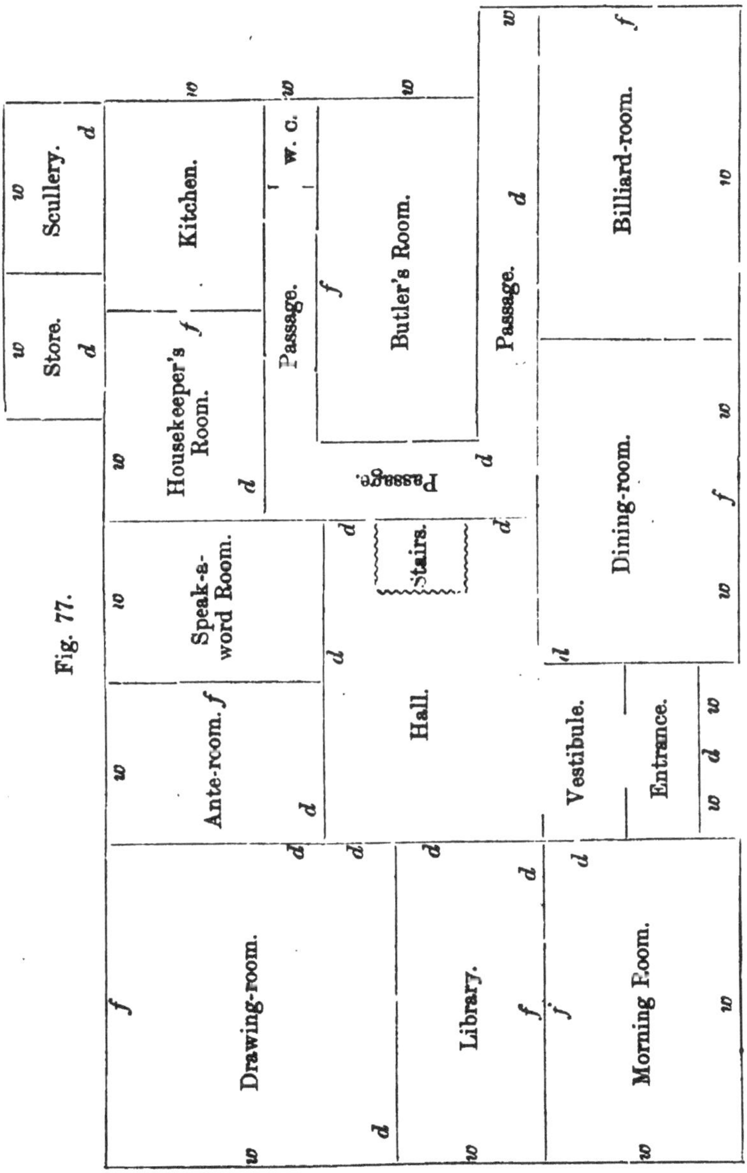

Ground Plan of Villa.

Fig. 78.

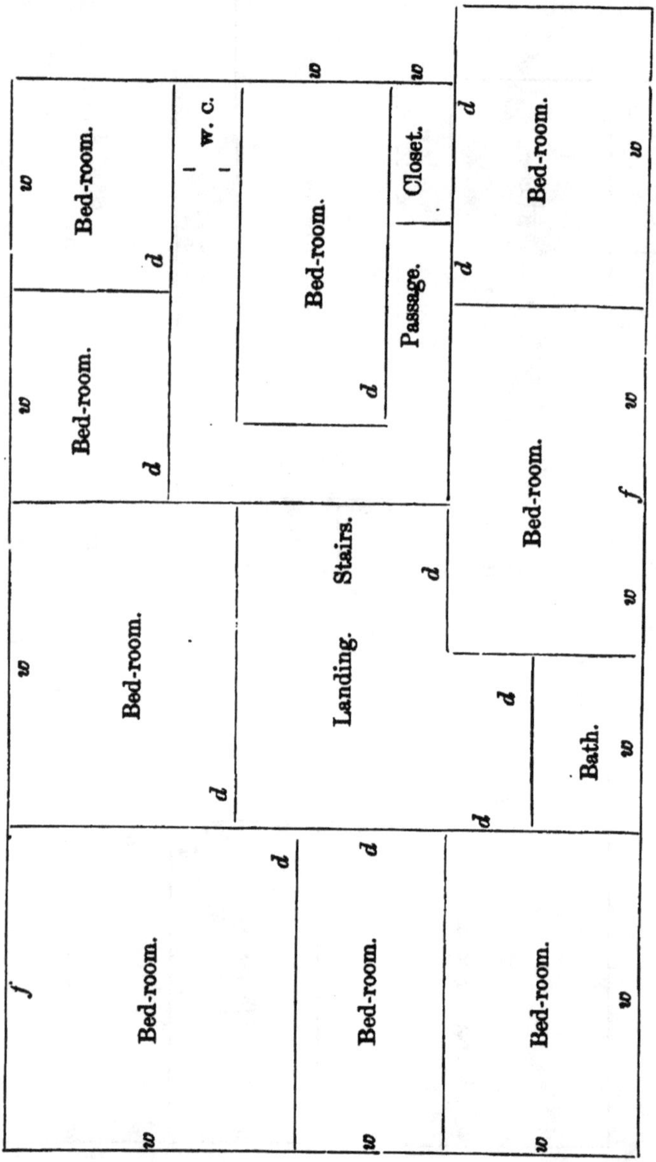

Chamber Plan of Villa in Fig. 77.

Space does not permit us to go here into a detailed notice of the principles which dictate architectural design as applied to the various purposes of domestic architecture—but as this work is designed to be as much a resumé of the opinions of others as of our own; and as the reader will find the subject of design discussed in Essay Second of "Working Drawings in Architecture and Building"—our purpose will be well served if we give here an extract from Mr. Downing's "Country Houses," an American work, which, although designed specially for the instruction of his countrymen, abounds in much that is of interest and value to all connected with the building arts. He asks:—"And what should the villa be, architecturally?" And then gives the following able and suggestive answer. "It should, firstly, be the most convenient; secondly, the most truthful or significant; and thirdly the most tasteful or beautiful of dwellings.

"The villa should indeed be a private house, where beauty, taste, and moral culture are at home. In the first outlines of the whole edifice either dignified, graceful, or picturesque, in the spacious or varied verandas, arcades, and windows, in the select forms of windows, chimney tops, cornices, the artistic knowledge and feeling has full play; while in the arrangement of spacious apartments, especially in the devotion of a part to a library or cabinet sacred to books, and in that elevated order and system of the whole plan, indicative of the inner domestic life, we find the development of the intellectual and moral nature which characterizes the most cultivated families in their country houses.

"It is therefore in our villas that we must hope in this country to give the best and most complete manifestation of domestic architecture. The cottage is too limited in size, the farm house too simply useful in its character, to admit of that indulgence of beauty of form and decoration which belongs properly to the villa.

"The villa, indeed, may be as simple and chaste as a cottage, and often, with a more satisfactory effect than if inlaid with sculpture; but its larger size, and the greater means devoted to its creation, will justify an embellishment that would be out of keeping in all respects with the cottage. The greater extent of the villa allows, for example, more intricacy of form and outline, as the greater completeness of the arrangement permits a luxury of space and decoration.

"Larger scope as the villa gives for the architect to indulge his love for the beautiful, there are yet limits beyond which he may not wisely go. He must not, for example, forget that it is domestic architecture which occupies him, and therefore that beauty must be united to convenience and comfort, or at least, must never be opposed to it. Instead of following the example of those who are always striving to make dwellings resemble temples and cathedrals, he will bestow on windows and doors, roofs and chimneys, porches and verandas—those truly domestic features—that loving artistic treatment which alone raises material forms from the useful to the beautiful.

"Both the architect and the amateur must recollect that proportion is the primary law of beauty. It should, therefore, be the first thing in the mere composition of the villa, as it is the universal chord which once struck, moves all beholders to instinctive admiration. After proportion comes decoration, or the enrichment of beautiful parts and details; which, however important, is still as much inferior to *proportion* as the shapes and colours of the clouds are to the grandeur and beauty of the arch form of the heaven in which they float.*

"And higher and deeper than either proportion or decoration, is that beauty of expression which indicates the spirit that lives within the country house. You may never have investigated it, but you have nevertheless tacitly recognized, that a spirit of frankness or reserve, a spirit of miserly care or kind hospitality, a spirit of meanness or generosity, a spirit of system or disorder, a spirit of peace or discord, may be found in the expression of every house, as well as every face in the country. Whatever gives to the villa its best and truest expression of human sympathy and affection confers on it its highest and most lasting character of beauty.

"We have said the *truest* expression, and this leads us to the most difficult question that arises in the mind of the artist in designing villas in this country. To unite the beautiful and the true, to make the outward form of all about us express our best

* Most especially do we recommend this fact to the notice of proprietors who are novices in architecture. It is an economical fact, as well as a principle. A perfectly proportioned building, with little or no decoration, being far more beautiful and satisfactory than one of equal bulk and cost, ill-proportioned, and with thousands lavished on the embellishment of its details.

ideal of life, to mould it so that it shall evince, not merely the borrowed and accepted forms of the books and schools of art, but the deeper essence of the life, and character, and manners of the people, and even the families that inhabit it—that should be the ambition and the goal of the domestic architect of any country. It is a result which can only be fully reached here, when the habits of the people have firmly crystallized, and when our people themselves understand the true meaning and the true beauty of architecture.

"The significance or truthfulness of a man's house, especially if that house be a villa, is a matter which he also should well consider, for in it lies the whole philosophy of both its beauty and its utility. He may easily build, or cause to be built, a pretty villa, in any one of a dozen styles—convenient and comfortable in its accommodation; and yet if there is no real fitness in the form and expression of the thing chosen, if it is foreign to the habits, education, tastes, and manners—in short, the life of the proprietor, he will, if he is a simple, unaffected man, sit foolishly in it, as he would in the church or town hall, wearing the court costume of some foreign ambassador. There is, for instance, something wonderfully captivating in the idea of a battlemented castle, even to an apparently modest man, who thus shows to the world his unsuspected view of personal ambition, by trying to make a castle of his country house. But, *unless there is something of the castle in the man*, it is very likely, if it be like a real castle, to dwarf *him to the stature of a mouse.**

" Shall we then have no variety, no latitude in the character and forms of our best country houses? Must all be bound with the common sense outline of a square or parallelogram?

" Far from it. The villa—the country house, should, above all things, manifest individuality. It should say something of the character of family within—as much as possible of their life and history, their tastes and associations, should mould and fashion themselves upon its walls.

* Almost all imitations of castles must, as private dwellings, be petty in this country. There is one lately erected, of grey stone, on the lower part of the Hudson. We had the pleasure of welcoming to the Hudson that accomplished daughter of Sweden, Fredrica Bremer, and as we were sailing past this spot some one near her remarked—" Do you see a castle?" "Ah!" she replied, " but it is a *very young* castle!"

"If we look into all the forms of architecture applicable to domestic life, we shall find but two elementary ideas—the rational, logical, sensible idea, bounded by the regular horizontal line of classical architecture, and the more poetic, aspiring, imaginative idea embodied in the upward lines of painted architecture. The man of common sense views only, if he is true to himself, will have nothing to do, in the choice or construction of his country house, with picturesque and irregular outlines. He will naturally prefer a symmetrical, regular house, with few angles, but with order, and method, and distinctness stamped upon its unbroken lines of cornice and regular rows of windows. He will do nothing without reason; he will have no caprices, and whims, either in his life or his house.

"The man of sentiment or feeling will seek for that house in whose aspect there is something to love. It must nestle in, or grow out of, the soil. It must not look all new and sunny, but show secluded shadowy corners. There must be nooks about it, where one would love to linger; windows, where one can enjoy the quiet landscape leisurely; cosy rooms, where all domestic fireside joys are invited to dwell. It must, in short, have something in its aspect which the heart can fasten upon and become attached to, as naturally as the ivy attaches itself to the antique wall, preserving its memories from decay."

On the subject of decoration of apartments the following from the pages of the 'Atheneum' will usefully and fittingly conclude this chapter:—"You are going to decorate your drawing-room or dining-room both with furniture and colouring. Before you speak to your upholsterer or house painter, have a perfect understanding and recognition of what is the aspect of the room. Let no circumstances make you regardless of this fundamental consideration. No cost will remedy the forgetfulness. Spend what you will, you will always repent having a cold colour in a room lighted from the north, or a very hot colour in a room lighted from the south. If the view be north, north-east, north-west, or due east, the general tone of colouring should be positively warm. Blues, greens, and all shaded colours which involve any predominant use of blues, must be avoided. There is a drawing-room in the Reform Club, looking north, which may convince any one of the mistake of forgetting aspect. The walls and curtains are blue;

with all its elegance—and its ceiling and cornice are beautiful—the effect of this room by daylight is always chilly. It would be just the reverse if it looked upon Carlton Gardens. In such aspects the choice should tend towards reds, and all their various combinations with yellow. As the aspect approaches east, and west, so the colour should verge towards yellow rather than red tints. In an eastern aspect, tints of light yellow, lemon colours, &c., are always effective and cheerful. If the aspect of the room be south, south-west, or west, and open to the sun, then we may venture on the use of cooler colours, even on positive blue, should our taste lead us in that direction.

"The supply of light, the size of the room, and its purpose, appear to be the chief circumstances which ought to regulate the strength or depth of the colours to be used. Where the light is strong, unobscured, and plentiful, the tone of the colouring may be full; on the other hand, where the supply of light is small, the tone of the colouring should be light. In the houses of the ancients, the strongest and darkest colours, even blacks, as we have already observed, were used on large surfaces when the apartment received a direct and full light from above. Under a strong and abundant light full-toned colours preserve their brightness and distinctive character, but when the light is feeble, and the supply of it limited, they become dull and gloomy. Full-toned colours lessen the apparent size of the room; light colouring enlarges it. A little attention to the proportion between the space to be coloured and the depth of the colouring becomes therefore of great importance. If you wish to make your room as large as possible, then exclude dark colouring, not only on the large surfaces, but even in the patterns of the paper hangings, and in the mouldings and ornamental parts. The nature of the use to which the room is applied should also influence the decision as to the tone of colouring. If the room is used mostly by artificial light, which being less pure than daylight, materially modifies the appearance of most colours—much or little according to their strength—then keep the colouring light. If, on the other hand, it is a room for occupation during daylight, then the tone of colouring must be deep. Red and green with black, appear dark and grave; with white they appear gay. We see these effects strikingly illustrated in book wrappers."

CHAPTER FOURTH.

PLANS OF FARM HOUSES.

We commence with plans showing the arrangement for small farm houses, and finish with those having a large extent of accommodation.

Fig. 79 represents a small farm house of one storey with a

Fig. 79.

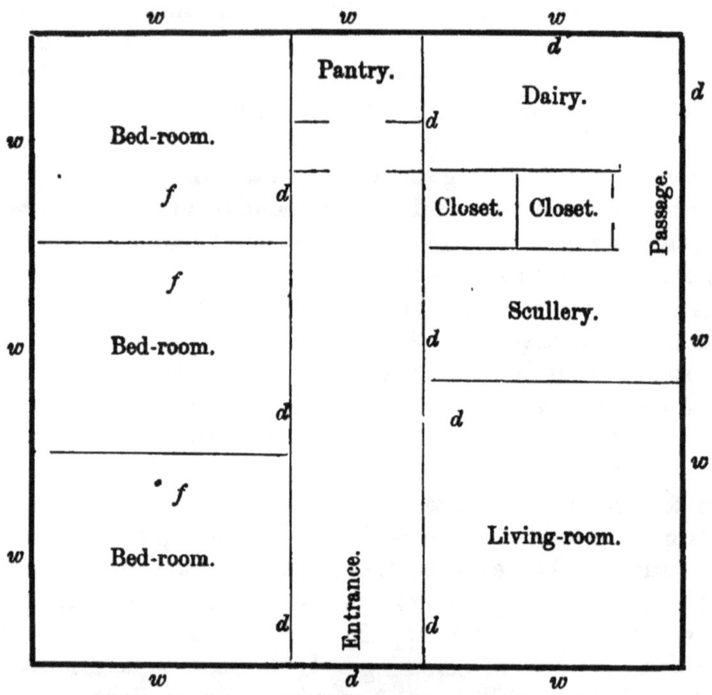

square outline. The working rooms of the house are all on one side of the central passage or lobby, and the bed-rooms on the other. On the working side, the scullery is placed next the kitchen or living room, and is entered therefrom by a door; or a second door may be made leading into the scullery from the passage or lobby. The dairy is at the (north) back of the house, and is separated from the scullery by closets, one of which enters from the dairy, or may be made to enter from the scullery, if more convenient; while the second of those closets enters from the passage leading from the scullery to the dairy. A large pantry (or bed closet) is placed at the end of the lobby, and is lighted by a small window, as indicated by the letter *w*.

Fig. 80.

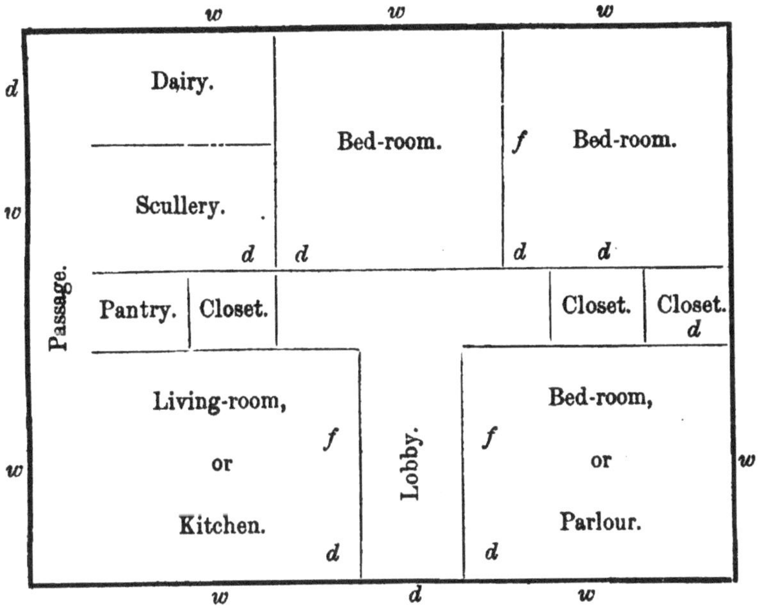

In Fig. 80 we give the plan of another form of square one-storeyed house, in which the kitchen, scullery, and dairy are all in direct communication with each other, as in Fig. 79. The bed-rooms in this case are at the back, while the room corresponding to the kitchen may either be made a third and principal bed-room or a parlour. A closet enters from the scullery, a pantry from the kitchen, while the principal and back bed-rooms have each a closet.

In Fig. 81 the square form is departed from, and projecting parts, or a set off, introduced. It is a one-storeyed house, as Figs. 79 and 80. There is a porch provided, opposite to the en-

Fig. 81.

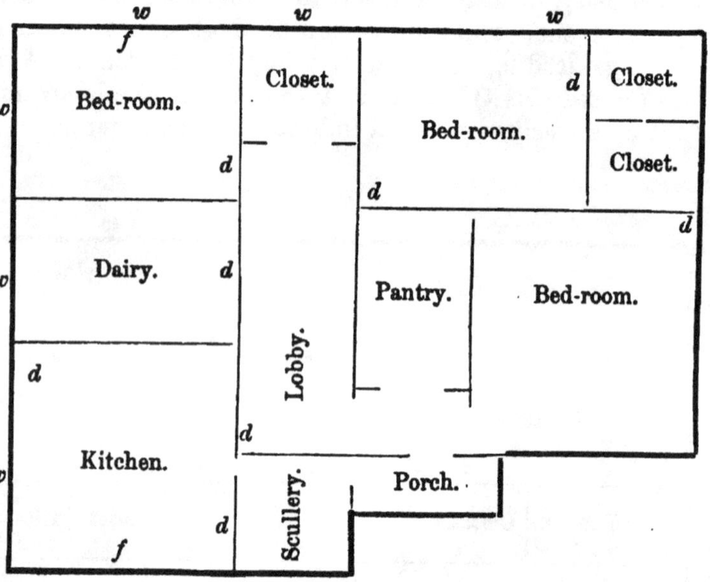

trance of which there is a pantry. To the left the kitchen is placed. The dairy enters from the lobby, at the end of which is

Fig. 82.

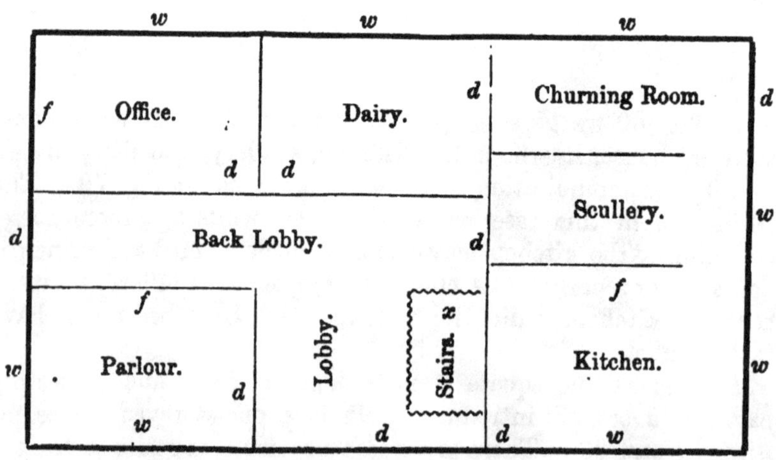

a closet, lighted with a window, and the door of which is provided with a casement to give light to the lobby. The scullery is placed next the porch, and enters from the kitchen. The two bed-rooms at the end have each a closet.

Fig. 83.

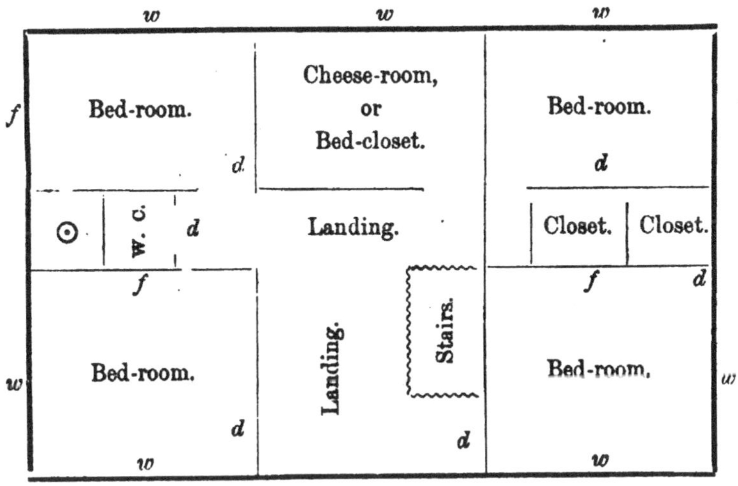

In Fig. 82 we give the ground plan, and in Fig. 83 the chamber plan, of a two-storeyed farm house. The kitchen, the scullery, and the churning room are all in connection. The dairy is entered from the back passage, as well as from the churning room. Next to the dairy, and close to the back door, is the office or breakfast-room. The parlour or sitting-room is opposite to the kitchen. In the bed or chamber-floor plan in Fig. 83 there is space obtained for two closets, one entering from the front or principal bed-room, the other from the back. A water-closet is situated between the other two bed-rooms; or if this is objected to, and a privy in the garden deemed the best, a clothes pantry may be put in place of it. The cheese-room is placed immediately above the dairy; or if cheese is not made in bulk, this may be made into a bed-closet. On comparing this accommodation in the ground or working part of the house in Fig. 82 with that in the plans in Figs. 79, 80, and 81, the reader will at once perceive that there is in Fig. 82 plan a kind of closet or pantry accommodation.

There is nothing which distinguishes a bad plan from a good one more strongly than the lack of accommodation of this sort. There cannot, indeed, in any house, be too many places of this kind: the careful and orderly housewife has always a use for them; and this, true of all houses, is remarkably so of farm houses.

Fig. 84.

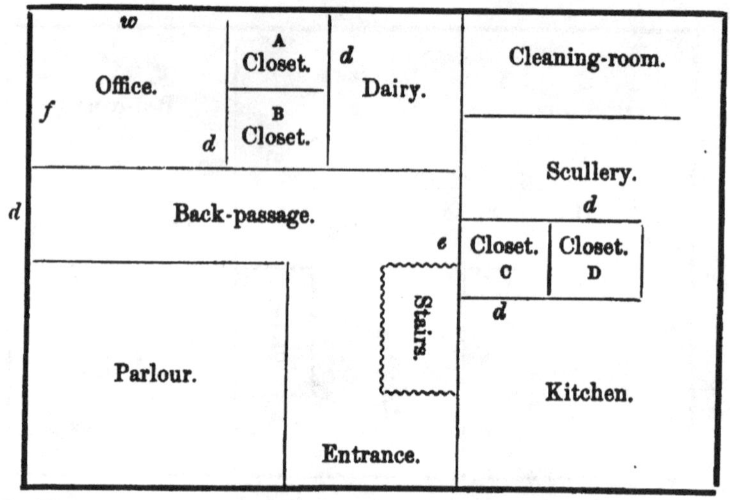

In Fig. 84 we give an alternative plan of Fig. 82, in which we obtain a closet (A), entering from the dairy, in which to store butter, &c.; another closet (B), entering from the office; a third (C), entering from the kitchen; and a fourth (D), entering from the scullery. As some housewives object to a back passage, on the score of the draught passing through the house, this in the plan before us might be done away with, and the space filled up with a pantry or store closet.

Fig. 85.

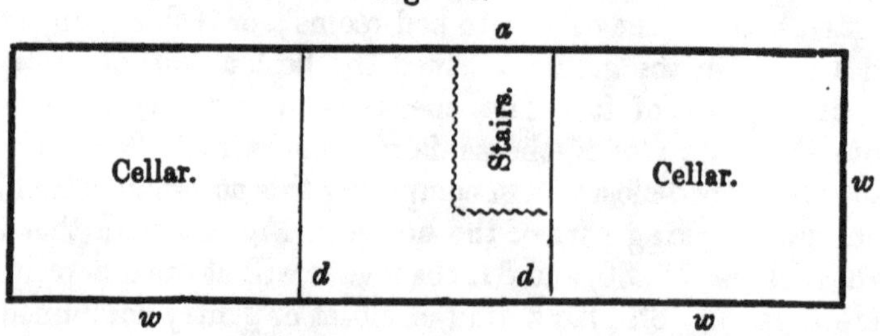

We have already, in a preceding chapter, adverted to the importance of having cellar accommodation in houses. In

Fig. 86.

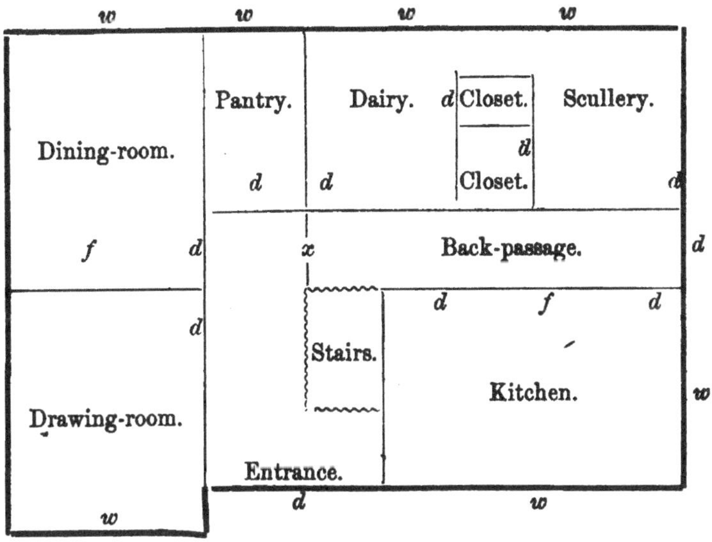

Fig. 87.

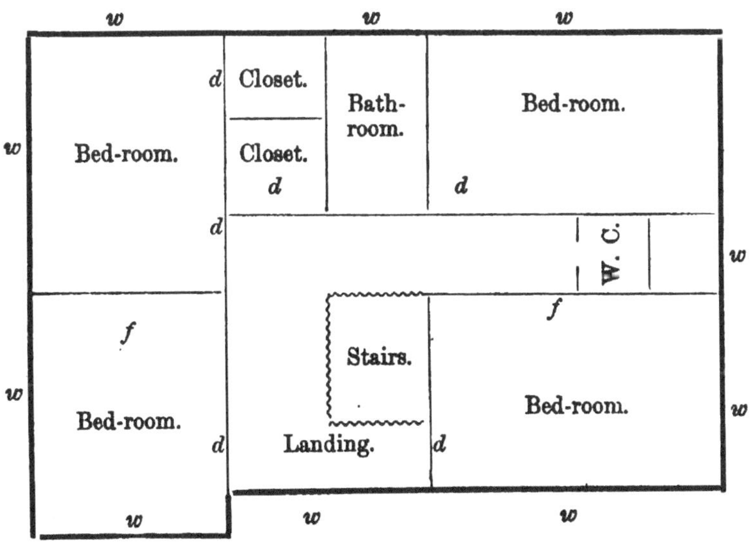

Fig. 85 we give the plan of cellar for the house in Fig. 82. The stairs enter at the end (*a*) corresponding to the part (*x*) in Fig. 82.

In Fig. 86 we give the ground plan, and in Fig. 87 the chamber plan, of a farm house, in which the working parts of the house

Fig. 88.

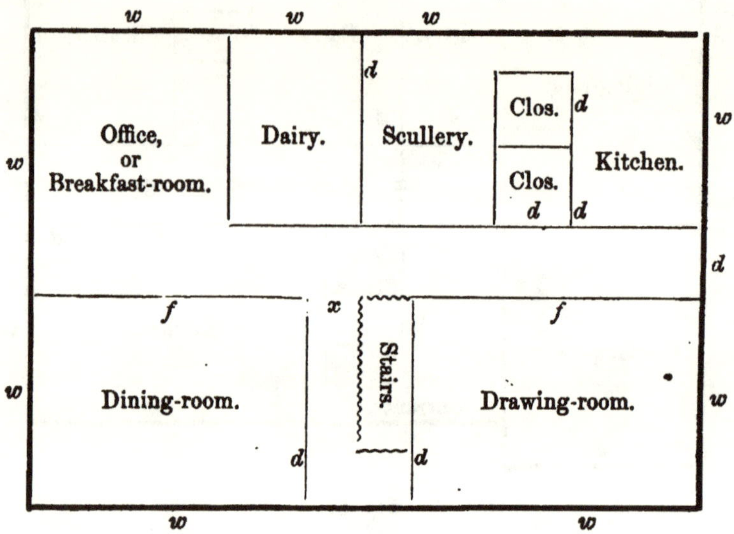

Fig. 89.

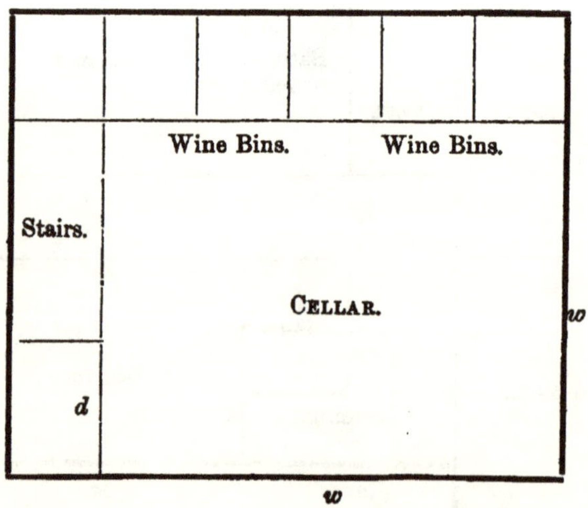

are isolated from the living apartments by a door placed at *x*. The scullery is opposite the kitchen, the back passage being between them; a door leads from the kitchen into the back passage, immediately opposite to which is the door of the scullery. The dairy is entered from the back passage, or from the scullery, and ample closet and pantry accommodation is provided.

In Fig. 88, which is the ground plan of a farm house, the isolation of the working parts from the living apartments is obtained by a back passage, which is shut off from the house by a screen door at the point *x*.

Fig. 89 illustrates the cellar arrangements of the house in Fig. 86; under the kitchen almost identically the same arrange-

Fig. 90.

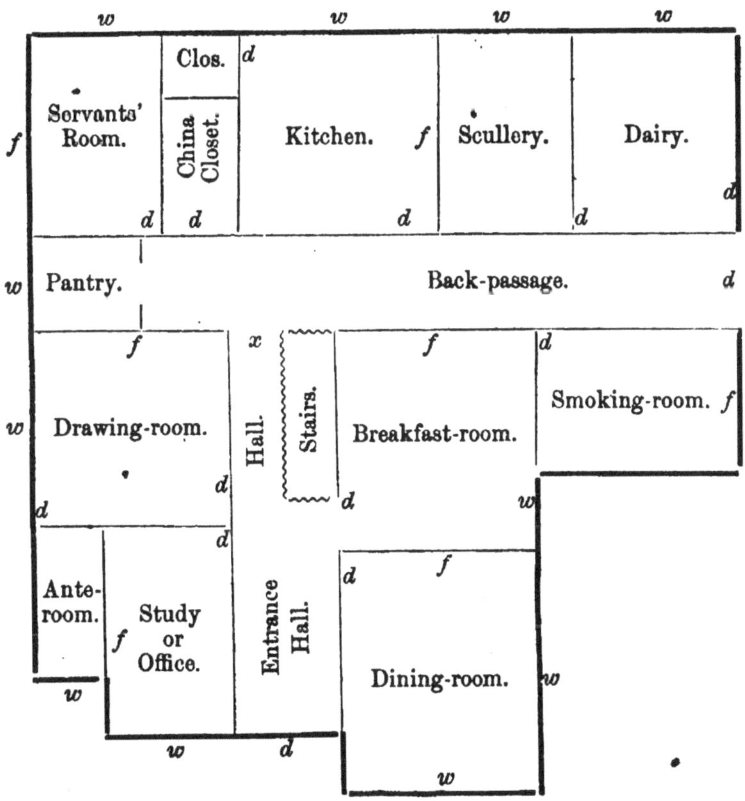

ment of cellar is required for the house in Fig. 88, the cellar of which would be under the drawing-room.

In Fig. 90 we give the plan of a farm house with superior accommodation. In this all the working apartments are isolated from the entertaining rooms by a door at *x*. The smoking-room may be dispensed with; or the servants' room may be used for this purpose. The smoking room and dairy are both of one storey in height, so that ample ventilation can be secured. The servants' room may be converted into a billiard-room.

Fig. 91.

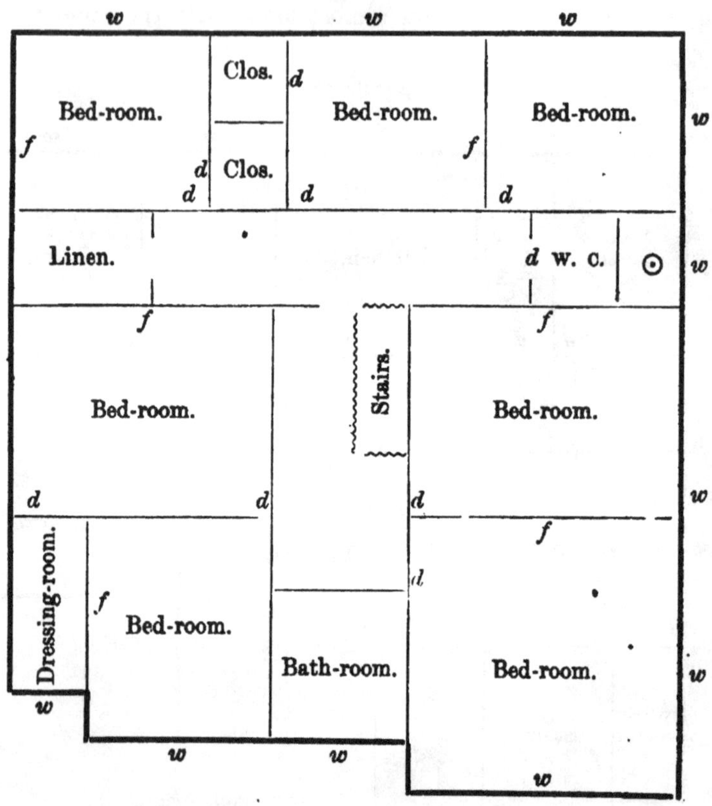

We have thus given a few suggestive plans; none of them will probably be fitting for particular purposes, some parts being redundant, some defective; but they will serve the purpose for which we have here inserted them, should they suggest an arrangement of apartments suitable for the case in view, by taking one part from one, and another from another plan. It is quite obvious that what will suit one farmer will not suit another. The first thing to do, then, is to ascertain how many apartments he requires, and the next how best they can be arranged to serve the purposes of economical management of the household. As we have said before, so we say again, do not plan in a hurry, but let your plans be well matured; and having drawn out a sketch of what you think you require in your house, endeavour to re-arrange the apartments in another form, and, after so doing, sit down quietly to study it, and you will probably find that the second arrangement was better than the first; and that you may, after all, find a third suggested which is better than both, or even a fourth better than all the three preceding.

A word or two on the design of the farm house may here be permitted before taking up the subject of the cottage. Whatever the style—so called—you adopt, let plain elegance be its distinguishing feature rather than affected ornate decoration. It should be thoroughly free from all pretension, and indicative of the great dignity and worth of the calling of its owner. If money is to be spent upon it liberally, let this be laid out so as to secure thoroughness of workmanship, and the avoidance of all "gingerbread" work. As a writer beautifully remarks, the farmer's dwelling should "suggest simplicity, honesty of purpose, frankness, a hearty genuine spirit of good will, and a homely and modest, though manly and independent, bearing. For the true farmer despises affectation; he loves a blunt and honest expression of the truth; and he shows you that he knows the value of a friend by shaking hands as if his heart acted like a magnetic machine on the chords of his fingers. It would be false and foolish to embellish highly the dwelling of such a man with the elaborate details of the different schools of architecture. We must leave this more scientific display of art and learning to villas and public edifices, and endeavour to make your farm house agreeable, chiefly by expressing in its leading forms the strength, simplicity, honesty, frankness, and sterling goodness of the farmer's character. Although we must recognise first of all the constant industry which gives so much dignity and independence to his life in the arrangements of the house mainly for useful ends, yet we would also introduce every comfort and convenience denoting the intelligence and ease of a farmer's life. The principles we would lay down for designing farm houses may be stated as follows, so far as the production of beauty is concerned: That the form of the building should express a local fitness, and an intimate relation with the soil it stands upon, by showing breadth and extension upon the ground rather than height; that its proportions should be simple and bold, and its ornaments, so far as they are used, should be rather rustic, strong, or picturesque, than delicate or highly finished. That in raising the character of the farm house, the first step which is really useful is to add the porch, the verandah, and the bay window, since they are not only significant of real but of refined utility." These remarks so thoroughly express our own sentiments, and express them so well, that we have chosen to borrow them as they stand, rather than to clothe them in language of our own.

To these remarks, however, we may add—and add with advantage—the following considerations affecting the accommodation of a farm house, for which we are indebted to the 'American Illustrated Annual Register for Rural Affairs:'—

"When a farmer is about to erect a house, he should, in the first place, make two leading inquiries. 1. What are the accommodations I want? 2. What is the amount of means for providing them? In order to assist in answering these questions properly, it may be well to classify houses, from the most simple and cheap, to the most expensive and complex. But it is necessary in the first place, to examine which of the apartments of a dwelling are most indispensable, and which are of various degrees of secondary importance.

"Every house must have a kitchen, or place for cooking food, a living room for day occupancy, and a lodging room for night—and a pantry and store-room. In the simplest log hut or board shanty, one room is made to serve all these purposes, the pantry being merely a cupboard, or tier of shelves against the wall. One step above this, is the separation of kitchen and living-room from the bed-room; and still better, is the appropriation of three distinct rooms for these purposes. As we continue to ascend in the scale, we find at last, that the largest and most complete houses, have most of the following apartments, although all may not be found in any single house:—

1. Kitchen, with appended iron closet, store-room, dairy, wood-room and laundry.
2. Bed-rooms, including nursery, and other sleeping apartments.
3. Dining-room.
4. Library, or office.
5. Bath-room.
6. Breakfast-room, parlour, sitting-room, or living-room.
7. Drawing-room and conservatory.
8. Entrance-hall and verandah. 9. Cellar.

"Now going back to the two leading inquiries already mentioned, let every one about to build, ask himself; How many of these different rooms will be indispensable for me; and 2. What can I expend in procuring them? We suppose that no man, even with quite moderate means, will be satisfied without,

1. Kitchen and small pantry. 2. Parlour.
3. Nursery, or bed-room on the ground floor.
4. Small entry.
5. Bed-rooms with closets above stairs. 6. Cellars.

"The cost of a house containing all these will of course depend much upon the nature of the materials, their cost, the size of the rooms, and the cheapness of the finish; but with a plain frame or wooden house, they could be had from six to twelve hundred dollars. A larger and more complete farm house, costing two thousand or more, would contain,

1. Kitchen, pantry, store-room, and iron closet.
2. Dining-room and china closet.
3. Parlour, or drawing-room.
4. Nursery, or bed-room below stairs, with ample closets; and with bath-room attached.
5. Bed-rooms above stairs, with closets to all.
6. Office or library—which may be simply a small business-room, for keeping account books, sitting with workmen, making bargains, &c.; or, a more complete library, with book cases and newspaper closets, and even cases for minerals, dried plants, shells, stuffed birds, &c., according to circumstances.
7. Verandahs. 8. Cellar.

"After the greater or less number of these rooms has been fixed upon, according to wants and circumstances, the next step is to arrange them in the most convenient and economical manner. This is a difficult task to a person of inexperience, but it may be greatly assisted by observing the following rules, and by an examination of published plans, such for instance as we are about to give in the present of the Register, or which have been furnished in the former numbers.

1. Let the kitchen (the most important apartment) always be on a level with the principal floor—and for strong light and free ventilation, it should have, if possible, windows on opposite or nearly opposite sides.

2. The pantry, or dish closet should be between the kitchen and dining-room, and easily accessible from both.

3. There should be a set of easy stairs from the kitchen to the cellar, and also an outer set into the cellar for admitting barrels, &c.

4. More attention should be given to the arrangement and disposition of such rooms as are in constant use, than those but occasionally occupied. Hence the kitchen and living-room should receive more attention on the ground of convenience, than the parlour.

5. Every entrance, except to the kitchen, should be through some entry or hall, to prevent the abrupt ingress of cold air, and for proper seclusion.

6. Let the entry or hall be near the centre of the house, so that ready and convenient access may be had from it to the different rooms; and to prevent the too common evil of passing through one room to enter another.

7. Place the stairs so that the landing shall be as near the centre as may be practicable, for the reason given for the preceding rule.

8. Let the partitions of the second floor stand over those of the lower, as nearly as may be, to secure firmness and solidity."

THE GRAMMAR

OF

HOUSE PLANNING:

HINTS ON ARRANGING AND MODIFYING PLANS OF

COTTAGES, STREET-HOUSES, VILLAS, MANSIONS, AND OUT-BUILDINGS.

By an M.S.A., and M.R.A.S.

1864.

PLATE I.

Fig. 1.

Fig. 2.

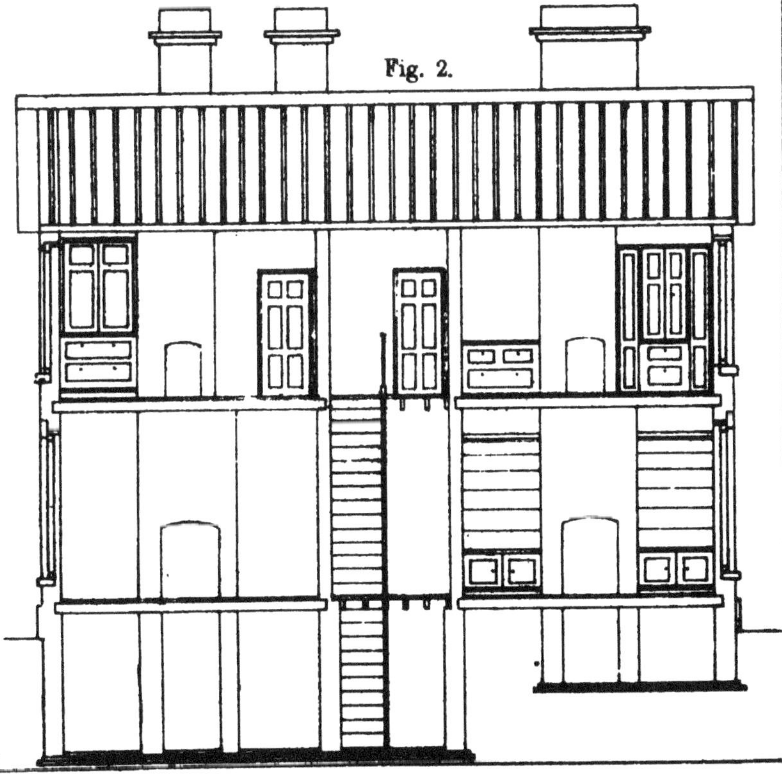

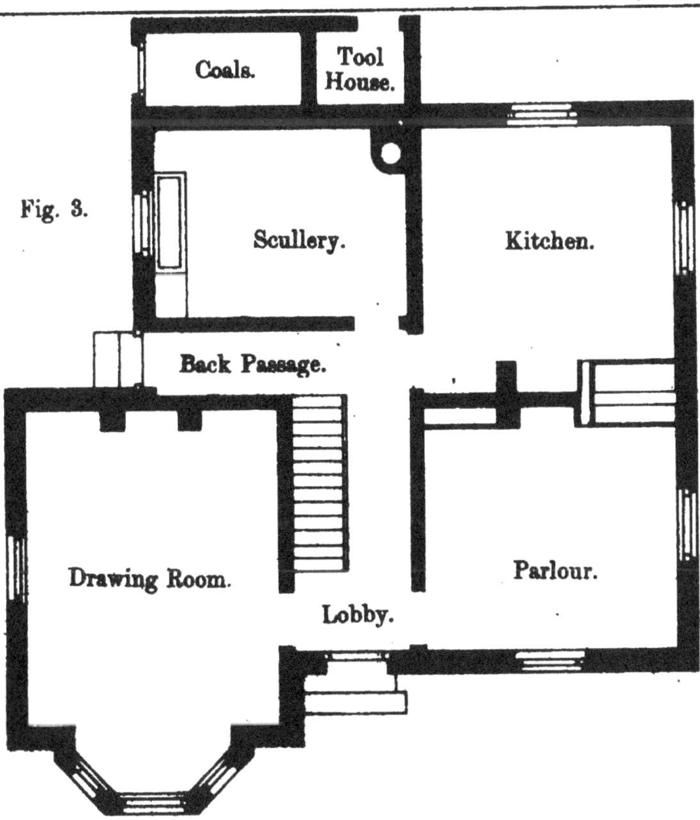

Fig. 3.

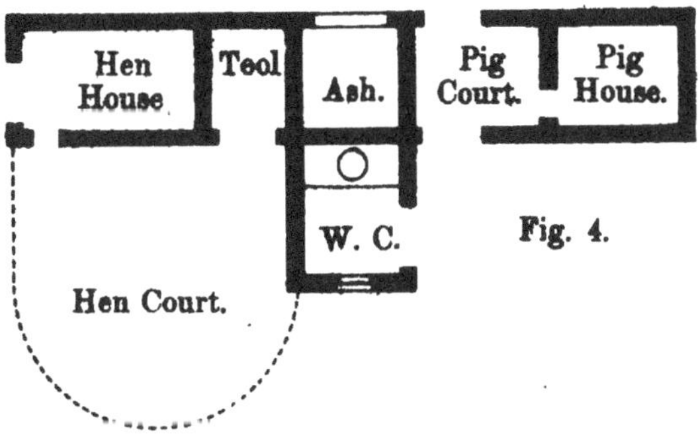

Fig. 4.

Fig. 5.

PLATE III.

Fig. 1.

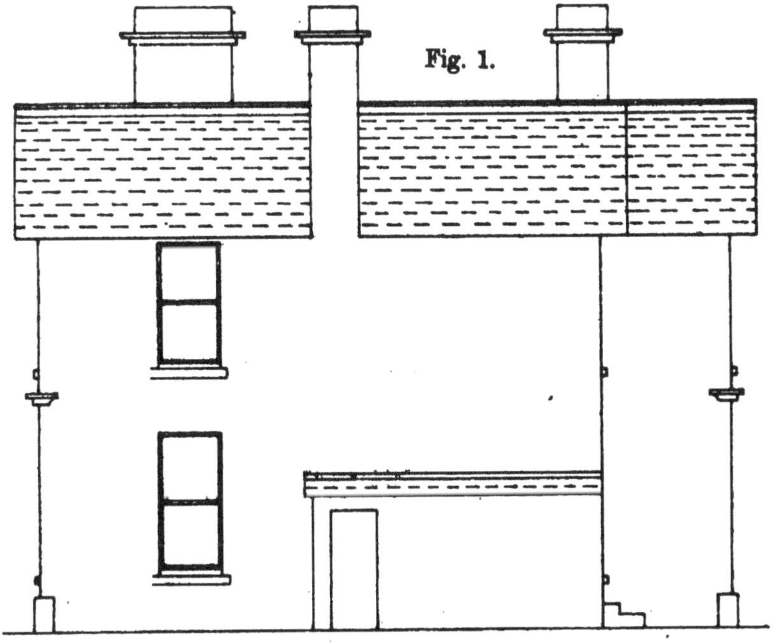

Fig. 2.

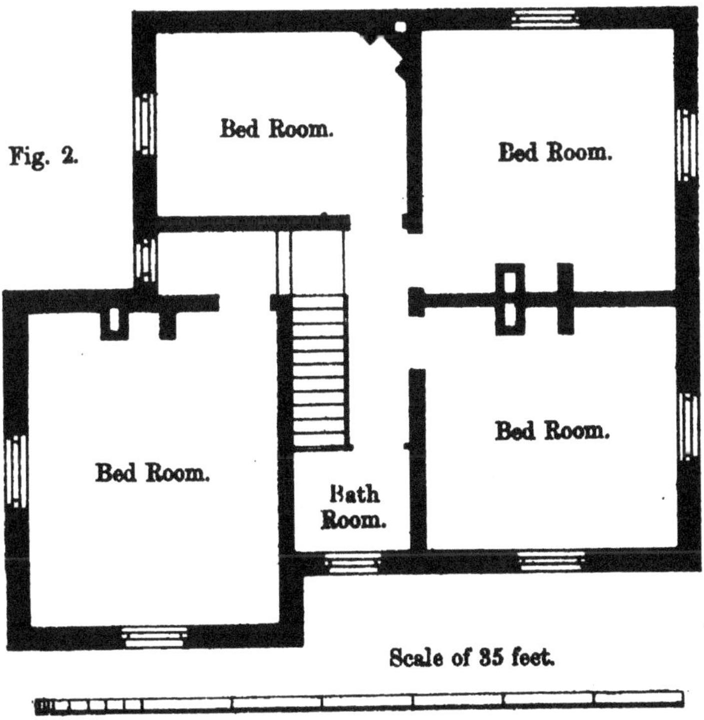

PLATE IV.

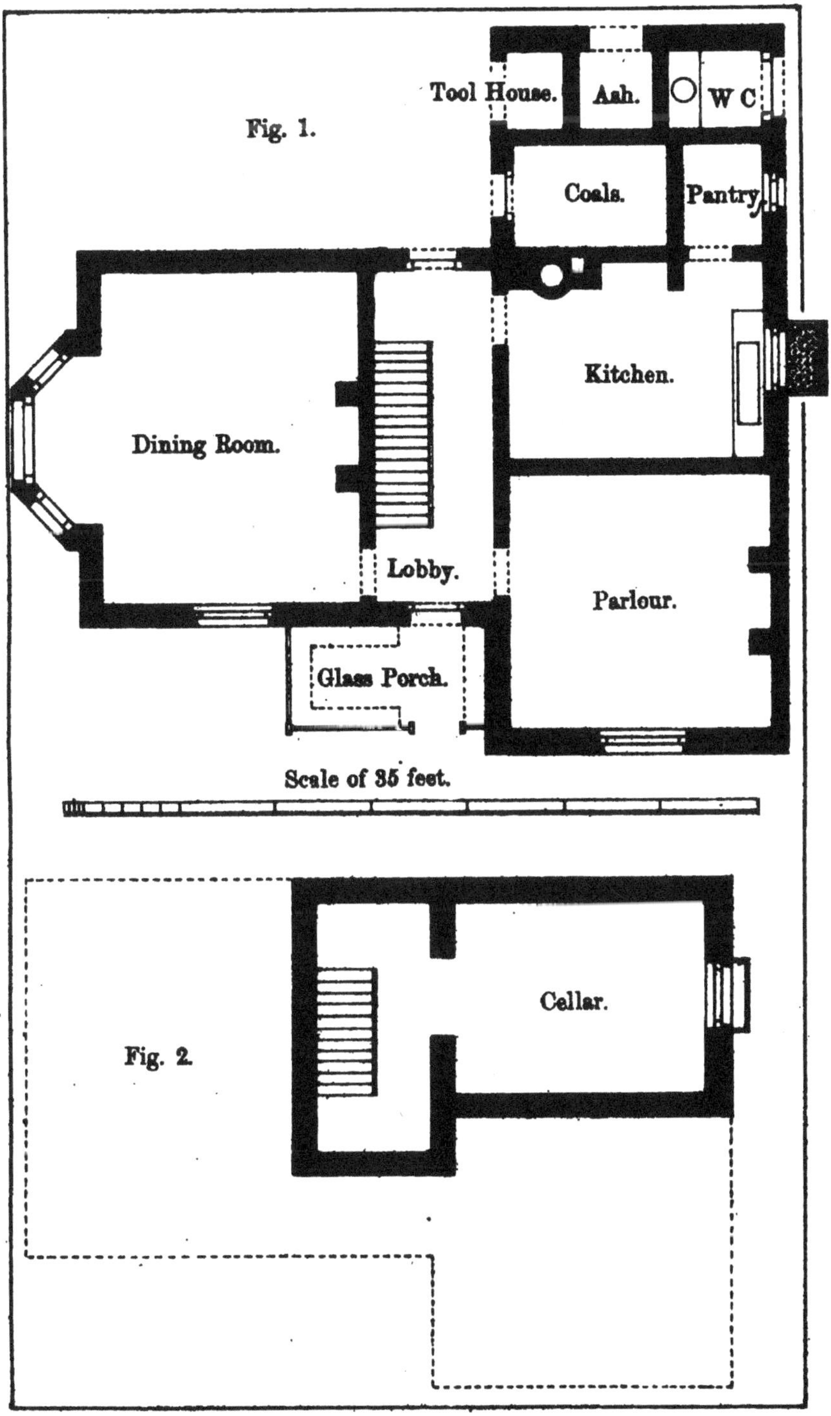
Fig. 1.
Tool House.
Ash.
W C
Coals.
Pantry
Kitchen.
Dining Room.
Lobby.
Parlour.
Glass Porch.
Scale of 35 feet.
Fig. 2.
Cellar.

PLATE V.

Fig. 1.

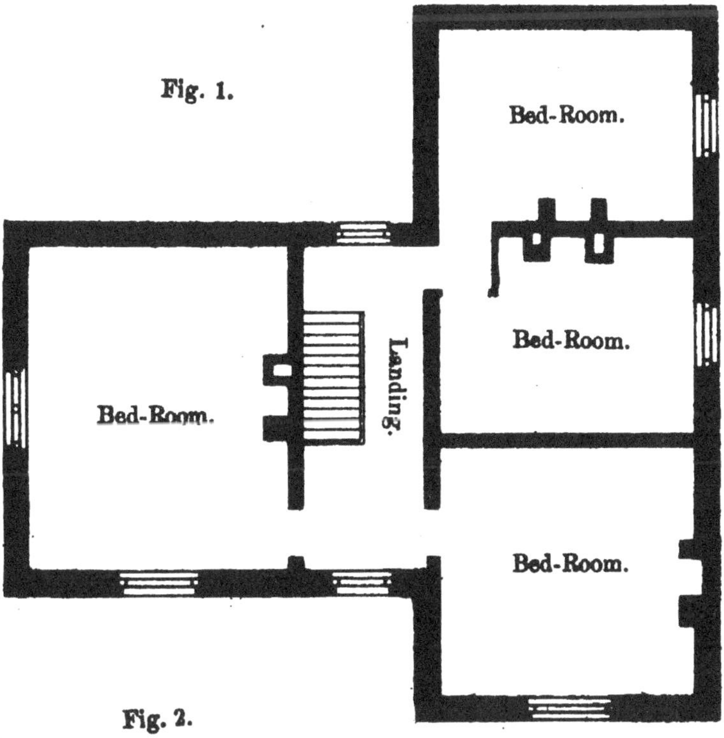

Fig. 2.

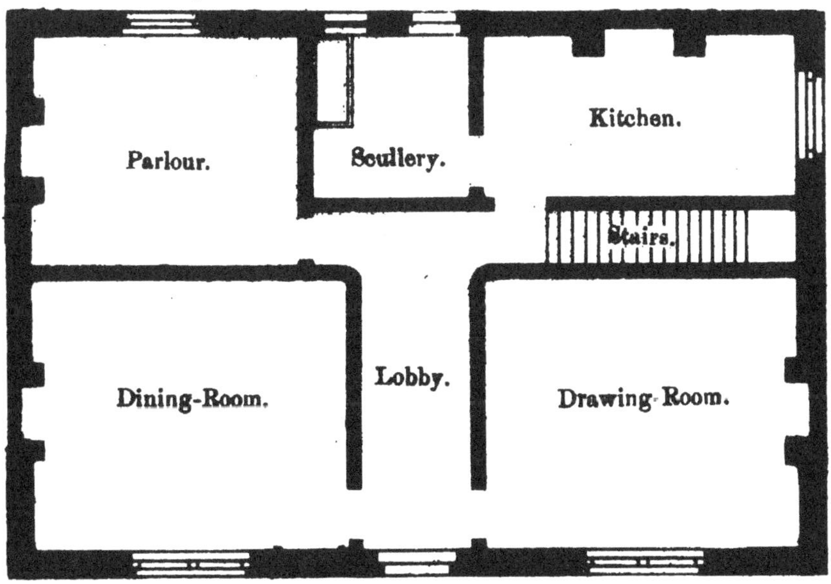

Fig. 1.

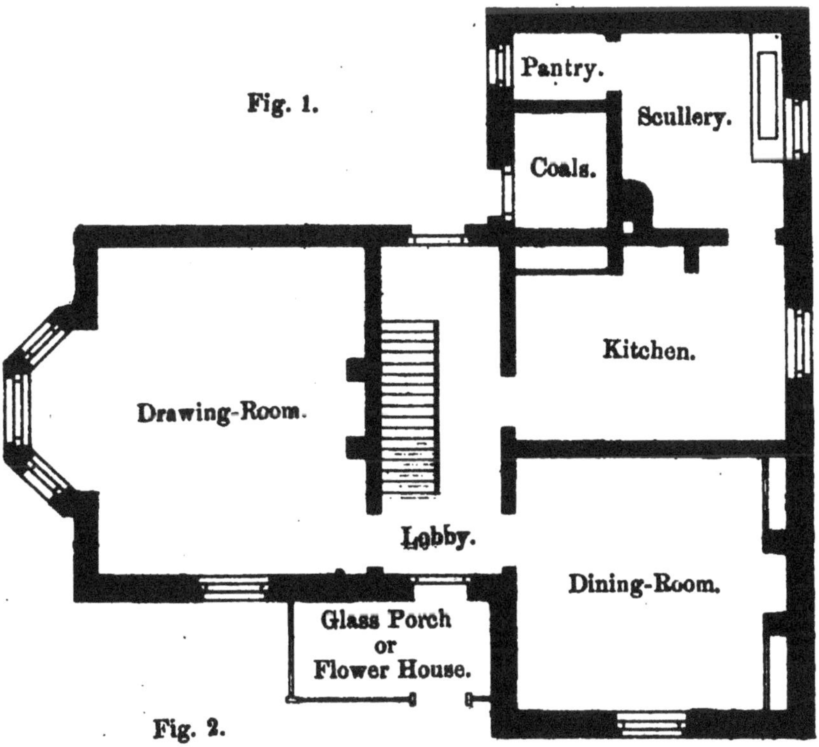
Pantry.
Scullery.
Coals.
Kitchen.
Drawing-Room.
Lobby.
Dining-Room.
Glass Porch
or
Flower House.

Fig. 2.

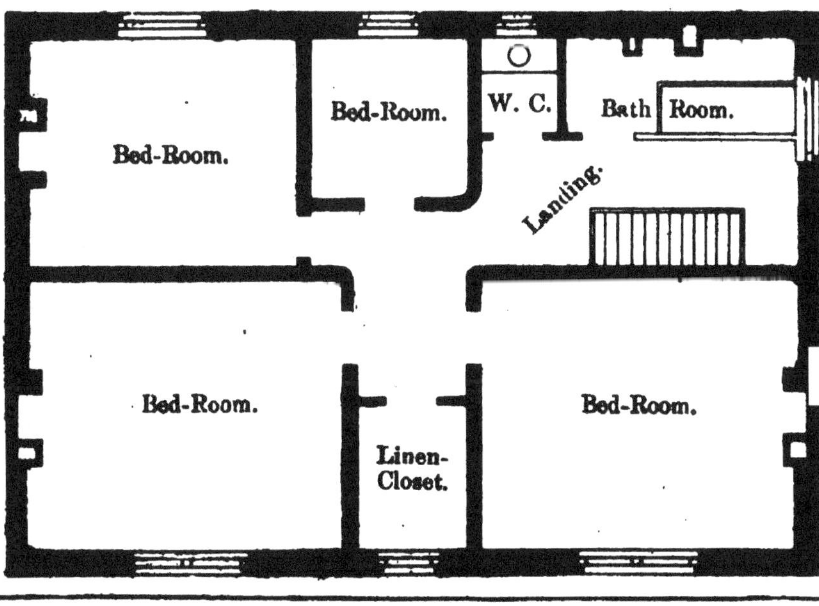
Bed-Room.
W. C.
Bath Room.
Bed-Room.
Landing.
Bed-Room.
Linen-
Closet.
Bed-Room.

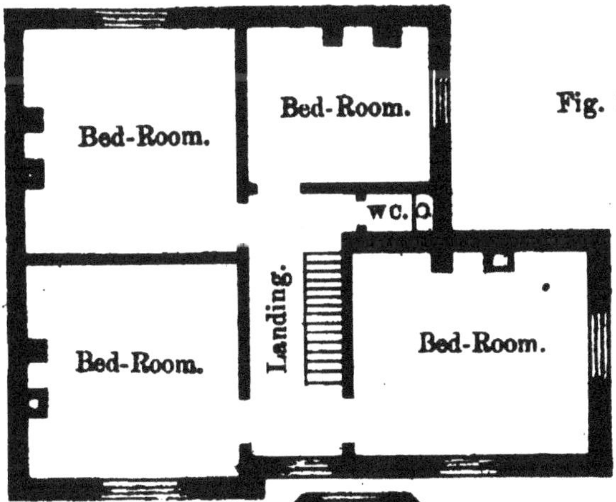
Bed-Room.
Bed-Room.
WC.
Landing.
Bed-Room.
Bed-Room.

Fig. 1.

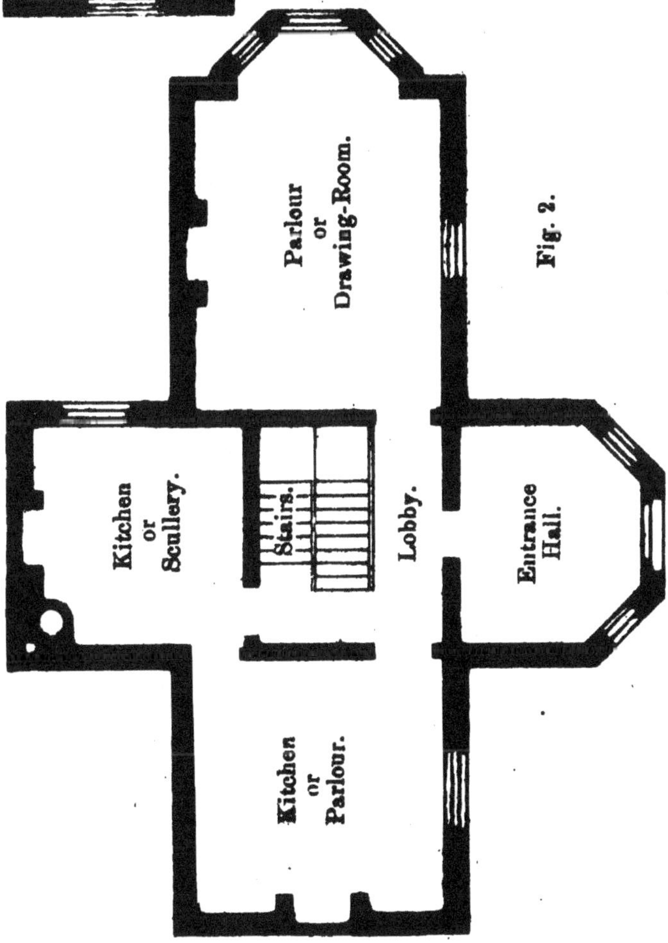
Parlour or Drawing-Room.
Kitchen or Scullery.
Stairs.
Lobby.
Entrance Hall.
Kitchen or Parlour.

Fig. 2.

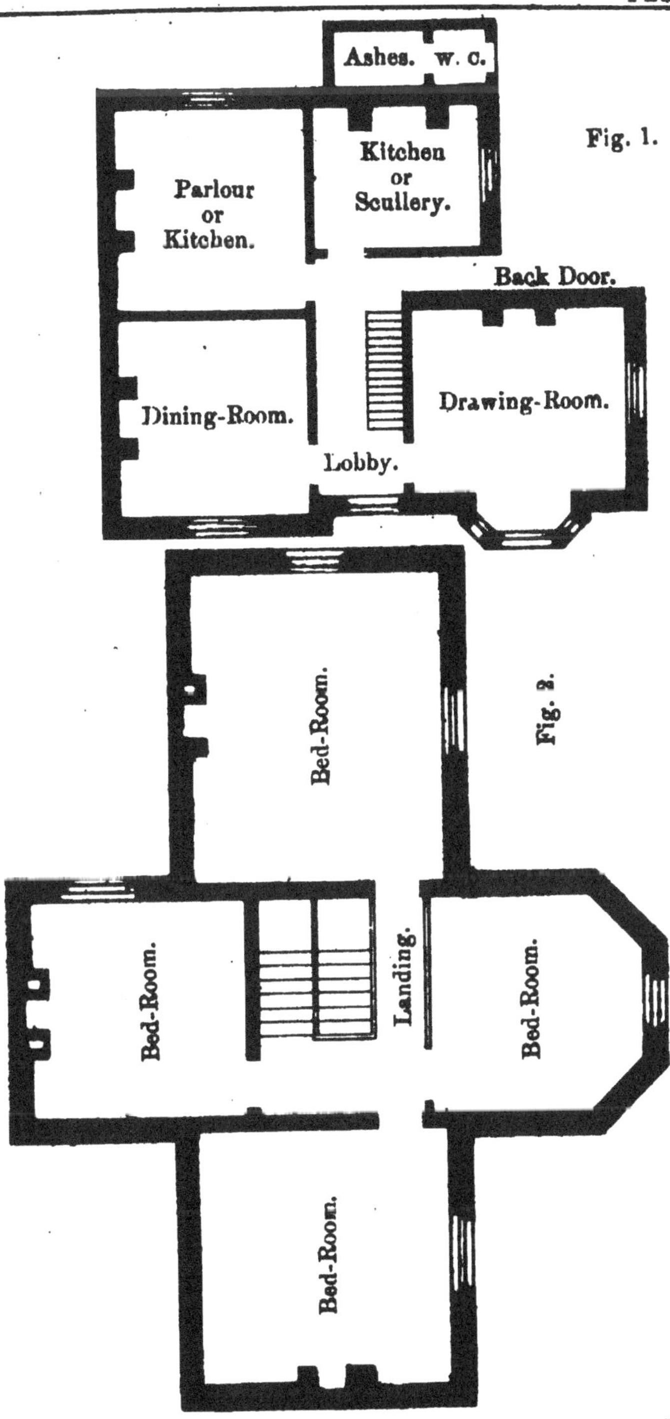
Ashes.
W. C.
Kitchen or Scullery.
Parlour or Kitchen.
Back Door.
Dining-Room.
Drawing-Room.
Lobby.
Bed-Room.
Bed-Room.
Landing.
Bed-Room.
Bed-Room.

Fig. 1.

Fig. 2.

PLATE IX.

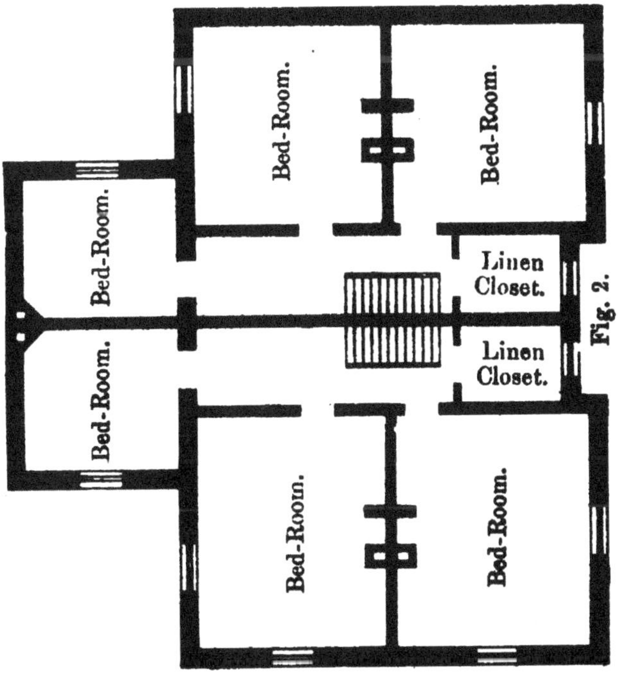

Fig. 2.

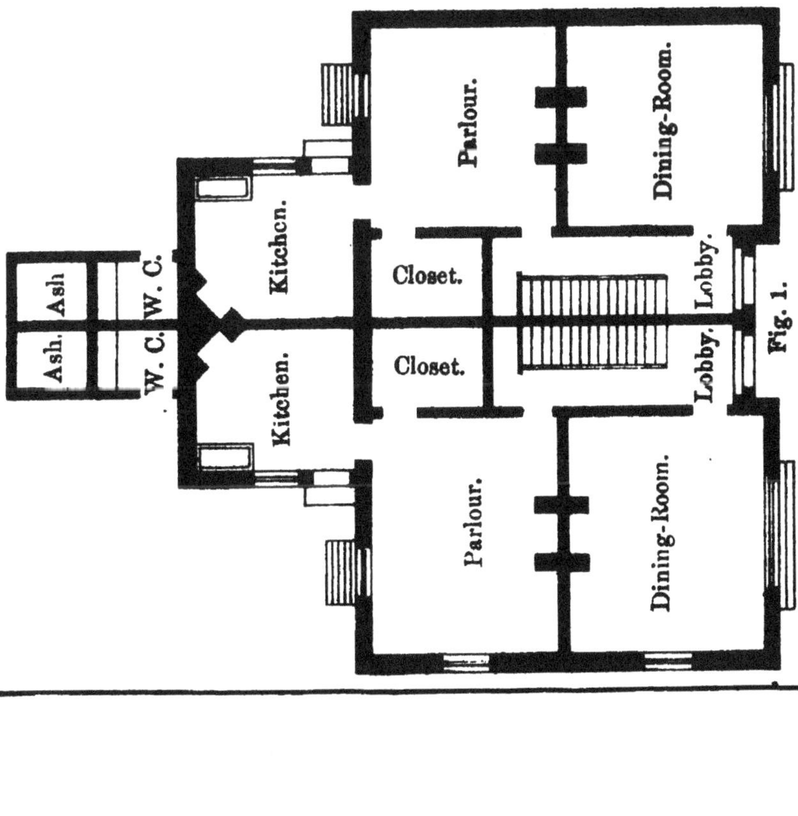

Fig. 1.

PLATE X.

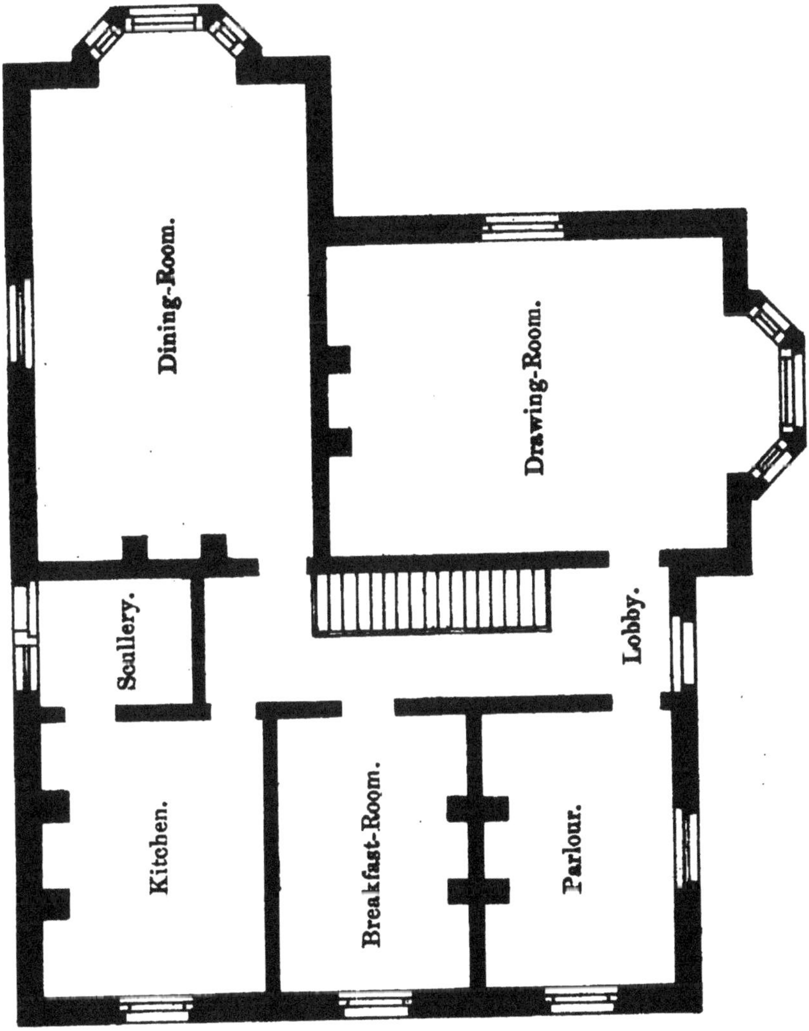
Dining-Room.
Drawing-Room.
Scullery.
Lobby.
Kitchen.
Breakfast-Room.
Parlour.

PLATE XI.

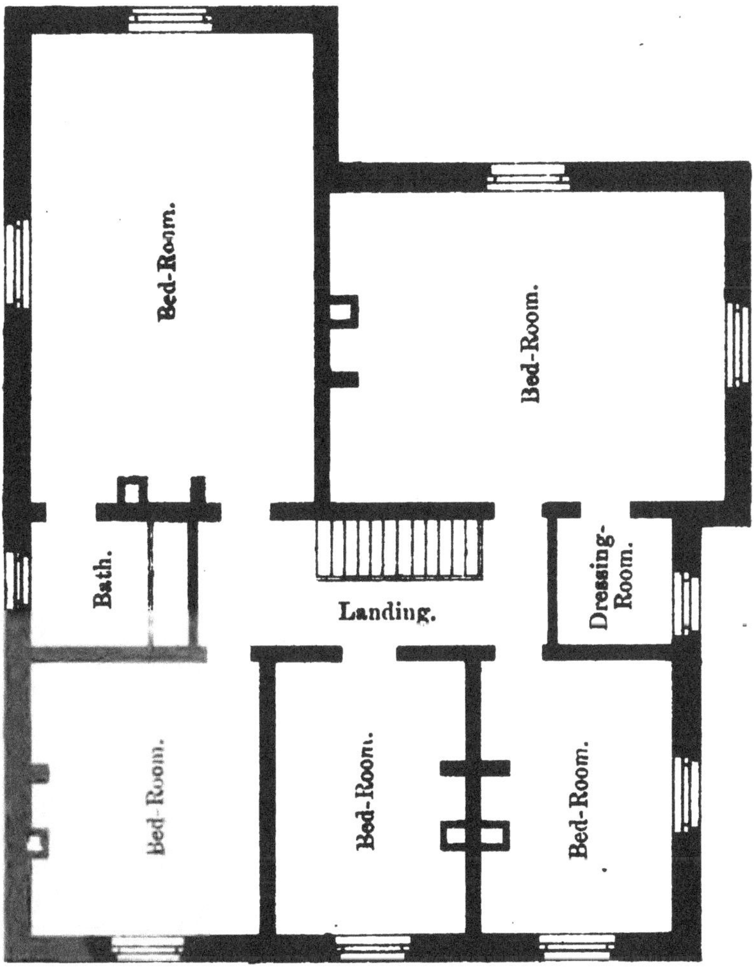

Bed-Room.
Bed-Room.
Bath.
Landing.
Dressing-Room.
Bed-Room.
Bed-Room.
Bed-Room.

PLATE XII.

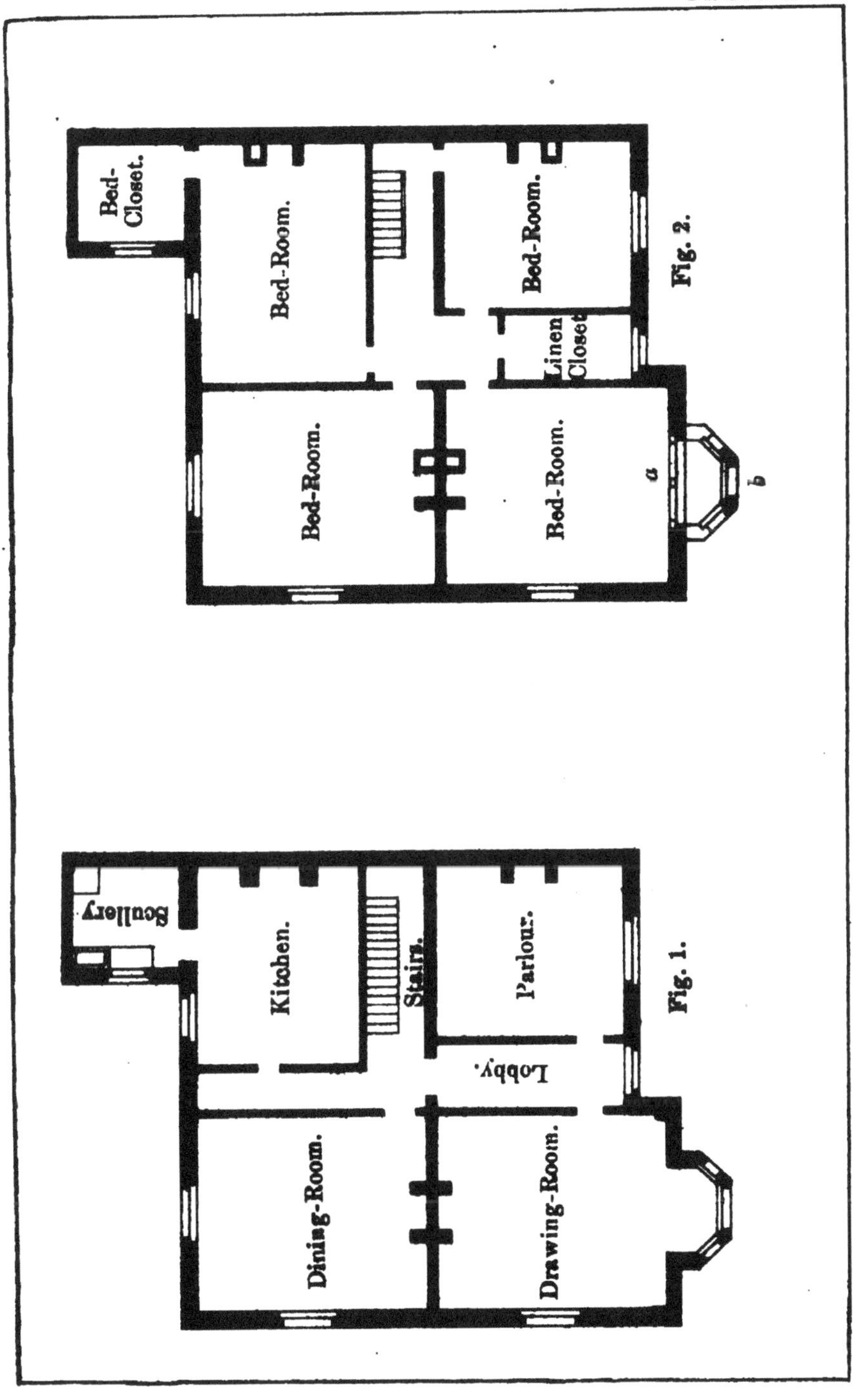

Fig. 2.

Fig. 1.

PLATE XIII.

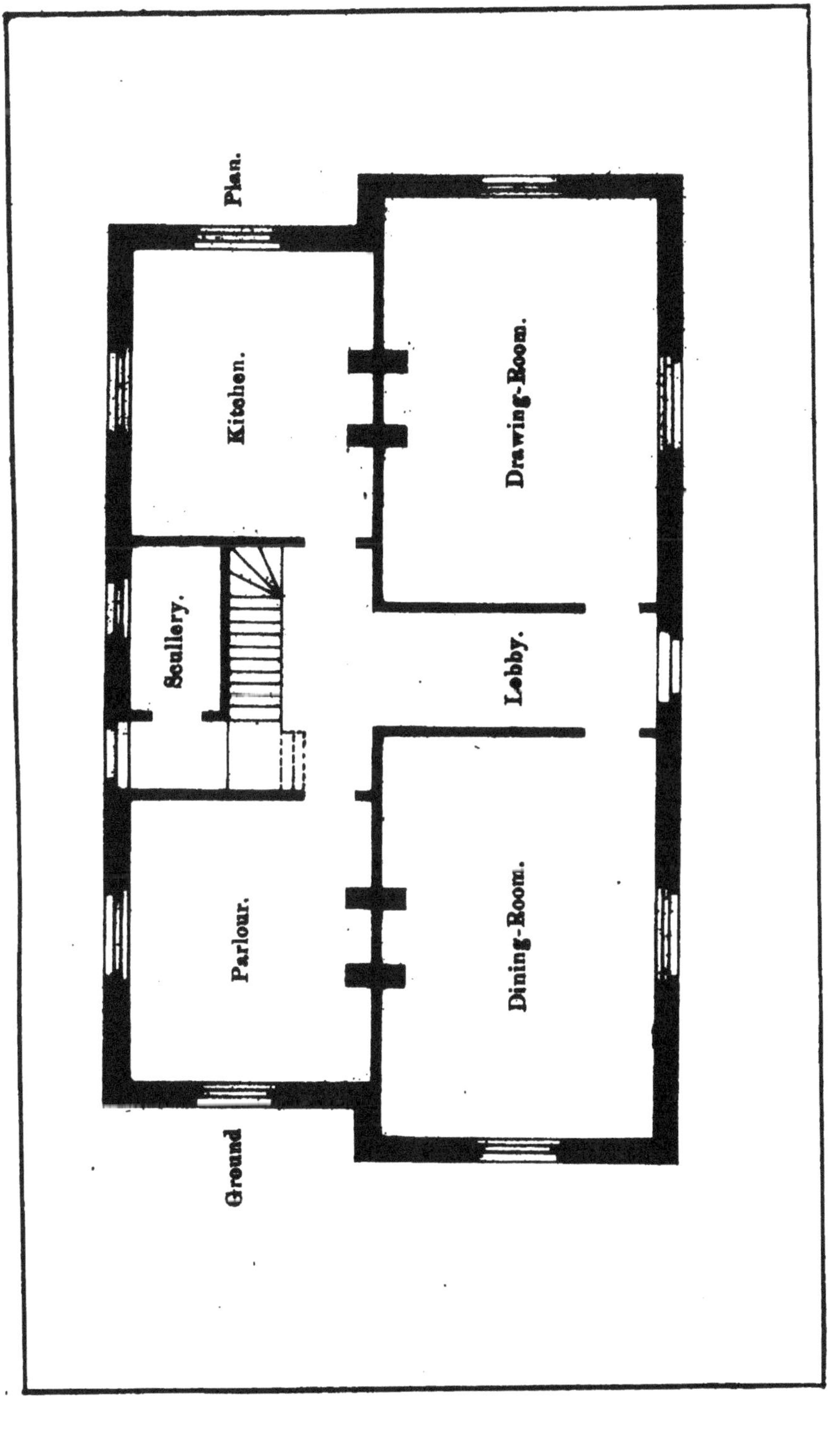
Ground Plan.
Kitchen.
Drawing-Room.
Scullery.
Lobby.
Parlour.
Dining-Room.

PLATE XIV.

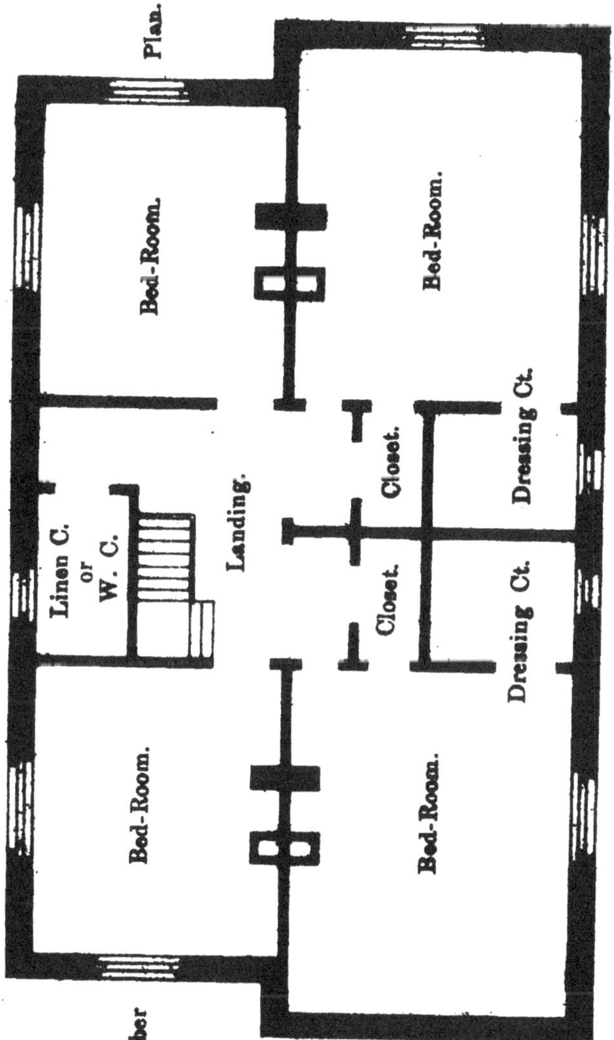

Chamber Plan.

PLATE XV

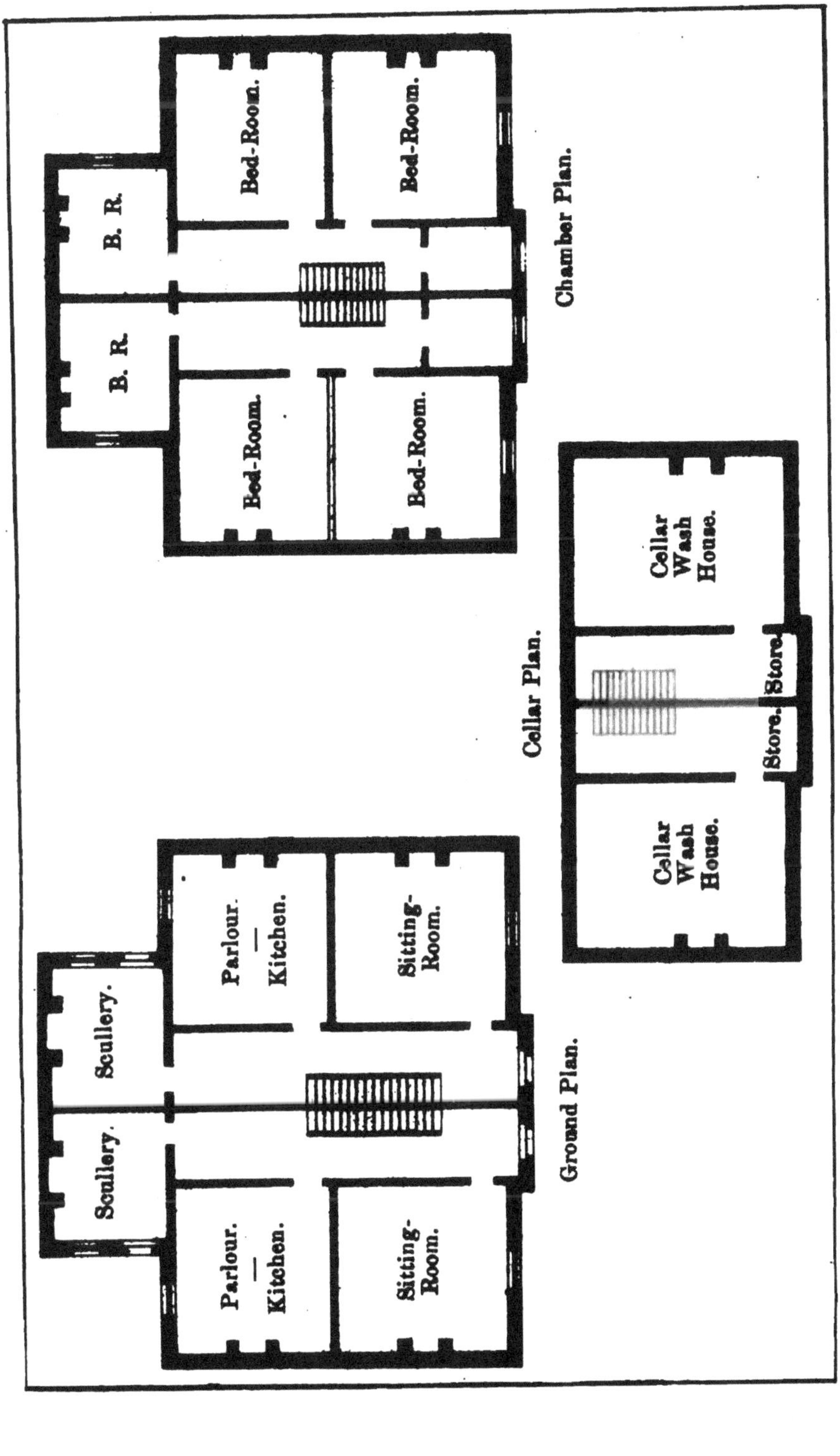
Chamber Plan.
Bed-Room.
Bed-Room.
B. R.
B. R.
Bed-Room.
Bed-Room.
Cellar Plan.
Cellar Wash House.
Store.
Store.
Cellar Wash House.
Ground Plan.
Parlour. — Kitchen.
Sitting-Room.
Scullery.
Scullery.
Parlour. — Kitchen.
Sitting-Room.

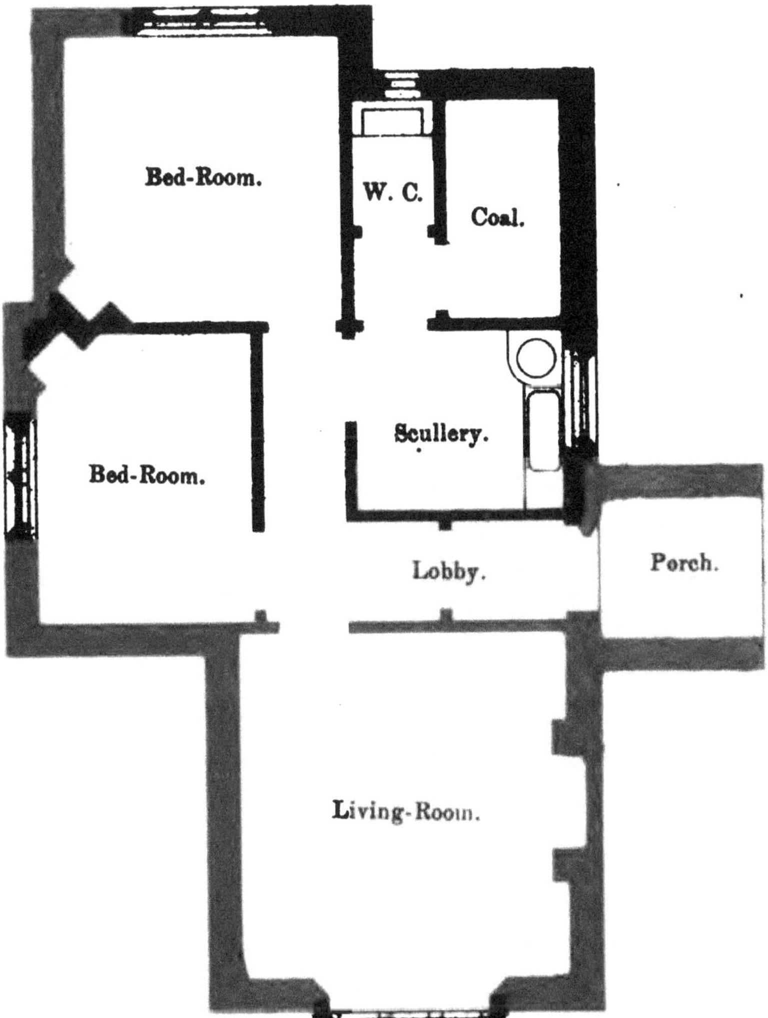
Bed-Room.
W. C.
Coal.
Bed-Room.
Scullery.
Lobby.
Porch.
Living-Room.

PLATE XVII.

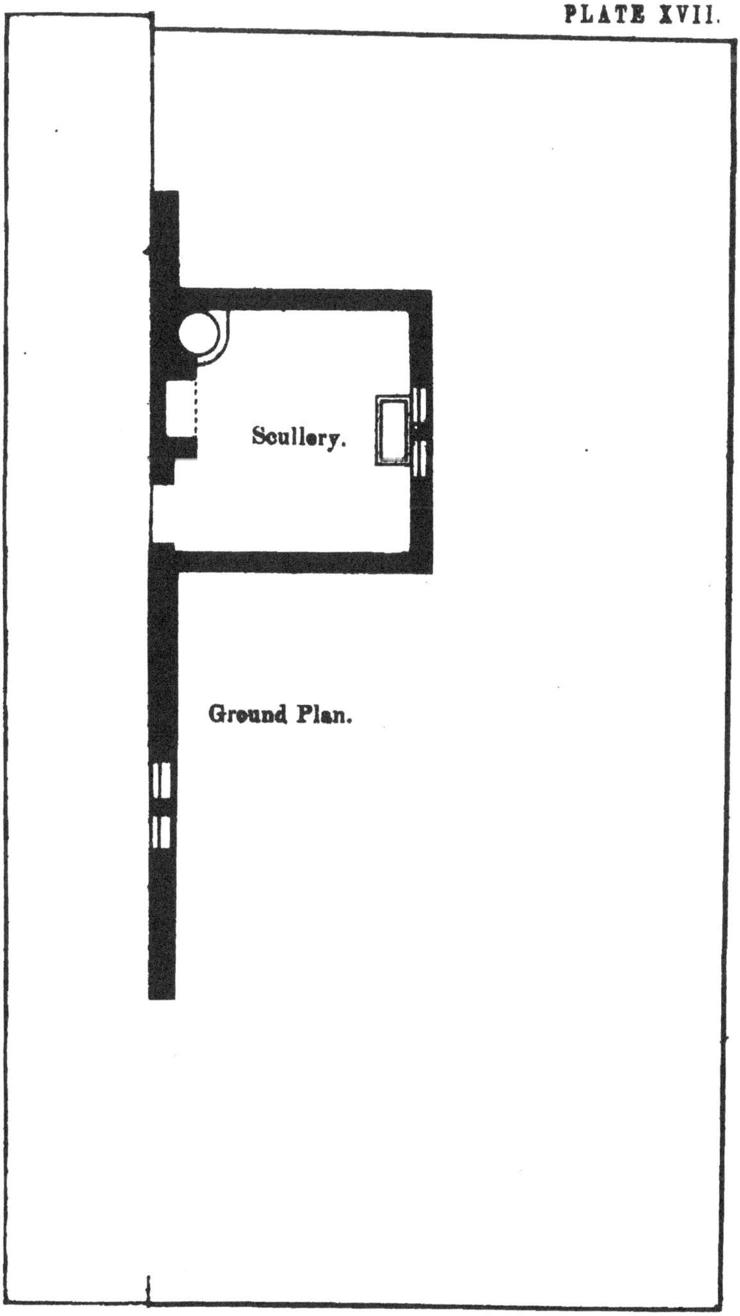

Fig. 1.

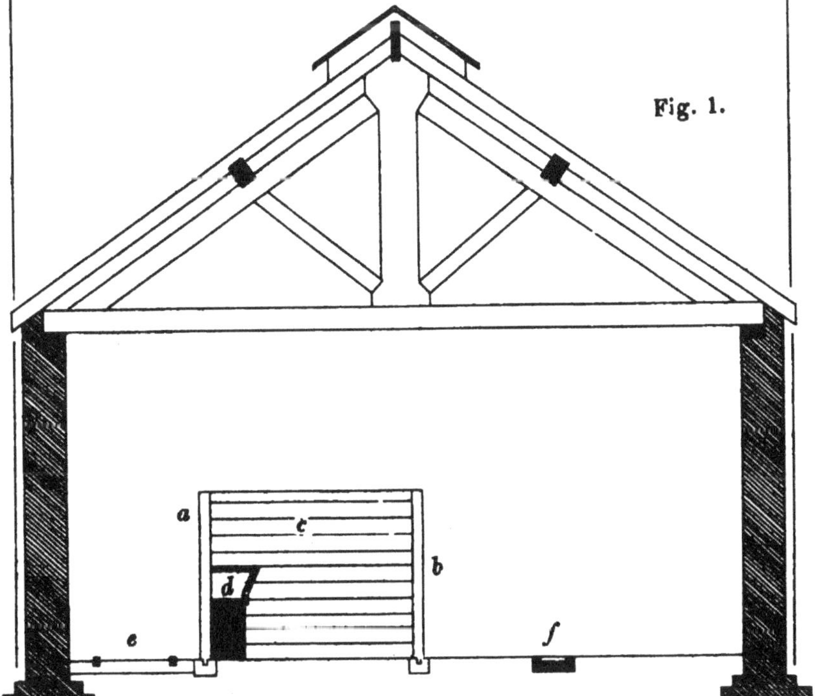
a
c
b
d
e
f

Fig. 2.

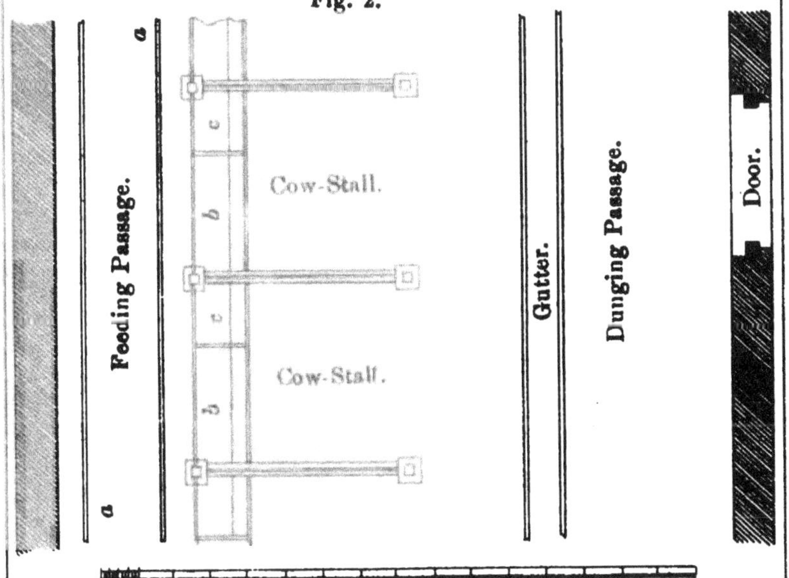
Feeding Passage.
a
a
c
b
c
b
Cow-Stall.
Cow-Stall.
Gutter.
Dunging Passage.
Door.

PLATE XXV.

Fig. 1.

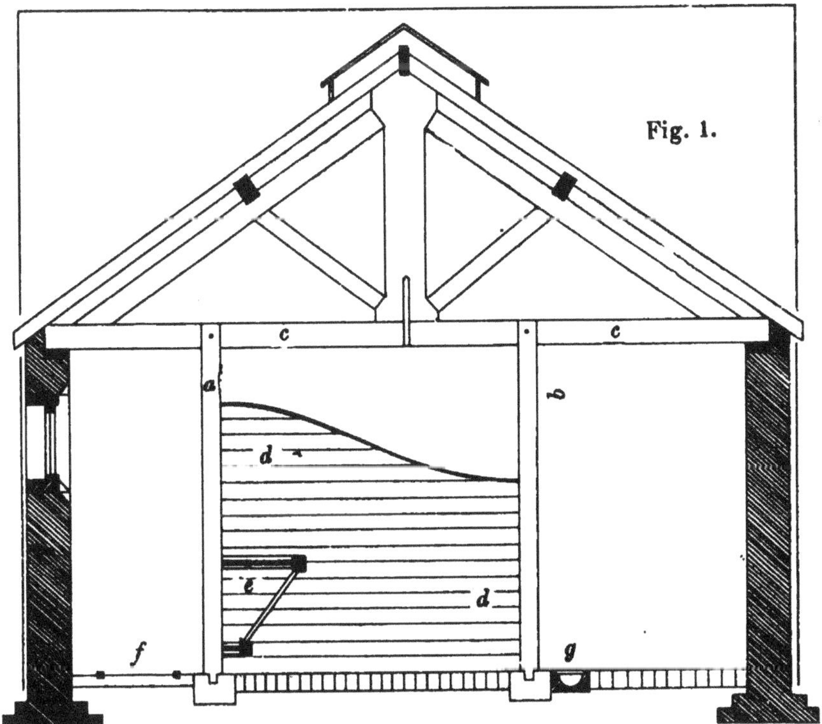

Fig. 2.

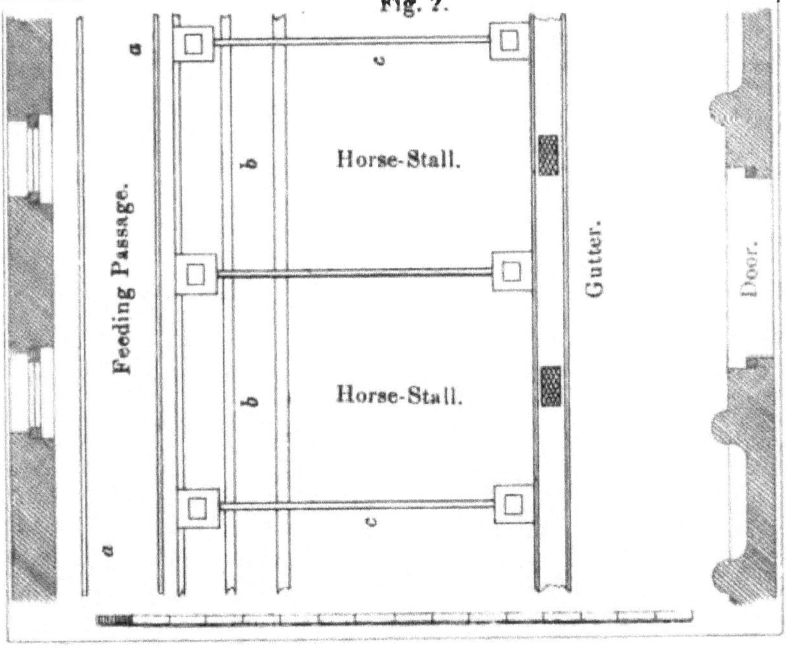

PLATE XXVI.

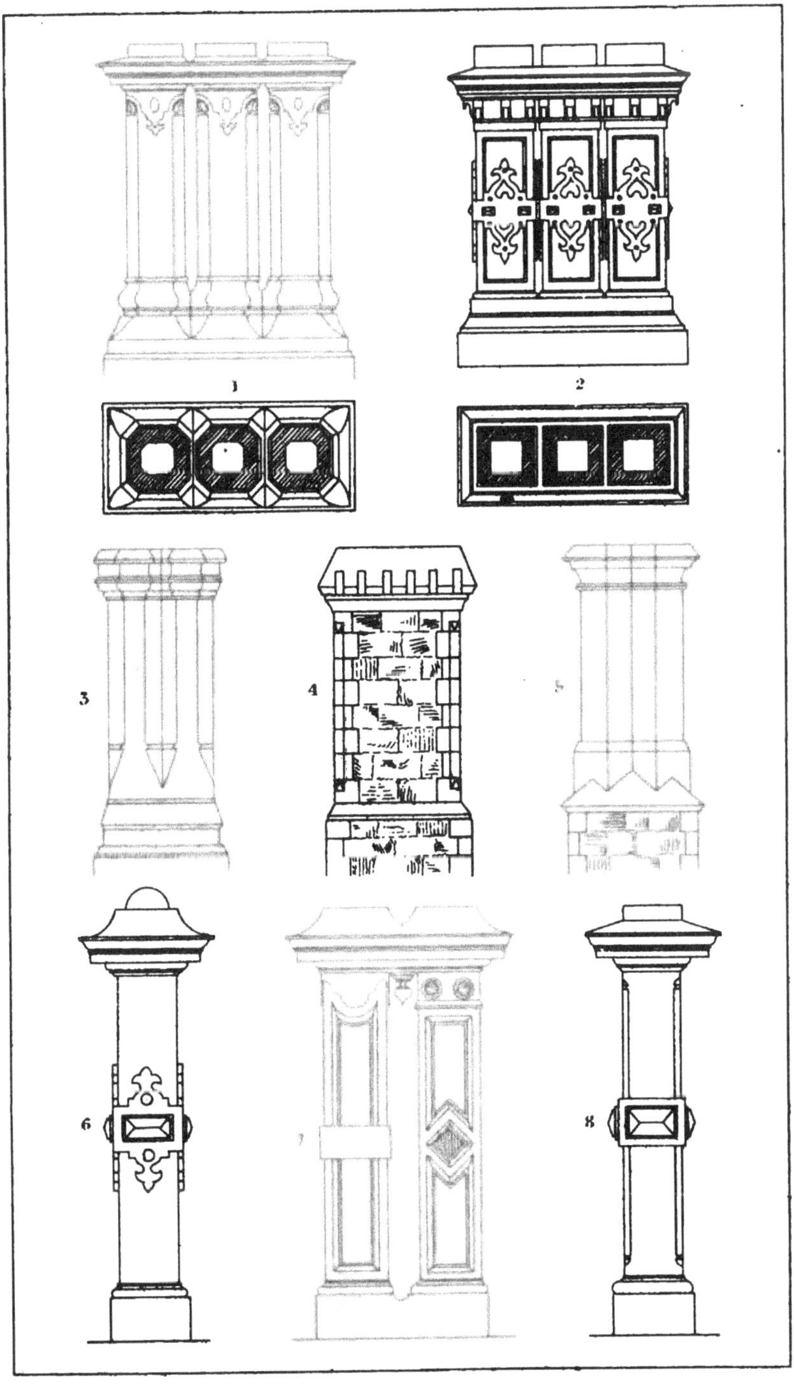

PLATE XXVII.

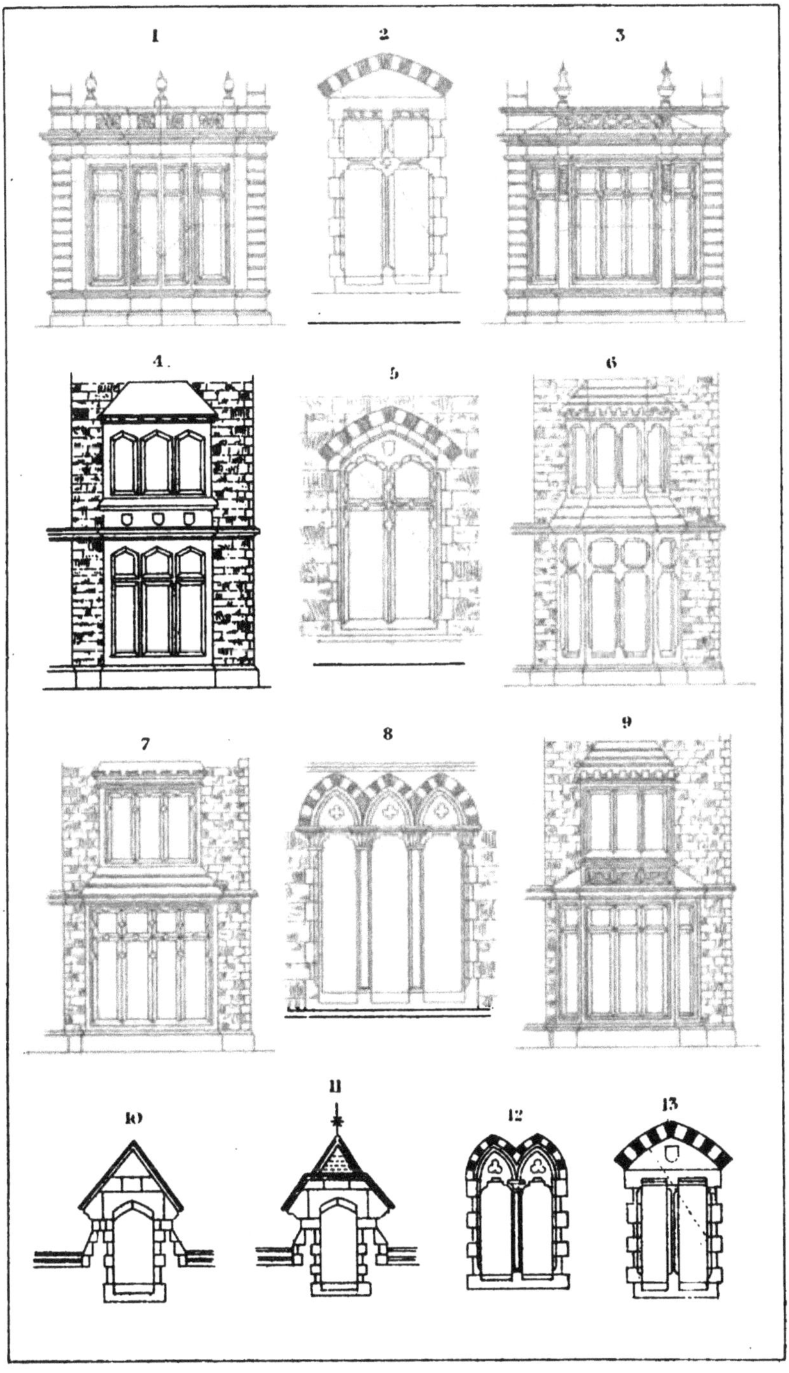

PLATE XXVIII

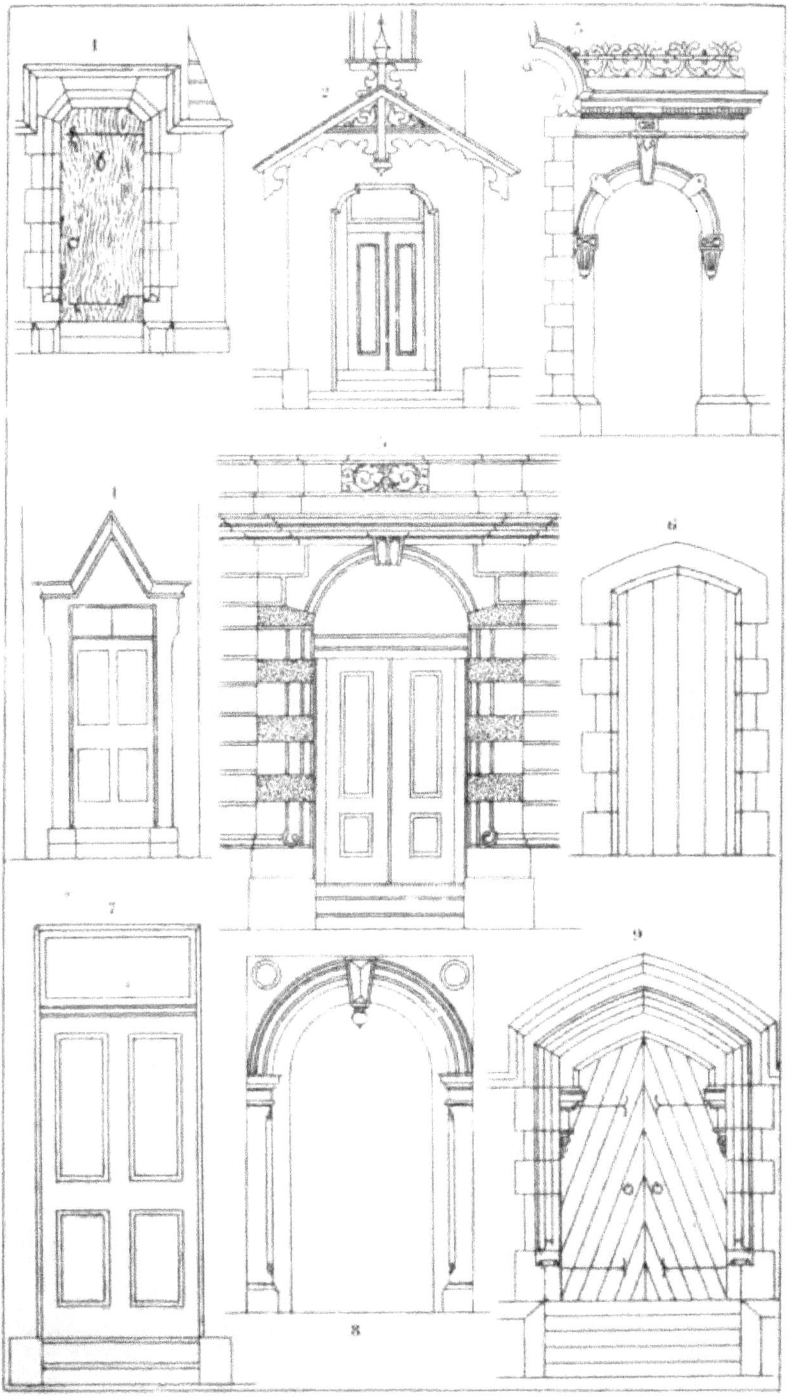

PLATE XXIX.

PLATE XXX

PLATE XXXI.

CPSIA information can be obtained
at www.ICGtesting.com
Printed in the USA
LVHW100515130422
716029LV00002B/119

9 783752 595017